The New Shell Guides

North-East England

The New Shell Guides
North-East England
Northumberland, Co. Durham,
Cleveland and Tyne & Wear

Brian Spencer

Introduction by Clayre Percy

Series Editor: John Julius Norwich

Photography by David Ward

Michael Joseph · London

First published in Great Britain by
Michael Joseph Limited, 27 Wrights Lane,
London W8 5TZ 1988

This book was designed and produced by
Swallow Editions Limited, Swallow House,
11–21 Northdown Street, London N1 9BN

© Shell UK Limited 1988

British Library Cataloguing in Publication Data:

Spencer, Brian, *1931*–
    New Shell guide to North-East England.
    1. England, Northern — Description and travel
    — Guide-books
    I. Title
    914.28′04858   DA670.N7

Cased edition: ISBN 0 7181 2909 1
Paperback edition: 0 7181 2973 3

Editor: Mary Anne Sanders
Reader: Raymond Kaye
Cartography: ML Design
Design: David Allen
Production: Hugh Allan

Filmset by Ampersand Typesetting Limited,
Bournemouth
Printed and bound by Kyodo Shing Loong Printing, Singapore.

A list of Shell publications
can be obtained by writing to:
Department UOMK/60
Shell UK Oil
PO Box No. 148
Shell-Mex House
Strand
London WC2R 0DX

John Julius Norwich was born in 1929. After reading French and Russian at New College, Oxford, he joined the Foreign Office where he served until 1964. Since then he has published two books on the medieval Norman Kingdom in Sicily, two historical travel books, *Mount Athos* (with Reresby Sitwell) and *Sahara*; an anthology of poetry and prose, *Christmas Crackers*; and two volumes on the history of Venice. He was general editor of *Great Architecture of the World* and, more recently, author of *The Architecture of Southern England*.

In addition, he writes and presents historical documentaries for BBC television and frequently broadcasts on BBC radio. He is chairman of the Venice in Peril Fund, a Trustee of the Civic Trust, and a member of the Executive and Properties Committee of the National Trust.

Brian Spencer, a Northerner by birth, has written several countryside books and four guides to family walking. His interests include industrial archaeology and the history of northern England. He is married with three sons.

Clayre Percy is a member of the Regional Committee of the National Trust for Northumbria and works for the Landmark Trust. She is married to Lord Richard Percy.

Frank Atkinson has written several books on industrial archaeology in North-East England. He is a member of the Museum and Galleries Commission and was awarded the OBE in 1980 for his services to museums.

Chris Given-Wilson has written many articles for historical journals and has published four books on medieval history. In 1985 he wrote and presented the Channel Four TV series, *The Making of Britain: The Middle Ages*. He is married with two daughters.

David Bellamy is a well-known television personality and distinguished botanist. His programmes have won many awards, among them the Richard Dimbleby Award in 1978. He is involved with many conservation organizations, including the World Wildlife Fund.

David Ward was born in 1960. He graduated with an Honours Degree in Photography from the Polytechnic of Central London in 1983. In addition to his recent work he is currently working on a series of books about walking – a personal passion.

*Front cover photograph: Durham Cathedral,
Co. Durham, see p. 96.
Back cover photograph: The Newport Bridge,
Middlesbrough, Cleveland, see p. 140.*

*Title page: Skyscape, Elsdon, Northumberland,
see p. 104.*

Contents

Introduction

CLAYRE PERCY

Visitors to the North East love its landscape and its castles. These two features impress them all. Some come on purpose to see Hadrian's Wall, that gaunt reminder of Roman occupation. A few associate the North East with Bede, the Jarrow genius who spent many an 8th-century winter writing about angels, Angles and early Christianity. The nature lovers make straight for the Farne Islands, England's most important breeding ground of those charming sea birds, the puffin and the eider duck. Industry has changed much of the North East, sometimes in quite surprising ways, so if you are at all interested in industrial history, this is the place for you.

The following four features give brief and expert accounts of Hadrian's Wall, early Christian history, wildlife and changing industry. You then get to the real meat of a Shell Guide, which is, of course, the gazetteer. But since, for the general public, views and castles are the thing, what better way to start than to have a look at both?

First you must arrive, and the manner of your arrival matters very much indeed. If you possibly can, come by train, sit on the east side of the railway carriage and make a point of being awake when you get to Durham. There you can look out of the window and see one of the great architectural sights of Europe: the view of Durham Cathedral from the train. The railway line curves as it leaves the station so you have not just a front view, but a view from two sides. And when you have sunk back in your seat, stunned by the beauty – because it is astonishing, the North's Norman answer to the Parthenon – the next view is upon you: the arrival into Newcastle over the river Tyne, with its four bridges, its ships, its round Georgian church and its high buildings by the quay. That is *the* way to arrive.

If you come by car, then take the A19, the road that runs parallel to and east of the A1 motorway. It will lead you along the edge of the Cleveland Hills, past the medieval Mount Grace Priory half-hidden in the woods, then suddenly you will be high in the air crossing the river Tees. In front of you will stretch one of the country's great industrial landscapes, mile after square mile of ICI works, giant cranes, cooling towers and chimneys spitting flame. Try to avoid the obvious approach by the A1: it is much the dullest.

Having arrived in the North East, the most tempting areas for the visitor, scenically, are the Cheviots to the north-west, the Pennines to the west, and the coast.

The landscape

The North-East coast has everything in its favour, with miles of yellow sand, interesting rock formations, splendid cliffs, marvellous castles and sea birds – everything, that is, unless you want to bathe. This is out of the question unless you have the constitution of a grey seal. But the very coldness of the sea has a counterbalancing advantage. Never, even on a sunny bank holiday, is the coast overcrowded. Little seaside towns like Alnmouth remain almost within their Victorian perimeters, with fields coming right up to their handsome, stone-built boarding houses.

Statues of Neptune and fishwives on the roof of the Old Fishmarket, Newcastle upon Tyne

Chillingham Castle (see p. 84)

The Cheviot Hills are steeped in history, much of it visible. They contain forts of all ages – Bronze, Iron, Roman and Norman and you can see peel towers, castles and battlegrounds from every stage of the Scottish wars. The hills themselves were volcanic at an earlier period of the Earth's history, but the craggy mountains have eroded away to their present shape: steep, smooth and rounded, with some heather, but mostly covered in white bent grass.

By contrast, the mid-Pennines are limestone hills, but this northern end of the range is mostly heather moorland. Teesdale, which runs up into the moors, is the richest part of the North East from the botanist's point of view – and also from the sportsman's, for here are some of the best grouse moors in the country.

The most striking feature of the country between the Pennines and the north Northumberland coast is the Great Whin Sill. It and the neighbouring 'dykes' are faults through which molten rock was forced upwards to form the rocky outcrops that are very much part of the Northumbrian landscape. The Great Whin Sill itself starts out at sea with the Farne Islands, then goes down the coast making a line of natural fortifications, which has been used to good effect by the castles perched upon it – Lindisfarne, Bamburgh and Dunstanburgh. Then it turns inland where more frivolously Robert Adam placed a folly, Ratcleugh, upon it. Further west it forms an escarpment upon which the Romans built the central stretch of Hadrian's Wall. The Great Whin Sill ends in the Durham Pennines, delighting the tourist in Teesdale where the river falls over it at High Force.

The hill country of the North East is divided up by drystone walls, or dry dykes as they are known in the North. They are sometimes built of whinstone from the Great Whin Sill, but more frequently of limestone or sandstone. Sandstone is the traditional building material of the North East, varying in colour from a warm golden brown to a darkish grey. In south Durham and Cleveland brick is traditional as well. If you are interested in building materials, the oldest brickwork in County Durham dates from 1499 and is in the kitchen in Durham Castle.

Spacious farmlands

Hedges replace the drystone walls as you go east across the region away from the hills, and arable land replaces sheep. The broad coastal plain has the best agricultural land and this is also where most of the coal has been mined. Farms are larger than they are in the South and the fields, particularly in Northumberland, are bigger too, giving the countryside a feeling of spaciousness. On the whole – and this is a sweeping generalization – it is a region of big landowners and they have brought a unity to their estates and a usually high level of maintenance. More than in most districts you are aware of the farming boom of the early 1800s. Not only was farming doing well then because of the Napoleonic Wars, but the great landlords, and smaller men as well, were making money in coal and industry and spending it on their land. It was then that the solid, square farmhouses so noticeable in Northumbria, stone built with slate roofs, and with generous farm buildings all of a piece beside them, were going up. That they are so noticeable is partly because farmhouses in the North normally stand by themselves in the middle of their land, rather than on the edge of a village, as they often do in the South, and partly because the surviving smaller and earlier farm-houses are so few in number.

The reason for this is that in those earlier centuries, particularly in the 300 years or so after 1296, when Edward I attempted to conquer Scotland, the area between Newcastle and the Border was devastated, first by the Scottish wars and then by the Border reivers. But if socially and agriculturally those three centuries were a disaster, from the present-day tourist's point of view they produced some splendid and romantic sights. To some extent the inhabitants lived either in very flimsy dwellings, virtually hovels, which could be rebuilt in a day if needs be, or in castles. The castles remain.

The great castles

There were two great castle-building periods in the North East: under the Normans from 1066 till about 1150; and then during the 14th century. Those of the first period were not necessarily built against the Scots but, like all the other castles constructed throughout England by William the Conqueror, and his barons and their immediate successors, to keep the peace in a conquered country. They mostly began as motte and bailey strongpoints – earthworks with a wooden keep and palisade. A good example can be seen at Elsdon, in the Cheviots. Here the wooden structures were never replaced with stone and they have, of course, disappeared, but the earthwork is on a grand scale, an impressive defence.

The chief Norman castles open to the public are Bamburgh and Newcastle, both royal; Durham and Norham, both of them belonging to the Prince Bishops of Durham; and Alnwick, which became a Percy stronghold in the early 14th century, when its outstanding barbican was built. The principal 14th-century castles that are open are Dunstanburgh, a royal castle, built in 1314 as a replacement for Berwick, which had fallen to the Scots after Bannockburn; Warkworth, another Percy castle; Raby, a Neville castle; Lumley, now a hotel; Chillingham; and Belsay.

The Great Whin Sill, near Cawfields (see p. 8)

Durham, begun in 1070, has a splendid site, on high ground in a loop of the river Wear, and an even more splendid neighbour in the shape of Durham Cathedral. It has been considerably restored, but there is much, even in the interior, that is very early and makes it possible to imagine what living in a Norman castle must have been like. So often, as at Norham, the Prince Bishops' romantic castle on the Tweed, only the keep remains intact, a grim place in which to live (as a rule this was only during sieges; in times of peace owners occupied comfortable quarters in the bailey). At Durham the Prince Bishop lived in something nearer to a palace. The great hall, although restored, is the size of one of the grandest dining halls at Oxford or Cambridge. The Norman gallery, built about 1150, and on one side untouched, is not a room for war, but one to sit in peacefully on a window seat between pillars, below decorated arches, and look out at what was going on in the bailey below. The chapel, built in 1080, before the cathedral was begun, may be primitive but, with its sandstone pillars and capitals with their engaging hunting scenes, it is far from austere.

But the Prince Bishops long remained men of war as well as being great grandees and men of God. When the Scots marched down to Durham in 1346 the Bishop swung his battle axe at the battle of Neville's Cross. Beside him, wielding a battle axe as well, was Earl Percy, and between them they defeated the Scots and King David was taken prisoner.

Shakespeare's *Henry IV, Part 2* begins with Rumour telling of Hotspur's death and calling Warkworth, which was his home, 'a worm-eaten hold of ragged stone'. Southerners were clearly as inaccurate then as they are now in their opinions of the North of England. No one, even after 400 more years of wear and tear, could describe Warkworth in these terms. Nikolaus Pevsner, admirably evenhanded in his praise and blame, describes the castle as: 'the acme of keep design in England and a successful attempt at combining the needs of defence with the comforts of the unfortified manor house'.

The Northumberland Household Book helps to bring alive the ancient inhabitants and the way they lived. This was written for the 5th Earl of Northumberland (1477–1527). It was his father who built the keep so admired by Pevsner. The 5th Earl was based in Yorkshire but he retained his great estates further north and came to Warkworth from time to time. The Household Book describes how when the earl travelled north the yeoman usher of the chamber, the clerk of the kitchen, the cook and the groom of the chamber were sent ahead to get in the food and prepare the castle for his arrival. A week later the luggage train would arrive, 17 carriages or carts and a great wagon, each filled with the particular goods assigned to it. Items ranged from furnishings, bedclothes and other linen, and furniture – even for the chapel – to pots and pans and other kitchen utensils and equipment.

Menus were laid down in detail for the whole year. The Lord and Lady had for their breakfast in Lent a loaf of bread, 2 pieces of salt fish, 6 baked herrings, 4 white herrings, a dish of sprats, a manchette (white bread), a quart of beer, and a quart of wine. The servants had bread, beer and salt fish. On 'Flesh days' there was a chine of mutton or boiled beef instead of fish, and on Saturdays a dish of buttered eggs.

A great variety of wild birds were eaten, but they seem to have been valued by weight rather than taste: the largest, herons, curlews, pheasants, and peacocks, were all a shilling each, while snipe were three for a penny.

A great castle like Warkworth was run by a bureaucracy of clerks, who arranged and ordered everything, even down to how many candles should be used by the porter at the gate.

The Border: wars and raids

The 6th Earl, son of the Percy of the Household Book, was Warden of the Marches and lived at Warkworth. In October 1532 he wrote a report to Henry VIII about a Scottish raid:

> Uppon Tuesday at nyght last came thirty lyght horsemen into a little village of myne called Whittell [now a mining village four miles from Warkworth] having not past sex houses in it, and there wold have fyred the said howses but there was no fyre to gyt there and they forgate to brynge any withe theym; and so take a wyfe, being grete with child in the towne, and said to hyr, 'Where we cannot give the Lord lyght, yet we shall do this in spyte of hym' and gave her three mortell woundes upon the head, and another in the right syde with a daggerr whereupon the said wyf is dede, and the child in her belly is lost.

Reprisals followed and on 15 December 1532 the Earl told the King that on their last raid into Scotland: 'Thankes be to God, we did not leave one pele, gentleman's house or grange unburnt or undestroyed.'

The feuding and the brutality continued right through the 16th century up to and beyond the accession of the Scottish James VI as James I of England. While the rest of England was peaceful and prospering under the Tudors, the Wardens of the Marches still needed their castles like Warkworth and Alnwick. The smaller landowners were not yet building manor houses, but strong peel towers with walls two yards thick. The parsons were building not vicarages but vicars' peels, as at Elsdon, Shilbottle and Corbridge. Even the church towers, like those at Edlingham and Longhoughton, were used as refuges against the Border reivers (also spelled 'reaver', the term comes from an Old English word meaning 'robber, despoiler').

Raids were so common that as late at 1570 an alarm system was enforced. In that year the Earl of Sussex, Lord President of the Council of the North, sent out an order to the Wardens of the Marches that, 'Every man that hath a castle or a towre of stone shall, upon everie fray raised in the night give warning to the countrie by fire in the topps of the castle or towre in such sort as he shall be directed from his warning castle, upon paine of 3s 4d.'

Quite how the Border Ballads emerged from this thuggery to form a chapter in the history of our literature it is hard to see. We can only accept the explanation of Sir Walter Scott, who collected ballads from old people who were still singing them in 1800, that the Borderers, like the Homeric Greeks, were cruel savages, but also poets.

Model fortifications

The most sophisticated work of architecture to be built during this period was, very appropriately, a military one. Queen Elizabeth and her advisers were worried by the chronic unrest on the Borders, and even more so by the possibility of French intervention, so in 1563 Berwick-upon-Tweed was fortified in the most up-to-date manner. Italian experts were consulted and the result was a model of 16th-century defence, very similar to the fortifications at Lucca in northern Italy. The population of Berwick has not exploded so the Elizabethan walls still almost encircle the town. The Royal Border Railway Bridge is as fine as a Roman aqueduct to the west; to the south is the old bridge built between 1610 and 1634. The story goes that in 1603 James VI of Scotland and I of England crossed over the Tweed by this bridge on his way to claim the English throne. It seems that it was so ruinous and alarmed him so much that he insisted that a new one should be built, and this is the result.

The peel tower at Elsdon (see p. 104)

The castles transformed

After the thrones of England and Scotland were united under the Stuarts, the North East became a more peaceful place. Only a very few years elapsed between the castles being used in earnest and their transformation into romantic country houses. In 1621 Chipchase, a 14th-century castle in the valley of the North Tyne, had a grand Jacobean house built on to it with big mullioned windows and no suggestion of defences. At about the same time Chillingham was partly remodelled as a country house. In 1720 Lumley, a castle of the same type, was altered by Vanbrugh.

By the mid-18th century grand country houses like Wallington were being built, but down the social scale conditions remained more primitive than in the South. The 1st Duke of Northumberland employed Charles Dodgson, Lewis Carroll's great-grandfather, as tutor to his son, and afterwards gave him the church living of Elsdon, near Otterburn in the Cheviots. He was a sophisticated young man, later becoming a bishop, and he was not impressed with his new home, the vicar's peel. On 20 March 1762 he wrote to his former pupil:

> The vestibule of the castle is a low stable, above it is the kitchen in which are two little beds joining to each other, the curate and his wife lay in one and Marjery the maid in the other, I lay in the Parlour, between two beds, to keep me from being frozen to death, for as we keep open house the winds enter from every corner, and are apt to creep into bed with us . . . my head is entrench'd in three nightcaps and my throat which has been very bad is fortifyed with a pair of stockings twisted in the form of a cravat, I wear two shirts at a time and for want of a wardrobe hang my great coat on my own back.

In the same year Alnwick was being gothicized by Robert Adam for the 1st Duke and his wife, the Northumberland heiress.

Two generations later, in 1854, Adam's work was thought to be too flimsy and a solid reconstruction was carried out by Salvin to great effect. Effective, too, was Salvin's work at Durham Castle, where he rebuilt the keep when the castle was transferred to the University. Raby, a castle on the same scale as Alnwick, was altered to suit both its 18th- and its 19th-century owners. Lindisfarne, a small Tudor castle, now owned by the National Trust, was almost rebuilt from a ruinous state by Edwin Lutyens in 1904. He created not a copy of a medieval castle, but a simple, solid and yet romantic building, rugged like the North East.

The future

What of the future? The most violent change to the landscape has been the planting of Kielder, the biggest man-made forest encircling the biggest man-made lake in the country. That part of the country now feels curiously alien – more like, say, Sweden than the Borders – with solid spruce covering the once bare hills. It is to be hoped that the future of the countryside does not lie in that direction. As for the castles, Chillingham is a hopeful sign. Here a castle, derelict for 40 years, is being restored and opened to the public and its gardens carefully remade, by a private owner. It is in a way comforting that the cliffs of the North East are still being used for our defences, but giant saucers sit on them instead of Norman castles, with radar instead of 'fire in the topps of the towers'.

Overleaf: The old bridge, Berwick-upon-Tweed (see p. 68)

The Changing Face of Industry in the North East

FRANK ATKINSON

One of the remarkable characteristics of Britain is the way its landscape has been changed by man over the course of centuries, and nowhere can this be better seen than in North-East England. Here is countryside once completely rural, with coastal plains and dales, and bearing as its crown one of the finest buildings in Europe, Durham Cathedral. Yet the North East was subjected to early industrial operations, as far back as Elizabethan times, and during the 19th century it became one of the richest, if blackest, parts of the richest country in the world. It is now struggling to find occupations for a population swollen by the demands of that Victorian industry, which itself has wasted away.

Early industries

Among the oldest industries still to be traced in North-East England is coal, for although the period of the greatest expansion of coal mining was the 19th century, it was a prosperous and active industry several centuries earlier. Thus Cockfield Fell, for example, near Bishop Auckland in County Durham, is now preserved as an archaeologically significant site (although it is by no means visually very exciting). Causey Arch, on the other hand, dating from 1727, is an impressive high stone arch spanning a deep gorge which once carried horse-drawn coal wagons from a nearby colliery towards the river Tyne, whence the coal was exported. These wagons, themselves of a characteristic shape to be found only in the North East, were drawn along wagonways which crisscrossed the landscape, along embankments and cuttings, from the growing numbers of coal mines down to the staithes built first along the banks of the river Tyne, and later along the Wear and the Tees. Traces of these wagonways of the 17th, 18th and 19th centuries can still be identified, many now in use as footpaths.

Along these graded routes tracks were put down, first of wood, then covered with iron, originally cast, and finally rolled as iron and steel rails. Of course little of all this remains on the ground, but the early railways that carried steam locomotives along these and similar tracks have left more pronounced remains and ruins of buildings and bridges. One of the earliest of such lines was that constructed by George Stephenson in 1825 and now known as the Stockton and Darlington Railway. This ran from Witton Colliery, crossed the river Gaunless by an iron bridge (the first railway bridge of its kind and now preserved at the York National Railway Museum) and came to the foot of an incline to the west of Shildon, where the buildings that housed a big steam haulage engine are still standing. From there, by way of Darlington, it eventually came to the river Tees at Stockton. Remains of this kind are a delight to the industrial arachaeologist and fortuitously exist because, at the time they ceased work, there was no economic or other pressure to clear the land.

In similar fashion the moorlands of west Durham and south-west Northumberland are scattered with remnants of 18th- and 19th-century lead-mining activities. One of the more dramatic is the giant (30 ft diameter) waterwheel at Killhope in upper

Causey Arch *(see p. 64)*

Killhope Wheel Mining Centre (see p. 134)

Weardale that once drove steel rollers to crush mined lead ore, which would then be 'washed' to separate off the ore from the associated stone and other minerals. Here is another example of building and machinery, in use probably until around 1890, which nevertheless stood rusting and rotting until the 1950s before anyone thought of clearing the site. By then, fortunately, an awareness of the value of such sites was growing and now 30 years later Killhope has been developed as a tourist attraction.

The early 19th-century lead industry has left other notable features on the moorland landscape: giant 'hushes' or scars where temporarily dammed water was allowed to scour the hillsides to expose veins of lead in the underlying rocks. And perhaps some of the most lasting features of that industry are the flues or 'pipes' that run up and over the hills from smelt mills in the valley bottoms to stubby chimneys near the tops of the fells. These mile-long flues were designed, not to protect the health of either workers or livestock, but to permit volatile lead vapour to condense and thus increase the productivity of the smelting process. 'Flue walking' as a special variety of fell walking can be fascinating as you trace the stonework up the hillsides and attempt to identify the curious features along the way, where the flues could be entered for cleaning.

An industry long gone, of which nothing visible survives, was that of saltmaking. In the 17th and 18th centuries seawater was boiled to produce salt, and a traveller in 1635 called at 'Tine-mouth' and 'the Sheeldes' and described 'panns which are not to be numbered, placed in the river-mouth and wrought with coals brought by water from Newcastle pits'. Ninety years later Lord Harley, while travelling north, visited South Shields: 'which is the chief place for making salt. The houses are poor little hovels, and are in a perpetual thick nasty smoke. It has 200 salt pans; each employs 3 men. Each pan makes one tun and a ¼ of salt at 8 boilings which last 3 days and a half

... The wages for Pumpers (pumping the salt water) is 5d per diem and the Watchers, who continually have an eye to the pans, have 6d a day.' This was obviously an industry that impressed travellers of its day, yet happily is no longer with us. Blyth must think itself particularly fortunate that it is not now noted for 'black skies and white salt'.

An early industry to be brought into the region was that of iron- and steelmaking and working. Ambrose Crowley, a Midlands ironmaster, established a nailmaking manufactory at Sunderland around 1685, although only a few years later he had moved it inland to Winlaton, where his works flourished until halfway through the 19th century, still run by the same family, making chains, anchors and other light and heavy ironwork. The Crowley firm must be unique among industrial firms in having had a written constitution. *The Law Book of the Crowley Ironworks* is a remarkable document by any standard and was an attempt to solve the problems of how to control large-scale industrial production from a considerable distance. This manuscript is now preserved in the British Museum: virtually the only remnant of that long-lasting and successful industrial empire.

Another industry that came early to the region was glassmaking. Until the 17th century, like so many industries requiring heat, wood had been the chief fuel, but when wood became expensive and legally forbidden for many purposes, coal began to be tried. However, its sulphur content often made it unsuitable as a crude fuel and it is therefore interesting to learn of one industrialist's technical struggle to use it. Sir Robert Mansell, according to his own evidence, obtained a patent in 1615 for making glass with coal and after trying to start works in London and elsewhere, he was 'enforced for his last refuge contrary to all man's opinion to make triall at Newcastle upon Tyne where after the expense of many thousand pounds, a worke for window-glasse was effected with Newcastle Cole.' The industry eventually prospered and one visible remnant, possibly of the late 18th century, is an enormous brick-built 'cone' at Lemington on the north bank of the Tyne to the west of Newcastle, within which glassblowers would cluster around the 'pots' of molten glass, each drawing out a blob of glass and blowing and shaping it into a bottle.

The industrial exports of the region – mostly coal, but also glass and later pottery – led to considerable riverside developments. The export of coal in particular necessitated elaborate staithes where the coal, brought by wagon, could be stored until the time was suitable for it to be transported further down river by shallow craft known as 'keels', to the colliers or seagoing ships awaiting the tide. And since the ships had probably arrived in ballast, that is bearing sand or similar cheap but weighty material, this ballast had first to be tipped and so ballast heaps began to grow on some of the river banks. To some extent the ballast heaps remain, although the early staithes have long been replaced by more modern structures such as quays and shipbuilding berths.

Geordie's heyday: the 19th century

Phrases like 'taking coals to Newcastle' or 'Newcastle Roads' (meaning colliery wagonways), or a once common saying like 'the world over you'll find a rat, a flea and a Newcastle grindstone', all indicate how Georgian England perceived the North East, personified by Newcastle, as being heavily industrialized.

Yet if the landscape of so much of Durham and Northumberland could then be thought of as an industrial region, how much more so when the developments of the

19th century got into their stride and labour was sucked into the region – from its own rural countryside; from other rural areas suffering bad times, like Norfolk; from depressed metal-mining areas like Cornwall and Derbyshire; from Ireland and from Scotland. Many of these Victorian 'invaders' brought young families and became part of a rapidly urbanized population that took on a character now thought of as indigenous. Many of those entering the region last century came without particular skills of use in their new environment, frequently being unskilled labourers. Yet from this workforce grew the skills that have been popularly accepted in the 20th century as having been such a pronounced feature of the North East.

As was the case in the previous century, coal lay at the centre of the region's industrial structure. Throughout the 19th century coal extraction grew and more and more pits were sunk. Before mid-century the 'concealed' coalfield of east Durham had been opened up, proving to have good thick workable seams, although at a greater depth than had previously been mined, and requiring heavy pumping to keep the pits clear of flooding. During that century of expansion not only the number but also the size of pits grew, steam came into its own as a power source for pumping, and now also for winding. One of the earliest successful designs of steam winders was that patented by Phineas Crowther of Newcastle upon Tyne in 1800. Before long these 'vertical winders' were in use across the coalfield in their characteristically shaped tall square stone buildings. Only one remains, built by Joicey of Newcastle in 1855.

During the second half of the 19th century, the Durham and south Northumberland coalfield took on the characteristics that have for long after lingered in the public mind. Colliery buildings sprang up, pitheaps grew both in height and area. So much so that one of the largest, at the Dean and Chapter colliery at Ferryhill alongside the old route of the A1, covered over 60 acres by the early 1900s. Across the smoke-laden countryside the horse-drawn wagonways were replaced by a less leisurely, steam-powered railway system. The advent of the first steam-hauled public railway system in the world was only to be expected in the region, since it was a natural successor to those 'Newcastle Roads' of more than a century earlier. Thus the Stockton and Darlington Railway of 1825 was only the first of many railways built across Durham and Northumberland. Many miles of track were constructed by colliery companies and many more by railway companies, and gradually all coalesced. The North Eastern Railway Company was formed in 1854 and at that point owned over 10,000 of the characteristically shaped 'chaldron' wagons. After further mergers, including the Stockton and Darlington itself in 1863, the number had increased to over 26,000, although gradually this fell as more efficient modern designs took over.

At first serving a local use for the transport of coal, and then becoming part of a national network, as George Hudson brought into being the London to Scotland link, this growing railway system built up its own industrial demands. Locomotive and wagon-building works sprang up at Newcastle, Darlington and Shildon: great sprawling engineering works, now closed or converted to other uses. Iron and steel were required in ever-growing quantities and blast furnaces were to be found developing in the most unlikely situations, such as Tow Law, Birtley, Tudhoe, and even Stanhope in Weardale. Perhaps the most rurally situated blast furnace was at Ridsdale in Northumberland near the A68. Remarkably the derelict engine house still stands by the roadside, looking rather like the keep of a Border castle.

Middlesbrough, near the mouth of the river Tees, began its explosive growth with the Quaker-inspired extension of the Stockton and Darlington Railway to the river

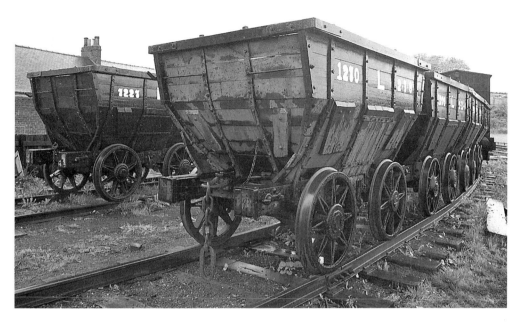

'Chaldron' wagon, Beamish Open Air Museum (see p. 63)

bank at what was at first called 'Port Darlington'. From two or three farming families in 1800, the population had grown to some 20,000 by the 1860s and 90,000 by 1900. The discovery of ironstone in the Cleveland Hills in the middle of the century led to a hasty development of blast furnaces at Middlesbrough, followed by other ironworking industries. A century later the 'ironmasters' district' is again clear of industry and, like so many one-industry towns, Middlesbrough is seeking a successor to iron and steel; although nearby Billingham, which has grown with the ICI chemical industry, is still reasonably prosperous.

After coal the North East has been particularly noted for its shipbuilding. The period of expansion for this industry stretched from around 1860 to the First World War. It had, however, begun much earlier than that. Colliery owners had themselves become interested in shipbuilding as a means of improving the export of coal, as well as taking part in a growing industry. Charles Palmer, a partner in the coal firm of John Bowes and Partners, set up his own shipbuilding company in 1851 at Jarrow, taking over a yard that had been building frigates since the turn of the century. An early name of the firm, the General Iron Screw Collier Company, speaks for itself, and only a year after starting work at Jarrow, Palmer was able to launch the *John Bowes*, a ship which – in modern terms – 'broke the mould'. It was a steam-powered collier, it used water ballast, pumped out by the engines used for the screw propeller, and the design of the holds was considerably improved.

Through the second half of the 19th century the banks of the Tyne became covered by shipyards, chemical works, coal shipment staithes and so on. Further inland the goods yards and railway systems linked everything, taking precedence over all else, while round about cheap mass housing sprang up. A glimpse of the crowded

Old iron-smelting works, Ridsdale

conditions and rough juxtapositions can be gained from old photographs showing huge ships being built virtually at the bottom of many a mean street.

From Daniel Defoe's description of Newcastle in 1727, 'They build ships here to perfection . . .', to a period a century and a half later, the shipbuilding industry had grown beyond comprehension. By 1889, for example, when the British Association visited Newcastle for the third time, British shipbuilding produced four out of every five ships launched in the whole world and the North East alone produced on occasion more than 40 per cent of the world total. Rarely, if ever, has a basic industry secured such a worldwide domination. Everything seemed ideal for such growth: the material resources of coal and iron ore were to hand and the need for shipping for the export of coal. Yet an additional catalyst was surely the men of that moment: William Armstrong, Charles Palmer, George Hunter, Andrew Leslie and a dozen others. Several had been born in the region and others came here. Around them sprang their firms and thus the industry. As Armstrong himself once commented of that time, there was 'something in the air'. And labour flowed in and work flowed out, the North East becoming for a short time just about the richest part of the richest country in the world. It has been said: 'If you wanted coal you came to the North East. If you wanted engineering goods you came, or if you wanted armaments or chemicals, iron or machinery. And, in particular, you came if you wanted ships.'

Yet by the time of the Second World War an end was in sight. Just as it is difficult to identify the secret of the region's growth and success, so it is not easy to trace the seeds of failure. Labour relations were soured; demarcation disputes caused great loss of working time, and the inventiveness and enterprise of the last century seemed lost.

Other industries similarly prospered and declined. One, clearly linked to iron and coal, was that of engineering which benefited from, and helped to feed the growth of, coal export, railways and shipping. Many names which were still to be found until comparatively recently included Losh Wilson and Bell, Robert Stephenson, W. G. Armstrong, Gilkes and Wilson, and several of their products may still be observed, although some now are only of industrial arachaeological interest. The Ryhope water-pumping engines, by R. and W. Hawthorn (1868) are preserved *in situ* and steamed occasionally; the Joicey colliery winder (1855) is steamed at Beamish (the North of England Open Air Museum); the Swing Bridge at Newcastle (1876) by Armstrong is still in working order and the fine High Level Bridge over the Tyne (1845) by Robert Stephenson still carries both rail and road traffic. Bridgebuilding had expanded as needs appeared and developed, and the Cleveland Bridge Company of Darlington, for example, is still active after more than a century of production.

Yet other industries that began or prospered on account of local materials were those of glass production, pottery and chemicals. On the banks of the Tyne the chemical industry, at one time known as the 'Alkali Trade', had found success largely on account of cheap coal and seawater: the making of salt and the use of copperas, or 'fool's gold', associated with coal. As the century drew on new chemical processes changed the emphasis and led to the industry moving to Tyneside, attracted by large underground salt deposits and supported in later years by deposits of anhydrite. A recent growth of pharmaceutical manufacturing in south Northumberland does not appear to have had any connection with this earlier chemical industry.

Naturally following the early success of the old chemical industry was that of soap manufacture, still happily to be found on Tyneside, if now rather attenuated. The simple formula 'alkali plus fat gives soap' helps to indicate why it developed here. This is another variation of the formula 'alkali plus sand plus lime gives glass', which explains that other expanding industry of last century, also still to be found at Sunderland, where heatproof glass for cooking vessels is made. This also helps to explain another once-enormous area of glass and copperas works, at Seaton Sluice where the Delaval family financed great industrial development and produced that 'sluice' or artificial harbour, traces of which can still be seen today.

The pottery industry flourished in common with glass, as the 19th century demanded more containers and higher standards, and more widespread use of domestic ware. Potteries were to be found along the Tyne and Wear in that century and one or two more self-conscious establishments around Middlesbrough. These expanded prodigiously into the present century, but have gradually been reduced as better materials and more efficient production techniques have been used elsewhere.

Between the wars

The period between the two world wars was no better for the North East and following a Conference of Christian Politics, Economics and Citizenship, held in Newcastle in 1924, a recommendation was produced that 'a most practicable contribution to the welfare of Tyneside would be a truthful and comprehensive survey of the facts'. A Bureau of Social Research was set up in the autumn of 1925 and Dr Henry Mess was appointed Director. His survey *Industrial Tyneside* was published in 1928. One of its conclusions may be compared and contrasted 60 years on: ' . . . the Tyneside population is [probably] the worst housed population in England and Wales. The health of the area is at least as bad as that of any other district, and the amount of tuberculosis is appalling.' At least some things have improved since then.

Ellen Wilkinson wrote of Jarrow in *The Town That Was Murdered* in 1939, following the Jarrow March of 1936. It was in 1936, too, that the Team Valley Trading Estate was funded by the Government 'against the unemployment and distress of Tyneside'. It is a remarkable example of planned architecture by W. Holford, very much of its period, although now undergoing much change and expansion.

Postwar New Towns, such as Peterlee and Newton Aycliffe, followed by Washington and Cramlington, have performed their part in broadening the base of manufacture in the North East, offering 'green field' sites for cleaner and lighter industries than the staple ones of the region. People may, however, be forgiven for repeating the not-very-old dictum 'when Britain sneezes the North East goes down with flu', as light and service industries come and go, helped or discouraged according to the amount and direction of Government grants and the shape of regional aid of the day. Meanwhile other dispersed but well-meaning attempts at establishing small industrial estates are to be found dotted around the region, for example one at Hexham (which is otherwise a small country town in rural Tynedale), where chipboard is produced.

More recent developments

The third quarter of the 20th century saw an increasingly rapid decline of traditional industries in the region and one of the first to show this was the coal industry, for long seen as the staple occupation of Durham and south-east Northumberland, which speeded its reduction as older pits were closed or amalgamated. Large-scale transfers of mining populations was one of the more humane ways of ameliorating this, as families and indeed whole communities were invited to move into the Nottingham-shire and other coalfields where expansion was still possible. Later miners from west Durham, where the older and increasingly exhausted pits were being closed in the 1970s, were offered jobs in coastal pits in east Durham, and for a time unemployment was contained within acceptable bounds. Government aid, encouraging factories to be established in the region, had its successes as, for example, with the large factory at Birtley making tractors and earth-moving machinery (alas closed in the mid-1980s); the ball-bearing factory near Consett of about 1950, which at one time employed over 1200 workers and is now closed; and the battery factory (1968) at Tanfield Lea, which at its most successful employed 1500 workers and exported a large percentage of its production, although it has suffered a steady decline since 1979 and is now down to about 350 employees. However, changes in international demands are blamed for reductions or closures at these and other similar factories.

Derwentside, in central west Durham, which at the height of its coal-mining prosperity had more than a dozen collieries employing perhaps several thousand workers, now has not a single pit within its boundaries. The figures for the whole north-eastern coalfield are even more noteworthy: in 1948, at the vesting date of the National Coal Board, there were 128 pits where now there are eight, all of them at or near the coast.

As the pits were being phased out other industries were still prospering, like the enormous iron and steel complex at Consett, which even as recently as the 1970s was employing more than 6000 workers, together with those other industries brought here by Government intervention – all flourishing for a time.

Yet further declines followed, seemingly inevitably, until the unemployment rate rose to its present cheerless figure of around 20 per cent.

The successor industries and the future

Nevertheless, all is not lost, for strenuous efforts to seek successor industries go on and small works are nursed and nurtured within the area once blackened by the prosperous, if heavy, iron- and steelworks at Consett. Around 200 small companies here now employ some 3500 men and women. In an area that once provided employment mostly for men, in heavy industry or underground, women are now increasingly required for many assembly jobs and similar light industrial work.

Three glimmers of light are to be spied, although only one of these may be termed 'real' industry, namely the new and promising car factory at Washington founded recently by Nissan from Japan, which began production in 1986. This company decided upon the North East as its European base and its first phase, assembling imported parts, appears to have gone according to plan and the second phase is about to begin, whereby an increasing percentage of British manufactured parts will be assembled. Like most manufacturing growth points, this should bring increased prosperity to the region.

The two other hopeful lightenings of the gloom come from service industries: something the North East has rarely provided in the past. The Eldon Square shopping development in Newcastle upon Tyne began trading in 1976 and now provides a prosperous facility in the city centre (not without controversy, however, as its construction destroyed the larger part of John Dobson's 1824 Eldon Square, which was once one of Newcastle's most attractive features, and it is argued that its very success has damaged other shopping streets by its concentrated prosperity).

The Eldon Square complex is now itself threatened by the Metro Centre development built on derelict, low-lying land to the west of Gateshead. Whether this should be praised or not cannot yet be determined. It is, however, undeniable that some 4500 jobs are provided by the enormous development and visibly true that every car parking space provided (and there are already 7000 of these) is filled for much of the week, while attractively designed and spacious galleries are thronged with well-dressed shoppers. It has to be assumed that for the employed of the region, shopping is now a pleasure as well as being a necessity; and presumably the 20 per cent or so of unemployed families subsist in their poorer areas, unable even to find the bus fare necessary to get to this new land of plenty.

Finally, an industry that seems to be undergoing world expansion – again tapping the pockets of the employed – is tourism. The difference, at least to the North East, lies in the fact that tourism brings funds into the region, whereas Eldon Square, Metro Centre and the many other shopping centres and malls that have sprung up, are largely recirculating money within the region, or withdrawing it to the headquarters of the national and multinational food and goods suppliers.

Hadrian's Wall and Durham Cathedral, as well as a number of castles, have long provided relatively minor attractions in the North East. Now, however, a more positive approach may be discerned. The Northumbria Tourist Board makes great efforts and a 'Prince Bishop's Land' initiative by Durham County Council shows promise. Undoubtedly a feather in the cap of the region is the North of England Open Air Museum at Beamish, which now attracts over 300,000 visitors annually, of which half are tourists to the region, and has a workforce of over 200.

So if service industries are to be the latest form of industrial development in a region once blackened by smoke, dazed by noise and scattered with unsightliness, then the face of the countryside may be changing at last for the better.

Early Christianity in the North East: The Golden Age of Northumbria CHRIS GIVEN-WILSON

As the official religion of the Roman Empire, Christianity came to the province of Britain in the 4th century AD, at which time bishoprics were established at York, Lincoln, London, and quite probably elsewhere. By about 410, however, the Romans had withdrawn from Britain, and the decline of cities and the widespread migration of pagan Germanic peoples (principally the Angles, Saxons, and Jutes) from the Continent to Britain during the 5th and 6th centuries meant that in much of lowland Britain Christianity either disappeared or was driven underground. There is no doubt, however, that some form of Christian practice was maintained in parts of the north and west. St Patrick, for example, who carried Christianity to parts of Ireland in the mid-5th century, came from the north-west of England. Christianity was widely established in Ireland and in 563 St Columba sailed over the Irish Sea to Argyll and founded a monastery at Iona, and from this Scottish island Christian influences began to reach down into Northumbria.

The kingdom of Northumbria

By the beginning of the 7th century, Anglo-Saxon Britain was broadly divided into seven major kingdoms: Northumbria (that is, the lands north of the Humber), Mercia (the Midland kingdom), East Anglia, Essex (the East Saxon kingdom), Wessex (West Saxon), Sussex (South Saxon) and Kent. Several of these incorporated other smaller kingdoms and Northumbria was a federation of two kingdoms, in the north Bernicia, which stretched from the Forth to the Tyne (modern Lothian, Borders and Northumberland, roughly speaking); and southern Deira, which reached from the Tyne to the Humber (modern Durham, North and West Yorkshire, and North Humberside). Ethelfrid (AD c. 593–616), the first Northumbrian king of whom we have any real knowledge, came from the Bernician royal line, but in 603 he succeeded in extending his rule over Deira as well, as a result of which his rival Edwin, the son of King Ælla of Deira, fled into exile at the court of Redwald, or Rædwald, king of the East Angles. Here Edwin came into contact with the new Roman Christianity which had begun to penetrate the south.

It was to the Kentish King Ethelbert (c. 560–616) and his Christian wife Bertha that Pope Gregory the Great had directed his famous mission under St Augustine in 597, which enjoyed considerable initial success. Ethelbert and many of his nobles were rapidly converted, and by the time of his death the new faith had also reached some of the southern kingdoms such as Essex and East Anglia. Ethelbert was at this time acknowledged as the *Bretwalda*, the nominal overlord of the English kingdoms south of the Humber, and thus had the ability to exert influence beyond the borders of Kent. This was always an important factor in the early spread of Christianity. The essential first task of the missionaries was to convert the kings and their nobles, for political or military superiority and religious conversion frequently went hand in hand.

Carpet page facing the beginning of St Matthew's Gospel, Lindisfarne Gospels, c. 698 (British Library, Cotton Ms. Nero D.IV, folio 26v.)

The reign of Edwin

Thus it was in Northumbria. In 616, Redwald helped Edwin to overcome King Ethelfrid, and for the next sixteen years Edwin ruled as king of the whole of Northumbria. Edwin's reign inaugurated what is often called the Golden Age of Northumbria: golden not only because it witnessed the political ascendancy of the kings of Northumbria (notably Edwin, Oswald and Oswy) in England, but also because it was marked by a flowering of Christian art and learning in the north which was to reach its pinnacle of achievement in such works as the Lindisfarne Gospels, and the scholar Bede's *Ecclesiastical History of the English Nation* – our main source for the period. Roman Christianity first came to Northumbria in 625, when Edwin married Ethelburga, the daughter of Ethelbert of Kent. Ethelburga was Christian, and it was agreed that she would be free to practise her religion at Edwin's court. Thus when she came north she brought with her a priest from Rome, the monk Paulinus. Paulinus had been in England since 601, having been sent by Pope Gregory in that year to assist Augustine, and before his journey north he was consecrated as bishop of York. Like Augustine in Kent, his success at court was remarkably rapid. Within a year Edwin had allowed his infant daughter to be baptized into the Christian faith, and in the spring of 627 – following a successful campaign against the West Saxons (which he was said to have attributed to the intervention of his new wife's deity) and a heavenly vision – Edwin held a council of his chief nobles to determine whether he ought to accept the new religion. Bede has left us a fascinating traditional account of this council. Foremost in arguing for the acceptance of Christianity was said to be Edwin's pagan high priest, Coifi, who declared that the new religion had proved itself more powerful than his own, whereupon the case for paganism crumbled. Coifi himself led the destruction of the old pagan temples, and on Easter Day 627, in the little wooden oratory that Paulinus had constructed at York, the king was baptized. According to Bede, he was swiftly followed by 'all the nobility of his kingdom and a large number of humbler folk'. This was followed by the building of a more permanent church at York, in stone, and by an evangelizing mission by Paulinus to the north, during which numerous baptisms were performed. A wooden church has been excavated at Edwin's palace site at Yeavering, Borders Region.

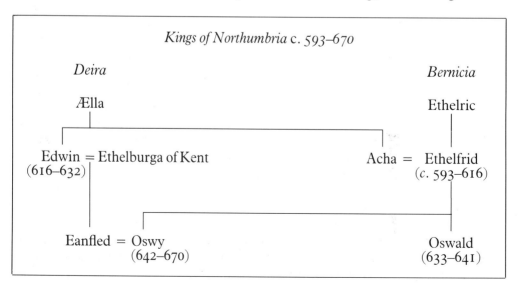

Kings of Northumbria c. 593–670

It is not always easy to know why some kings embraced Christianity and others refused to but politics and prestige were certainly important. The promise of eternal life was also influential. Thus, according to Bede, one of Edwin's nobles at the council of 627 compared the life of man on earth to 'the swift flight of a single sparrow through the banqueting hall where you are sitting at dinner on a winter's day with your thanes and counsellors':

> This sparrow flies swifly in through one door of the hall, and out through another. While he is inside, he is safe from the winter storms, but after a few moments of comfort, he vanishes from sight into the wintry world from which he came. Similarly, man appears on earth for but a little while, but of what went before this life or of what follows, we know nothing. Therefore, if this new teaching has brought any more certain knowledge, it seems right that we should follow it.

Yet the Christian God, like the pagan deities whom be superseded, also had to prove his worth to his supporters, and nowhere more so than on the battlefield. While he lived, Edwin's stature and influence as *Bretwalda* did much to encourage the acceptance of Christianity in England; but when he was slain by the pagan King Penda of Mercia at the battle of Hatfield Chase (near Doncaster) in October 632, it marked not only the temporary eclipse of Northumbrian dominance in England, but also the official collapse of Christianity in the north. Paulinus fled south, taking with him Queen Ethelburga and her daughter Eanfled, where they found refuge at the court of the Kentish King Eadbald (Ethelburga's brother). Only the courageous James the Deacon was left behind by Paulinus to care for his church at York, but there was little that James could achieve against the resurgence of paganism. During the next year Northumbria was ravaged by Penda and his ally, the Welsh Christian King Cadwalla. 'At this time,' says Bede, 'a terrible slaughter took place among the Northumbrian church and nation.'

Oswald and Irish Christianity
Within little more than a year, however, Christian worship was re-established in Northumbria, and once again it was through military strength that this was accomplished. At the time of his victory over Ethelfrid in 616, Edwin had driven into exile the princes of the Bernician royal house, Oswald and Oswy. Oswald took refuge at the monastery of Iona, where he was brought up by monks of St Columba's foundation, but on hearing of Edwin's death he marched south and killed Cadwalla at the battle of Heavenfield (near Hexham) late in 633. He was soon ruling the whole of Northumbria and was even acknowledged as *Bretwalda*. The re-adoption of Christianity in Northumbria from Iona brought with it a new problem, however. It was to the Irish monks of Iona, not the Roman missionaries of the south, that Oswald looked to restore the faith to his kingdom; and in 634, in response to the king's request, a party of Ionan monks led by Aidan arrived at the royal court. Oswald gave them the island of Lindisfarne as their base where they established the first documented monastery in Northumbria. Further monastic foundations soon followed: during the next 30 years about a dozen religious houses were founded in Oswald's kingdom, of which the most celebrated were Tynemouth, Gilling, Old Melrose, Lastingham, and the 'double houses' of monks and nuns at Hartlepool and Whitby, both of which were under the rule of Abbess Hilda, the great-niece of King Edwin. Little is known about the rules followed in these early monasteries, but they

were certainly of the unreformed Irish type, with the monks or nuns living in separate cells grouped around the church (rather than in a dormitory), the abbot's or abbess's cell a little distance apart, and the whole complex surrounded by a wall to cut it off from the world outside. Excavations at Whitby in 1924–5 revealed the foundations of some of the cells, although they have since been reburied.

Because of the lack of towns in early Christian Ireland, monastic communities had become the centres of the church, giving rise to an unusual structure where bishops and priests were under the authority of abbots. It was also an evangelizing church, and missionary work, as Bede tells us, was very much a part of Aidan's life:

> Whether in town or country, he always travelled on foot unless compelled by necessity to ride, and whatever people he met on his walks, whether high or low, he stopped and spoke to them. If they were heathen, he urged them to be baptized; if they were Christians, he strengthened their faith, and inspired them by word and deed to live a good life and to be generous to others.

The piety and humility of Aidan and his fellow Celts undoubtedly appealed greatly to the Northumbrian people. But what the Celtic church really lacked was the diocesan and organizational structure that underlay the church in the rest of Western Europe. The difference between the two churches is encapsulated in the differing ideas concerning the functions of a bishop. A Roman bishop was above all the administrator of his diocese, a defined area within which the clergy were directly responsible to him. The church in parts of Wales and Ireland accorded this title to those who, through the purity of their lives, proved themselves especially worthy of it. Thus there might, for example, be several bishops living in one monastery, under the rule of the abbot. There were other differences between the two churches, such as the style of the monastic tonsure and, most pressing of all in the short term, the means of calculating the date of Easter. Whereas the Roman church by the 7th century had adopted the 19-year cycle to calculate the date of Easter, part of the Celtic church still used the antiquated and less accurate 84-year cycle. Thus in Britain, where Christians of the two traditions mingled, they could be celebrating the most important festival of the church at different times.

Under King Oswald the Celtic church was dominant in Northumbria, but after his death in 641 (also at the hands of Penda of Mercia), the problem of reconciling the two branches of northern Christianity became more insistent. Oswald was succeeded by his brother Oswy (642–70), the most powerful of the 7th-century Northumbrian overlords, who succeeded in 654 in defeating and killing Penda, the scourge of English Christianity, and thus became *Bretwalda* of the southern English kingdoms. Oswy married Eanfled, that daughter of King Edwin who had fled to the Kentish court with Paulinus in 632, and it was this that brought the question of Celtic unorthodoxy to the fore. Naturally Eanfled had been brought up as a Roman Christian, and when she came north she brought her chaplain Romanus with her. As Bede tells us, this created a great problem in the royal household:

> It is said that the confusion in those days was such that Easter was sometimes kept twice in one year, so that when the king had ended Lent and was keeping Easter Sunday, the queen and her attendants were still fasting and keeping Palm Sunday . . . This dispute rightly began to trouble the minds and consciences of many people, who feared that they might have received the name of Christian in vain.

Moreover, Oswy's son Alchfrith, who had been set up by his father as under-king in Deira, was greatly influenced by the teaching of Wilfrid of Ripon, an uncompromising supporter of Roman practice, decided to call a council to resolve the problem.

The Synod of Whitby: Roman practice triumphant

This council, the celebrated Synod of Whitby, met in the year 664 at Abbess Hilda's newly founded double monastery high on the east cliff overlooking the 'Bay of the Beacon', as Whitby was then called. Wilfrid spoke on behalf of the Frankish bishop Agilbert and became chief protagonist for the Roman cause; Colman, bishop of Lindisfarne (Aidan had died in 651), defended Celtic practices. Also present, as well as Oswy, Alchfrith and Hilda, were James the Deacon, Cedd, bishop of the East Saxons, as well as Agilbert, bishop of the West Saxons. Thus it was more than just a Northumbrian occasion. It concentrated on the calculation of the date of Easter. 'King Oswy,' according to Bede,

> opened by observing that all who served the One God should observe one rule of life, and since they all hoped for one kingdom in heaven, they should not differ in celebrating the sacraments of heaven. The synod now had the task of determining which was the truer tradition, and this should be loyally accepted by all. He then directed his own bishop Colman to speak first, and to explain his own rite and its origin.

Bede, brought up in the Continental tradition, has left us a fuller and more coherent account of the arguments advanced by Wilfrid than of those of Colman. In the end it

Left: Pectoral cross of St Cuthbert, 7th century (see p. 37). Right: The figure of Jonah on the 10th-century stole which was also found in St Cuthbert's coffin (Both items by courtesy of the Dean and Chapter of Durham)

came down to a choice between the teaching of St Peter and the practice of St Columba. Not surprisingly Peter emerged as the authority.

'Then I tell you,' concluded the king, 'Peter is the guardian of the gates of heaven, and I shall not contradict him. I shall obey his commands in everything to the best of my knowledge and ability; otherwise, when I come to the gates of heaven, there may be no-one to open them, because he who holds the keys has turned away.' When the king said this, all present both high and low signified their agreement and, abandoning their imperfect customs, hastened to adopt those which they had learned to be better.

Thus was Roman practice triumphant at Whitby. Colman and several of his followers retired to Ireland via Iona in order to practise what they regarded as the true customs of the church, and it took another 50 years to persuade the monks of Iona to adopt the Roman Easter. Nevertheless, the Synod of Whitby was a watershed in early English Christianity, for it meant that it was now possible to organize the English church as one body. It was to this task that Theodore of Tarsus, who came over from Rome in 669 to be Archbishop of Canterbury, addressed himself. At a Synod at Hertford in 672 he laid down the outlines of a proper diocesan structure in England. It was in Northumbria, however, that he found it most difficult to secure acceptance for his ideas; and paradoxically the man whom he found most difficult to accommodate was Wilfrid of Ripon.

St Wilfrid

The late 7th-century Northumbrian church was dominated by three utterly different characters: St Wilfrid, St Cuthbert of Lindisfarne, and Benedict Biscop. Born in 634, the son of a Northumbrian nobleman, Wilfrid was a domineering, persuasive and often worldly monk whose career was full of controversy and highly political. In about 670, Theodore made him bishop of York, but it was also part of Theodore's plan to break down the enormous diocese of York into smaller units. Wilfrid objected strongly to any diminution of the power of York, and quarrelled so violently with both Theodore and the king that he appealed to Rome and was twice exiled from Northumbria. Yet such was his energy that even his years of exile bore fruit; he took the opportunity to found a number of monasteries in Mercia; to convert the people of the Isle of Wight (one of the last remaining outposts of paganism in England); and even to begin the conversion of the people of Frisia (the modern Low Countries), a task that was soon to be taken up by other Englishmen. In his native Northumbria he introduced the strict Benedictine rule at his monastic foundations at Hexham and Ripon and ensured that these houses were richly endowed.

St Cuthbert of Lindisfarne

St Cuthbert, who was born in the same year as Wilfrid, could hardly provide more of a contrast. Originally a shepherd boy, he entered the monastery at Old Melrose in Scotland in 651, where he became so renowned for his piety and asceticism that he was summoned to rule the monastic community at Lindisfarne. Despite his own upbringing in the Celtic tradition, he fully accepted the authority of the reformed Northumbrian church and performed his duties as bishop of Lindisfarne unstintingly, winning fame and respect for his missionary zeal and his miracles. Yet it was as a hermit that he was happiest; and it was as a hermit that he died, early in 687,

The fragments of St Cuthbert's coffin, 7th century (By courtesy of the Dean and Chapter of Durham)

having spent his last few months alone on the island of Inner Farne in a stone hut 25 feet in diameter with a roof of timber and straw. Initially he was buried at Lindisfarne in a stone coffin. Eleven years later, when the monks opened his tomb to remove the remains to a wooden coffin, his body was found to be still intact. His bones were later to be venerated as the chief relic of the Northumbrian church, just as he was to become its patron saint.

Benedict Biscop

Benedict Biscop was, like Wilfrid, born into the Northumbrian nobility, and was a great collector and builder. He made six journeys to Rome and was for a short while abbot of St Augustine's Abbey at Canterbury, but it was in the North East that he established the two great monasteries upon which his real fame rests. Monkwearmouth was founded in 674 and Jarrow in 685. The original inscription stone recording the dedication of Jarrow church on 23 April 685 may still be seen repositioned above the western arch of the tower there. Benedict intended his new monasteries to be great houses. Local building tradition was in wood but he brought stonemasons and glaziers from the Continent to build 'in the Roman manner' and the glass, painted plaster and sculpture from these splendid buildings can be seen in the Bede Monastery Museum at Jarrow. Benedict Biscop summoned John, archcantor of St Peter's in Rome, to teach the Roman chant to his Northumbrian monks. The Benedictine rule was a major influence in his monastery. His greatest contribution to the Northumbrian church, however, was the splendid library that he built up at Monkwearmouth–Jarrow, supplied largely with books that he had acquired on his journeys to Rome. It was this library that made possible the work of Bede. Indeed, before his death he personally taught Bede: as the latter tells us, 'on reaching seven years of age, I was entrusted by my family first to the most revered Abbot Benedict for my education.'

The dynamic Northumbrian church

The vitality of the Northumbrian church in the late 7th and the early 8th centuries is abundantly clear. Monasticism was flourishing, especially at Monkwearmouth and Jarrow, which were united under Benedict's successor Abbot Ceolfrith. By the time of Ceolfrith's death in 716 there were apparently 600 monks living under his rule at the two houses. And increasingly Northumbrian churchmen were making their presence felt abroad. Wilfrid had shown the way on his visit to Frisia in 678, and around 690 he was followed by St Willibrord, the 'Apostle to the Frisians', a Northumbrian monk who was born about 658 and educated under Wilfrid at Ripon. In 695 the Pope made Willibrord archbishop of Frisia with his see at Utrecht, and he spent the rest of his long life in missionary work on the Continent. By the time of his death in 739, at his own monastery of Echternach in modern Luxembourg, great strides had been made in the conversion of the peoples of these areas of north-west Europe. Willibrord's work was continued by St Boniface, a West Saxon who worked mainly in Germany before his martyrdom at Dokkum in 754, and by Willehad, another Northumbrian whom the Frankish King Charles the Great (Charlemagne) asked to undertake the conversion of the Old Saxons of northern Germany. Willehad became bishop of Bremen in 787. There is a pleasing irony in the fact that those peoples who had come as pagans to Britain in the 5th and 6th centuries were in turn converted to Christianity by their own Anglo-Saxon descendants.

Meanwhile Theodore and his successors at Canterbury had been reorganizing the northern church. From the 670s onwards, Northumbria proper (that is, excluding those parts of the kingdom that passed to the Scots) was normally divided into three dioceses, with their episcopal sees at York, Hexham and Lindisfarne. In 735 the pre-eminence of York was officially acknowledged when it was elevated to the status of an archbishopric (as had been intended by Pope Gregory the Great as early as 601), and it has remained to this day the chief seat of the northern English church. However, the parochial structure of Northumbria at this time was probably very limited. The early Northumbrian church was centred on monasteries or 'minsters' before the establishment of parish churches, many associated with magnificently decorated stone crosses that still survive in parts of the north. The most famous is at Bewcastle in modern Cumbria, which stands to a height of 15 feet. Substantial fragments of a similar cross from Rothbury in Northumberland, dating probably from the first half of the 9th century, can now be seen in the Museum of Antiquities in Newcastle upon Tyne and at All Saints church at Rothbury. One of the earliest surviving churches in the North East to have remained in any way close to its entirety is Escomb, Durham, which, although slightly altered and added to in later centuries, is still essentially 7th or 8th century. Seaham church, too, has a complete Saxon nave, and less substantial remains of early churches can be seen at a number of other sites. These include Bywell, Corbridge, Whittingham and Heddon-on-the-Wall (all in Northumberland); and Staindrop, Aycliffe and Norton (Durham). Most of these are late rather than early Anglo-Saxon and most of the stone-built structures were monastic in origin rather than parochial churches – as were also, of course, the more notable survivals at Hexham, Monkwearmouth and Jarrow. Humble parish churches were probably originally built in wood.

The Lindisfarne Gospels

It is in the fields of learning and pictorial art that the most impressive survivals from

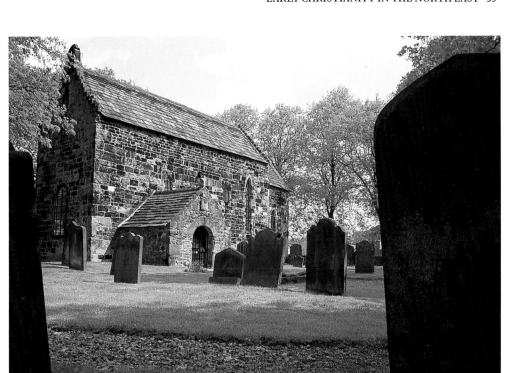

Escomb Church (see p. 106)

Northumbria's golden age are to be found. As the meeting point of Christianity introduced from Italy and Ireland, Northumbria became the melting pot of markedly different artistic styles, the interlace and geometric ornament of the Germanic and Celtic craftsmen, and the more naturalistic birds, beasts and foliage patterns of the Mediterranean tradition. It is the fusion of these styles that gives Northumbrian manuscript painting of the 7th and 8th centuries its unique character, nowhere more readily apparent than in the Lindisfarne Gospels. These were probably written and illuminated by Eadfrith, Bishop of Lindisfarne from 698 to 721, in the last decade of the 7th century. The so-called carpet page (illustrated) from the beginning of St Matthew's Gospel shows clearly the blend of geometrical symmetry and naturalistic power that is characteristic of Northumbrian art at the time. Here the writhing forms of the animals actually provide the interlace, but despite the intricacy of the intertwining forms, the whole pattern falls into easily distinguishable and symmetrical units. The Lindisfarne Gospels are now in the British Library, but a replica may be seen in the island's museum. Another splendid product of this time is the *Codex Amiatinus*, written and decorated by order of Abbot Ceolfrith at Monkwearmouth–Jarrow in the early 8th century. Ceolfrith took the *Codex* with him on his last journey to Rome in 716, intending it as a gift for the Pope to demonstrate the quality of Northumbrian workmanship of the time, but he died on the way and his book eventually found its way into the Biblioteca Medicea Laurenziana in Florence.

The Venerable Bede
The great figures of Northumbrian scholarship in the 8th century were Bede, Egbert and Alcuin. Bede was born about 672 at Monkton, Durham. At the age of seven he

was entrusted to the care of Benedict Biscop at Monkwearmouth, but in 687 he moved to Jarrow where he spent the rest of his life. He became a deacon at the age of eighteen and a priest at thirty. By this time he had already begun to write, and for the next 30 years, until his death in 735, his energies were devoted almost entirely to learning. He wrote numerous works, scientific, theological and hagiographical as well as historical, and thought of himself primarily as a teacher; but it is for his *Ecclesiastical History of the English Nation* that he is now chiefly remembered. The *History* is an astonishing achievement for its time. A large text of about 100,000 words, it records the history of Christianity in Britain from Roman times until 731 (although about nine-tenths of the book deals with the 7th and early 8th centuries). Although he never travelled beyond the borders of Northumbria he managed, through persistent inquiry and painstaking scrutiny of the sources available to him in the Monkwearmouth–Jarrow library (some 80 different authorities are represented in his works), to compile a scholarly, reliable, yet sympathetic and eminently readable account which is still, and will always remain, the indispensable primary source for the England of his age. Bede's aim, as he states in his preface, was to inspire others to act as good Christians:

> For if history records good things of good men, the thoughtful hearer is encouraged to imitate what is good: or if it records evil of wicked men, the devout, religious listener or reader is encouraged to avoid all that is sinful and perverse and to follow what he knows to be good and pleasing to God.

Egbert and Alcuin

The same sentiments, we can be sure, motivated Bede's successors. After his death, the centre of Northumbrian learning shifted to York where Egbert, the first Archbishop of York, and himself a former pupil of Bede, established a school based on a library as splendid as that at Monkwearmouth–Jarrow. Egbert's brother was Eadberht, king of Northumbria, who proved a generous patron to the school and was eventually to resign his throne in order to become a monk. One of Egbert's pupils at York was Alcuin, who succeeded him as Master there in 767. Such was Alcuin's reputation as a scholar that in 784 Charles the Great (Charlemagne) invited him to become head of the palace school of Aachen, where he remained until 796 before moving to the monastic school at Tours, where he died in 804. Thus did the Northumbrian renaissance of the 8th century make its own special contribution to the Carolingian renaissance of the 9th century. Alcuin's appointment as Master of the most prestigious school in Western Europe says much for the intellectual climate in which he was reared.

The Viking onslaught and the rise of Wessex

By the time of Alcuin, the golden age of Northumbria was drawing to a close. Northumbrian politics in the 8th century were, with the exception of one or two periods such as the reign of Eadberht (738–57), a time of dynastic feuding and rebellion, and by about 750 the balance of power among the island's kingdoms had shifted decisively southwards, to Mercia. However, Mercian supremacy, which reached its height under King Offa (755–96), was also to be brief. It was to be the kings of Wessex, descended from Egbert (802–39) and Alfred the Great (871–99), who emerged in the 9th and 10th centuries as the dominant power in England and eventually managed to unite the Anglo-Saxon kingdoms under their rule.

Northumbrian monasticism was also in decline by the second half of the 8th century, and it may be that too many of its brightest spirits had been drawn off to missionary work on the Continent. The growth of the parochial system in this period is unrecorded. The Viking raids of the 9th century provided the death blow. As pagans, worshipping the same gods as the Anglo-Saxons had done before their conversion, the Vikings treated monasteries and churches as nothing more than easy sources of movable riches. The first Danish raid on Northumbria came in 793, when Lindisfarne was sacked, followed by Jarrow in 794. After this there was a lull for 40 years, but from 835 the Danish raids became more frequent, and after 865 the pattern changed from simple raiding to conquest and settlement. It was at about this time that the words, 'From the fury of the Northmen, Good Lord deliver us', were added to the litany, but there was to be no deliverance. During the next 15 or so years, every important centre of Christianity in the North East was destroyed: York was devastated in 866, Whitby in 867, and so on. The great Hiberno-Norse kingdom of York was established, isolating north Northumbria. Although Norse settlers accepted Christianity it was to be another two hundred years before monasticism once again became an integral part of the northern church.

Only two dioceses were continuously occupied through the 10th century. The first was York where, despite its devastation in 866, there was at least an unbroken succession of archbishops – yet the fact that every archbishop of York from 972 until 1016 was a southerner by origin suggests that the northern church at this time was far from thriving. The second was the see of Lindisfarne, which moved to Chester-le-Street.

The founding of Durham

In 875, the few remaining monks at Lindisfarne had been forced to flee from yet another Viking attack. Carrying with them St Cuthbert's coffin, a number of his relics and the Lindisfarne Gospels, they spent the next eight years wandering about the Northumbrian countryside, unable to find a haven, until in 883 they settled at Chester-le-Street. Here they remained for over a century. It was this community that King Athelstan of Wessex visited on his way to Scotland in 934, when he presented the monks with a maniple, a stole and a number of other gifts including a copy of the works of Bede. With the renewal of Viking raids after 980, however, they were forced to look for a less vulnerable site. The one that they chose was some ten miles to the south, the steep outcrop of land known as Durham, almost encircled by the river Wear: where, on 4 September 998, the 'White Church' of the monastic community was dedicated. St Cuthbert's remains had at last found a secure resting place. His tomb still occupies the place of honour in the cathedral, just to the east of the high altar, while on display in the Treasury are several of the relics carried around inside Cuthbert's coffin by the monks of Lindisfarne on their wanderings – his portable altar, pectoral cross, his comb, as well as the pieced-together fragments of his original carved oak coffin. It was here at Durham, almost exactly a century after the dedication of the White Church, that the foundations were laid for one of the architectural masterpieces of Europe: the massive Norman cathedral which is the enduring monument to early Northumbrian Christianity and to its favourite son, the shepherd boy Cuthbert.

Un-natural Natural History

DAVID BELLAMY

I will not enter into the complex argument as to the exact birthplace of the Industrial Revolution, but will state with my hand on my heart that despite the massive part it played throughout that period of creative destruction, North-East England still holds a unique place in the natural history of Europe.

From Cross Fell, the highest point of the Pennines, to the depths of the seas around the Farne Islands and all environments between, there are massive scars of enterprise and misuse, scars that have in many cases healed in a most miraculous way to provide 'natural' history for the present and hope for the future.

The Northumbrian islands

The Farne Islands, sanctuary for St Cuthbert in the 7th century AD, now performs the same function for the grey seal and for hosts of sea birds. Not so long ago *Halicoerus gryphus* was one of the rarest large mammals in the world, an endangered species; now, thanks to the protection afforded by the Grey Seal Acts and the vision of the National Trust, their numbers have increased – some would argue too much. Along with myriad nesting and resting birds, cormorant, shag, eider, ringed plover, kittiwake, common, arctic, roseate and sandwich terns, razorbill, guillemot, puffin and rock pipit, to name but a few, they provide a year-round spectacle for an ever-increasing number of tourists from all parts of the world.

As they are islands set in difficult waters, human pressure is more readily controlled and contained, but not so the conflicting pressures of seal haul-outs and puffin burrows. The combined effects of these two forms of natural land use have already stripped the soil from some of the islands to the detriment of the birds and the vegetation, and the visitors.

On nearby Holy Island, human visitors are less easy to control, for at low tide cars can stream across the causeway to visit one of Europe's last wonderlands of dune, grassland and seascape. In the wet hollows among the dunes curved sedge, an arctic alpine plant, finds its southern limit set among drifts of orchids, some, like the northern fen and fen orchids, not uncommon, while others are so rare that they must be protected by fences and wardens. Moonwort, lamb's lettuce, viper's bugloss, birdsfoot trefoil, marram and lime grass: the rare and the common grow cheek by jowl, each adding colour to this pastiche of nature, each doing their bit to bind and hold the drifting sands in check. No wonder St Cuthbert made this his home; no wonder it was here the Lindisfarne Gospels were illuminated in all their colourful detail.

Today signs of change are everywhere, many for the good, but some for the bad. The hooked fruits of the pirri-pirri burr, an introduction from New Zealand, threatens the birds – especially the eider chicks, catching and clogging their feathers. Out on the broad mud- and sandbanks that provide a varied diet of eelgrass, cockles, laver spire shell, crabs, tellins, lug- or ragworms for many birds, another alien is leaving a trail of destructive change. Hybrid cord grass, which had its origin in

Inner Farne, the Farne Islands

Grey seals, the Farne Islands (Roger Wilmshurst, Bruce Coleman Ltd)

Southampton Water, now grows here in spreading clones. These bind the mud and threaten both the birds' food supply and even the isolation of this National Nature Reserve, for if this aggressive grass spreads unchecked, it could turn Holy Island into a mere peninsula.

Holy Island, jewel of the Northumbrian coast, itself the best wilderness coastline left in Europe, is a haven of rare solitude and delight. Headlands of Whin Sill surmounted by yesterday's castle homes provide a place for the spring squill to bloom and many birds to nest. Great sweeping areas of clear, clean sand, on which you can catch the breath of cold east winds blowing clear across from the Urals and wander lonely except for the knots of knots, the clockwork rush of sanderling and the plaintive call of whimbrel. It is a place where nature still holds its breath in hope, as yet untainted by tomorrow's problems. Inland from this sacred coast, the broad farmscapes of Northumberland have more than any other shrugged off the excesses of the recent years, retaining much of their landscape shape, an inheritance of good sense and good husbandry. Hedgerows, broadleaved trees, wet bits, dry bits and winding lanes still welcome migrants and residents alike: fieldfares, hobbies, redstart, redpoll, goldfinch, siskin, linnet, goldcrest, spotted flycatchers, tawny, barn, little, long- and short-eared owls fly the day and night away, while badgers dig their dung pits, red squirrels make their drays, otters hunt the clear waters, home of fish both game and coarse, and foxes give His Lordship's hounds a run for their money. This is still England in good heart, with all its rights and wrongs, watered by westerly winds that just make their way over the Cheviot Hills, bringing rain, which is neither too acid nor too alkaline, to flow back down the Tweed, Till, Aln and Coquet to the majesty of that coast.

Seal Sands

About 80 miles to the south as more than 200,000 migrants fly each autumn there is another sanctuary for sea birds, although it is in a less idyllic setting. Seal Sands welcomes those migrants twice each year, with a backdrop of heavy industry in all its current manifestations, complete with an atomic power station standing sentinel over a dying coalfield. Almost hidden among the cooling towers, cracking plants, retaining walls and bunds a maze of tidal waterways leads the ebb and flow of every tide in silver defiance of the filth of centuries.

These precious head-just-above-water acres are all that is now left of natural Teesmouth, although it is easy to think of a more appropriate suffix. Of all the rivers in the region, the Tees has transported an ever-more-complex fricassee of the products of 18th-, 19th- and 20th-century effluence than any other. Despite all this, and thanks to the work of conservationists, and in recent years of local industry and the authorities, these acres still remain, attracting birds in their thousands. Some drop in for a short time to refuel, others stay longer for repairs, preening and moulting, while many make this their home for the winter, perhaps deriving some benefit from the urban microclimate and the warmed waste waters.

These murky waters become especially important in bad winters when the Continental ports of call are frozen over. Then an ever-larger fraction of the shore birds that overwinter around the North Sea crowd in to enjoy the Tees. This is especially true of the smaller birds like knot and dunlin which, in order to retain their inner warmth, need to eat more regularly than their larger cousins.

It is, however, not just the common birds that come to this not-so-desolate spot. Every year the rare and ultra-rare drop in in their twos or ones, attracting the twitchers, the most fanatic of bird spotters who turn up in their thousands drawn from all over Britain and further afield for the glimpse of a new record.

Birdwatchers of another sort also stalk this coast, which attracts more than its fair share of the 200,000 wildfowl that make the east coast their winter home. They take much more than a Latin binomial and help boost the level of lead poisoning in the area. It must, however, be borne in mind that it is in part their voice and the work of the Wildfowl Trust that has helped protect coastal sites like this from total desecration.

A coastline of great interest

Not far north of Seal Sands scraps of dune and cliffs of sand and limestone form the ramparts of one of the most polluted and degraded coastlines in the world. Yet miraculously it is still a coastline of great wonder and interest, where bloody cranesbill, sea milkwort and burnet rose brighten the dullest summer day. Here, too, old-man's beard, yellow-wort, erect brome and three of out most fascinating orchids, fly, bee and burnt-tip, find their northern limit in Britain, for the coastal strip shares a similar climate with the North Downs, nearly 200 miles to the south. Some of these plants brave the open coast while others are hidden in the protective dampness of the coastal denes. These narrow karst-like valleys snake their way inland incised into the soft yellow limestone, which is rich in magnesium and provides Hartlepool with raw materials for its last two major industries: water in which to brew fine ales; and magnesia, fashioned by skill and expertise into firebricks to line the hearths of furnaces that still make steel.

This special limestone also provides a habitat for some very special plant communities. Within the narrow recesses of the denes, woodlands of beech, yew, ash, oak and even elm provide shelter for sheets of wild garlic, dog's mercury and hart's tongue fern. Here, too, our largest and most showy orchid, the lady's slipper, once grew until collected to extinction. Perhaps it may one day return – or be returned – to Castle Eden Dene, which was the first local nature reserve in Britain and now, with the new town of Peterlee perched on its rim, is a National Nature Reserve, no less.

Further inland the vast majority of the woodland has long since disappeared, destroyed to make way for agriculture, quarrying and other sorts of industry. Yet miraculously on the margins of some of the quarries, on the quarry spoil on roadside verges and waste spots, limestone grassland has survived and developed. Grassland dominated by blue moor grass complete with a strange admixture of plants, dusky red helleborine, frog orchid, English flax and mountain everlasting and, at the damper end of the soil spectrum, globe flower, bird's eye primrose and flea sedge: grassland more reminiscent of arctic alpine climes than a lowland situation near the coast.

Upper Teesdale and the Great Whin Sill

These scraps of grassland form a direct link with what must be regarded as the high spot of the region's history. Upper Teesdale is the focal point of the largest National Nature Reserve in England and of pilgrimage by all would-be naturalists who are worth their salt.

Say Teesdale anywhere near a botanist and he or she will immediately conjure up pictures of spring gentians, shrubby cinquefoil, bog sandwort, alpine forget-me-not, and almost 140 other plants of phytogeographical interest. This means that their occurrence in the area is of special interest and it is for this reason that Widdybank, Cronkley, Great and Little, and Dun Fell are sites of world importance. A heritage of arctic alpine, montane and southern plants that have remained marooned in place since the ice sheets of the last glaciation gave way first to forest and then, under the hand of primitive cultures and changing climate, to the open moorscape we now know.

The reasons for the survival of this special assemblage of plants are many and complex. They revolve around the subarctic aspects of the contemporary climate and the presence of the Great Whin Sill, which outcrops all across the region. Whin Sill, a very hard and durable rock, forms the foundations of many of the local landforms. High Cup Nick, a now dry valley of fluted dolerite, like Fingal's Cave without a roof, is one of the geological wonders of Britain as are the great waterfalls, Cauldron Snout and High and Low Force, the lips of which are formed of the same black rock.

As the Whin Sill was injected by some volcanic upheaval molten into the surrounding strata, it baked the adjacent rocks, metamorphosing, changing them into other forms. At that time rich lodes of silver lead, zinc, barytes and fluorspar came into being: geological wealth that first brought industry to this place, pockmarking it with hushes, drifts, adits, shops, tailing yards and spoil heaps.

The miners, who had names for all the rocks among which they made their living, christened one of these fresh-baked strata that outcrops across the fells 'sugar limestone'. As its name suggests it is of granular structure and so forms friable, freely draining soils which can give little or no support to the roots of trees or to the development of wet blanket peat. So it is argued that these sites, along with the

Spring gentians (Gentiana verna) *(Eric Crichton, Bruce Coleman Ltd)*

dolerite cliffs and those areas tainted with toxic heavy metals, would have remained open throughout the past ten thousand years as refugia for the arctic alpine and other special plants which, although tolerant of harsh climate and poor soils, are unable to tolerate shade or competition by larger, faster-growing plants.

Research has shown that much of the contemporary grassland that is rich in what have come to be styled 'the Teesdale Rarities' is characterized by low levels of annual production. This could be controlled by harshness of climate, by soils poor in available nutrients or rich in toxic chemicals: it is probably a permutation of all three which together make this a very special place.

Man in the uplands

People came to these uplands many thousands of years ago, and using technologies of polished stone, bronze and iron, hunted the wild animals and cleared the forest to make way for their domesticated animals and for their agriculture. A gradually deteriorating climate, cooler and much wetter, leached the upland soils now devoid of a canopy of trees and gradually replaced the richness of the forest with a blanket of wet peat; a blanket so poor in nutrients and acid in nature, that trees could never grow again and so the uplands remained open, their grandeur bared for all to see, an area of outstanding natural beauty.

The same is true of all the other upland areas of the region, from the Cheviots in the north to the North York Moors in the south, and all along the backbone of the high Pennines, moorland rules the roost, deep peat filling the valley bottoms and softening all but the steepest breaks of slope. Domain of buzzard, curlew, lapwing, blackcock and of course Britain's only endemic bird, the red grouse. In the past golden eagles hunted these high hills and even today the smallest of all our raptors, the merlin, makes this its major retreat, while peregrines are beginning to make a comeback.

Although in part created by people, and used and scarred by industry, it was not until the invention of the breech-loading gun that these areas became subject to regular management. Each year small patches of heather were set on fire in order to produce a patchwork of heather stands of different age to feed and shelter the grouse in their windswept home (*see p. 74*). This, together with overgrazing by sheep and drainage, or gripping as it is locally called, has taken its toll on the peat blanket, speeding erosion and the development of peat hags and immense channels in places. The boots of the many walkers, climbers and orienteers who now tread the Pennine and Cheviot Ways and the Lyke Wake are doing nothing to arrest this process of degradation and now other forms of management are having to come on line in the shape of a new environmental factor, The British Trust for Conservation Volunteers.

Peat still grows in lone wet places complete with cotton grasses, bog mosses, bog asphodel, cranberry and sweet gale. There bog bean and mud sedge reflect in pools of peat-stained water from which dragonflies drag themselves to run the gauntlet of the sundews ringing the open water.

The plantations

You can see it all for yourself the hard wet way, or in comfort in your car, or from the carriages of the railway lines that are still in operation, and everywhere you will see change, the most extensive of which is coniferization. Kielder, the largest plantation in Europe, now swathes the shores of Europe's largest reservoir. The trees were planted to provide pit props in times of war and blockade, and the reservoir to provide water for future industrial growth. Both are now redundant: modern pits use hydraulic props and big, thirsty industry is on the decline, not on the increase.

Like the reservoir, the plantations are now on stream and are finding other uses, the wood for pallets and for pulp, and the broad acres of water and forest for recreation of all types. A well-managed plantation, even when pure conifer, provides not only jobs for people but, in a patchwork of forest stands of different ages, a home for red squirrel, long-eared owl, crossbill, coaltit, siskin, redpoll and goldcrest, and even for nightjars, sparrowhawks, goshawks, pine martens, polecats and deer. Add to this the expertise of the new Wildlife Rangers of the Forestry Commission, complete with mixed contour planting and hardwood blocks and corridors along streamsides, and all is not bad. The countryside has lost a lot, but with care diversity can once again replace uniformity and the landscapes can live once more, attracting the discerning visitor to return again.

Conservation and challenge

Despite its industrial history, the North-East region holds much to captivate the attention of the natural historian. Most of the key sites are at least in part protected within the bounds of National Parks, Nature Reserves, both national and local and Sites of Special Scientific Interest. There are, however, smaller special places, scraps of unofficial countryside still waiting for you to discover them for yourself.

A small ox-bow lake with crystalwort covering the surface of the water, home ground of kingfishers; a roadside verge overflowing with butterburr both male and female, a place where badger cubs play beneath the great rhubarb-like leaves every summer; another verge where adders sun themselves among bilberry and bell heather. Hanging woodlands complete with all the lichens that should be there, yet within the sight and sound of past heavy industry; old meadowlands with as many flowers as you could ever want, a calendar of colour with a backdrop of natural topiary, juniper in all its shapes and

Coniferization, the Kielder Forest

forms. Under and among the juniper there is a wealth of ferns, oak, beech, hard, lemon-scented, broad buckler, male and lady, also the fern allies the club mosses, fir, common and lesser with horsetails thrown in, marsh, wood, common and shady: a fitting complement of plants to grow in an area that has produced so much coal in the past, for it was the ancestors of these same plants that helped form the coal so many millions of years ago. Another meadow has giant ant hills as medieval as the palace in whose yard it lies; and while on the subject of ants, there are nests of the wood ants, each one piled high with pine needles and twiglets, the air suffused with formic acid and the whisper of millions of marching feet. Other ants tend the caterpillars of a very special butterfly, keeping them clean and free from disease; they allow the Durham argus the freedom of the fields and food in plenty from the rockrose garden. Go to Hadrian's Wall to sense the presence of Rome, but also to see a wealth of willows, their catkins covered with insects sipping nectar in the spring sunshine. Brambles there are, bird cherries, crabs, rowans, haws and rosehips galore, enough to nurture the visiting waxwings, and a lifetime of study sorting out the species, varieties and hybrids.

I know all this, for I live there, Honorary Professor at the University that sits astride the river Wear: Durham, a site of World Heritage ranking, grey towers that received the bones of St Cuthbert and have looked down across the centuries of change.

The North East is a well-used landscape; much has survived and now some of the most precious acres are in danger of being loved to death. The challenge of the future is to face up to the opportunities of conservation. We cannot put the clocks back but we can learn from the lessons of these landscapes, conserve what we have and together with industry and government, both local and national, put the whole thing back into working order. Teesside can have its industry and its birds; Teesdale its farms and National Nature Reserves; Northumberland its unpolluted coasts and its new enterprise; the uplands their beauty and new rural industry. It is a challenge that will create jobs and hope, and a fitting place for civilization to develop into and beyond the 21st century.

A Walk on Hadrian's Wall

BRIAN SPENCER

A visit to Hadrian's Wall is an excellent way of bringing to life some of the cold historical facts about the Roman period in Britain. The wall was built to defend Roman Britain from attacks from the unconquered North and was probably completed around AD 138. It ran across the relatively narrow neck of land between what is now Carlisle in the west and Newcastle upon Tyne. The wall was not intended as a final frontier (in fact at one stage the Romans extended their occupation further north and built the Antonine Wall between the Forth and the Clyde); and in addition to its defensive function it was used to control the movement of people and the flow of trade. In peaceful times cattle, sheep and wool from the north would pass through, heading for Roman towns further south; metal goods, pots and luxury items would go north into Caledonia. The wall was also a customs barrier: tolls were no doubt levied to help pay for the thousands of troops who manned it.

In planning a walk on Hadrian's Wall it is a good idea to try to fulfil two criteria, especially where 'first-timers' or young people are involved. Firstly, the walk should be interesting and cover an area where the Roman remains are easily understood; secondly, it should not be too long or difficult. Both of these requirements are met by the easy, 7½-mile walk from Once Brewed to Housesteads along Hadrian's Wall and back by way of Vindolanda.

Further and often exciting evidence of Roman life is continually being brought to life in this area. Archaeological digs are in progress more or less every summer and Roman features are in view for most of the way. Ideally, a whole day should be spent on this walk into the past as there are so many things to see and appreciate.

The Walk

The numbered text relates to the map; features of interest and importance are indicated by a ●.

① Start the walk from the Northumberland National Park Information Centre at Once Brewed. You will find it on the corner of the B6318 and the Bardon Mill Road. There is plenty of space to park the car and for a picnic afterwards.

● Visit the Information Centre before setting out. Its displays are always imaginative and easy to understand. Recently, for example, the display described Hadrian's Wall through the simple story of stone and the landscape was depicted in terms of the people who lived in and worked the area both before and after the Roman era.

② From the Information Centre cross the B6318. (Watch out for traffic along this road, which can be busy, even though it is only a 'B' class road.)

● On the far side of the staggered crossroads, Hadrian's Wall, the main objective of the walk, follows the skyline from left to right, about a half mile in front.

● A broad overgrown ditch runs on either side of the Steel Rigg road, just beyond the junction with the B6318. This is the Vallum, originally a flat-bottomed ditch about 10 ft deep and 20 ft wide. Soil from the ditch was piled in a single high mound to the

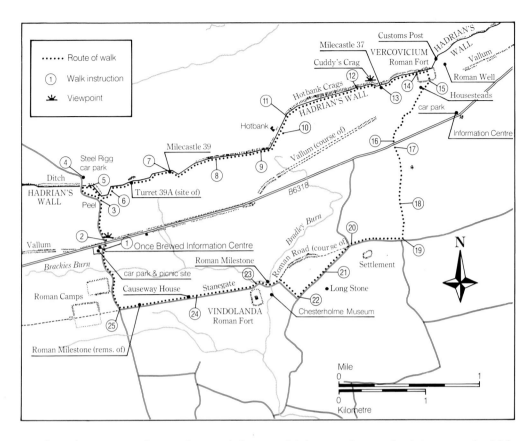

north and two mounds, one low and the next higher, to the south giving a total width of about 120 ft from north to south. This important feature in the Northumbrian landscape follows a course roughly parallel to Hadrian's Wall from coast to coast, sometimes only a few yards south of the Wall, at other times anything up to half a mile. There is no apparent reason for these diversions, which seem quite deliberate. At this point the diversion south might have been to enclose flat land on either side of what is now the Steel Rigg road. One suggestion as to the purpose of the Vallum is that it indicated the southern limit of the military zone. Others argue that it was a fiendishly designed trap for anyone who illegally crossed the Wall. Intruders would have been forced into the ditch, giving the defenders time to regroup between the southern mounds. At several points the Vallum was deliberately filled in and the mounds breached on either side, making what appear to be crossing places. Who made these infills or for what purpose is not clear. Some of the crossings, however, were made so that roadways could be carried over the Vallum. Others are spread over a considerable distance, such as those on either side of Shield on the Wall, about 2 miles west of Once Brewed. It is thought the crossings were made *c*. AD 140.

(3) From the Vallum, the road climbs towards the skyline, first passing a cottage on the left, and then another on the right of the sharp left-hand bend.

● Peel, formerly a farmhouse, marks the line of the narrow Roman road just south of the Wall. This was a service road designed to provide rapid access to the Wall and was built after the rest of the installations had been completed. As the modern road bears left, still uphill, you will be following this Roman Military Way.

④ The surfaced road turns right at the top of the hill and leaves the line of the Military Way. Walk on towards Steel Rigg car park.

● On your left before you leave the road, the line of a ditch can be seen just inside a clump of trees. This was the forward obstacle of Hadrian's Wall, also designed to increase its effective height. The ditch was V-shaped, around 27 ft wide and lay about 20 ft in front of the wall. Earth and stones from its construction were thrown on to the forward bank; anyone approaching from the north would have to cross this obstacle. Recently discovered evidence suggests that the Wall was also whitewashed.

⑤ Turn right away from the road and walk through the car park, then follow the footpath towards what at first appears to be a grass-topped boundary wall. Turn left and follow the course of Hadrian's Wall.

● This is the first, and perhaps disappointing glimpse of Hadrian's Wall, but the full impact is gained as you walk down into the narrow gap below Peel Crags. Although it is possible to walk along the grassy top of the Wall, you should heed the National Trust's request and use the path at the side to help prevent further erosion.

● When Hadrian's Wall was built it stood about 15 ft high to a 6 ft parapet. Locally – not along its full length – it would have been about 10 ft wide, built from stone quarried near by. The Wall was built in sections by individual units who were responsible for seeing that their work linked with that of their neighbours. Unfortunately Roman survey methods were far from perfect and many sections are misaligned by as much as 1 ft! Despite this, the Wall has stood the test of time.

⑥ For the next stage you have to scramble up the steep natural steps of Peel Crags.

● The view from Peel Crags is one of the finest in Northumberland. Hadrian's Wall snakes along the craggy north face of the Whin Sill. To the south, rolling moors beyond the Tyne Gap reach out towards the Pennines, and northwards, mile upon mile of pine forest continue towards the hazy outlines of the Cheviot Hills.

● There was once a lookout turret on the top of Peel Crags. Known today by its official title of Turret 39A, it was one of a pair placed equidistant, about 540 yd on either side of Milecastle 39. Eighty milecastles, each with a pair of turrets, guarded Hadrian's Wall; they are numbered from east to west. The turrets were of standard design, about 20 ft square and recessed into the wall. They were usually occupied by four soldiers, two of whom patrolled the wall on either side while the other two rested in the upper storey or cooked on the ground floor.

⑦ Walk a little further to the excavated foundations of Milecastle 39.

● As the name suggests, milecastles were spaced about one Roman mile (1620 yd) apart. Each milecastle was built as part of the Wall with north- and south-facing gates, the northern one guarded by a lookout tower. Up to 64 soldiers would live in each milecastle, relieving those doing guard duty in the turrets, or acting as reserves when other parts of the Wall came under attack.

⑧ The next section of the Wall is missing above Crag Lough, but scramble on to Highshields Crags for the view of this tree-lined natural lake. Take care not to go too close to the edge of the crag as the smooth rock can be very slippery.

The B6318 follows the course of Hadrian's Wall

(9) Bear right away from the top of the crag, to reach a well-preserved section of the Roman Military Way.

● The broad green track of the Roman Military Way is easy to recognize, still following its original course after more than 18 centuries.

(10) Turn left along the Roman Military Way and go downhill until you reach a farm road. Cross the road and walk on until the Wall and Military Way join each other. At this point it is easier to follow the line of the Wall again. In front and slightly to your left are the sturdy buildings of Hotbank Farm, and if you turn round you can again see Crag Lough at the foot of Highshields Crags.

● There are few traces of the Wall near Hotbank Farm and you cannot help wondering how many of its stones were used to build the farm.

(11) Climb again towards a small plantation at the top of the rise and go to the left of the wind-blown trees. Almost on the lip of Hotbank Crags, a well-preserved section of Hadrian's Wall crosses the hilltop and then drops steeply into Rapishaw Gap.

● The Pennine Way, the long-distance footpath from Edale in Derbyshire to Kirk Yetholm in Scotland, turns left in Rapishaw Gap and heads north towards Wark Forest. The path joins Hadrian's Wall near Greenhead.

(12) The last climb follows the low remains of the Wall across Cuddy's Crags.

● Two more natural lakes, Broomlee and Greenlee Loughs, are to the north on either side of Ridley Common; like Crag Lough, both are excellent fishing waters.

● Milecastle 37's distinctive outline is the next feature to be visited.

(13) Go past Milecastle 37 and then along a narrow path between a belt of trees and the lip of Housesteads Crags. Again take great care along the top of the rocks.

(14) As you reach the eastern edge of the wood, the Wall continues its way along the craggy escarpment, but on your right are the ramparts of Vercovicium Roman fort – Housesteads as it is known today. There are several ways to enter Housesteads. The nearest is a ladder stile on the site of an angle tower near the point where the fort's western or Decumana wall joins Hadrian's Wall. Another entrance is lower down the field on your right. This is the West Gate, but you may prefer to use the North Gate, the Porta Principalis Sinistra.

● The fort is built on a steep, south-facing slope and the layout is gradually coming clearer with each successive stage of its excavation. Oblong in shape, its longest face is built slightly forward of the wall. Turrets and gate towers bolster the defences at each corner with extra turrets on the northern and southern walls, and two more on the eastern side overlooking open country beyond Knag Burn. The western wall was adequately defended by the corner turrets and those on either side of the gate. Each of the four walls has a heavily defended gate, although the South Gate opens on to the top of a steep slope and was only used by pedestrians or horse riders. All other gates coped with wheeled traffic, which wore deep ruts in their threshold stones.

● A causeway, later removed, led downhill from the North Gate. Originally this gate had two portals, but one was blocked soon after work started on strengthening the northern defences. As you pass through the North Gate and go between the outlines of its twin guard chambers, the first feature inside the fort is a worn stone water

Steel Rigg

trough, which would have been filled by rainwater draining off nearby rooftops.

● Directly in front of the gate as you enter is the Via Principalis, the fort's main street which leads downhill to the South Gate, the Porta Principalis Dextra. Another street, to the west and parallel to the Via Principalis, is the Via Quintana; the two streets divide the fort into three roughly equal parts. The main buildings are in the central portion, with the headquarters or Principia in the middle. Here is where the commandant would control the administration of the section of Hadrian's Wall under his control; columns and heavy masonry indicate the importance of his imposing office. To its rear is a well-ventilated granary, or Horrea, and the hospital, Valetudinarium, is on the western side facing the Via Quintana.

● The commandant lived inside the fort in its largest building, the Praetorium, near the South Gate, and his troops lived in barrack blocks. About 1000 men were accommodated in 10 blocks, each building divided into about 12 rooms. Eight men had to squeeze into each room together with their equipment; their officers and non-commissioned officers had the two end rooms.

● Cleanliness and sanitation were of great importance to Romans. The latrine at Housesteads is one of the best-preserved buildings in the complex. Wooden benches with holes in them lined both walls and clean water flowed along a narrow channel in front of them.

● Life in Housesteads was not all parades and guard duty. In more peaceful times a civilian settlement, or Vicus, grew around the South Gate and land on both sides of the shallow valley was terraced and farmed.

● At least one murder took place at Housesteads. When one of the civilian houses was being excavated, the skeletons of a man and a woman were found beneath the stone floor. What caused their death will possibly never be known.

● Before moving off, take a walk from the East Gate towards Knag Burn and the Wall. Here there is a customs post. The small gate and its guard chambers are well preserved. Notice also the well-made culvert that allows Knag Burn to flow through Hadrian's Wall.

(15) Return to the South Gate and go down to the museum along the broad track south-west of the fort.
● Visit the museum (where you pay to look around Housesteads) and have a look at the model of the fort and items found during archaeological digs.

(16) Follow the surfaced lane away from the museum as far as the main road, the B6318. Take care as you cross this road.
● The B6318 follows the line of another military road, not as old as the Roman Military Way, but still an important piece of British history. During the Jacobite rebellions in the 1700s, it was realized that the important cities of Newcastle upon Tyne and Carlisle had no proper contact with each other. General Wade, a brilliant young engineer, designed this road. As with his Roman predecessors, he planned the route across the narrow neck of the country. Unfortunately he fell to the temptation that was offered by the ready-made material and built the eastern portion of the road on top of the ruined remains of Hadrian's Wall. The Jacobite rebellions were over by the time the road was finished in 1753.

(17) Climb a ladder stile and follow the narrow footpath across the field and up the rocky hillside. Walk across an undulating stretch of rough grazing, then go down towards the farmhouse of East Grindledikes.

(18) Keep to the left of the farm buildings and cross a shallow valley by the farm's access drive.

(19) Join a metalled road and turn right.
● You are now on Stanegate, the Roman road that linked the east–west line of forts before Hadrian's Wall was built. Stanegate (this English name was, of course, acquired long after the Romans left) runs from Corstopitum outside modern Corbridge as far as the fort of Petriana across the river Eden from Luguvallium, the Roman town that became Carlisle. Corstopitum was the main supply base for the central section of the Wall and also outlying units to the north. Supplies were brought by sea to Arbeia, on the site of modern South Shields, and transferred to flat-bottomed barges which were hauled by manpower up the Tyne. At Corstopitum goods were then transferred by road, either in carts or on pack animals.

(20) Follow Stanegate around a steep hillside on your left. Keep left at the next road junction.
● A Roman signalling station occupied the site of a British settlement on the prominent height to your left. Part of a sophisticated cross-country system of signalling posts, it was able to send messages either by fire at night, or smoke on bright days, with great speed and accuracy from one side of the country to the other. Beyond it is the Long Stone. It still points like a solitary finger, no doubt once acting as an unofficial marker for anyone travelling along Stanegate.
● Stanegate, which continues ahead at the road junction, down into Bradley Burn valley, has been abandoned in favour of the modern road.

㉑ Continue walking along the macadamed road for about half a mile. As the road descends towards the valley, look for the sign directing cars and buses to the Vindolanda parking place.

㉒ Turn right and follow the lane downhill past a Roman milestone as far as Chesterholm, a beautiful country house surrounded by attractively laid-out gardens, now the Vindolanda museum.
● Look through the museum before going out on to the site of the Roman fort, as it will make everything much simpler to understand.

㉓ Move out on to Vindolanda site.
● Originally the fort was part of the northern defences of Roman Britain before Hadrian's Wall took over that duty and Vindolanda became a rear echelon garrison, holding about 500 soldiers and acting as a back-up for the Wall. Divided into two sections, the main, and almost completely excavated, part has buildings as diverse as the commanding officer's house and a military bathhouse with a complex central heating system together with hot and cold water plunges, a great luxury on this wild northern frontier. Retired soldiers and friendly natives settled close to the fort; some must have been fairly well off, if the size of the houses are anything to go by. Workshops have been found and an inn or Mansio has been uncovered.

㉔ In the final stages of the walk you will need to use about 1½ miles of road from Vindolanda to Once Brewed. There is a bus service along it in summer, but if you have the energy and time to spare, there are still more examples of the Roman occupation to be found.
● There was a Roman cemetery in a field behind Causeway House, the first building on the right as you walk along the lane from Vindolanda car park. There is nothing to see, but the next object you will come to is easy to recognize. This is a tall stone column standing upright on the grassy right-hand verge, the base of a Roman milestone marking the course of Stanegate. Most of the old milestones have disappeared or been moved from their original sites and this one is unique; it has stood in this position for around 18 centuries indicating that you have walked one Roman mile from Chesterholm.

㉕ Turn right when you reach the Once Brewed road and follow it downhill across the steep valley of Brackies Burn. The car park is on the left at the top of the next rise. Do not drive off immediately, but sit down at one of the picnic tables and look across the valley.
● Ridges in the fields on the opposite side of Brackies Burn are the outer walls of a temporary camp. These camps were built by Roman soldiers when travelling cross-country in an area without any suitable accommodation, or if they needed a temporary base. Turf ramparts were quickly thrown up in the traditional square design of all Roman forts and the soldiers would pitch their leather tents in an ordered pattern with the commanding officer's tent in the middle. The layout would be similar to that in the permanent stone forts and every soldier could find the exact position for his tent even in the dark.

Overleaf: Hadrian's Wall, near Housesteads

Back street, Alnmouth

Note on using the Gazetteer

Entries in the Gazetteer are arranged in alphabetical order. 'The', if part of the name, follows the main element: **Cheviot Hills**, **The** (alphabetized under C).

Entry headings consist of the name of the place or feature in **bold** type, followed by the county name in *italics* and a map reference in parentheses: **Newton**, *Northumberland* (4/2C). The figure 4 is the map number; 2C is the grid reference, with C indicating the across and 2 the down reference.

If a name mentioned within the text of an entry is printed in capital letters – i.e. CONSETT – this indicates that it has its own entry in the Gazetteer.

Bold type is used for certain places, buildings or other features of interest or importance referred to within Gazetteer entries.

Every effort has been made to ensure that information about the opening to the public of buildings, estates, gardens, reserves, museums, galleries, etc., and details of trails, walks and footpaths, and of ferries, were as accurate and up to date as possible at the time of going to press. Such particulars are, of course, subject to alteration and it may be prudent to check them locally, or with the appropriate organizations or authorities.

Gazetteer

Acklam, *Cleveland* (8/2C) Nowadays a suburb of MIDDLESBROUGH, but mentioned in the Domesday Book and existing long before its now larger partner. Acklam and the neighbouring district of Linthorpe were separate entities until 1830.

Acklam Hall was built by the Hustler family in 1678. It remained in the family until 1929, when it was bought by Middlesbrough Corporation for use as a school. Features include carefully preserved fine plasterwork and the mile-long avenue of trees leading to the hall.

Acomb, *Northumberland* (4/1C) Built mostly along a side road east of the A6079, just to the north of HEXHAM, the village is in two parts, old and new, the latter being closest to the main road. Acomb was once a coal-mining community, but is now favoured by Tyneside commuters. The original village is built mostly of 18th-century houses, set around a pleasant square marked by a Victorian drinking fountain.

The manor house dates from 1736 and the opulently decorated church, a little to the south of Acomb, was designed by the Newcastle architect John Dobson and built in 1875. It was enlarged ten years later. There is a caravan and camp site near by on reclaimed colliery land.

Aesica *see* Hadrian's Wall

Allen Banks *see* Beltingham

Allendale Town, *Northumberland* (3/3C) Former lead-mining town on the B6295 and on the banks of the East Allen river, with rolling heatherclad Pennine moors as its backcloth. A sundial in the market place claims the town to be the geographical centre of Britain.

Lead mining was the main industry in the area until cheaper imports killed it off as late as the 1920s. The strongly Nonconformist religious outlook of its management is still reflected in the number of temperance hotels here, which were opened in the belief that milk was an antidote to lead poisoning. A smelt mill at Thornley Gate across the valley had an underground flue almost 2½ miles long, designed to produce the intense draught required by the furnaces and also to collect valuable arsenic deposits, a by-product of lead smelting. Men had to scramble along the steeply angled flue in order to scrape the poisonous arsenic from its walls.

There are many festivals and ancient customs in the area, the strangest being the Guizers, who carry blazing barrels of tar on their heads throughout the town every New Year's Eve. The parade culminates in a massive bonfire in the market place. Dancing and 'first footing' continue throughout the night, part of a festival that has links with the pagan past.

Sheepdog trials and an agricultural show are held here. The golf course is attractively situated above the west side of the dale. Nearby moors usually have a good covering of snow in winter and skiing is a well established sport in the area. Pony trekking across the moors is a popular summer activity.

Allenheads, *Northumberland* (5/3A) Small village in the sylvan upper reaches of the river East Allen. A former lead-mining community, Allenheads is now simply the estate village for Allenheads Park. Some of the mines have been reopened to extract fluorspar, valuable for use as a flux to remove impurities in steel making, or as a source of fluorine gas for the chemical industry.

With the declining fortunes of the valley and a much smaller population, several redundant schools and chapels now serve as Field Study Centres, covering activities in the area. Pony trekking takes place from Allenheads in summer and skiing on the surrounding moors in winter.

Alnmouth, *Northumberland* (2/3C) Unspoiled seaside village on a south-facing peninsula east of ALNWICK at the estuary of the river Aln. Its roots go back to the earliest days of Christianity's arrival in Northumbria; the sculptured shaft of an 8th-century cross was found near by and is now in Alnwick Castle Museum.

Alnmouth was an important seaport in medieval times, and still was in the 18th century, when the behaviour of its roistering mariners shocked John Wesley during his visit there.

The privateer Paul Jones bombarded the harbour during the American War of Independence, as part of his impudent attack on the North-East coast. Today, Alnmouth harbour is a popular anchorage for pleasure craft and inshore fishing boats. Sandy beaches and sheltered rocky havens stretch along the coast to the north and south of the estuary. The town has a 9-hole golf course; Foxton Hall, to the north, is a championship course.

Alnwick, *Northumberland* (2/2C) The town, pronounced 'Annick', is strategically placed at a crossing of the river Aln. It grew beneath the guardian walls of its castle, and narrow streets and intimate market squares still evoke an atmosphere of the medieval past, a past that is re-enacted each year during the costumed Alnwick Fair. Alnwick has been an important commercial centre since its first market charter in 1291. In a corner of the market place the stepped Market Cross looks out on to the Northumberland Hall, an imposing building erected in 1826. To one side is the older Town Hall, dating from 1771. Beyond the square are the Shambles, where the butchers were concentrated in medieval times.

The parish church of St Michael is mostly Perpendicular in style and dates from the 14th century, probably replacing a Norman building on the same site.

The Great North Road used to pass through Alnwick, which lies halfway between NEWCASTLE UPON TYNE and BERWICK-UPON-TWEED, but the modern AI(T) bypasses the town in a broad sweep along an embankment to the east. Many of Alnwick's inns, notably the Nags Head, have catered for travellers since the 16th century. Old Cross Inn in Narrowgate is better known as 'Dirty Bottles', from the row of bottles in a small bow window that have remained untouched for almost 200 years.

Alnwick Castle as we see it today is the result of careful restoration in the 18th century, then internal alterations in the Victorian era by Anthony Salvin for the 4th Duke of Northumberland. Originally dating from the 11th century, it is the home of the present duke, who still lives under the protection of warlike statues lining the battlements, carved by James Johnson in the mid-1800s. The castle is open to the public at advertised times and the interior is richly decorated in the Classical style, and there are paintings by Canaletto, Van Dyck and Titian. There are also dungeons, an armoury and an interesting museum of local remains dating from pre-Roman times; the Royal Northumberland Fusiliers Regimental Museum is housed in the Abbot's Tower. The park was landscaped by 'Capability' Brown and stretches away to the north across the Aln; the best view is obtained from the castle terrace.

Alnwick was built to withstand siege and was frequently under attack by raiding Scots. It was enclosed by a wall with several towers, some of which still exist, notably the Hotspur, Constable's and Postern Towers.

In the past Alnwick had to be self-reliant: being a long way from London and constantly under threat from the north, it found that help was always very slow to arrive. Its leading family, the Percys, have featured throughout much of England's history; Harry Hotspur (1364–1403) was immortalized in Shakespeare's *Henry IV*. He imprudently backed the Welsh Prince Mortimer and his ally Owen Glendower at the battle of Shrewsbury.

Visitors arriving by road from the south cannot fail to notice the 83 ft tall tower at the roadside. Surmounted by a lion with its tail stiffly outstretched, it is the symbol of the Percys, the Dukes of Northumberland. The tower rises from a base of five other lions; built in 1816 it was the gift of ducal estate tenants after their rents had been reduced after the Napoleonic Wars. Many stories surround this gift. One is that the duke regretted the reductions, feeling that if the tenants could afford the tower, they could well afford to pay full rents. Percy lions feature in Turner's painting of Alnwick Castle viewed in moonlight from the bridge. The castle is open from May to October.

Modern Alnwick is the commercial centre for a rich agricultural region and its industries are mostly connected with farming. It also makes fishing tackle and, perhaps rather unexpectedly, distils rum.

Parkland fills the northern aspect beyond the town. Abbeylands is part of the castle park, with the scant riverside remains of Alnwick Abbey, founded by monks of the Premonstratensian order. Upstream, Hulne Park stretches on either side of the Aln and here are the remains of a monastic house, **Hulne Priory**, a fortified abbey founded by the Carmelite order of White Friars in 1240. Although very much reduced in size, a considerable portion of the site is still well preserved. The massive curtain wall is complete, although most of its defences are gone, except Lord's Tower; this was added in 1488. The priory was something of a pleasure garden for later Percys and the 1st Duke added a pseudo-Gothic summerhouse in 1777. The priory church is aisleless, in keeping with the Carmelite order, and is a mixture of styles from medieval to Victorian. From the priory, a riverside walk leads upstream

Alnwick Castle

to Brislee Tower, a further pseudo-Gothic orna-mentation, built for the 1st Duke by Robert Adam.

Alwinton, *Northumberland* (1/3C) Remote village in the upper Coquet valley about 9 miles north-west of ROTHBURY. It sits on a sunny plateau above the junction of the Coquet with the river Alwin. Being enclosed by high Cheviot moors on all sides gives the village a general air of tranquilli-ty and makes it an ideal centre for walks in central Cheviot, and for trout fishing in the local rivers. The village church was founded in the 12th century, but was very much altered about 1851.

The valley road continues north-westwards, following the Coquet to reach ever more remote hamlets and sheep farms in the upper dale. Tracks from the dalehead spread out like a fan to reach the Scottish border. Windy Gyle (2032 ft) and Auchope Cairn (2418 ft) are the highest points on the actual border ridge. The Cheviot is higher (2674 ft), but not on this ridge.

Amble-by-the-Sea, *Northumberland* (7/2A) A small seaport at the mouth of the river Coquet, where the esturial harbour of WARKWORTH is busy with pleasure craft and inshore fishing boats. Coal is still exported from here, taken from mines exploiting the northern edge of the North-umbrian undersea coalfield. Some of the local seams are close enough to the surface for coal to be washed ashore during winter gales, providing free fuel for anyone hardy enough to brave the elements.

Coquet Island is about a mile offshore. The haunt of eider duck and other sea birds, it still has the foundations of a 12th-century Benedictine monastery. Now guarded by a lighthouse, the island, which is directly in line with the harbour entrance, was once a notorious hazard to ship-ping.

Arbeia *see* Hadrian's Wall

Ashington, *Northumberland* (7/2A) The town was built between 1890 and 1946, and lies between MORPETH and the coast. It became known as 'the largest pit village in the world'. Even though it has spread over both sides of the river Wansbeck, and has grown into a fair-sized town, Ashington still keeps its village-like character. Its amenities are the large shopping centre together with an adjacent sports complex. Wansbeck riverside Park is set along a 2-mile, partly wooded stretch of the tidal Wansbeck. Waterside facilities include picnic sites, sailing, river fishing and a caravan site.

Aydon Castle *see* Halton

Bamburgh, *Northumberland* (2/2B) The red sandstone bulk of Bamburgh Castle hangs over this village and gives it an almost medieval atmosphere. Pleasant low stone houses line its two main streets and the village fits snugly behind a natural rocky barrier and sand dunes, screened from harsh north-easterlies blowing off the North Sea.

Grace Darling was born in the village and on her death from tuberculosis in 1842 she was buried with much Victorian pomp in St Aidan's churchyard. The Grace Darling Museum opposite the church commemorates her epic rescue when, together with her father, keeper of the Longstone lighthouse, she saved the lives of a number of survivors of the SS *Forfarshire*, which went aground on the FARNE ISLANDS in 1838.

St Aidan's Church is a mid-7th-century foundation, but the present building is mostly 13th century with some Victorian alterations. The vaulted crypt contains tombs of the Forsters, a notable Northumbrian family.

Bamburgh Castle, the home of Lord and Lady Armstrong, is dramatically set on its high rock and is a landmark for miles along the Northumbrian coast. Its present romantic appearance is largely the result of restoration: some in the 18th century, more by the 1st Lord Armstrong, the engineer, who paid for the last and most ambitious work.

Once the home of monarchs of the Anglo-Saxon kingdom of Bernicia, the stronghold is steeped in legend. It is certainly mentioned in the Anglo-Saxon Chronicle as being founded by King Ida in AD 547 and his successors reigned here until the seat of government was moved to CORBRIDGE in the mid-8th century. The castle was inherited by Ida's grandson, Ethelfrid, who united the kingdoms of Bernicia and Deira to the south to form Northumbria. He apparently gave

it to Bebba and it is from her the early form of the name, *Bebbanburh*, derives. Constantly in the front line, it was frequently attacked by the dreaded Norsemen. The Anglo-Saxon fortress was replaced by a Norman castle and in 1095 it was besieged by William Rufus, in the course of putting down a rebellion. In the early part of the 12th century Bamburgh Castle became a possession of the English Crown, used by several kings in their wars with Scotland. It was a Yorkist stronghold during the Wars of the Roses, but the rest of its medieval history was peaceful.

From the reign of James I (1603–25) it was in the care of the Forsters. It was Lord Crewe, Bishop of Durham, who inherited the castle by marriage in 1704 and began the long process of reconstruction, entrusting most of the work to Dr John Sharp, Archdeacon of Northumberland. Lord Armstrong bought Bamburgh Castle in 1894 and spent the following 30 years on its final restoration.

Viewed from the village, the castle fills the whole of the upper crag on which it sits, an outcrop of the Great Whin Sill sheet. This volcanic rock is also very dramatically exposed at places as far apart as Cauldron Snout in upper Teesdale and the Farne Islands, as well as the escarpment crossed by a large section of HADRIAN'S WALL. The massive square keep dominates the outer works; restored by Dr Sharp, it was originally built about 1164 in the reign of Henry II. Inside the main gate and on the north aisle of the Inner Ward are the remains of St Oswald's Chapel. (Oswald was king of Northumbria 631–42 and died fighting the Mercians at Oswestry.) The main room within the castle proper, panelled with teak and hung with rich tapestries and paintings, is known as the King's Hall. The next building of note is the Armoury. This has an astonishing collection of weapons and armour.

Bamburgh Castle is open to the public from Easter to October and also contains the Armstrong Museum, depicting the life and times of the 1st Lord Armstrong.

Banna *see* Hadrian's Wall

Bardon Mill, *Northumberland* (3/3C) Former mining village above the north bank of the South Tyne, on the A69 about halfway between HEXHAM and HALTWHISTLE. An important drove road once crossed the river at this point. Cattle were fitted with iron shoes at Bardon Mill to help them on their way, on the hoof, to southern markets. Since the loss of its coal mine the village

Bamburgh Castle

has diversified its industries in keeping with current economic demands. An old brickworks is now producing garden containers and plant pots of all shapes and sizes.

Bardon Mill is a convenient starting point for HADRIAN'S WALL. A tourist bus runs on a circular route between the Tyne valley and the Wall, calling at most of the important features *en route*, including the nearby Vindolanda site and museum, also Housesteads Fort.

Barnard Castle, *Co. Durham* (6/1C) Marking the division between fell and plain, this charming market town on the A67 DARLINGTON–Brough road developed within the protection of a Norman castle. This was rebuilt in the 12th century by Bernard de Baliol, hence the name. The original grant of lands surrounding Teesside was made by William II in 1093. Built on a commanding height above the Tees, the castle controlled an important north–south river crossing, still marked by a venerable bridge dating from 1569. Warwick the Kingmaker acquired the castle in the 15th century and through his daughter it passed to Richard III: his emblem, the wild boar, decorates the wall of the Great Chamber. Now maintained in immaculate condition by English Heritage, it is possible to gain an accurate impression of its original size from the surviving walls and neat lawns that were once the site of crude buildings and stables housing the castle's retainers and their animals.

Streets radiate away from the castle with names like Bridgegate, Newgate and Thorngate. Stately 18th-century town houses line Thorngate, which descends past an old watermill to an attractive

footbridge over the Tees and then leads on to The Bank and its quiet riverside walks. On the left as you descend is 16th-century Blagroves House, a venerable building with gabled bay windows on three storeys, giving the appearance of a tall narrow tower butted on to the main structure.

The substantial octagonal Market Cross was built in 1747 and stands in the Market Place at the top of The Bank. Crowned by a cupola and weathervane, the colonnaded shelter has been used by generations of local people selling their farm produce on the ground floor. The Town Hall, lit by elegant Venetian windows, fills the upper storey.

Barnard Castle's parish church is to the east of the cross; much altered in the 19th century, it is built on Norman foundations.

Uphill, beyond the Market Place, the street becomes Horsemarket and on the left is the King's Head, where Charles Dickens stayed in 1838 when collecting material for his novel *Nicholas Nickleby*. In Newgate a plaque marks the site of a shop owned by the man who was the inspiration for Dickens' *Master Humphrey's Clock*, intended as a frame for both *Barnaby Rudge* and *The Old Curiosity Shop*.

A little to the east of the town, along Newgate from the Market Cross, is a building that would be more in keeping with the French provinces than a quiet North of England market town. This is the **Bowes Museum**, built originally by the French architect Jules Pellachet for George Bowes, who inherited vast Durham estates and coal-mining interests from his father, the 10th

The Bowes Museum

Earl of Strathmore. Bowes laid the foundation stone of the museum in 1869, but both he and his wife (a French actress) had died before it was completed. In accordance with his wishes, the museum opened in 1892. Now run by Durham County Council, it is filled with objects ranging from local Roman relics to paintings by El Greco, Goya and other masters, as well as period furniture and fashions. Pride of place in the main entrance is a lifesize working model of a silver swan. A park and gardens surround the museum. Open daily except Christmas and New Year.

Cotherstone (6/1C) lies 3½ miles north-west of Barnard Castle, on the B6277. A charming group of stone cottages, and one or two larger houses, stand above the south bank of the Tees, near where the Balder flows into it. Of its 12th-century castle only a few small mounds remain.

Barningham, *Co. Durham* (6/2C) Secluded village on a minor road off the A66, about 5 miles south-south-east of BARNARD CASTLE. The quiet loop road leaves the bustle of the A66 at Greta Bridge to travel south for a little over a mile to reach the village, marking the division between pasture and moor. There is a wide green lined with stone cottages in a charming grouping of styles and sizes. The church is Victorian Gothic with a graveyard of venerable, moss-covered tombstones. Barningham Park, home of the Milbankes, is late 17th century with an 18th-century stable block. The whole is set in attractive

gardens and terraced woodland walks.

A series of Roman shrines have been discovered on Scargill Moor to the west of Barningham. Altarstones and details of the excavation are on display in Bowes Museum (*see* Barnard Castle). Nearby **Stang Forest**, astride the minor road from Barnard Castle to Arkengarthdale in North Yorkshire, has a short waymarked forest walk from the upper of the two roadside car parks.

Barrasford, *Northumberland* (4/1B) Village of stone houses on a side road west of the A6079, north of HEXHAM. Barrasford faces the sun above a bend of the North Tyne and its tributary, the Swin Burn. A ferry used to carry foot passengers across the river to Haughton Castle, but it is now closed. The castle is one of the great houses of Northumbria and is in private ownership.

A right of way still exists from the ferry landing and around the boundary of the estate, passing close to Haughton. The castle is built on ancient foundations, which were destroyed in the 16th century. The present battlemented building was designed by Anthony Salvin in the 19th century.

Pity Me (4/1B and 6/3A) is a woodland estate hamlet on a minor road off the A68, about 8 miles north of Hexham. There is a camping and caravan site on its northern edge. 'Pity Me' may indicate a former pond or lake (*petit mere*), as in the case of its Durham namesake.

Beadnell, *Northumberland* (2/3B) A caravan site dominates the shoreward side of Beadnell, which lies on the B1340 coast road south-east of BAMBURGH, and many of its houses are second homes; but the rocky foreshore and sheltered sandy beach around Beadnell Bay to the south more than compensate for this. The small harbour is overlooked by 18th-century lime kilns, now cared for by the National Trust. The village church is mainly Victorian Gothic, and the remains of ancient St Ebbe's Chapel also overlook the harbour. A pleasant 18th-century inn, the Craster Arms, is in the main street and a 15th-century peel tower stands to the west of the village.

An unspoiled sandy beach leads to Newton Links above Snook Point, a little over one mile south of Beadnell; here there are 55 acres of sand dunes owned by the National Trust.

Beamish Open Air Museum, *Co. Durham* (7/2C) The museum is within the grounds of Beamish Estate, off the A693 to the east of STANLEY. Still developing, it is attempting to re-create northern life as it was around the turn of the century. The buildings, vehicles, together with farming machinery and early industrial heavy plant, have been collected throughout the region and rebuilt or reassembled, usually in full working order, in the open air. The museum's pride is the 1920s Town Street, a collection of furnished houses, including a dentist's surgery and solicitor's office, a working pub and the fully stocked cooperative shop moved lock, stock and barrel from Annfield Plain. An electric tram takes a short rural ride to connect Town Street with Home Farm, where there is a collection of farm implements and unusual breeds; beyond is the colliery area with its row of miners' cottages furnished to show the changing styles of furniture throughout the last 100 years. Visitors can travel underground into a drift mine on the small colliery train. Rowley

Two reconstructions at the Beamish Open Air Museum
Above: The nursery, the Dentist's House
Below: The kitchen, Miner's Cottage

Station, near the museum, nostalgically re-creates the atmosphere of steam railways.

Beamish – its full official name is the North of England Open Air Museum – was awarded the European Museum of the Year title in 1987.

Beamish Hall is across the access drive and houses an interesting collection of objects ranging from miners' safety lamps to handmade Durham quilts, a traditional craft the museum is at pains to preserve. The hall was, until death duties led to its sale in 1952, the home of the Davison, Eden and latterly Shafto families. Lord Avon, formerly Sir Anthony Eden MP, was a frequent visitor to the hall and Bobby Shafto, immortalized by the famous Northumbrian sea shanty, was an ancestor of the last owners. Records show that a house has stood on the site of Beamish Hall since 1268, when Guiscard de Charron first lived there.

Footpaths link Beamish Museum with the single-span Causey Arch about 1 mile to the north. Built in 1727 to carry horse-drawn railway wagons from a local colliery, it is considered to be the oldest stone railway bridge in the world.

Not part of the museum, but seen on the approach road from the A693 through Beamish village, is a Georgian public house, The Shepherd and Shepherdess. The inn sign has two romantically styled figures.

The Shepherd and Shepherdess public house, Beamish

Bearpark, *Co. Durham* (6/3A) Mining village developed a little more than a century ago on a hilltop a mile to the west of DURHAM. The name has nothing to do with bears, but is a corruption of *beau repaire*: this was the country seat of Durham priors in the Middle Ages. Little now remains of a once proud building that stood above the Browney valley to the north-east of the present village. The famous Roman Catholic seminary of Ushaw College is half a mile west of Bearpark. Founded by Bishop Allen in 1568, and originally based at Douai in France, the seminary first moved to Crook Hall, near STANLEY, after the French Revolution.

Pontop Hall is the simple stone building that next housed the seminary. It is near **Dipton**, a scattered ridge-tip community on the A692.

The present site was chosen in 1808 and among its buildings are the Chapel and Refectory designed by A. W. N. Pugin; and the Library and Exhibition Room are by Hansom. The school buildings were the work of E. W. N. Pugin. The college still retains many of the traditions established at Douai, including its own form of squash: the Douai Game, as it is known. Ushaw is open to visitors by prior arrangement.

Bedlington, *Northumberland* (7/2B) A mining town built above the deeply cut wooded valley of the river Blyth, a few miles inland from the port of BLYTH. Bedlington was once the capital of Bedlingtonshire when this was part of the County Palatine of Durham, before the boundary reorganization of 1884. A miners' gala is held every June in Attlee Park, where speeches by miners' leaders and prominent Labour politicians compete with beauty contests, jazz bands and other colourful events, which make this the biggest function of Bedlington's year.

Bedlington terriers take their name from this town; renowned for their tenacity, the dogs are still great favourites among miners.

Font Street, the main street in Bedlington, climbs away from the river and heads towards the market cross and the ancient church dedicated to St Cuthbert, where Victorian improvements have destroyed the oldest features. Interesting old houses line the rest of Font Street, parts of which have been designated a Conservation Area.

Plessey Woods Country Park follows a wooded dene along the banks of the meandering Blyth. The country park is about 1½ miles to the south-west of the town, beyond Bedlington's 18-hole golf course. Woodland and riverside walks are aided by interpretive displays of the natural history of the area.

Belford, *Northumberland* (2/2B) Now bypassed to the east by the A1, this small agricultural and busy market town a few miles inland from BAMBURGH surrounds a wide main street. This was originally formed by the Great North Road and leads past a simple market cross towards the ivy-covered Blue Bell Inn, once a coaching hostelry.

Belford Hall was built in 1756 to a design by James Paine. After being neglected over the years it has now been tastefully reconstructed by the Northern Heritage Trust Ltd. The land to the north-west of the village rises towards the wooded **Kyloe Hills**, an excellent area for short walks.

Bellingham, *Northumberland* (3/3A) A small market town – pronounced 'Bellinjam' – on the North Tyne river, once the centre of a busy coal- and ironstone-mining area. The railway that served Bellingham has now gone; sheep and cattle sold at the regular livestock markets are moved instead by massive road vehicles.

St Cuthbert's body is supposed to have rested here during its long travels around the North before reaching its final resting place in DURHAM;

Bellingham

the village church, as tradition decrees, is therefore named after him. The church came under attack many times by Scottish raiders and the present building is designed to withstand a siege. Its arched roof is made of unusually heavy stone slabs, supported by massive hexagonal ribs, and the narrow slit windows are like those found in castle walls. Historically, there has been a church on this site since the 11th century; however, nothing remains from that time, the oldest features dating from the 13th, and most of the present building is early 17th century with 19th-century 'improvements'. There is a curiously shaped gravestone in the churchyard associated with the 'Long Pack' story; it traditionally marks the grave of a pedlar who was secreted into a local house inside a travelling pack, with the intention of later letting in a gang of robbers. Seeing the pack move, servants fired a gun at it and on opening the pack, found the body of a man.

Near to the church is St Cuthbert's, or Cuddy's, Well whose waters were once claimed to have healing properties and are still used for baptisms.

A quiet town, Bellingham is the kind of place where you naturally look for bygones. The Boer War Memorial, together with a gingall, a Chinese gun captured at Fort Taku by a local worthy

during the Boxer Rebellion, are just two of the unusual items to be found.

Hareshaw Linn (3/3A) is a 30 ft high waterfall at the end of a secluded wooded dell immediately beyond the old railway siding to the north of the town centre, which makes an attractive 1½ miles' walk. Sturdier walkers pass through Bellingham during the later (or earlier, if travelling south) stages of the Pennine Way. Most will be seeking accommodation either in the town or at the nearby Youth Hostel.

The annual North Tyne Agricultural show is held on the riverside meadows below the town, usually on the last Saturday in August.

Belsay Castle and Hall, *Northumberland* (4/2B) Ruined castle and early 19th-century hall standing in parkland 6 miles to the north-west of PONTELAND. The site has been populated for thousands of years, each successive development moving east across the centuries. The first was a prehistoric circular mound to the west, used as a settlement by Neolithic people, and a standing stone associated with it later became a Christian cross. In the 14th century a castle was built to shelter the tenants and a village clustered around its defensive walls. All that remains of the castle is

Opposite: Belsay Castle

The stables, Belsay Hall

the impressively ruined tower house and its adjacent wings. The last stage in the development came in the early 19th century when the village was demolished to make way for Belsay Hall, home of Sir Charles Monck, a member of the Middleton family. Designed by John Dobson, its south front is adorned by Doric pilasters and the spacious central hall surrounded by Ionic and Doric columns in the romantic style of the time. The grounds are particularly fine, with a lake and a quarry garden. Hall, castle and gardens are open to the public from mid-March to mid-October, together with an exhibition of the development of the estate. The demolished village was replaced in 1830 by the single arcade of Italianate sandstone buildings seen on the A696.

The view of Belsay Castle is particularly impressive when obtained from the Belsay–STAMFORDHAM road (B6309).

Beltingham, *Northumberland* (3/3C) Small village on the south bank of the South Tyne and only accessible by a minor road off the A69, 10 miles west of HEXHAM. The church, although much altered in the 19th century, was probably founded in the early part of the 16th century as a chapel of ease. Dedicated to St Cuthbert, it is reputed to have Saxon origins; the age of a yew tree in the churchyard certainly seems to bear that out. Two

Roman altarstones, also in the churchyard, link the building to even older times. Next door an elegant Georgian house belongs to the Bowes-Lyon family, relatives of the Queen Mother.

Eighteenth-century **Ridley Hall** is over the fields from Beltingham and close to the confluence of the river Allen with the South Tyne. The mock castle is now a college and holiday centre. A mile south from Ridley Hall, and best reached on foot by a riverside path through the National Trust's **Allen Banks** property, is the woodland beauty spot of Plankey Mill. Beyond the mill another riverside path, again of about 1 mile, leads to **Staward Pele**, a ruined tower. Field paths or quiet side roads could be used for the return to Ridley Hall, but the valley is so attractive that it scarcely matters if the same path is used twice.

Berwick-upon-Tweed, *Northumberland* (2/1A & 2/3A) England's most northerly town sits at the mouth of the Tweed and astride the A1, the Great North Road. Once a 'shuttlecock', changing hands 13 times between the two contending nations, it had the special status of a 'free burgh' from 1482 until the Reform Act of 1885. The national border now follows the line of the Tweed to a point about 4 miles west of Berwick and then makes an unnatural loop northwards.

A curious anomaly created by the 1885 act was that Berwick remained officially at war with

Russia for 110 years, from 1856 until 1966. Apparently, official documents declaring war on Russia at the start of the Crimean War were in the name of Victoria, Queen of Great Britain, Ireland, Berwick-upon-Tweed and all the British Dominions. When war ended in 1856, by oversight the Paris Peace Treaty made no mention of Berwick. This omission was rectified in 1966 when a Soviet official made a special goodwill visit to the town. The town's mayor, Councillor Robert Knox, told the Russian people that they could now sleep peacefully in their beds.

The AI now follows a more westerly route and heavy lorries no longer bring chaos to this bustling market town. Four bridges cross the Tweed; the oldest is furthest downstream and was built between 1610 and 1634, although there had been bridges before that date. Next are the four spans of the Royal Tweed Bridge opened in 1928, below which the famous Berwick Swans keep pace with the tide. The London-to-Edinburgh railway enters the town by way of the 28-arched Royal Border Bridge; this was built by George Stephenson's son Robert, who demolished most of Berwick Castle to make way for Berwick station. The castle's Great Hall is now the waiting room; a plaque records the decision by Edward I to give the throne of Scotland to John Balliol rather than to his most serious rival Robert Bruce. The most up-to-date bridge is furthest upstream and carries the AI bypass.

Stately Georgian town houses, restored under a joint scheme by the National Trust and the Berwick-upon-Tweed Preservation Society, line the quayside on the north side of the river. Narrow cobbled streets lead away from the river towards the town centre, where the 18th-century Town Hall dominates the bottom end of Marygate, the broad main shopping street. The Town Hall was once a jail and is unique in having a spire where the bell is rung to announce services at the parish church of the Holy Trinity, a few streets away, which has no bell. This 17th-century church is one of the few built during the Commonwealth period after the Civil War, and has some remarkable stained glass.

Uphill along Marygate is a gate in the town wall which was a notorious bottleneck before the bypass was built. It is an opening in the Elizabethan ramparts, the last word in military architecture in their time and unique in Britain. The thick earth and stone-faced walls and emplacements were built against possible attack by the joint armies of France and Scotland, and could withstand artillery bombardment. Built

between 1558 and 1566, they replaced earlier defences constructed around 1296 during the reign of Edward I. Traces of these older walls can still be seen around the town. The best way to see Berwick and its river is by a circuit of the ramparts using a footpath along their crest. Guided tours of the ramparts, starting from Berwick Barracks, are organized from mid-March to mid-October.

Sir John Vanbrugh, architect of Blenheim Palace and Castle Howard, designed these barracks in 1717, after the first Jacobite uprising. Something of a show place in its day, it became the home base of the King's Own Scottish Borderers and now houses a museum telling the story of organized army life from Cromwellian times until the present day. Part of the Burrell Collection (the rest is in Glasgow) is on display in the Clock Block of the Barracks.

The Tweed is a famous salmon river. The fish swim annually upstream to spawn in its headwaters. Commercial fishing is by net; sportsmen use flies and there are several specialist tackle shops around the town. Berwick has a fishing fleet and also a small boatyard. The dock and industrial area of the town is between Tweedmouth and Spittal on the south side of the river. There is a fine sandy beach beyond Spittal. The football team, Berwick Rangers, is in the Scottish League.

The Border ceremony of Riding the Bounds, which has continued since the reign of Henry VIII, takes place each year on 1 May. Horsemen follow the town's 10-mile boundary with the mayor and civic party following by more sedate transport.

Haggerston (2/1A) is a small village east of the AI, about 7 miles south of Berwick. A caravan site now surrounds the lake and a peel tower, the remains of a castle built in 1345.

Billingham, *Cleveland* (8/2B) A traveller crossing the river Tees by Newport Bridge, a single-span, vertical-lift bridge opened in 1934, or by the more modern bridge that carries the dual carriageway of the AI9 northwards, cannot fail to recognize that Billingham is a town devoted to the manufacture of chemicals. The smoke and steam, the weird skyline of distillation towers, storage tanks and electricity pylons, all dazzlingly lit at night, spell 20th-century industrial alchemy.

It is hard to realize that Billingham has its roots in the 9th century AD, or even further back in history. St Cuthbert's has a Saxon tower and nave

Overleaf: The Newport Bridge, Middlesbrough

and still stands beside a village green in the town centre, a church that reflects the development of the town down to the present time.

Billingham began to expand in 1834 when the Clarence Railway was built to carry coal to Clarence Staithes, a deepwater dock on the north bank of the Tees. An iron foundry, opened three years later at Haverton Hill, was soon followed by a glassworks and blast furnace, and ever more foundries. It was the First World War that led to the development of Billingham's chemical industry, when a factory was opened to make nitrogen, a component of explosives and fertilizers. After the war the plant was taken over by Brunner, Mond & Company, which later became part of the Imperial Chemical Industries (ICI). Since then a massive complex of oil refineries and chemical plant has grown, spreading from the town towards the flat marshlands of Seal Sands and along the north bank of the Tees.

At the same time as this industrial development was taking place there was a rapid expansion of housing; and the town has practically been rebuilt since 1945. Billingham Forum caters for the town's leisure and intellectual needs; it is an imaginative complex of theatre and sports halls where the Billingham International Folklore Festival is staged every August.

The famous Transporter Bridge, opened in 1911, dominates the Teesside skyline and crosses the river from Port Clarence to MIDDLESBROUGH; the 571 ft gap is spanned by a mobile deck. The bridge is still in operation, but the massive traffic jams it once created by its stately progression backwards and forwards across the river have eased with the opening of the A19-based inner ring road.

Cowpen Nature Reserve lies off the A178 HARTLEPOOL road, a haven for wildlife on marshland almost surrounded by 20th-century industry. Waders and other wildfowl visit the site each year from as far away as northern Scandinavia and Siberia.

Cowpen Bewley is almost surrounded by industrial Billingham to the south-west, but the village has retained its agricultural base since the 18th century. The regular layout of its farms and cottages on either side of the wide green follows a pattern established soon after the Norman Conquest. Village Farm House and Little Neuk Farm Cottage, dating from the early 18th century, and 17th-century Ivy House, are its most notable buildings.

Wolviston (8/2B) is a small, compact village on the northern outskirts, proud of winning the Britain in Bloom award several times. A well-kept green and attractive gardens make a pleasant oasis in Teesside's industrial belt.

Billsmoorfoot, *Northumberland* (4/1A) Camping and caravan site next to the B6341 OTTERBURN–ROTHBURY road, in what was once a deer park surrounded by a 7-mile-long wall. Heather moors climb on either side of the road and natural birch and alder woodland are near by where, occasionally, shy roedeer can be seen. Abandoned peel towers once guarded the surrounding farms from attack from the north.

Bishop Auckland, *Co. Durham* (6/3B) The town's foundations are ancient, but you must look hard to find them beneath industrial sprawl and housing developments. Bishops of Durham have used Auckland Castle and its surrounding Bishop's Park since the 12th century. The castle is to the north-east of the town, and is approached through an imposing gateway; beyond it is the Deer Cote or Sanctuary, set in 800 acres of riverside parkland and woods. The park and deer sanctuary are open to the public, but Auckland Castle, the official residence, is private and only open from May to September. It was originally a Norman manor house but was largely rebuilt in 1760. Within are splendid state rooms with delicate tracery in their plaster ceilings. Bishop Cosin designed much of the magnificent woodwork and panelling in the chapel of St Peter, a building of breathtaking proportions, much larger than you would expect for a private chapel. It was in fact the banqueting hall, converted by Cosin.

The town has had a market since medieval times and grew from a scattered group of hamlets between the steep south bank of the river Wear and its tributary the Gaunless. The Wear is spanned by a 15th-century road bridge and 19th-century railway viaduct. The latter is now used as a footpath, part of the 9½-mile Bishop Brandon Walk from Bishop Auckland to Broompark picnic area on the outskirts of DURHAM. This passes through the southern outskirts of **Brandon**, a small colliery town south-west of the city.

The parish church of St Andrew is Saxon in its origins. Said to be the largest church in the county, its greatest feature is the Saxon cross reconstructed from fragments found during rebuilding work in 1881. Carved on the base are three haloed figures and, on a panel above, is the Crucifixion, finally surmounted by two figures, one holding a cross. Animals and birds within Celtic scrolls embellish the sides.

Roman Dere Street passed northwestwards through here from York to CORBRIDGE. To the north of the town, between Binchester and the Wear, are the partly excavated remains of the Roman fort of Vinovia, which means 'pleasant spot'. The most easily understood outlines are those of the hypocaust, a Roman central heating system. Nearby 19th-century Binchester Hall is now a hotel with excellent views of Auckland Castle.

Bishop Middleham, *Co. Durham* (8/1B) An industrial village between the A177 and A1 motorway, to the east of BISHOP AUCKLAND. The title 'Bishop' in this case refers to a medieval castle belonging to the Bishops of Durham; the only remains are vague grass-covered mounds in a field to the south-west of the village. What is intact, however, is the 18th-century Hall in the older part of the village and the 13th-century church of St Michael, with a font made from Frosterley marble and memorials to the Surtees family, who lived at Mainsford Hall a mile to the west. The hall is now demolished. Robert Surtees (1779–1834) was a famous historian especially interested in County Durham.

Bishopton, *Co. Durham* (8/1C) Rural village on high ground in pleasant countryside, about 3 miles west of STOCKTON-ON-TEES. Although the village is old, its church is only 19th century, but fragments of medieval stones hint at an earlier building.

Castle Hill, a prehistoric site, is to the south of the last houses of the village; man-made, it covers 7 acres with double ditches and a 40 ft high mound or bailey.

Bishopwearmouth *see* Sunderland

Blackhall, *Co. Durham* (8/2A) A small town in from the coast south-east of PETERLEE New Town and supportive to Blackhall Colliery, one of the big undersea coal mines of the North East. The A1086 and the SUNDERLAND to HARTLEPOOL railway line run parallel to the coast, at this point a polluted stretch of rocks and sandy coves.

To the west on the CASTLE EDEN road is the two-storey 18th-century façade of 16th-century Hardwick Hall (*see also* Sedgefield).

Blanchland, *Northumberland* (6/1A) A small moorland village in the wooded upper Derwent

Blanchland…'a timeless serenity about the place…'

valley, about 10 miles west of CONSETT. There is a timeless serenity about the place; mellow grey stone houses fit snugly around an open square opposite the Georgian Lord Crewe Arms, and a narrow hump-backed bridge completes the tranquil rural scene. The present layout of the village dates from the early part of the 18th century, when the trustees of the Crewe estate built the cottages to house lead miners.

The name Blanchland links the place with its ecclesiastical foundations. White canons of the Augustinian order of Premonstratensians founded an abbey here in the 12th century. After the Dissolution, the monks were driven away, but the abbey church remained in use for the devotions of the local community. As with many old churches, Blanchland's was renovated in the 19th century and little remains of its ancient fabric apart from the tower and north transept.

Blaydon, *Tyne and Wear* (4/3C & 7/1C) Industrial town on the south bank of the Tyne above its confluence with the river Derwent. The town was immortalized by the Geordie anthem 'Blaydon

Below: Each year small patches of heather are set on fire (see p. 44)
Opposite: The 18th-century lighthouse, Blyth

Races', but unfortunately the last race was in 1916 and the famous racecourse is no more; Stella Power Station occupies the site. To appreciate the town and its residential suburb of **Winlaton** you must climb the steep hillside above the A695. The Geordie dialect is very much at home here in the pubs and working men's clubs of Blaydon. A Southerner could well have problems with this language of soft 'r's and its vocabulary where, as in the other Northern dialects, there are many more words of Scandinavian origin than in Standard English. The town has a small but modern shopping centre and swimming pool.

In Winlaton's Hood Square a chain forge has been preserved. Once part of the cottage industry that flourished in the town, it can be seen on application to the Winlaton Branch Library.

Countryside quickly reasserts itself in the Derwent valley south of Blaydon, where Thornley Wood Country Park and Woodland Centre covers 82 acres of woodland and reclaimed colliery spoil above the Derwent. Derwent Walk Country Park is a linear park adjoining Thornley Wood and follows the track of an old railway line above the valley side, away towards the woodland of ROWLANDS GILL and beyond to CONSETT. The track is ideal on foot, cycle or horseback; some sections are suitable for invalid chairs.

Blenkinsopp Hall; **Blenkinsopp Castle** *see* Haltwhistle

Blyth, *Northumberland* (7/2B) The town spreads to the south of the elongated estuary of the river Blyth. To the north, across the river and reached either by passenger ferries or road, is the massive power station at Cambois, converting undersea coal into electrical energy for the National Grid. Coal is still exported from Blyth, but not in the quantities of a century ago; timber is imported from Scandinavia and eastern Europe and the rest of the river is given over to pleasure craft. The Royal Northumberland Yacht Club has its headquarters at Blyth, based on a converted lightship. Sea angling and inshore fishing boats complete the maritime scene.

The oldest part of Blyth is built around Northumberland Street and near by is an 18th-century lighthouse, standing a little incongruously inland behind some terraced houses. South of the town and well away from industry, sandy beaches, a golf course, and camping and caravan sites on the foreshore beyond the Nautical School give this part of the town a holiday resort atmosphere.

Bolam Lake Country Park, *Northumberland* (4/2B) An artificial lake in a woodland setting. Access is along a country lane linking the A696 and the B6343 about 2 miles north-west of Belsay; there are picnic sites and limited car parking facilities. The lake and nearby estate of Bolam Hall were created by the Newcastle architect John Dobson in the 19th century.

Bolam Hall, a mile to the north-east of the lake, is now a guesthouse; the house and St Andrew's Church are the only remaining links with an older village. The church dates from 960 and is one of the best-preserved Saxon churches in Northumberland. Its tower is the oldest feature, but much of the Saxon work can still be found within the later Norman interior.

Shortflatt Tower to the south of the lake is a private house, built into the remains of a 14th-century peel tower. **Shaftoe Crags**, a prominent outcrop topped by a prehistoric fort to the west of Bolam House, can be aproached along a public footpath beyond a gate in the access lane leading to Shaftoe Hall. Near by is the standing stone with the strange name of Poind and his Man.

Bothal, *Northumberland* (7/1B) Model village on the side road between ASHINGTON and MORPETH. Bothal is at the end of a spur between the wooded denes of Brock's Burn and the river Wansbeck.

The tiny village is centred on its Saxon church and also the ruins of Bothal Castle, which was built in 1343 by Robert Bertram, but later became the seat of the Ogle family. Little of its central bailey and defensive wall remain, but the fortified gatehouse is now used as a guesthouse. The wooded denes of the Wansbeck and Brock's Burn are accessible by footpaths between Pegswood and Morpeth, or from below the castle.

Boulby, *Cleveland* (8/3A) A cluster of buildings close to the highest cliff on the east coast (679 ft). The rocky foreshore and cliff face here are a

The potash mine, Boulby

treasure ground for fossil hunters. The district was once the scene of intensive alum mining, used as a mordant or fixative for Turkey Red dyes. Eighteenth-century smugglers lived on this remote stretch of coast, an ideal place for illicit deals in wines and spirits and other contraband.

Across the busy A174 the complex of modern pithead gear and silos is only a small indication of the vast and very deep series of shafts and galleries of the Boulby Potash Mines, which stretch far out beneath the sea. The potash and salt deposits are moved underground by huge dumper trucks and are carried to the Teesside chemical industry along a still operating clifftop railway, the last relic of the scenic Yorkshire coast route.

Boulmer, *Northumberland* (2/3C) Small coastal village once the haunt of smugglers, about 5 miles east of ALNWICK along a minor road. Only a few single-storey fishermen's cottages remain in what was once a busy fishing village. Today's fishermen are mostly engaged in inshore fishing for crabs, lobster and sea salmon, and they still use the traditional coble (pronounced 'cobble') of the Northumbrian and Yorkshire coast, a beach boat with a transom stern. Boulmer has no harbour and craft must be hauled ashore. Sandy beaches alternate with a rocky foreshore, habitually the home of sea birds.

Bowes, *Co. Durham* (6/1C) Bowes lies just off the A66 trunk road south-west of BARNARD CASTLE. This important east–west link route across the high Pennines has been in constant use from prehistoric times down to the present day. The Roman fort built here to command the eastern end of wild Stainmore was known as Lavatrae and covered about 4 acres; its site encloses the rectangular Norman keep built in the reign of Henry II, as well as the village church and vicarage. The massive walls of the keep are still standing and the grassy outline of the Roman fort's perimeter is easily recognized. The site is maintained by English Heritage and access is free. William de Arcubus became the first commander of Bowes Castle.

Before the advent of motorized transport, horse-drawn coaches braving the crossing of Stainmore paused at the 18th-century Unicorn Inn, which still graces the quiet village street. Charles Dickens left the east–west mailcoach at the Unicorn when he was researching material for *Nicholas Nickleby*. There was a boys' academy in this remote place run by its owner, William Shaw. He became the sadistic Wackford Squeers in the novel and the house, alleged to be the model for Dotheboys Hall, can still be found at the western end of the village.

Safe from the hazards of the main road, Bowes makes an ideal base to explore footpaths and lanes on either side of the river Greta, or the wilder moors to the north and west. God's Bridge is 2½ miles to the west, a natural stone arch over the Greta, used by generations of cattle drovers and now walkers along the Pennine Way. It can be reached on foot by a short moorland path opposite Pasture End Farm at the side of the A66, or along a pleasant series of interlinked rights of way from Bowes, by way of the camp site at East Mellwaters Farm.

Bowes Museum *see* Barnard Castle

Brancepeth, *Co. Durham* (6/3A) Village built mainly to the east of the A690, it lies south-west of DURHAM. It is dominated by the massive strength of its castle and its 'chessmen' watchtowers. The castle's origins go back to Saxon times, with a history linked to the fortunes of famous Durham families. Much of the present

Below: Bowes
Opposite: Brancepeth Castle

building was altered in the 19th century, but the castle has been a dwelling house since its original owners passed it by marriage to the Nevilles in the 13th century. Following the disastrous Rising of the North in 1569, Brancepeth was confiscated and sold by the Crown. It passed through various hands until the wealthy coal owner William Russell took over in 1796. His son, Matthew, was responsible for the alterations that took place in 1837 under the care of John Patterson, an Edinburgh architect. In 1927 it became the headquarters of the Durham Light Infantry, but more recently a private dwelling.

The church of St Brandon is old, mostly 13th century, but its main attractions are the excellent 17th-century interior panelling and carved ceiling, the double-decker pulpit and splendidly carved chancel screen. The carving is a fine example of Cosin style woodwork (John Cosin was rector here, 1626–44). Tombs of several important Nevilles lie within the church, which is within the Brancepeth Castle grounds.

Brandon *see* Bishop Auckland

Brinkburn Priory

Branxton, *Northumberland* (1/3A) Tiny village lining a side road surrounded by rich farmland between the river Tweed and the Till, near the site of the battle of FLODDEN FIELD in 1513.

The 18th-century mansion Pallinsburn House is a mile to the north, across a wide, shallow valley; the walled and partly wild gardens are open on advertised days, usually in spring when the display of daffodils is at its best. Another mile along the A697 Coldstream road beyond the house, a 7 ft high standing stone, known as the King's Stone, is in a field to the right.

Bremenium *see* Rochester

Brinkburn Priory, *Northumberland* (4/2A & 7/1A) Access is along a lane south of the B6344 about 5 miles south-east of ROTHBURY. Brinkburn Priory stands above a tight loop of the river Coquet and was founded in about 1135 by William de Bertram, 1st Baron Mitford. After the Dissolution of the Monasteries in the 16th century it became a private house, but later fell into disuse and was a complete ruin in 1858; its roof was missing and part of the nave had collapsed.

The priory was restored by Thomas Austin, a

Newcastle architect, and the building now stands as an almost perfect example of early Gothic architecture. Today Brinkburn Priory is cared for by English Heritage and is open to the public from mid-March to mid-October.

Brotton *see* Saltburn-by-the-Sea

Budle Bay, *Northumberland* (2/2B) Esturial Nature Reserve surrounded by sand dunes between BAMBURGH and HOLY ISLAND. Access is from the B1342 at Waren Mill. The bay and nearby saltings and dunes are visited annually by thousands of migrant waterfowl, many of them rare, which can be seen together with local sea birds and waders.

There are camp sites at Waren Mill, once an important port, given its charter by Henry III in the 13th century. The busy harbour has long since disappeared, silted up beneath the sands of the estuary. Spindlestone Heugh (pronounced heuff), to the south of Waren Mill, features in the Northumbrian ballad of the 'Laidly Worm'.

Byrness, *Northumberland* (3/3A) Forestry Commission village at the side of the A68 NEWCASTLE UPON TYNE to Edinburgh road and about 1 mile south-east of Catcleugh Reservoir. The small village church to the south-west dates from 1786; it has a pretty churchyard, filled with wild daffodils in spring. The 12-mile-long Forest Drive (toll road) from KIELDER joins the A68 near by, above the very sturdy-looking farmhouse of Blakehopeburnhaugh. When broken down, Blakehopeburnhaugh means: a farm called Blake (a commonly used name in Northumberland), in a sheltered valley (hope) near a hill stream (burn), on riverside flat land (haugh).

Bywell, *Northumberland* (4/2C) Village, castle, hall and two churches cluster around the south-facing promontory above a bend in the Tyne. The castle is a 15th-century tower with four turrets built mostly from Roman stones; it is privately owned and not open to the public. Bywell Hall, one of the seats of the Fenwick family, is a 1760 conversion of an older house with 19th-century alterations and beautifully landscaped gardens. Again this is a private house, now owned by Viscount Allendale, but the gardens and riverside walk are open to the public on advertised days. Because of a quirk in the parish boundaries, the village has two churches known locally as the Black and White. St Andrew's was founded by the White Canons of Blanchland and is Saxon (the tower is particularly good) with 13th-century and

later additions. St Peter's was founded later by Black Dominican monks in Norman times and also has to serve nearby **Stocksfield**, on the opposite side of the river Tyne. This is a commuter village with a blend of old and new houses along wooded Stocksfield Burn.

Callalay Castle, *Northumberland* (2/1C) Castellated mansion reached by a minor road signposted from the A697, 15 miles south of WOOLER and about 2 miles from WHITTINGHAM. Here is an interesting building with a complex history. The present structure is basically a 13th-century peel tower that with the easing of Border raids was extended in 1676 and again in 1835. However, the tower itself stands on the site of a much older stronghold. The castle was originally owned by the Callalay family, who lived here from before 1161, and then an Essex family, the Claverings, acquired the property in the late 13th century. They continued to own it until the 19th century when it transferred to the Brownes, an old Northumbrian family. Today the castle is a gracious home in a beautiful setting, an attractive mixture of styles down through the ages. The entrance hall, built in 1750, is sumptuously decorated in the Italian style. The Georgian and Victorian interior of the rest of the building contains exquisite plasterwork and many notable items of furniture, as well as paintings by Morland and Hogarth and also a Gobelin tapestry dated 1787. The house and its pleasant gardens are open most days from May to September.

Callalay Park was enclosed in 1704 and extends from the castle towards the slopes of Callalay Hill where there are traces of prehistoric settlements. In a sandstone crag near by there is a cave that was hewn out as a safe place for Catholic priests to hide from persecution in the 17th century.

Cambo, *Northumberland* (4/2B) A snug village at the junction of the B8342 with the B6343 about 10 miles to the west of MORPETH. It was built around 1740 as a model village associated with the nearby WALLINGTON HALL estate. Rows of neat cottages and a 19th-century hilltop church tell of its wealthy patronage. Cambo was the birthplace of Lancelot 'Capability' Brown, the landscape gardener, who designed the gardens at Kew, Richmond and Blenheim, and many others. He was Royal Gardener to George III and eventually became High Sheriff of Huntingdon and Cambridge.

Camboglanna *see* Hadrian's Wall

Carter Bar, *Northumberland* (1/1C) Carter Bar marks the highest point, at 1370 ft above sea level, on the A68 trunk road from DARLINGTON to Edinburgh. A notorious place in winter, it is frequently blocked by snows. It also marks the border between England and Scotland.

It was previously called Redeswire ('swire' from an Old English word meaning 'col' or 'neck') and was the scene of a Border skirmish in 1575, a battle commemorated by one of the old Border ballads. Carter Bar was one of the meeting places of the Wardens of the Middle Marches, a kind of policing system that operated – sometimes none too fairly – during the times of Border disputes. The main duties of the March Wardens were to determine the rightful ownership of cattle stolen from one side or the other of the Border. Another important task was to negotiate the return of hostages.

Castle Eden, *Co. Durham* (8/2B) A neat little village on the B1281 to the south of PETERLEE New Town. It has its own 'real ale' brewery housed in a whitewashed cupola-topped group of buildings, used as a cotton mill in the 18th century. The church is ancient, but was rebuilt after being found in ruinous decay by Rowland Burdon in

A fountain at Cambo (see p. 81)

1764, or so says a plaque over the vestry door.

North of the road is the Castle, which gives Castle Eden its title. It is a three-storeyed late-18th-century castellated hall, built by the first Rowland Burdon to the designs of a local architect, William Newton of Newcastle. Sash windows and a Gothic palmhouse feature towards the front of the structure. At one time the castle was used as a regional office by the National Coal Board, but it now belongs to the Peterlee Corporation. A golf course covers part of the park. Beyond the castle is Castle Eden Dene, a deeply cut wooded valley created by meltwater at the end of the last Ice Age. The Dene was landscaped in the late 18th century by the younger Rowland Burdon, who lived at the Castle. It can be followed for much of its length along easy footpaths that wander past such features as Ivy Bridge, Devil's Lap Stone and Dungy Bridge. Eden Dene has been classified as a Nature Reserve, a haven of wildlife, the haunt of over 70 species of birds and many rare moths and butterflies.

South of Castle Eden village another wooded valley, that of Crimdon Beck in its lower reaches, marks the boundary between County Durham and Cleveland.

Castles, The *see* Hamsterley

Cauldron Snout *see* Langdon Beck

Chatton, *Northumberland* (2/1B) Estate village of mellow stone houses surrounding a small village green, east of WOOLER and above the west bank of the river Till. The Norman church was 'beautified' in the late 19th century. An old house associated with the derelict watermill to the east of Chatton, along the B6348 BELFORD road, has been tastefully converted into a private dwelling.

Chester-le-Street, *Co. Durham* (6/3A) Bustling market town crammed around the confluence of Cow Burn and the river Wear, restricted from eastward development by the A167 trunk road and the A1 motorway. The main railway line to the north crosses the town centre on a massive viaduct. Chester's 'Street' is the Roman road later followed by the Great North Road, from Binchester to Pons Aelius or modern NEWCASTLE UPON TYNE. The town's roots reach back to the *vicus* or civilian settlement that developed close to the protective shelter of a Roman fort.

When the Danes attacked Lindisfarne in the 9th century, monks brought the coffin of their beloved St Cuthbert to a site close by the Roman

Castle Eden Dene

fort, where they established a small wooden church. Here it remained for 113 years, until further attacks forced the monks to move first to Ripon in Yorkshire, and then to find a final resting place for the saint at DURHAM.

With the departure of St Cuthbert's body, Chester-le-Street, which for a century had been the centre of Northumbrian Christianity, declined until Bishop Egelric decided to build a new church here in the 11th century. Finding a hoard of Roman coins during the excavation, he abandoned the work and returned to his native Peterborough to live in luxury with his ill-gotten gains, but was subsequently imprisoned by William the Conqueror. The church, despite the wayward bishop, was comlpeted and later rebuilt in the 13th century. Further restoration work was carried out in Victorian and more recent times. The spire was built around 1400 and is considered to be the finest in County Durham. Inside, the atmosphere is dark, giving the row of tombs of 14 medieval knights lining the north aisle a rather macabre effect.

Pride of place in modern Chester-le-Street is the Civic Centre. The all-glass, open-plan municipal office is readily accessible to the public, in an attempt to make local government less intimidat-

ing. Indoor trees and a restaurant all add to the informal nature of this courageous experiment.

Waldridge Fell Country Park is about a mile south-west of the town, the county's last surviving lowland heath. Access is open to the whole of its 300 acres by waymarked footpaths. **Lumley Castle** lies to the east of the town on the opposite side of the river Wear. Now a hotel with a golf course in its grounds, the castle is set in elevated parkland and dates from the 14th century. A popular venue for Elizabethan banquets, it has its own ghostly white lady, the Lily of Lumley!

Several Georgian and Victorian houses can be found around the town. Once the homes of rich coal owners, the most notable are the Hermitage, a mock Tudor manor house to the south; and Southill Hall a fine late-Georgian house, standing in well-wooded grounds.

Chesters *see* Chollerford

Cheviot Hills, *Northumberland* (1/2C & 3C) A region of wild remote hills roughly bounded by the North Tyne and the A68 in the west and in the east by the A697. The two roads are linked by the

Chillingham wild white cattle

B6341 in the south and a series of 'B' roads complete the northern boundary. Deeply cut valleys drain eastwards to feed some of the finest trout and salmon rivers in the country. The Cheviots are included within the NORTHUMBERLAND NATIONAL PARK.

The underlying rocks are mostly decomposed old red sandstones, accounting for the rounded shapes of most of the Cheviot summits. Volcanic activity was once prevalent throughout the land that eventually became the Borders and Scottish Lowlands; this activity is highlighted by the dramatically outcropping crags of Hen Hole and The Schil, to the north of The Cheviot (2674 ft), the main summit in the range. Wild goats are frequently seen in the quieter parts of the northern Cheviots, especially around the ravines of Hen Hole and the Bizzle. Bird life is plentiful; ravens live among the high crags and birds of prey such as buzzards and sparrowhawks are seen.

A rather incongruous fence follows the watershed of the main range and marks the border between England and Scotland. For most of its length, often across impenetrable bogs, it is followed by the last stage of the Pennine Way, England's first official long-distance path linking Edale in Derbyshire with Kirk Yetholm over the Scottish border.

The Ministry of Defence owns large areas of the western moors, using them for military training, and although many of the paths and trackways are still rights of way, pedestrians and motorists must take due heed of warning signs and red flags that indicate when live firing is in progress. The Cheviots have a long tradition of military use: Roman legions marched across these moorland wastes and left their mark by a series of superimposed temporary camps at Chew Green, on the line of Dere Street at the head of Coquetdale. Modern Redesdale Camp is next door to both a Roman marching camp and Bremenium fort, thus continuing the military link into the 20th century (*see also* Rochester).

Rough moorland grasses and great tracts of purple heather cover most of the hills. Unsuitable for arable farming, the moors are given over mainly to sheep rearing and for fattening beef cattle. Pine forests have been planted around the upper reaches of Coquetdale and above Redesdale, outliers of the huge KIELDER FOREST further west. Lonely farmsteads and remote villages in deep moorland valleys are linked to the rest of the world by long, traffic-free roads.

The Cheviots end abruptly along a line running south-east of OTTERBURN, eventually giving way to wide fertile valleys draining towards the North Sea through the broad coastal plain. The Cheviots have their last south-eastern fling in the craggy SIMONSIDE HILLS above ROTHBURY.

Chillingham, *Northumberland* (2/1B) Peaceful group of cottages, the home village of Chillingham Castle, away from a minor road south-east of WOOLER. The Norman church of St Peter has been beautifully restored to its former simplicity and fits snugly between the village and the spreading boughs of mature specimens of imported pines that mark the boundary of Chillingham Park. The finely carved tomb from about 1450 with figures of Sir Ralph and Lady Elizabeth Grey seems not a little out of place in such a simple church; in fact it almost fills the tiny side chapel.

Chillingham Castle was originally a small peel tower and was first developed as a fortress in the 14th century. The one-time home of the Greys and later the Tankervilles, Chillingham Castle fell into disuse. The present castle is basically a 14th-century construction of four massive corner towers dominating the main wings surrounding a central courtyard. It has suffered greatly from neglect over the last decade or so, and also from a bad fire that occurred during the Second World War, when it was used by the army. The castle is slowly being restored by its present owner, Sir Humphry Wakefield, and a dedicated team of helpers, and was due to be open to the public from 1987 onwards. Of special note is the Italianate Garden, which has already been brought back to its former glory.

Chillingham is probably best known for its herd of wild white cattle. This is claimed to be the purest surviving herd of native British cattle, a breed that has remained unchanged since the Bronze Age. It is thought that when the park wall was built in the 13th century, a wandering herd was trapped inside the 365 acres of parkland and has remained there ever since. It is possible to see the cattle but, for reasons of safety, only in the company of a keeper: details are posted at the park entrance. Another feature of the park is the 260 acres of wild woodland and grassland, a unique environment, almost completely free from the impact of any form of husbandry. No dogs are allowed in the park.

Ross Castle, an Iron Age hilltop fort owned by the National Trust, stands to the south-east, above Chillingham Park; access is on foot from the minor road across Hepburn Moor. There are wide-ranging views of the CHEVIOT HILLS, Chillingham Park, BAMBURGH Castle, Lindisfarne and the FARNE ISLANDS.

Chipchase Castle, *Northumberland* (3/3B) On a minor road south-east of WARK (access via the B6320), the castle stands at the head of parkland rising above the east bank of the North Tyne. Considered to be the finest example of Jacobean architecture in Northumberland, it was built in 1621 around a 14th-century peel tower for the Heron family, official 'keepers' of Tynedale. The first owner, Sir George Heron, was killed at Redeswire near CARTER BAR in 1575, during the last Border skirmish. The castle and its 18th-century chapel are in private grounds, but can be seen from the roadside across the North Tyne. The name Chipchase may derive from Old English words meaning 'beam' or 'log' and 'heap'.

Chollerford, *Northumberland* (4/1B) A small group of buildings and an inn around the northern abutment of the single-track bridge carrying the B6318 HEDDON-ON-THE-WALL to GREENHEAD road, the Military Way, over the North Tyne. A traffic island opposite the George Hotel marks its junction with the B6320 BELLINGHAM road. The bridge dates from 1778 and replaced an earlier one washed away by flood in 1771. The

Below: Chipchase Castle
Overleaf: The Cheviot Hills

George, a comfortable hotel on the north bank, is much favoured by anglers and is a former post-house. River fishing is available to guests staying at The George.

Further west is **Chesters**, the 18th-century home of John Clayton who began the careful excavation of Cilurnum, the Roman cavalry fort within the grounds of Chesters, and four other forts along HADRIAN'S WALL. His timely action prevented their further exploitation as a cheap source of building material. Many of the foundations of this once extensive fort are exposed; of special interest is the strong room beneath the unit's chapel and the palatial bath house closer to the river.

On the opposite bank of the North Tyne from Chollerford, a short footpath below the road bridge leads to a pile of stones, the remnants of a Roman bridge.

Chollerton, *Northumberland* (4/1B) Tiny hamlet above the eastern bank of the North Tyne, about 8 miles north of HEXHAM. The village is reputed to be the site of the battle of Heavenfield, where King Oswald (later canonized) of Northumbria defeated the North Welsh King Cædwalla in 634. The battlefield is marked by a wooden roadside cross at the side of St Oswald's Chapel. Chollerton's church is Norman, incorporating Roman pillars to support its south arcade. A Roman altar stands immediately inside the church door.

Cilurnum *see* Hadrian's Wall

Coalcleugh, *Northumberland* (5/2A) Little remains of this one-time lead and coal mining settlement at the head of West Allen Dale, but what is left stands 1750 ft above sea level, and can claim to be the highest village in Northumberland.

Cockfield, *Co. Durham* (6/2B) Hilltop village on a minor road south-west of BISHOP AUCKLAND. Its main street runs west to Holymoor, a place once famous for its geese. The church is 13th century – but does not look it at first glance. A local family, the Dixons, descendants of the 17th-century steward of nearby RABY CASTLE, achieved fame in various ways. George Dixon, born in 1731, was a colliery owner, chemist and engineer who invented coal gas. His brother Jeremiah was an astonomer and surveyor, who with Charles Mason surveyed the boundaries of Pennsylvania and Maryland in North America, giving their names to the Mason-Dixon line. Another George

Dixon brought Cleopatra's Needle to London in 1878.

Condercum *see* Hadrian's Wall

Consett, *Co. Durham* (6/2A) Nothing remains of the steelworks that once stretched over a mile across the broad ridge, lighting up the night sky with its furnaces and dulling the daylight with its belching smoke and steam. Terraced houses are still coated by grime, but the only tangible links with the steel industry are a firm making refractory bricks for lining furnaces elsewhere, and the Smelter's Arms in the Castleside suburb lower down the hill from Consett. Land reclamation schemes have all but replaced this huge steel complex; its attendant slagheaps are now green hillsides dotted with plantations of young trees.

Local supplies of iron ore and coal determined the birth of this town in 1837; it grew in a few decades from a population of 200 to over 10,000.

Consett has hardly any buildings of note, its chapels and churches all date from the early to mid-1800s – it was the people who made Consett. This is a tight-knit community where the world's first Salvation Army band played in 1879. It is this community spirit that is gradually helping the town to recover from the almost mortal blow of losing its livelihood. New technologies are slowly moving in, with companies taking advantage of the concessions made by the Manpower Services Commission and the local authority.

A redundant railway line north of the town is now a walkway linked to the Derwent Walk Country Park (*see* Rowlands Gill). To the south, the Waskerley Way follows an old ironstone railway out on to the moors above Weardale.

Coquet Island *see* Amble-by-the-Sea

Corbridge, *Northumberland* (4/1C) An ancient town on the north bank of the Tyne and once the capital of Anglo-Saxon Northumbria. It is now a delightful jumble of styles and many of its older houses are built from Roman stones taken from nearby Corstopitum. The excavated site of this important Roman fort, together with an excellent museum devoted to finds there, is to the west of the town centre. The site is under the care of English Heritage. Roman Dere Street, which ran north from York, crossed the Tyne to the west of Corbridge to reach the supply base of Corstopitum. It then continued northwards across HADRIAN'S WALL and on towards Caledonia. Corstopitum was the headquarters for troops guarding the eastern half of Hadrian's Wall; Luguvallium on the site of modern Carlisle was its western counterpart. A civilian town that later became Corbridge developed around the fort from the 3rd century AD, but the place was often the scene of bloodshed. On the site of an important river crossing, Corbridge was constantly on the line of march of invading Angles, Vikings and Scots.

Time has left a wealth of historic buildings, not only at Roman Corstopitum, but in the town itself. Vicars of Corbridge built themselves a peel tower, using Roman stones, as protection against Scottish raids. The tower now houses the more peaceful Information Centre. The church is dedicated to St Andrew and is Saxon, with parts dating from before 786, but with later additions mainly from the 13th century onwards. A Roman gateway arch taken intact from Corstopitum is used to support its tower.

The cast-iron market cross in the town square bears the Percy lion and is dated 1814. The

Above: The peel tower, Corbridge
Below: Roman remains, Corbridge

Cragside House

seven-arched bridge below the town dates from 1674, the only one over the Tyne to survive a disastrous flood in 1771. A Bailey bridge next to it now protects the old structure from the excessive weight of modern traffic. A little further upstream, and visible during periods of drought, are the remains of piers of the original Roman bridge.

Jacobean plotters are said to have held secret meetings in the Angel Hotel in Main Street. The present building is 18th century, but built on older foundations. Old shops and the Heron House Art Gallery complete the attractions of this interesting and historic town. A riverside footpath connects Corbridge with Roman Corstopitum.

Cornforth, *Co. Durham* (5/3B) The village is close to the AI(M), east of SPENNYMOOR, and is dominated by a cement works and the nearby motorway. Its standardized miner's cottages were built to serve collieries that have since closed. Despite the nearness of industry and noisy traffic, Cornforth still has one or two Georgian and Victorian houses lining an unexpected and attractive village green, the relic of a more rural village before the development of the Durham coalfield.

Corstopitum *see* Corbridge; Hadrian's Wall

Cotherstone *see* Barnard Castle

Cow Green Reservoir *see* Langdon Beck

Cowpen Bewley, **Cowpen Nature Reserve** *see* Billingham

doors are typical of an era that managed to combine prosperity and opulent living conditions for the successful together with low labour costs. Armstrong was fascinated by electricity, then in its infancy, and Cragside was the first building in England to be lit by it. He had a series of ornamental lakes built on the hillside above the house and used their water to power the necessary generators. Many of the original electric lamps designed by their inventor, Joseph Swan of Newcastle, are displayed in the library; some are adaptations of antique Chinese vases. Hydraulic machinery, one of Armstrong's inventions, was used to operate household equipment at Cragside, such as the lift and roasting spits in the kitchen. Armstrong surrounded his retreat with landscaped gardens and forest. The 910 acres of woodland (famed for rhododendrons and azaleas) and nearby farms and forests, all part of the estate, are now owned by the National Trust.

Visitors to Cragside should allow themselves plenty of time so as to be able to see not only the house, but also explore the laid-out walks that follow gentle gradients throughout the gardens and forest, and admire the lakes or call at the children's playground.

Cramlington, *Northumberland* (7/2B) The Co-operative movement took early root in this north-eastern mining village, which still retains its character, despite the growth of what is correctly styled Cramlington New Town. This is laid out within the confines of four dual carriageways and is roughly divided into four rectangular zones. So far, the northern and south-eastern zones are residential, the north-west industrial. Farmland and a golf course, mainly to the south-west of a minor cross-country lane, retain a green belt in the remaining section of the town.

Cowshill, *Co. Durham* (5/3A) Village of stone cottages astride the A689, in upper Weardale, and once the scene of intense lead-mining activity centred on Killhope at the head of the dale. Moorland scenery surrounds the village and rocky streams feed into the river. The counties of Northumberland, Durham and Cumbria meet above the dale head about 5 miles to the west of Cowshill.

Cragside, *Northumberland* (4/2B) Cragside House, near ROTHBURY, was built between 1864 and 1884 by Norman Shaw for Sir William (later Lord) Armstrong, the armaments king. Combining elements of mock Tudor and Norman features, the house is very much in the 'Old English' Revivalist style favoured by the Victorians; its heavy décor, massively ornate fireplaces and large

Craster, *Northumberland* (2/3C) A signposted minor road off the B1339 winds down to the coast. This pleasant fishing village, famous for its oak-smoked kippers, does not reveal itself until the last possible moment. The Whin Sill blocks the view, outcropping above the village; this was once quarried and the dolerite-based stone was shipped from the tiny stone-jettied harbour. The Arnold Memorial Trail leads through the quarried crags to show the geological formations and also visits the nearby woodlands.

Sandy beaches appear between outcropping rocks of a coastline much favoured by sea birds. Their calls accompany walkers on the easy coastal path to DUNSTANBURGH CASTLE.

Craster, the 'pleasant fishing village...' (see p. 91)

Cresswell, *Northumberland* (7/2A) Coastal village with Druridge Bay to the north and a rocky foreshore to the south. It has a spacious village green where Cresswell Tower, a 14th-century fortified dwelling, stands above a tunnel-vaulted ground floor. The church is neo-Norman, built in 1836, and contains some fine stained glass.

Druridge Bay (7/2A) is a broad, 7-mile sweep of unspoiled sandy beach. A mile of coastline consisting of 99 acres of sand dunes and grass hinterland 2 miles north of Creswell was bought by the National Trust in 1972 with funds provided by Enterprise Neptune.

Crook, *Co. Durham* (6/2B) Spacious little town on the A689 north-west of BISHOP AUCKLAND where new industries have taken over from coal mining. Its central feature is a wide square surrounded by pleasant greens and flowerbeds. It probably took its name from a crook, or bend, in the river. The quaintly named Billy Row to the north of the town centre is a typical Durham coalfield hamlet of miner's cottages.

Croxdale, *Co. Durham* (6/3B) The village is about halfway between DURHAM and SPENNYMOOR on the A167. Rows of miner's cottages line the main road (the Old Great North Road). The main features here are dramatic bridges crossing the deep cleft made by the river Wear. Sunderland Bridge is 13th-century and lies below a modern road bridge; then upstream a railway viaduct carries the London–Edinburgh line towards Durham. Hidden in a wooded park is 18th-century Croxdale Hall, home of the Salvin family who have lived on this site since the early 15th century. Burn Hall, built in the early 19th century by Joseph Bonomi, was another Salvin property, but is now a Roman Catholic seminary.

Cullercoats *see* Whitley Bay

Darlington, *Co. Durham* (6/3C) First impressions are of a mixture of Victorian houses and a part modern, part older, central shopping area of 'gates', as the streets are known (from an Old Norse word meaning 'road' or 'street'), surrounded by the fast inner ring road.

Although Darlington's origins lie in the Anglo-Saxon period, starting as a settlement on the river Skerne, a tributary of the Tees, and becoming an important market in Norman times, it is better known for its rapid expansion during the development of the railways. The first fare-paying passenger steam trains ran from here to STOCK-TON-ON-TEES in 1825, an era commemorated by the North Road Station Museum off Northgate, where George Stephenson's original *Locomotion Number One* is on display together with many other examples of railway memorabilia. The station – reminiscent of a Hampshire country gentleman's house – was redesigned in 1887 by the railway architect, William Bell. Development of the railway to Stockon was not as straightforward as might be imagined. In the late 18th century the canal system was the main transport network for heavy goods. Canal owners fought a strong rearguard action to preserve their interests. It was a far-sighted Quaker, Edward Pease (1767–1858), who championed steam locomotion as a means of carrying coal from the Durham coalfields in the west of the county to the Tees for shipping to London and the Continent. He supported George Stephenson, morally as well as financially, and was therefore one of the many unsung heroes of the early railway system. The house where Pease was born stands on the corner of Bull Wynd and Houndgate, opposite a row of Georgian town houses.

The Wynd, one of the town's oldest streets, where there was once a bull ring, leads to the marketplace with the Old Market Hall and Victorian Town Hall cheek by jowl. Bennet House is a fine example of a three-storeyed Georgian dwelling and stands in the Horse Market. Tubwell Row, on the north side of the market, houses the Darlington Museum with its collection of local, natural, and social history items. Darlington Civic Theatre is in the New Hippodrome, a building in the original music hall tradition dating from 1907. The modern conversion is classed as one of the best examples of civic theatres in the British Isles.

The church of St Cuthbert is a splendid example of Early English architecture; dating from 1192 it probably replaced an older building. The church is on the west bank of the Skerne and can be reached by a short riverside walk.

Darlington's position as the railway centre of the world lasted for almost 150 years. Its skilled craftsmen produced locomotives not only for British use, but for export. With the demise of

A First Class coach built in 1846 for the Stockton & Darlington Railway

steam, its workshops closed in 1966, and new industries, ranging from electronics to chemicals, furniture and bridge fabrication, have replaced the traditional engineering crafts. Darlington was a leading wool-spinning centre in the 18th century, a skill that has lately re-emerged.

Darlington is well served for public recreation: 6 parks and 18 playing fields and open spaces are available. Nature trails are usually organized every summer and the annual Darlington Show is held each August in South Park.

Denton, *Co. Durham* (6/3C) Whitewashed farm buildings and cottages fit snugly around the Cocker Beck in this quiet village set in rolling country off the B6279 DARLINGTON–STAINDROP road. The Norman church, although much rebuilt in the 19th century, has some interesting medieval relics, especially the blue marble 12th-century tombstone built into the vestry wall.

Derwent Reservoir, *Co. Durham* (6/1A) Access is off the A68 about 5 miles west of CONSETT. Opened in 1967, the reservoir was planned for tourists, as well as providing water for industrial County Durham. Sailing, fishing, picnic sites and bird watching are all catered for on and around this now naturalized feature.

Pow Hill Country Park lines much of the southern shore. Roughside Hall, further west along the B6356 BLANCHLAND road, was a shooting box in Georgian times, but it is now a private house.

Derwent Walk Country Park, *Co. Durham/Tyne and Wear* (4/3C) This follows the course of the former Derwent Valley railway between Winlaton, near BLAYDON, and CONSETT in the south-west. The track is used, with linking footpaths and minor roads, either as a footpath, bridleway or a cycle track. The route passes through more than 10 miles of woodland and unspoiled valley scenery, with many interesting features of the old railway still remaining. Opened as a railway in 1867, the track passes through a 60 ft deep, half-mile-long cutting, north of ROWLANDS GILL and over four large viaducts. The one near Lintz Green, over the Pont Burn, is over 120 ft high and more than 600 ft long.

Beyond Consett the **Waskerley Way**, another railway walkway, continues south-west towards the moors above Weardale.

Dilston, *Northumberland* (4/1C) Dilston is a tiny hamlet off the A69 between CORBRIDGE and HEXHAM. The name means 'homestead on Devil's Water', a stream that flows north through the village to join the Tyne. Devil's Water itself is believed to be an Anglicization of a Celtic name meaning 'black water'.

Near by are ruins of an incomplete castle that was being built for the 3rd Earl of Derwentwater at the time of his execution for his part in the 1715 Jacobite Rebellion. The more up-to-date building, Dilston Hall, is now an advanced Social Training Unit, but was formerly the home of Viscount Allendale.

Dipton *see* Bearpark

Doddington, *Northumberland* (2/1B) Village of stone-built houses at the junction of a minor road with the B6525, 3 miles north of WOOLER. It sits snugly away from harm above the floodplains of the river Till and to the east Doddington Moor protects the village from the harsh easterly winds off the North Sea. Several moorland rocks are marked with enigmatic cup and ring carvings. There is a great concentration of these in this area.

The 13th-century church of SS Mary and Michael is unique, for its altar is situated at the west end.

Druridge Bay *see* Cresswell

Duddo, *Northumberland* (1/3A) Tiny village built on rolling farmland on a sharp bend of the B6354, a little under 8 miles south-west of BERWICK-UPON-TWEED. To the south-east of a belt of trees lining the B6354, near its junction with a minor road that links Duddo to the A698 Berwick–Coldstream road, are the remains of Duddo Tower. This was built in the 16th century but replaced an older watchtower.

Dunstanburgh Castle, *Northumberland* (2/3B) Isolated and dramatic ruins on an 11-acre clifftop site, east of EMBLETON. The original castle was built in 1313 by Thomas Earl of Lancaster as part of the coastal defences of the North East against Scottish attack. In 1362 John of Gaunt took on the title of the Duke of Lancaster and began to enlarge Dunstanburgh by blocking off the original gatehouse and enlarging it into the keep; he placed the new entrance in the south-west corner of the outer wall. The heavily fortified castle became an important stronghold in the Wars of the Roses and, in 1462, withstood a siege from

Cup and ring carvings, Doddington

troops led by Margaret of Anjou, Henry VI's Queen. This warlike lady eventually sheltered within the walls of Dunstanburgh after losing the battle of HEXHAM in 1464; she waited in the castle for a ship to take her back to France and safety.

Most of the damage caused by artillery bombardment during the Wars of the Roses was never repaired, although the place must have had some appeal to Henry VIII, whose fleet anchored in the tiny harbour below the castle. The harbour silted up many years ago. The artist J. M. W. Turner painted the ruins, capturing the North Sea scene in evening light. Sea birds nest on the seaward-facing rocks and also in the dunes further inland.

Dunstanburgh, under the guardianship of English Heritage, is a National Trust property, as are the nearby Embleton Links – 214 acres of dunes and foreshore – together with the tiny fishing village of Low Newton-by-the-Sea and Newton Links, 55 acres of dunes to its north. The freshwater Newton Pool to the south of the village, also a National Trust property, is of special ornithological significance, attracting

The Norman castle, Durham

visiting migrant birds from the Arctic and Siberia as well as northern Europe.

There is no road access to the castle; the best approach is by the easy 1½-mile seashore footpath north of CRASTER, or by a slightly longer path around Embleton Bay, which starts near the Embleton Golf Course clubhouse.

Durham City, *Co. Durham* (6/3A) Even though recent excavations indicate there was a Roman settlement at Durham, we have the Danes to thank for the origins of the present city. When they stormed across the North Sea around AD 875, monks living on Lindisfarne fled inland, carrying with them the coffin of St Cuthbert. After wandering about the North of England for over a century, the monks eventually settled on Durham in 995. The site chosen for their abbey was perfect and used the natural defences offered by a steep rocky peninsula, almost surrounded by a sharp meander of the river Wear. William the Conqueror established a palatinate or semi-autonomous region based on Durham to protect northern England against the Scots. Prince Bishops ruled in this county palatine until 1836,

formulating their own laws, levying taxes and minting their own coins. They even had powers to raise their own army. The original wattle church, the simple building erected by the wandering monks from Lindisfarne, was pulled down and in 1093 the Norman Prince Bishop William began the building of Durham Cathedral. This magnificent soaring construction, the greatest piece of Norman architecture in Britain, took only 40 years to build – lasting testimony to the devotion of its creators.

The Norman castle was built near by, soon after the Conquest, and became a key defensive point against attacks from over the Border.

Durham grew as a city around both cathedral and castle, the narrow streets or 'vennels' reaching down to the Wear. Easily protected by gates, the vennels closed off the city at night or whenever danger threatened.

Today the city is still centred upon its ancient bastion and original street pattern. More recent development has been on the relatively flat ground away from the river. The city grew first to the east around Elvet Bridge and, later, to the west around the London–Edinburgh railway line. The railway skirts the older part of Durham on high viaducts on either side of the station. Passengers are offered a tantalizing glimpse of cathedral, castle and rooftops.

Durham University grew around the cathedral, its antecedents in the teaching activities of monks and clergy. It was established as England's third university by an 1832 Act of Parliament. Outgrowing their ecclesiastical foundations, the modern colleges and campuses spread themselves across the wooded slopes of Elvet Hill to the south of the river. A striking modern bridge by Ove Arup links Palace Green with Dunelm House across the river.

The most natural way to explore Durham is on foot, starting at its oldest and finest building, the cathedral. A monster's head in bronze serves as the sanctuary knocker on the main door. Only a replica (the original is preserved inside the cathedral's Treasury Museum), it is a faithful copy, including a hole made by a Scottish arrow. The first impression a visitor has on entering the cathedral is of massive strength embodied in the Romanesque pillars supporting the nave roof. At the west end beyond the font, a line of Frosterley marble is the demarcation beyond which women were once not allowed to pass. At that time they had to worship in the Galilee Chapel, built in 1175 and now the resting place of the Venerable Bede. In the south transept an astronomical clock from

The sanctuary knocker, Durham Cathedral

about 1500 only displays 48 minutes. Behind the high altar is the beautiful Neville Screen, carved in 1375 from Caen stone. It acts as a backing for the simple tomb of St Cuthbert who has rested here since 1104. Traditionally, St Cuthbert's body did not decompose while it was being carried around the North, but when the tomb was opened in 1827, only the remains of a skeleton and a second skull, thought to be that of St Oswald the great Northumbrian king, were found. Relics of the saint, including his maniple and cross, are on display together with other precious items in the Treasury Museum. The Chapel of the Nine Altars, built in Early English style, fills the eastern transept and dates from 1242. Since the Dissolution, monks no longer live in close proximity to the cathedral. Their dormitory, dating from 1400, now serves as the Library. Behind the cathedral are several elegant private houses, together with the 18th-century water tower and the well-kept memorial garden to the 7th Durham Light Infantry.

Palace Green fronts Durham Cathedral, leading by cobbled ways to the castle. Begun as a motte and bailey mound, the fortress withstood

attacks by the Scots as late as the 17th century, when it was held for the Crown during the Civil War. Later maintenance and additions to the castle were the prerogative of incumbent bishops until it became University College and Bishops of Durham made Auckland Palace, in Bishop Auckland, their official residence. The castle is open as advertised throughout the summer.

Georgian buildings line North Bailey, which leads to the Market Place where the 14th-century Guildhall is incorporated within a Victorian Town Hall. Downhill and to the right of the Market Place is the 12th-century Elvet Bridge, surrounded by some fine medieval buildings. Further along is Hallgarth Street where the medieval Tithe Barn stands.

There are pleasant footpaths below the cathedral on both sides of the Wear and all are well away from the traffic, the river banks linked by bridges at Kingsgate and Framwellgate. A less energetic way to view the city and surrounding countryside is from a launch or rowing boat on the river.

One of the finest views of the cathedral is from the river opposite the Corn Mill, or from Prebends Bridge below Watergate. Floodlighting at

Right: Coats of arms, the University Library
Below: The Venerable Bede's tomb, the Galilee Chapel
Opposite: Durham Cathedral in winter

The Corn Mill and weir from below the castle walls

night picks out the intricacies of the stonework and delicate pinnacles surmounting the towers and roof. As can be expected in an ecclesiastical city there are many ancient churches. St Nicholas is on Claypath, St Margaret of Antioch in Crossgate. St Mary le Bow in North Bailey is where the body of St Cuthbert rested while the cathedral was being built.

Durham has a wide range of museums: the Cathedral Treasury; Durham University's Museum of Oriental Art and Archaeology on Elvet Hill; the Heritage Centre in St Mary le Bow; the Durham Light Infantry Museum at Aykley Heads; and the Old Fulling Mill on the river bank.

To the west of the city stands Neville's Cross, commemorating a decisive Border battle fought near by in 1346, when the army of David II of Scotland was beaten by the mixed forces of the Archbishop of York together with followers of the Nevilles and Percys.

Durham is the annual venue for the Durham Miners' Gala, an event that happily mixes politics with all the fun of the fair. Durham Regatta, on the broad waters of the Wear to the north of the city centre, is the oldest of its kind in the country.

Mining villages, many with unusual names, surround Durham and Pity Me on the Old North Road (A167), is perhaps the one whose name most fascinates visitors. The village is a disappointment architecturally, simply rows of miner's cottages mostly built in the 1930s. The name is thought to be a corruption of *Petit Mere* – a little lake or pond – but this has since disappeared.

Eaglescliffe *see* Egglescliffe

Easington, *Cleveland* (8/3A) The village straddles the A174, on a hilltop site halfway between LOFTUS and Staithes in North Yorkshire. The parish church of All Saints was established in Anglo-Saxon times, but the present building dates from 1888. A farmhouse stands close by, on the site of an ancient moat marking the position of a medieval manor house. Other old buildings are mainly on the south side of the village.

Easington, *Co. Durham* (8/1A) The view from the A19 to the north of PETERLEE New Town is of a pleasant group of houses around the 13th-century church, showing that colliery districts can be attractive. The village is divided between Easington proper and Easington Colliery. In 1951 this pit village was the scene of the worst modern mining disaster, when over 80 men were killed or trapped following an explosion in the Five Quarter Seam. The accident is commemorated by the brilliantly coloured and gilded screen and altar, specially commissioned for the red-brick Church of the Ascension.

Easington was long represented in Parliament by the eminent Labour politician, the late Emanuel Shinwell, who became Lord Shinwell.

Crumbling 13th-century Seaton Holme in the centre of Eastington village is supposed to be built on the site of an 11th-century house once owned by Nicholas Breakspear. He became Adrian IV (died 1159), the only English pope.

Eastgate, *Co. Durham* (6/1A) The village is the eastern 'gate' of the Bishop of Durham's 16th-century deerpark in Weardale (**Westgate**, once the site of the Bishop's hunting lodge, is the other). Eastgate sits beneath rolling heather moors at the junction of narrow Rookhope Dale with Weardale. The valley is dominated by the chimney of a cement works; its hillside quarry is partly screened to the south, but nothing seems to escape the ever-present dust. Fluorspar was once a waste product but is now extracted from nearby redundant lead mines. It is then processed in plant close to the village, for use in both the chemical and steel industries. The Low Linn waterfall on Rokehope Burn is near Eastgate.

Edward III faced a Scots army on a hillside above the village in 1327, but the Scots withdrew without either side losing a man.

Westernhopeburn, on the opposite side of the Wear, is probably the least altered farmhouse in the dale. Dated 1601, it is one continuous low stone structure in the medieval style, built to house animals and family under one roof.

East Rainton *see* West Rainton

Ebchester, *Co. Durham* (4/2C) The village follows the A694 on a ledge between a steep hillside and the Derwent. The river was crossed at this point by Dere Street, the Roman road from York to HADRIAN'S WALL. Vindomora fort was established to guard the river crossing and the church and churchyard are built into its south-west corner. The church is basically Norman, but was much altered in the 19th century and has many fragments of Roman stones in its fabric.

Access to the DERWENT WALK COUNTRY PARK here is from the Information Centre and picnic site at the old station yard.

Edlingham, *Northumberland* (2/2C) The B6341 moorland road from ALNWICK to ROTHBURY crosses Corby's Craggs, where there is one of the finest views in Northumberland. The vast panorama encompasses the CHEVIOT HILLS in the north, then further south a rolling landscape of heather moors and crags stretches towards HADRIAN'S WALL. High tops of the northern Pennines, such as Cross Fell and its satellites still further south, can be glimpsed on a clear day. About a mile further on and to the right of the road, you come to the straggling village of Edlingham. To one side is a curved viaduct across Edlingham Burn, which once carried the railway line to WOOLER. Next to a peel tower and the tree-ringed vicarage is the church of St John, largely Norman but founded by King Ceolwulf in the 8th century. There is a small burnside campsite below the village.

Edmundbyers, *Co. Durham* (6/1A) Moorland village south of DERWENT RESERVOIR, with fine views of the heather moors of MUGGLESWICK and Edmundbyers Commons. It once had two pubs, but the older one is now a Youth Hostel. The church was founded in 1150 and has the remains of one of the last witches, once common in this remote area, buried in its graveyard. A single eye decorates the squint of its circular west window.

Egglescliffe, *Cleveland* (8/1C) A pleasant backwater of red-tiled farms and cottages centred around a village green, on rising ground above the meandering river Tees. Since the A19 took the through traffic on a more direct route to the industrial belt beyond the Tees, Egglescliffe has become a quieter place. Its elevated position gives it wide views of the Vale of York, across the rooftops of neighbouring YARM.

Egglescliffe

The river is crossed by a 15th-century road bridge and a brick railway viaduct with 43 arches. The church of St Mary is mainly Perpendicular in style with a good array of woodwork (notably a barrel roof of oak) and an 18th-century three-decker pulpit.

Egglescliffe is a gentle place and so contrasts with its burgeoning infant **Eaglescliffe** (8/1C) to the north and west. This is an industrialized suburb of STOCKTON-ON-TEES, with a handful of older cottages surviving among modern housing. Preston Hall Museum is to the north-east of the town along the main A135, which separates Eaglescliffe from Egglescliffe, and here the social history of the region is depicted through the use of a period street assembled in the open, together with reconstructed rooms in the main building.

The Stockton & Darlington Railway ran along the boundary of the park by the Stockton–Yarm road and so transport is an important theme in the museum. Indoor galleries have displays ranging from toys to costume and pewter. There are play areas, a small zoo and riverside walks in a parkland setting.

Eggleston, *Co. Durham* (5/1B) Teesdale village about 7 miles north-west of BARNARD CASTLE. Its position marks the boundary between the wild moors and lush lower reaches of the dale. A 17th-century packhorse bridge crosses the tiny village stream. The Victorian church replaced one of earlier date; its ruins can be seen within the grounds of Eggleston Hall to the south.

The Hall, a private residence, is 19th century and a fine example of a Victorian country gentleman's house.

Egglestone Abbey, *Co. Durham* (6/1C) Ruined 12th-century abbey founded by Premonstratensian canons 1 mile south-east of BARNARD CASTLE on the south bank of the Tees, near where the Thorsgill Beck flows into it. The setting is tranquil and much of the cruciform, aisleless church still survives, especially the nave and chancel. The windows are Early English although the matching east window is thought to be 17th century. Further monastic buildings on the site were converted into a house after the Dissolution. Access to the abbey is either by the minor road from Barnard Castle, or by riverside footpaths on both banks of the Tees. The nearest road bridge is a quarter of a mile downstream from the abbey, and there is a footbridge upstream, near Barnard Castle. English Heritage maintains the site.

Opposite: Egglestone Abbey

Eglingham, *Northumberland* (2/1C) An attractive village of stone cottages lining the B6346 ALNWICK–WOOLER road. It is at its best in spring when alpines bloom on garden walls, and the whole aspect makes a most pleasing contrast to the stark moors beyond. Eglingham Burn runs alongside the main road and is noted for its well-cared-for trees. The church dates from around 1200, but is built on earlier foundations granted by King Ceolwulf of Northumbria to the Lindisfarne monks in 738.

On the Wooler side of the village, Eglingham Hall is mostly 18th and 19th century, but has an unspoiled panelled Jacobean chamber where Oliver Cromwell stayed during the Civil War, the guest of the owner Henry Ogle. Parliamentary troops frequently moved through Northumbria on their way to fight the Scots, who had been persuaded to support King Charles I.

Elishaw, *Northumberland* (3/3A) The farmhouse of Elishaw marks an important junction between the NEWCASTLE UPON TYNE and CORBRIDGE roads to Jedburgh in Scotland. There has been a

Preston peel tower, Ellingham

river crossing at this point since the Roman occupation. Their Dere Street, which is still followed for most of its length south of the river Rede by the A68, has a series of marching or temporary camps near by. The modern road leaves Dere Street at Blakehope, near Elishaw, and then crosses it 2 miles north-west of the modern junction at the hamlet of Horsley, where the church has a Roman altar in its porch. Beyond Horsley, Dere Street climbs to the Roman fort of Bremenium near ROCHESTER, before continuing into Scotland. Several marching camps, some superimposed on each other, mark what is now the Border crossing at Chew Green.

Ellingham, *Northumberland* (2/2B) Small agricultural village just east of the A1, around the restored Norman church of St Maurice, which has a central tower instead of the usual west one. Ellingham Hall is at the end of a quiet lane beyond the village and is the home of the Haggerston family, whose Roman Catholic chapel is built on to it. Hall and chapel date from the early 17th century. Preston peel tower is nearby and can be seen to the south-east across the fields and a shallow valley from Ellingham. One of the few of these defensive structures to survive from less law-abiding times, the tower is open to the public during the summer months, a graphic example of life under constant threat from Border Reivers, who roamed the district pillaging and stealing cattle until the late 17th century.

Elsdon, *Northumberland* (4/1A) A compact village, built mainly to the west of Elsdon Burn, Elsdon was once the capital of Redesdale. At one time more than five roads crossed Elsdon Burn at this point; the village was then a much busier place, a staging post for droves of Scottish cattle and sheep walking their way to English markets. The traffic was not one way, for Elsdon was on an important salt road into Scotland, and wool and finished products travelled in both directions. This busy trade died when turnpike roads (which later became the A696 and A68), and later railways, marked the end of drove roads and packhorse trails. The only tangible link with this bygone traffic is the large village green in the centre of Elsdon, the former cattle-holding area. A pinfold or pen for stray cattle still stands in one corner.

Today the village is mostly a cluster of 18th-century houses around the pleasant green. There is a 14th-century church with a half-barrel vaulted ceiling. About 1000 skulls, thought to be those of soldiers slain at the battle of Otterburn in

The motte and bailey, Elsdon

1388, were discovered when the church was being restored about a hundred years ago. The rectory is a fortified tower: one of the best-preserved peel towers in the country, it dates from the turbulent Border days of the 14th and 15th centuries. Even older are the remains of a Norman motte and bailey. It was once topped by a pallisaded wooden castle and outer buildings held by the de Umfravilles, Lords of Redesdale, but was abandoned after Henry II transferred his regional headquarters to HARBOTTLE in 1157. Edward I granted a weekly market charter to Elsdon in 1287 and the Lords of Redesdale were able to charge market tolls and exact a 'crossing tax' from Scots who came across the Border.

Elton *see* Stockton-on-Tees

Elwick, *Cleveland* (8/2B) Here is a pleasant rural backwater, a picture postcard village of old cottages and a 17th-century hall. Elwick is off the A19, north of BILLINGHAM and west of HARTLE-POOL. The main street is lined with a narrow greensward on either side and backed by attractive properties. The village was established long before the Norman Conquest, part of the wapen-take (an old subdivision of a shire) of SADBERGE.

The church is away from the centre of the village on a prominent rise, an interesting mixture of styles dating from the 13th, 17th and 19th centuries. Look for two small, intriguing Saxon carvings on either side of the chancel arch.

Embleton, *Northumberland* (2/2B) A charming village of sturdy stone-built houses on the B1339 about 7 miles north-east of ALNWICK. Its position on an exposed ridge means that the village is open to gales sweeping in off the North Sea, and the houses and gardens seem to crouch low in an attempt to escape them. The large late-Norman church dates from the 12th century, but much restoration work was carried out by Victorian 'improvers'. The fortified vicarage, in common with a number in the region, is built on to an old peel tower. The living is in the gift of Merton College, Oxford.

Do not expect to buy an alcoholic drink in the Working Men's Club. It is one of the few dry clubs in England.

DUNSTANBURGH CASTLE is close by and can be reached by a footpath above Embleton Bay golf course. There is an excellent sandy beach.

Escomb, *Co. Durham* (6/2B) Industrial village to the north-west of BISHOP AUCKLAND, composed mostly of modern houses and estates set on a north-facing hillside above the river Wear. Escomb's main attraction is the finest and least altered Saxon church in the country. Probably built during the lifetime of the Venerable Bede, it features many of the stones plundered from Vinovia, the Roman fort at Binchester. One of them is inscribed 'Leg VI', indicating the 6th Legion, which was based there. The construction of the church is typical of its time, with a tall narrow nave and chancel, the additions being confined to two or three larger windows. Parts of the original cobbled floor are intact and the sundial is still in position, the oldest of its kind in England. Escomb owes its happy preservation to being neglected by the Victorians who, despite their zeal for 'improving' churches, abandoned this one in favour of a new building higher up the hill. The wheel of fortune has now gone full circle. The Victorian church has been demolished, the Saxon one carefully restored to its former glory.

Esh, *Co. Durham* (6/3A) Tiny hilltop village between the Browney and Deerness rivers and on the minor road from DURHAM to LANCHESTER. The tiny parish church, although much restored, still bears traces of its ancient foundations. St Cuthbert's body is said to have rested here, the spot marked by an ancient cross on the village green. The Hall, originally owned by the Smythe family, is 17th century, but only traces of a once great building are left, the remaining fragments incorporated within the farmhouse on its site. The elaborately ornamented gate piers are the only tangible links with the more glorious past of a family who numbered Mrs Fitzherbert, morganatic wife of George IV, in its ranks. The unusual village name is from the Old English for 'ash tree'.

Eston, *Cleveland* (8/3C) MIDDLESBROUGH claims this ancient village as its suburb, but its history goes back at least to the Bronze Age when there was a camp on top of Eston Nab, the prominent hill to the south-east above the busy A174. Eston grew with the 19th-century industrial expansion of Teesside, when ironstone was mined beneath the escarpment and carried by rail to riverside furnaces in Middlesbrough. The church and hospital, together with many of the red-brick buildings, date from that time and now blend with modern developments.

Etal, *Northumberland* (1/3A) Charming model village on the B6354 and the east bank of the river Till. Attractive whitewashed cottages lining the picturesque street lead down to a ford across the river. There was once a bridge at this point, guarded by a 14th-century castle, but the bridge collapsed during floods in the 16th century and was never replaced. The castle had a turbulent history, frequently besieged by the Scots and eventually destroyed in 1497 by James IV; only ruins remain.

The garden of Etal Manor, the 18th-century home of Lord and Lady Joicey, is open to the public on advertised days. This woodland garden with rhododendrons and flowering shrubs is at its best in May and June, and also September and October.

The Black Bull is in Etal's main street and is the only thatched inn in Northumberland. A working smithy stands near by.

Falstone, *Northumberland* (3/2A) Small North Tyne village below the dam wall of Kielder Reservoir, a little to the north of the minor road to BELLINGHAM, and rather dominated by holiday

Puffins, Inner Farne

Sea stack, the Farne Islands

cabins associated with KIELDER WATER. In 1813 a Saxon cross dating from about the 8th century was found close by the village; inscriptions call for prayers for the souls of Hroethberht and Eoma. The cross is now kept in the Newcastle Museum of Antiquities. The countryside in the upper North Tyne valley was obviously well settled in Anglo-Saxon times, as witness further stone fragments in Falstone Church.

Two electricity generators in the valley bottom are powered by water from Kielder Reservoir.

Farne Islands, *Northumberland* (2/2A, 3A & 2B) A group of basaltic islands and rocks, the final outliers of the Great Whin Sill, which occurs throughout the North East. They lie between 2 and 5 miles offshore to the north of SEAHOUSES. The islands are divided into two main groups, the Inner and Outer Farnes; their actual number varies according to the state of the tide. The largest, which gives its name to the whole group, is Farne Island. It has a lighthouse built on to an ancient tower near the remains of a 14th-century chapel. Knock's Reef and several groups of other rocks, Knocklin Ends, Little Scarcar and The Bush, complete the inner group of islands.

Beyond Staple Sound the northern, Outer Farne group is composed of Staple Island and Brownsman. These are linked at low water; the latter is the only fertile island in the outer group. Further out are the North and South Wamses, also joined at low water, and Big and Little Harcar, which lead on to a complex group of rocky islets known as Longstone. A second lighthouse marks the position of the Longstone group. Knivestone rocks are the furthest point offshore in the Farnes. Smaller rocks surround the main groups, their names often an indication of their lethal potential. Rocks like the Callers and Fang guard the south-eastern approach and Megstone, Islestone Shad and Glororum Shad, together with Oxscar, Elbow and Gun Rock, lie in wait for careless navigators.

Probably the best-documented shipwreck on the Farne Islands was that of the ill-fated SS *Forfarshire*. Drifting in a violent storm on the night of 7 September 1838, and with its engines out of commission, the vessel struck Harcar Rocks. At that time the lighthouse on Longstone was manned by Grace Darling and her father. Despite the violence of the storm, they rowed out to the *Forfarshire*. After many difficult journeys,

Felton

they managed to rescue a number of the passengers and crew. Grace Darling became something of a national heroine and her story is recorded in a simple museum in BAMBURGH.

The first inhabitant of the Farnes was St Aidan, Bishop of Lindisfarne from AD 635 to 651. He built a simple stone cell on Farne Island to pray and meditate in peace. His successor was St Cuthbert, who made the island his home from 676 to 685. In 1255 a brave attempt was made to establish a small Benedictine monastery on the island, but the harsh conditions of this isolated rock in the North Sea were too much for the monks.

For centuries, the Farnes were an easy source of eggs and as a result the bird population had declined alarmingly by the late 1800s. St Cuthbert befriended the nesting birds and eider ducks are known locally as 'St Cuthbert's chicks'. The Farne Islands Association was formed in 1880 to protect the wildlife of the islands. In 1925 the National Trust acquired the Farnes, with the exception of the Longstone lighthouse, and in 1964 the islands became a bird sanctuary.

It is possible to visit Farne Island and Staple Island (with restricted access during the nesting season from mid-May to mid-July). Information about sailings and landing tickets can be obtained from the Information Centre at Seahouses. Trips take about 2 hours and usually go past rocks where grey seals can be seen basking in the sunshine. A Nature Trail provided by the National Trust has been established on Farne Island. (For details of longer visits for the purposes of birdwatching or botany, contact the National Trust Warden, c/o The Shieling, 8 St Aidan's, Seahouses, tel. Seahouses [066 572] 651.)

Featherstone Castle *see* Haltwhistle

Felling, *Tyne and Wear* (7/2C) Industrial Tyneside town of terraced streets and tower blocks on a steep hillside above the south bank of the river. **Pelaw**, to the east of the town centre, was once synonymous with the Cooperative Wholesale Society, which had a number of model factories here. Changing fortunes and marketing patterns have greatly reduced their number.

A mine disaster in the early 1800s took the lives of 92 people who are buried in a mass grave at Heworth, south of Felling town centre.

The North East Bus Museum is in Leam Lane at **Wardley**, where there is a representative collection of historic motorbuses from the area.

Felton, *Northumberland* (4/3A & 7/1A) Straggling village built mostly east of the A1, north of MORPETH. Two bridges, one modern and the other dating from around the 15th century, cross the river Coquet in the centre of Felton.

English barons met here in 1215 to plan the transfer of their allegiance from King John to King Alexander of Scotland, a rash decision, for King John had the town burned down as punishment soon afterwards. Possibly with this in mind the village, which supported the first Jacobite Rebellion in 1715, switched sides in time for the '45, even going so far as to entertain the Duke of Cumberland on his way to Culloden. Felton Park was used by the Jacobites in 1715 as a temporary base for their northern operations.

St Michael's, the parish church, is 13th century, with many later alterations.

Ferryhill, *Co. Durham* (6/3B) The Old Great North Road, now A167, runs through a cutting 7 miles south of DURHAM. Terraces of miners' cottages and council houses cover the hilltop. A steep hill leads to a long narrow market place with the Victorian town hall and a war memorial. The land around is slowly recovering from the ravages of coal mining; a massive slagheap of the Dean and Chapter mine has been landscaped and is now an attractively wooded green hillock.

Finchale Priory, *Co. Durham* (6/3A) Finchale (locals pronounce it 'Finkle'), a Benedictine priory first established by the hermit St Godric in the 12th century, and enlarged in the 13th, which developed into a retreat for Northumbrian monks until the Dissolution. The ruins are situated in lovely woodland on a bend of the Wear about 5 miles north of DURHAM. Access is by way of a minor road north-east of Framwellgate Moor. There is a camp site near by and the river bank is an ideal place for picnics. Open daily except Christmas and New Year.

Flodden Field, *Northumberland* (1/3A) Site of the battle of Flodden between the Scots and English on 8 September 1513, where James IV of Scotland lost his life together with those of 9000 of his followers. It was the last and bloodiest battle fought in Northumberland, a battle commemorated by the Scottish lament 'The Flowers of the

Flodden Field memorial (see p. 110)

Red-roofed cottage, Ford

Forest'. The spot where the king was slain is marked by a simple granite cross, inscribed 'To the Brave of Both Nations'.

The site of the battle is often confused with Flodden Hill, about 1¾ miles south-east of BRANXTON. If James IV had stuck to his original plan, this could well have been the case and the outcome of the battle might have been different. The story is that the king, looking for an opportunity to wage war on England, crossed the Border at Coldstream with, it has been said, between 60,000 and 100,000 men, after his Warden of the Eastern March had been killed in an argument. (March Wardens were a kind of peace-keeping force along the frequently disputed Border.) Destroying many of the castles on the English side of the border, the Scots camped on the strategic heights of Flodden Hill. Meanwhile, the English troops, assembled under the command of the Earl of Surrey, marched north and encircled the hill. Thus separated from the Border, King James unwisely left his secure hilltop for the open meadows near Branxton, where the battle began at about four o'clock in the afternoon. Still on comparatively high ground, the Scottish archers had some initial success, but

along with the rest of the army were quickly outmanoeuvred by the English.

By nightfall, the battle was over and 9000 Scots lay dead together with 5000 English. In August a simple service marks this tragic event.

Flodden Field is half a mile south of Branxton village. Access to the latter is by a side road off the A697, 2 miles west of Crookham.

Ford, *Northumberland* (1/3A) Estate village on the B6353 above the east bank of the river Till, with brown stone and red-roofed cottages, built in the mid-1800s for Louisa, Marchioness of Waterford. She was an accomplished artist, a friend of the Pre-Raphaelite Brotherhood, and decorated the old schoolhouse with frescos of Biblical themes using villagers and their children as her models. The building, now known as the Lady Waterford Hall, is open to the public throughout the year.

Lady Waterford lived above the village at Ford Castle, which dates from 1338. Built by Sir William Heron, High Sheriff of Northumberland, and destroyed several times during Border feuds, only three of its original corner towers are left. However, thanks to the careful efforts of Lady Waterford, the present castle is a good Victorian adaptation of the original quadrangular style. The 13th-century church of St Michael in the castle grounds has an interesting bell tower.

Heatherslaw Mill is about 1 mile north of Ford on the ETAL road. This 19th-century double-acting flourmill is powered by a massive undershot waterwheel, which operates when water conditions allow. The mill is open to the public, together with a local craft shop and café.

Fourstones *see* Newbrough

Frosterley, *Co. Durham* (6/1A) A straggle of terraced cottages on the A689 in upper Weardale, mostly the homes of quarrymen whose grandfathers quarried the famous Frosterly black marble. This unique marble is in fact a limestone speckled by thousands of fossils, and is still in demand for its beauty, although not in the quantities of Victorian times. Its sombre black when polished appealed to Victorian tastes and it found its way into churches all over the country.

Frosterley is old and was even worth a mention in the Boldon Beuk, the 1183 equivalent of the Domesday Book, but no buildings survive from that time. A stone bridge, hundreds of years old,

crosses the Wear to the east of Frosterley carrying the once important road (now the B6278) south towards Teesdale.

A mast on the hilltop to the north of the village transmits radio and television signals over Weardale and the surrounding moors and dales.

Gainford, *Co. Durham* (6/2C) Here is a group of pleasant Georgian houses above the river Tees, around a wide village green and considered by many to be the most attractive village in County Durham. The main road from BARNARD CASTLE to DARLINGTON (A67) divides most of the older village from its modern development. The church is Early English, built, it is rumoured, from stones taken from the Roman fort at nearby PIERCEBRIDGE. The church is on the site of a Saxon monastery; inside are memorials to the local gentry, notably the Middletons, a family who owned Jacobean Gainford Hall at the west end of the village. About 1 mile upstream from the village, and only accessible on foot over rough ground, is Gainford Spa, a group of sulphur

Gainford Hall

springs which can be detected from some distance. The spa achieved fame in the early 19th century during the vogue for 'taking the waters', however foul.

Gateshead, *Tyne and Wear* (7/2C) Administrative centre for the group of industrial towns south of the Tyne and west of the A1 motorway as far as, but not including, PRUDHOE. Gateshead developed around coal deposits discovered in the 14th century, and heavy industries that grew along the riverside during the Victorian era. Most of these no longer exist and the town is struggling to redevelop its industrial base. Many tangible relics of bygone industrial achievement still remain, such as the solidly built warehouses and remaining jetty timbers of this once thriving port. In 1814, the first river steamboat in England was launched at Gateshead, and one of its native geniuses, Sir Joseph Swan, invented the incandescent lamp in 1878. Thomas Bewick, famous for his woodcuts of British birds, also lived here.

The modern Gateshead skyline is dominated by its concrete tower blocks, but the oldest part of

Metro Centre, Gateshead

the town is built around St Mary's church, itself dwarfed by the single steel span of the Tyne Bridge, one of the eight road or rail bridges linking the town to its bigger neighbour, NEWCASTLE UPON TYNE. The church is of medieval date but with a lot of 18th- and 19th-century work. Poignant 19th-century memorials to local dignitaries tell of the times when health care was less efficient than today.

Industry is now mostly confined to the Team Valley Industrial Estate, of prewar layout and the firmly established forerunner of similarly designed estates throughout the country.

The town boasts a number of firsts, from its international sports stadium and nearby Leisure Centre to the Metro Centre, a vast shopping complex built on reclaimed industrial land close to the A69. The arts are catered for with the Little Theatre at Saltwell View and Caedmon Hall, in the Central Library complex, has programmes ranging from concerts by visiting orchestras to photographic exhibitions. Shipley Art Gallery has a permanent collection of paintings of the British, Dutch and French Schools.

Windy Nook Nature Park is an unexpected area of countryside within an urban setting to the south-east of the town. Bowes Railway Heritage Museum is near Springwell village, further to the south-east of Gateshead. This unique museum is devoted to the only remaining standard gauge rope-hauled railway left in Britain. Dating from 1826 and partly designed by George Stephenson, it carried coal from 13 collieries to the river for shipment. There are audio-visual displays, exhibitions, locomotive workshops and steam-hauled passenger trains. Access is from the A1 motorway–A69 Birtley interchange.

Gibside, *Tyne and Wear* (4/3C & 7/1C) The chapel and adjoining woodland have been maintained by the National Trust since 1966. Designed in the Palladian style for Sir George Bowes, the chapel is the Bowes family mausoleum and was given to the Trust by the executors of the 16th Earl of Strathmore and Kinghorne. Sir George Bowes began work on the mausoleum around 1760, but it was discontinued seven years later, then eventually completed in 1812.

Beyond and on private property are the ruins of Gibside Hall, which was built around 1620, altered in 1750 and again in 1805, by various members of the Bowes family who were wealthy Durham colliery owners. Architects such as James Paine, who also designed the mausoleum,

Gibside Chapel

and landscape artist 'Capability' Brown were employed in the construction of the mansion and its parkland. Gibside Hall is closed to the public at the time of writing, but the nearby statue of British Liberty, on top of its 140 ft tall column, is visible to anyone following the DERWENT WALK, a waymarked route around the Gibside Estate.

Gibside Chapel is best approached from the B6314, the road between Rowlands Gill and Burnopfield.

Gilsland, *Northumberland* (3/1C) Small village – the most westerly in Northumberland – on the western side of the Tyne–Solway gap, 2 miles north-west of GREENHEAD along the B6318 Langholm road. HADRIAN'S WALL passes through the village and a section of it can be found in the vicarage garden. For reasons either of economy, or possibly for speedier construction, the Wall, although on a broad foundation, is built narrower here than those sections visible further to the east.

The Roman fort of Camboglanna is a mile to the west, across the river Irthing and therefore part of Cumbria. A bridge abutment near Willowford, back towards Gilsland, stands incongruously in an open field. The bridge once crossed the Irthing, but the modern course of the river is about 100 yd to the west of this point.

Gilsland has romantic links with the novelist Sir Walter Scott. He met his future wife, Charlotte Carpenter, here and mentions the village in *Guy Mannering*.

Glanton, *Northumberland* (2/1C) The quiet village stands at the junction of five roads, about 10 miles west of ALNWICK and west of the A697 MORPETH to Coldstream road. It shelters beneath the south-eastern shoulder of Glanton Hill, an outlier of the Cheviots, and its elevated position commands extensive views across the Aln and Breamish valleys.

Royalist troops camping overnight in Glanton during the Civil War woke to find themselves prisoners. Parliamentary troops, hearing of their movements, came under cover of darkness and surrounded their unguarded camp.

The World Bird Research Station was opened here in 1930 for the study of wild bird life in the Border region. The station organizes the annual recording of dawn and dusk choruses throughout the British Isles and is open from June to mid-October.

Gosforth, *Tyne and Wear* (4/3C & 7/2C) A mainly residential suburb in a rural setting, about 2½ miles to the north of NEWCASTLE UPON TYNE along the A6125, the old Great North Road. Its most interesting feature is the 800-acre High Gosforth Park and racecourse, where the famous Northumberland Plate, the 'Pitman's Derby', takes place every June. The park lake is home to wildfowl and is edged by dense woodland. Parts of the lake and the woodlands are designated as a Nature Reserve. It is surprising that large numbers of badgers, deer, woodland birds and waterfowl can be found so near the Newcaslte conurbations. Arrangements to visit the Reserve should be made through the Natural History Society based at the Hancock Museum in Newcastle.

The town centre has a modern, well-laid-out, covered shopping precinct which is served by the Metro transport system. Central Park offers tennis and bowls as well as a children's play area.

Greatham, *Cleveland* (8/2B) A village (its name is pronounced 'Greet'em'), between BILLINGHAM and HARTLEPOOL, which retains its tranquil atmosphere despite the proximity of acres of salt-based chemical plant on the flat marshlands of Seal Sands. The salt is extracted from vast deposits deep beneath this corner of Teesside and led to the foundation of the substantial Teesside chemical industry.

Several fine late Georgian houses fill the village and the 'Hospital of God' was founded in 1272 by Robert de Stichil, Bishop of Durham. The hospital was rebuilt in Gothic style early in the 19th century and a new long wing designed by Francis Johnson was added in 1973. Although the present parish church was built in 1855 and the west tower added in 1905, its foundations are 12th century, or earlier.

Greatham holds an annual Feast, a festival whose origins are lost in the mists of time.

Great Swinburne, *Northumberland* (4/1B) The woodland hamlet, some 8 miles north of HEXHAM, stands at the end of an unclassified road to the west of the A68 and, with an added 'e', takes its name from the Swin Burn, which flows through a wooded ravine below the village. Most of the houses are inhabited by workers from the estate of the 17th-century manor house. The house is privately owned; its earliest owners, the Swinburne family, took part in the 1715 Jacobite Rebellion.

Half a mile to the south is the largest standing stone in the county. The red sandstone monolith is 12 ft high and 3 ft wide, with incised grooves running down its sides and decorated by a series of enigmatic 'cup and ring' markings.

Greaves Ash *see* Ingram

Greenhead, *Northumberland* (3/2C) Greenhead lies west of HALTWHISTLE and sits in a tight green hollow beside the Tipalt Burn. The site is a natural river crossing for roads built from before Roman times, and is still used by the modern A69. Both the Maiden Way and Stanegate Roman roads crossed the river at this point, to serve HADRIAN'S WALL. Stones from the Wall were removed by General Wade in the 18th century to build a military road, which later became the B6318. Wade's road gave Hanoverian troops a rapid east–west crossing of northern England between NEWCASTLE UPON TYNE and Carlisle at the time of the Jacobite Rebellion.

Now bypassed by the busy A69, Greenhead has returned to being a sleepy place, a useful starting point to explore the middle part of Hadrian's Wall. Its church is 19th century, built to the design of John Dobson of Newcastle.

Fourteenth-century Thirlwall Castle, to the north of the village along Tipalt Burn, is a romantic ruin guarding a natural gap in the east–west escarpment.

Edward I, Hammer of the Scots, is said to have stayed here on a foray into Scotland in 1306.

The Roman Army Museum stands next to the site of Carvoran Fort and can be reached either by following Hadrian's Wall east from Thirlwall Castle for a little under half a mile, or along the signposted access road off the B6318.

Grindon, *Cleveland* (8/1B) A scattered hamlet of a handful of cottages set in green rolling country, off the A177 about halfway between STOCKTON-ON-TEES and SEDGEFIELD. The church of St Thomas à Becket, dating at least from the 12th century, is in ruins and stands in open fields.

WYNYARD PARK is near by.

Guisborough, *Cleveland* (8/3C) 'Capital' of Cleveland since Anglo-Saxon times and now part of the new borough of Langbaurgh. A busy town, part market, part dormitory for nearby Teesside. The town centre spreads on either side of wide and cobble-verged Westgate, its main street.

The ruins of the priory (open daily) stand in their own grounds, and not far from the parish church, at the head of Westgate. Nearly 900 years old and now grassed over, the outlined nave and chancel are still recognizable for much of their 145 ft. Along their length the view is towards the graceful ruined tracery of its once magnificent east window. The priory is a place of serenity, and the medieval octagonal dovecot that stands in the priory grounds still attracts those gentle birds.

Gisborough Hall (without the 'u') is behind the priory. It was the home of the Chaloner family, who founded the town's cottage hospital. They were supporters of Charles I during the Civil War and suffered accordingly.

Tockett's Mill is a wooded dell about 1 mile east from Guisborough along a side road off the A173. Cleveland's only surviving working water-mill, it is owned by a private trust and open to the public on advertised days.

Gunnerton, *Northumberland* (4/1B) An agricultural village at the junction of minor roads about 8 miles north of HEXHAM and west of the A68. Wooded Gunnerton Burn flows through the village on its way to join the North Tyne. St Christopher's Church was built in 1900 to the prize-winning design of a young architect named Hall, who later took holy orders and became a hermit. A motte and bailey defensive site can be found in private woodland half a mile to the north.

Guyzance, *Northumberland* (4/3A & 7/1A) The ruins of an ancient priory and St Wilfrid's Chapel lie to the south-west of this attractive farming community a few miles from the estuary of the river Coquet. The village faces south, high above the wooded north bank of the Coquet, and is built around a loop in the minor road that runs north from the river. Guyzance Hall is famous for its rose gardens and herbaceous borders, and is open on advertised days.

John Sneaton, the 19th-century water engineer, almost ruined the salmon fishing on the Coquet when he built a high weir to control the river's flow, but a salmon ladder now eases their way upstream.

Hadrian's Wall, *Tyne and Wear*; *Northumberland* By AD 90, Rome had virtually conquered southern Britain, but further advance north was prevented by the warlike tribes, notably the Picts, who could carry out guerrilla attacks under the cover offered by their wild mountains and glens. In order to mark the northernmost limits of the Roman Empire, walls were built in the northern part of the Black Forest in Germany; and in Britain across the conveniently narrow neck of land between present-day Newcastle and Car-

lisle, its central section being based on the steep north-facing crag of the Whin Sill. Originally this frontier was marked by a line of forts, such as the one at **Vindolanda**, connected by Stanegate and roughly following a parallel course to the south of the eventual position of the wall. The decision to strengthen them by a wall was made soon after Emperor Hadrian's visit to Britain in AD 122.

Hadrian's Wall has something of a modern counterpart in the wall that marks the East–West divide of Berlin: a means of delineating a frontier between two ideologies, of controlling movement, and acting as a customs or trade barrier.

The actual work of building what we refer to as Hadrian's Wall was carried out under the control of Aulus Platorius Nepos, who planned that it would stretch 80 Roman miles (about 74 of our miles) from Pons Aelius (on the site of modern NEWCASTLE UPON TYNE) to Maia (Bowness) on the Solway Firth. The width was to be 10 Roman ft (one Roman ft equals 11.7 in) and its height about 15 ft, rising to a 6 ft high battlemented parapet backed by a walkway. Along its front, about 20 ft to the north, was a broad, deep ditch only omitted where steep crags or the sea made it unnecessary. Milecastles provided both defensive cover and habitation for troops stationed along the Wall. As a means of strengthening the Wall's defending forces extra forts, such as the one at

The standing stone, Great Swinburne

Vercovicium, better known today as House-steads, were built on or close to the Wall. The Vallum, a complex ditch, lies to the south of the Wall at distances varying between a few yards and a half of a mile. The Vallum was basically a deep ditch with a single high mound to its north and two lower ones to the south. The true use of this structure is not absolutely clear, but popular theories suggest that it was either designed as the southern boundary of the military zone, or that it was built as a means of trapping anyone who had breached Hadrian's Wall. Whatever its purpose the Vallum, built later than the Wall, had cross-ings made during more peaceful spells and then was eventually abandoned. To aid rapid troop movements, a narrow road – still clearly visible in many places – was built immediately south of the Wall, and was the final stage of this massive undertaking.

Recent research suggests that a line of coastal forts in the west continued beyond the end of the Wall at Maia, and on towards St Bees Head in Cumbria.

Hadrian's Wall was built in sections by detach-ments seconded from the three legions based in the area. Each legion was responsible for its own length, which in turn was broken down into subsections, allotted to individual centuries of troops, who often left carved centurial stones to mark their work. Once the actual construction began, lack of convenient stone prevented its being built to the planned width of 10 Roman ft: many sections remain narrow, but on a wide base. In other places, especially to the west of **Camboglanna**, at Birdoswald near GILSLAND, the Wall had to be made from turf when stone was in short supply, although later, sections of this turf wall were rebuilt in stone. Roman surveyors were not always as accurate as their modern counter-parts: some stretches of the Wall show consider-able discrepancy where the work of individual builders join as much as 10 in to 1 ft out of line.

When finished, Hadrian's Wall needed about 13,000 troops to man it, many of them based on the extra forts built to accommodate them. In more peaceful times, civilian settlements grew alongside the forts where retired soldiers married local girls and set up home. Tradesmen also moved in to supply the needs of the civilians and off-duty soldiers. Small farms developed on the southern slopes beneath the protection of the Wall.

Hadrian's Wall was breached many times by attackers from the north, the major defeats being in AD 197, 300 and 367, but the Roman with-drawal is agreed to have taken place about 409.

With the withdrawal of troops from Britain, Roman law and order broke down as Scots, Angles and Saxons invaded and settled. Although people still lived within the comparative shelter of the abandoned forts for another 1300 years, Hadrian's Wall gradually fell into disrepair. Its stones became a ready-made building material for local farmhouses and churches in the area. The final act of vandalism occurred when General Wade built the Military Road (B6318), from HEDDON-ON-THE-WALL on the western outskirts of Newcastle upon Tyne to Carlisle, during the 1715 Jacobite Rebellion. The road follows the line of the wall for much of its length, especially in the east where it is actually built over it. Despite the protests from 18th-century archaeologists, Wade's roadbuilders used the convenient stone from the wall for their foundations. Before the B6318 was macadamed, it was possible to make out the oblong blocks of wallstones; and many still lie buried beneath the modern surface.

In more enlightened times work began on preserving what was left of Hadrian's Wall and also excavating its forts. What remains is an exciting link with the Roman period in Britain. Even though there are few places where the ruins are more than the outline of a building's founda-tions, or perhaps only part of the final height of the Wall, it does not need much imagination to see them as they were over 1500 years ago.

With the aid of the excellent strip map of Hadrian's Wall, published by the Ordnance Survey, it is possible to follow most of it on the ground. However, care should be taken not to trespass where the Wall runs across private land.

The list opposite and overleaf covers the main accessible sites on Hadrian's Wall, from east to west; also those sites that are in Cumbria and therefore outside the scope of this guide.

Haggerston *see* Berwick-upon-Tweed

Halidon Hill, *Northumberland* (2/3A) Prominent hill above the A6105 Duns road, about 3 miles north-west of BERWICK-UPON-TWEED. The hill is the site of a battle in which the Scots suffered a terrible defeat at the hands of the English on 19 July 1333. Access is from a small car park near Camphill along a public footpath through the battlefield. The 'Bendor', a stone commemorat-ing the battle, can be found in the hedgerows alongside the A6105. From the top of Halidon Hill (535 ft) there is a magnificent view of Berwick-upon-Tweed and the CHEVIOT HILLS further to the south-west.

Site	Roman name	Situation	Details
SOUTH SHIELDS	**Arbeia**	Signposted from town centre	Excavated fort. Not on the line of the Wall, but an associated seaport
WALLSEND	**Segedunum**	Buddle Street and roadside features in town centre	Outline of tower and sections of the Wall
Benwell	**Condercum**	Roadside A69	Preserved gateway stones and foundation of a temple
Denton Burn (Tyne and Wear)	–	Roadside A69	55 yd of Wall and part of Turret 7B
HEDDON-ON-THE-WALL	–	Roadside B6528	110 yd of Wall and rock-cut Vallum
Wall Houses	–	Near junction of B6318 and B6321	2 miles of ditch and Vallum with crossings
CORBRIDGE	**Corstopitum**	South of A69 and west of A68	Important Roman town, 2½ miles south of Hadrian's Wall, still only partly excavated
Whittington Fell	–	¾ mile west of junction of A68 and B6318	Ditch, Vallum, Roman Military Way and Milecastle 23
Roman Quarry	–	Written Crag	Rock inscription: *Petra Flavi Carantini* – now moved to Chesters Museum
Chesters	**Cilurnum**	B6318 CHOLLER-FORD	Excavated site of Wall fort. Bath house and bridge abutment
Limestone Corner	–	B6318	Unfinished ditch due to hardness of rock
Carrowbrough	**Brocolitia**	B6318 3 miles west of Chollerford	Partly excavated fort. Mithraeum and Coventina's Well
Sewingshields Crag	–	B6318 68½ miles west of Chollerford	Ditch, Vallum, Roman Military Way. Turret 34A. Good viewpoint
Housesteads	**Vercovicium**	B6318 Once Brewed	Best-preserved section of Wall, excavated fort, Vicus (civilian settlement), Vallum, Roman Military Way. Limited access for disabled.
Steel Rigg	–	East of Steel Rigg Car Park	Milecastle 39 and well-preserved section of Wall
Winshields Crag	–	½ mile north-west of Once Brewed Information Centre (B6318)	Highest point on wall, 1230 ft above sea level

Site	Roman name	Situation	Details
Chesterholm	**Vindolanda**	1½ miles north of Bardon Mill (A69)	Excavated fort and settlement, Stanegate, Roman milestones
Great Chesters	**Aesica**	Off B6318, 2 miles north of HALTWHISTLE	Fort, Wall ditch, Roman Military Way
Carvoran	**Banna**	½ mile east of GREENHEAD (B6318)	Excavated site of fort
Walltown Crags	–	North-east of Greenhead	Well-preserved section of Wall
Thirlwall Castle	–	½ mile north of Greenhead (B6318)	14th-century castle built of stone taken from Hadrian's Wall
GILSLAND	–	B6318 5 miles west of Haltwhistle	Wall. Milecastles 48 & 49. Bridge abutment to the east of the present course of the river Irthing
Birdoswald (Cumbria)	**Camboglanna**	Minor road west of Gilsland (B6318)	Fort and sections of stone wall with earlier turf wall to its south-west
High House (Cumbria)	–	Alongside minor road south-west of Birdoswald	Turrets 51A & B and 52A and the tallest section of Wall

MUSEUMS DEVOTED TO ROMAN FINDS IN THE AREA OF HADRIAN'S WALL

South Shields   Arbeia Roman Museum on site of an extensive Roman excavation
Newcastle upon Tyne   Museum of Antiquities, near site of Pons Aelius
Corbridge   Museum devoted to finds on Corstopitum site
Hexham Abbey   Roman altar stones and columns
Chesters   Museum devoted to finds on the site of Cilurnum
Housesteads   Interpretive museum next to Vercovicium Roman fort
Once Brewed   Northumberland National Park Information Centre and Roman Wall Museum
Chesterholm   Museum devoted to finds on Vindolanda site
Carvoran   Roman Military Museum and also finds from nearby Banna fort
Lanercost Priory (Cumbria)   Museum on the site of an Augustinian abbey, founded in 1160. Includes Roman remains found in the area
Carlisle (Cumbria)   City centre museum on site of Roman town of Petriana

Halton, *Northumberland* (4/1C) Secluded hamlet at the end of a minor road to the north of CORBRIDGE, guarded by two ancient castles with HADRIAN'S WALL to its north.

Halton Tower is a Jacobean manor house added on to a 14th-century peel tower. Although the house is privately owned, the gardens usually take part in the Northumbrian Gardens Scheme each July. **Aydon Castle** to the south is a fortified manor house of similar age and is due to re-open after restoration by English Heritage. Wooded denes and lanes lead back to Halton and its 17th-century chapel, built on 8th-century foundations.

Previous page: Hadrian's Wall above Cawfield Craggs

Haltwhistle, *Northumberland* (3/2C) Haltwhistle is a busy little industrial and market town, supplying the needs of nearby villages and farms on the remote surrounding fells. A former colliery town, its industry tends to be the manufacture of materials that require a skilful labour force, such as industrial paints and chemicals.

The town is not all industry and is an ideal centre for visiting the north Pennines, HADRIAN'S WALL, or the upper reaches of the South Tyne valley. Notable buildings in and around the town centre range from the Old Courthouse in Central Place to the Red Lion Hotel, which incorporates a peel tower, a relic from the turbulent past of this district. Townspeople and their animals would shelter in the safety of the tower when threatened by attack from marauding cattle thieves. Until the late 18th century, lands on both sides of the Border were completely lawless, not unlike the American West during the last century.

Holy Cross, the parish church, is 13th century and claims to have been founded by William the Lyon, King of Scotland, in 1178. (At one time the Scottish kingdom included most of Cumbria and Northumberland, and the border was far to the south of its present position.) The plain exterior gives little or no indication of the spacious interior; its pride is the painted roof of the nave, a Victorian embellishment.

Bellister Castle, owned by the National Trust,

Roman bath house, Chesters

is half a mile to the south of Haltwhistle, across the South Tyne. The Victorian castle is on the site of an older building of which a peel tower, incorporated into the house, still remains. The estate, castle, three farms and cottages are not open to the public.

With Hadrian's Wall so close there is a Nature Trail that starts on the outskirts of the town and follows Haltwhistle Burn, across Stanegate, the Roman supply road and then the Vallum, to reach the wall near a picnic site close to Aesica Roman fort (Great Chesters). The South Tyne Show is held on the local show ground, close to the town.

Blenkinsopp Hall (3/2C) is a privately owned 19th-century house standing in attractive gardens that open on advertised days. Access is off the A69 about 1½ miles west of Haltwhistle. **Blenkinsopp Castle**, 1 mile further west along the A69, predates the hall by 500 years. The group of buildings is part 16th-century ruin, part private 17th-century manor house.

Featherstone Castle (3/2C) is a large, castellated private dwelling 2½ miles south-west of Haltwhistle, along an unclassified road. The present structure is romantic in style, but based on the site of a castle built 800 years ago to guard the river crossing; some parts date from the 13th century, and the south-west tower from 1330.

Hamsterley, *Co. Durham* (6/2B) Single-road Weardale village 7 miles west of BISHOP AUCKLAND, on a broad ridge between Linburn and Bedburn Becks. The dense coniferous plantations of Hamsterley Forest stretch to the west above Bedburn Beck. The church is Early English. A mile north-west is the 19th-century Bedburn Mill. This watermill has some considerable architectural and archaeological merit; it is currently being restored by a conservation society.

To the north of the mill, about 1 mile along the WOLSINGHAM road, a lodge looking as though it came out of a fairy tale once guarded the drive to Hoppyland Hall. Only the mellow ruins of this 18th-century Gothic house remain, and its parkland has gone back to nature. Naturalized rhododendrons in the lower valley blaze with colour each spring. Just over 1 mile to the north of Hamsterley, and above the Harthope Beck, **The Castles** is a large, enigmatic mound, ancient but of uncertain date, surrounded by a wooded moat. A scenic forest drive follows the Bedburn Beck valley, through Hamsterley Forest from Bedburn village, to a series of short waymarked walks in the southern upper limits of the forest.

Hamsterley Forest

Hamsterley, *Co. Durham* (4/2C) Derwent Valley village in a pleasant setting north of CONSETT, not to be confused with its Weardale namesake. The village was home of the celebrated 19th-century novelist Robert Smith Surtees, creator of Jorrocks, the sporting grocer. Surtees lived at Hamsterley Hall to the east of the village. Latterly the hall was the childhood home of one of Surtees' descendants, Field Marshal Viscount Gort VC, hero of Dunkirk, who commanded the British Expeditionary Force in France at the beginning of the Second World War. The late 18th-century hall is set in dense woodland almost 2 miles to the east of the village. It is built in Gothic style, but delightfully enhanced by the addition of Elizabethan bay and mullioned windows from demolished Beaudesert House in Staffordshire; 18th-century doorways and canopies, from London houses that suffered a similar fate to Beaudesert, also embellish the hall.

Handale *see* Loftus

Harbottle, *Northumberland* (1/3C) An attractive village, on an unclassified valley road in upper Coquetdale, with light-brown sandstone cottages that nestle beneath a ruined castle. Only a grassy mound now remains to mark the position of the

fortification which was first built by Robert de Umfraville, one of William the Conqueror's knights. Later, Henry II had a stone castle built on the site following the transference of Northumberland from Scotland to England in 1159.

There is another castle in Harbottle, to the east of the village, but this is comparatively recent and was built in 1829 as a shooting lodge. It is now used as a private house together with a craft centre.

The Drake Stone is a rock formation near a small lake, about 1 mile uphill by a footpath to the west of the village. It is considered locally to be misnamed: it should be 'Dragon Stone', and is a place where primitive rites are supposed to have taken place.

Forested slopes lead out towards craggy Harbottle Moors. Several rights of way climb them from the village, but take heed of the warning signs erected by the Ministry of Defence before you follow any moorland footpath. The Otterburn and Redesdale Artillery ranges occupy large areas of moorland to the west of Coquetdale.

Hareshaw Linn *see* Bellingham

Hart, *Cleveland* (8/2B) A small peaceful commuter village in a rural setting, built on rising ground 2 miles inland from HARTLEPOOL. Its situation gives the village wide views over the surrounding fields towards the North Sea. The 7th-century church of St Mary Magdalen was originally the mother church of Hartlepool; and though the village remained small, its offspring grew. Very little remains of the original Saxon church apart from a few traces in the tower, but there is a Saxon sundial and a plain-looking Norman font, together with another rather more ornate font dating from the 15th century; the rest of the church is 17th and 19th century.

The name of 19th-century Brewery Farm indicates the part-time occupation of one of its previous owners.

Hartburn, *Cleveland see* Stockton-on-Tees

Hartburn, *Northumberland* (4/2B) Sheltered rural village west of MORPETH on the B6343, at the top of a steep hill that leads down to a bridge across the Wansbeck. There is a delightfully unspoiled, mainly 13th-century church here that is associated with the Knights Templar. Dogtooth moulding decorates both sides of the south doorway and in the nave the cup-shaped font is supported by a central pillar and three shafts. There are tomb

The old sea wall, Hartlepool

brasses of interest and a memorial to John Hodgson. He was a local historian who wrote extensively about Northumberland and also traced the line of the Devil's Causeway Roman road, which crossed the Wansbeck near Hartburn. The road ran north-east from a point near CORBRIDGE, on HADRIAN'S Wall, to the coast at what became BERWICK-UPON-TWEED.

Hartlepool, *Cleveland* (8/2B) If you approach from the north along the coast, the first sight of Hartlepool is a strange conglomeration of concrete storage tanks and chimneys. This is the Steetley Refractories plant, where dolomitic limestone is reacted with sea water, to form special heat-resistant magnesia-based powders. Beyond and on the north side of the harbour is The Heugh, the oldest part of the town where St Aidan founded an abbey in AD 640; nothing remains since its destruction by the Danes in 790, but the parish church built on its site in 1185 is dedicated to St Hilda, who went from there to found her abbey at Whitby.

Hartlepool is based on ancient foundations and was the first fortified harbour on the North-East coast. Streets in this the oldest part of the town are still laid out within the original pattern dictated by a defensive wall, built to the orders of King John in the 13th century to keep both seaborne and Scots attackers at bay. When finished, the wall with its 10 watch towers was a formidable barrier, only falling into disuse after its capture and destruction by the Scots during the Civil War.

The prosperity of Hartlepool as a port grew in the mid-1800s, when a railway linked it to the Durham coalfields. Victoria Dock, its main harbour for coal shipments, was opened in 1840, but coal is no longer a major export. What little traffic uses the harbour now is mostly related to North Sea oil exploration. The dignified Victorian Customs House still watches over shipping movements in and out of the old harbour, protected to the south by a long curving pier, but there is much dereliction. Part of the docks are put to use for reconstructing old ships, in particular HMS *Warrior*, a massive ironclad of 1860 that was discovered in use as an oil jetty at Milford Haven in Wales, then lovingly rebuilt at Hartlepool. Returned to its former glory, it now takes its place alongside HMS *Victory* and *Mary Rose* at Portsmouth. The *Warrior*, the equivalent in its day of the nuclear bomb, never fired a shot in anger. Plans are in hand to extend the skilful work of renovating old ships.

All Saints, the 13th-century church at Stratton, has the grave of the clockmaker from BARNARD CASTLE who was the subject of Charles Dickens' *Master Humphrey's Clock*. The Maritime Museum is in Northgate and the Gray Museum and Art Gallery concentrates on scenes of local industry and landscapes. Its name commemorates Sir William Gray, one of the founding fathers of Hartlepool's prosperity. Another was Ralph Ward Jackson, whose name is remembered in the Ward Jackson Park on the eastern outskirts. Hartlepool's parks and public places are a subject of justifiable local pride, usually a blaze of colour throughout the summer.

West Hartlepool, the industrial suburb to the south-west, was originally a separate borough. The similarity of names often led to confusion, but bureaucracy for once found the right answer by amalgamating it with its older brother.

Haydon Bridge, *Northumberland* (3/3C) The place developed around a river crossing a few miles west of HEXHAM and its church is on the site of the hallowed ground where St Cuthbert's body rested on its long journey around Northumbria. The A69 crosses the South Tyne by a utilitarian reinforced concrete bridge here, which leaves the old six-arched stone bridge to pedestrians. Frequent heavy flooding by the South Tyne damaged this 18th-century bridge and the structure has been deemed to be unsafe, as well as awkward, for heavy traffic.

Haydon Bridge, a former spa, has snug greystoned houses filling the level ground on both sides of the river. The Shafto Trust founded the Grammar School in 1685. The song 'Bobby Shafto's gone to sea' was written about one of the family as an election ditty.

Headlam, *Co. Durham* (6/2C) Small village in a charming rural setting, reached by side roads between DARLINGTON and BARNARD CASTLE. It is a good vantage point for views of the north Pennine moors across Teesdale. Headlam Hall, a private house, surrounded by high stone walls broken only by an attractive wrought-iron gate, stands on the southern outskirts of the village. It is a fine example of a Jacobean manor house.

Hebburn, *Tyne and Wear* (7/2C) Shipbuilding and heavy engineering town on the south bank of the Tyne. Its industry is now centred around the modernized Swan Hunter shipyards, once famous for building warships in the days of British naval might. Much of the old riverside dereliction has been cleared; it is now turned into an attractive walkway and marina, backed by open grassland, a good place to watch the waterfront activities.

South of the town, at **Monkton**, is the site of Bede's Well from where the monks of Jarrow Priory are reputed to have taken their water. Monkton is also home of the Hebburn Athletic Club, which numbers Steve Cram, 1500 metre World Champion, and 1 mile and 2000 metre record holder, among its members.

Heddon-on-the-Wall, *Northumberland* (4/3C & 7/1C) This was originally a small agricultural village that developed into a residential suburb of NEWCASTLE UPON TYNE after the Second World War. The first village was built on ancient foundations and the hilltop parish church of St Andrew dates from Anglo-Saxon and Norman times. A terrace of miner's cottages, dated 1796, was allocated to French Royalist refugees, an act of charity commemorated by the name Frenchmen's Row.

The most easterly visible section of HADRIAN's WALL, and over 100 yd of rock-cut Vallum, are to the east of Heddon and can be approached by either the B6318 from THROCKLEY or from the

Heddon exit of the A69. A hoard of 5000 silver coins, dating from AD 244–75, was found beneath a nearby milecastle in 1879.

Hedgeley Moor, *Northumberland* (2/1C) An information board in a layby at the side of the A697 near Wooperton, 6½ miles south of WOOLER, marks the site of a battle on 25 April 1464, during the Wars of the Roses, when a Lancastrian army was defeated by a Yorkist force. Two nearby stones, about 10 yd apart, are known as Percy's Leap and are supposed to mark the gap across which the horse of Sir Ralph Percy, Earl of Northumberland, jumped when its rider was killed. The battle is also commemorated by the 15th-century Percy's Cross, which stands by the side of the road a little further south.

Heighington, *Co. Durham* (6/3B) The A6072 and gently rolling countryside separate the village from its industrial neighbour NEWTON AYCLIFFE, a mile or so north-east. Attractively grouped cottages and terraced houses line a series of wide sloping greens. The church is Norman with additions dating from the 13th to the 19th centuries; the pulpit, with six linenfold panels, and the brass memorials, are noteworthy. Heighington Hall, north-east of the church, is early 18th century and has some interesting stonework. The descendants of Captain Cumby, Commander of HMS *Royal Sovereign* at the battle of Trafalgar, still live at Trafalgar House, a pleasant 19th-century squire's house behind high walls on the Aycliffe road. A mile north of the village is Redworth Hall, part 16th century, part 19th, a stone-gabled dwelling, once the home of the Surtees family, but now used as a school.

Stephenson's *Locomotion Number One*, on 27 September 1825, the first steam engine to haul a fare-paying passenger train (*see* Darlington), was first put on the rails at Heighington. Built at NEWCASTLE UPON TYNE, it was brought to this point by road.

Hett *see* Spennymoor

Hexham, *Northumberland* (4/1C) Administrative centre for the Tynedale district and 1300 years old, a market town living comfortably hand in hand with modern industry. Hexham developed around a crossing of the Tyne, where for centuries passengers were ferried over the river. The first bridge was built in 1770 but it did not last long, being washed away by floods a year later. The next, erected in 1780, survived only two

years before suffering a similar fate. However, the third dates from 1793 and still stands, although it had to be widened in 1967 to cope with the needs of modern traffic.

St Wilfrid built his abbey here in 674; it was a very early use of stone by the Anglo-Saxons. The abbey suffered from many attacks by marauding Danes, and later Scots, who seemed to have a penchant for setting fire to it. Despite its problems, the abbey gradually developed into the majestic focal point of today. Many of the stones used in its construction are Roman; a Roman tombstone at the foot of the night stairs, which linked the monks' dormitory to the abbey, is dedicated to a 25-year-old standardbearer called Flavinus, clearly a man of importance. The oldest remains of the original abbey can be found in the Saxon crypt; and St Wilfrid's chair, once used as a frith or sanctuary stool, is at least 1300 years old and it is reputed to be the coronation seat of the kings of Northumbria. Rich ecclesiastical wooden furnishings fill the choir, and especially interesting are the medieval misericords, the backs of which were sold for firewood during a misguided attempt to tidy the building in the early part of the 19th century. The abbey has a Breeches Bible, dating from 1612 (so called because in Genesis 3:7 Adam and Eve, instead of clothing themselves, are said to have made breeches). Only the Priory Gate and parts of the Chapter House remain from the once extensive monastic buildings that supported the abbey. Their demise dates from the Dissolution of the Monasteries by Henry VIII.

The market place is to the front of the abbey. The site is centuries old, continuing a tradition dating back beyond the Middle Ages. Past it is the gate-like Moot Hall, built in 1335 using convenient Roman materials. Its wall are 11 ft thick, and it was once a debtors' prison. Around the corner is the Manor Office, also 14th century, a fortified tower again made from Roman stones. The building now houses the Middle March Centre, a museum of Border history.

Narrow streets lined with Georgian buildings and interesting shops radiate out from the market place. The town also holds busy agricultural markets for the produce of surrounding farms, selling thousands of sheep and cattle each year.

On a broad ridge to the south of the town, Hexham racecourse hosts racing under National Hunt rules. The course is used as a caravan and camp site between race meets.

Many of Hexham's inhabitants took part in the Pilgrimage of Grace in 1536, demanding the

Sheep sale, Hexham

restoration of the monasteries, an act that led to its leaders' betrayal and execution. A similar fate befell the 3rd Earl of Derwentwater, who supported the wrong side during the Jacobite Rebellion of 1715. Anya Seton based her novel *Devil Water* on his exploits.

In the late 18th century the Riot Act was read to lead miners in the market place who were protesting against conscription, introduced to raise troops for the war against Napoleon. Soldiers guarding the magistrates panicked and opened fire, causing many casualties, some of them fatal.

High Coniscliffe, *Co. Durham* (6/3C) The village sits on a high cliff on the north bank of the Tees west of DARLINGTON, straddling the A67. The name means 'King's cliff'. The church spire can be seen for miles as you approach from the south. The church, which was rebuilt in 1846 in the Early English style, is dedicated to St Edwin, a king of Northumbria who did much to encourage the early spread of Christianity. Strangely, this is the only English church dedicated to him. Fragments of Saxon stonework and a Norman window and north door help to show its age. There are interesting 15th-century chancel stalls, a 12th-century tomb cover in the porch, as well as a late 17th-century monument to one of the Bowes family, who lived at Thornton Hall.

High Coniscliffe's main street is lined with Georgian houses and cottages. Thornton Hall is a tall, gabled structure, spanning three centuries

from the 16th, and stands back from the B6279 to the north-east.

High Force *see* Langdon Beck

Hilton, *Cleveland* (8/2C) A sleepy MIDDLESBROUGH commuter village of modern properties mingling with older cottages, set in pretty gardens. It is roughly halfway between the bustling market towns of YARM and Stokesley in North Yorkshire. St Peter's Church stands on a little hill overlooking the road and probably dates from before the 12th century; certainly some of its stonework is from that period. Of special interest is a curious but simple carving of a dragon biting its own tail.

Holwick, *Co. Durham* (5/3B) Village at the end of an unclassified road, 3 miles west-north-west of MIDDLETON IN TEESDALE. A tiny group of stone cottages and farms fit snugly beneath the vertical whinstone crags of Holwick Scars. A short walk through Mill Beck Wood, to the east of Holwick, leads to a hidden rocky gorge and an attractive waterfall. Known as Fairy Dell, it is on private land, but permission is usually granted to anyone wishing to ramble or picnic there: enquire at the Strathmore Arms in Holwick.

Holy Island, *Northumberland* (2/2A) The island is approached from Beal, 1 mile east of the A1, and

9 miles south of BERWICK-UPON-TWEED. To reach the island it is necessary to cross the sands by a causeway which is only open at low tide. Do not, therefore, attempt the crossing other than at authorized times; lives have been lost by people disregarding the tide tables, which are posted at each end of the causeway.

The ancient name for Holy Island is Lindisfarne. It was early Celtic missionaries who first brought Christianity to the north-east of England. However, it took many years, years that were not without bloodshed, before St Aidan was able to establish a priory on Lindisfarne in 635. The island was comparatively safe from mainland attack, but prey to marauding Vikings in later years. A crude, graphic stone carving in the priory museum conveys the terror the monks felt about the Viking raids. Cuthbert, the saintly missionary, came to Lindisfarne in 664.

On his death in 687, St Cuthbert was buried on Lindisfarne and 11 years later, when the monks wanted to move his coffin to a more honoured place, his disinterred body was found to be still whole.

From that time onward his remains became

The Castle, Lindisfarne (Holy Island)

something of a sacred relic and when the monks fled from the island to avoid attack by the Danes in 875, they took St Cuthbert with them. For the next 125 years monks carried the coffin around the North of England, rarely settling for long in any one place, until a divine revelation instructed them to take St Cuthbert's remains to Dunholm. The site later became the magnificent cathedral city of DURHAM.

Most of the work of developing the priory of Lindisfarne took place under St Cuthbert's successor, St Wilfrid. It was during his reign that many wonderful works of art were made, such as St Cuthbert's Cross, which is now in Durham Cathedral, and the Lindisfarne Gospels, in the British Museum. A modern facsimile of the latter is in the priory church. The priory has been in ruins since it was dissolved by the edict of Henry VIII, but St Mary's, the abbey church, still stands and Lindisfarne has become a place of pilgrimage. St Cuthbert is the patron saint of Northumberland and his feast day is celebrated on 20 March, when special services are held throughout the county.

The sole village here uses Holy Island as its name. Originally the service village for the priory, its inhabitants are mostly fishermen, or look after

the visitors who come to the couple of pleasant pubs and the handful of tearooms there. A market cross in a tiny square to the south of the village dates from 1828, but rises from a medieval socket. The island's one farm uses grazing on Chare Ends, between the sand dunes to the north and Lindisfarne Castle in the south. The little harbour shelters inshore fishing boats and pleasure craft. Local fishing is mostly for crabs and lobsters, which are sold in village hotels and tearooms.

Holy Island is half bird sanctuary. Migrants and local sea birds nest in the seclusion of the sand dunes and foreshore, which are now part of the Lindisfarne National Nature Reserve.

The Whin Sill, a vast extrusion of doleritic basalt that appears throughout northern England in places as far apart as Teesdale, HADRIAN'S WALL and the FARNE ISLANDS, has created the highest point of Holy Island. Lindisfarne Castle sits romantically on the top of rocky Beblowe Crag and was built as part of the coastal defences in 1550. It was transformed in 1903 into a magnificent private house for Edward Hudson by the architect Sir Edwin Lutyens. The castle and its fine collection of oak furniture is now open to the public. It was given to the National Trust in 1944 by Sir Edward de Stein and his sister Miss Gladys de Stein.

Storerooms, Lindisfarne (Holy Island)

The Trust also owns the surrounding 30 acres of land, together with the tiny walled garden near by. Sheltered from winds off the North Sea, it was developed by Gertrude Jekyll between 1906 and 1912. For further details enquire at: National Trust Information Centre, Elm House, Marygate, Holy Island, Berwick-upon-Tweed, Northumberland; (0289) 89253.

Holystone, *Northumberland* (4/1A) Secluded hamlet by the side of the river Coquet, where the missionary St Paulinus is supposed to have baptized 3000 Northumbrians during Easter week in AD 627. The site of this mammoth task was at Lady's Well, a rectangular pool fed by clear spring water and reached by a footpath beyond the Salmon Inn. There is a stone cross in the centre of the pool and a statue dedicated to St Paulinus at the side. Lady's Well is now owned by the National Trust.

Holystone Common, a forested outlier of the CHEVIOT HILLS, is reached along a quiet forest track to the south-west of the village. The group of tumuli here known as the Five Barrows yielded evidence of a highly civilized population that lived in the area between 1600 and 1000 BC. Many other prehistoric relics stand enigmatically on the windswept moorland heights, such as the line of stones known as the Five Kings and the earth ramparts of a fort above Harehaugh.

A ruined peel tower stands in the grounds of Holystone Grange.

Houghton-le-Spring, *Tyne and Wear* (8/1A) The dual carriageway of the A690 cuts the town in two, with colliery dereliction near by and modern development to the south-east, but Houghton retains its ancient atmosphere. Groups of old stone-built houses surround the large, mainly 13th-century church where Bernard Gilpin, the 'Apostle of the North', preached in the 16th century. Gilpin inaugurated the annual Houghton Feast and Ox Roast, which is held on the first Friday in October. He is buried within his church, in a tomb chest near to the memorials of two ancient knights. Eight lancet windows pierce the south wall of the church and a passageway leads to the two-storeyed, battlemented 15th-century chapel of the Guild of the Holy Trinity.

Howick Hall, *Northumberland* (2/3C) A private house on the winding road between CRASTER and LONGHOUGHTON. Howick Hall, built in 1782 on the site of a 15th-century tower, is the home of Lord Howick, a descendant of the Grey family –

Lady's Well, Holystone

the 2nd Earl Grey was Prime Minister at the time of the Reform Bill. The gardens are open to the public from April to November, although the best time to visit is in May, when the rhododendrons are in full bloom.

Hulne Priory *see* Alnwick

Humshaugh, *Northumberland* (4/1B) Small village on gently rising ground between the B6320 CHOLLERFORD–BELLINGHAM road and the North Tyne river. Humshaugh House is a red-brick, comfortable-looking Georgian manor house. Haughton Castle, a riverside stronghold to the north of the village, dates from before the 14th century, but frequent sackings and burnings led to its abandonment in the 16th. The present building is a 19th-century restoration together with additional features by Anthony Salvin, an architect who was responsible for many fine Victorian mansions. Both Humshaugh House and Haughton Castle are privately owned.

The village church was built in 1818 to a design by John Dobson but, like many churches in the region, probably has older foundations.

Hunwick, *Co. Durham* (6/2B) Village in the decayed industrial landscape between BISHOP AUCKLAND and CROOK – landscape now undergoing a long-needed change that should eventually bring the village back to its former rural self. Several old buildings denote its earlier charms. Hunwick Old Hall, a medieval manor, is now a farmhouse; its former chapel has been relegated to being a barn, but still retains the stones of its traceried east window. Outside the farm gate is a 'gin', an engine designed to operate farm machinery and worked by horses. Helmington Hall to the north is again a farm, all that remains of a large house dating from 1686.

Hurworth-on-Tees, *Co. Durham* (6/3C & 8/1C) Here is a spacious, attractive village on the bank of the Tees to the south of DARLINGTON. It has several fine Georgian houses built around a long, bright village green where the parish church of All Saints, which was rebuilt in 1831, has foundations that go back at least to the 15th century. Effigies on the church wall are said to be from nearby Neasham Abbey, founded by Benedictine nuns, which was dissolved by Henry VIII. The coal-owning Millbanke family pew stands boxlike on columns above the nave. William Emerson, eccentric mathematical genius, was buried in the churchyard in 1782, his Hebrew and Latin epitaphs indicating his classical education. Hurworth's bay-windowed manor house, one of the finest dwellings lining the village green, was built in 1728; it is now a preparatory school.

Hutton Magna, *Co. Durham* (6/2C) Set in a wide rolling landscape of lush farmland, the village is a single street of low stone cottages and pretty gardens to the south-east of BARNARD CASTLE. The church is almost hidden by the village inn. A Tudor hall to the west of the churchyard is a private house.

Ingram, *Northumberland* (2/1C) A secluded village of stone-built houses at the end of a side road off the A697, south of WOOLER. Ingram fits snugly above the southern bank of the river Breamish and at the foot of the east-facing slopes of Ewe Hill, an outlier of the CHEVIOT HILLS. The village is a natural gateway to the moors and high tops of the Cheviots, and useful data about local conditions can be obtained from the National Park Information Centre outside the village.

Numerous hut circles and other prehistoric sites can be found on the nearby moors – most notable is the **Greaves Ash** (1/3C) site near

Linhope Farm at the head of the Breamish valley. This is the largest complex in Northumberland and contains traces of no fewer than 40 huts, which were occupied from the Iron Age until Roman times. A medieval farmstead is super-imposed upon the circle.

Davidon's Linn is an attractive waterfall about 7 miles from Linhope, at the head of Usway Burn in the Coquet valley. It is only accessible by a lonely moorland path, the Salter's Road, climbing out of the Breamish valley beyond the remote High Bleakhope Farm. The walk is only suitable in fine weather and could include an exploratory visit to the Greaves Ash Iron Age site.

Irehopeburn, *Co. Durham* (5/3A) Former lead-mining village on the south bank of the Wear. Two entirely different establishments vie for the visitor's attention: the Rancho del Rio, a converted farmhouse offering Western-style entertainment; and, near by, High House Chapel, which has been converted into the Weardale Museum, devoted to local customs and to lead mining. Built in 1760, the chapel has strong links with John Wesley who used to preach regularly in the area – at first beneath a hawthorn tree a short distance from the village. A commemorative plaque now identifies this protected tree and quotes 1749 as the date of his visit.

Burnhope Reservoir is attractively surrounded by a small plantation of pine trees; it can be approached from Irehopeburn either by footpath, or along a short moorland road that rejoins the valley road at COWSHILL.

Jarrow, *Tyne and Wear* (7/2C) The ruins of the priory that Bede entered as a boy of 12 stand above the marsh of Jarrow Slake, but today these tranquil ruins, and the church of St Paul that adjoins them, are surrounded on their landward side by oil storage tanks. Fortunately the trappings of modern industry are partly hidden behind a low hill and so this place where the Venerable Bede (AD 673–735) wrote his history of the English people, *Historia Ecclesiastica Gentis Anglorum*, remains a haven of peace. As well as compiling his unique record, Bede also produced some 40 scholarly works on subjects ranging from theology and music to astronomy and medicine.

The simple yet dignified ancient church contains much that has stood since Bede's day, or even earlier. The oldest part is the Saxon chapel at the east end built, it is thought, around 681 with Roman stones. Bede's Chair is on the south wall; experts disagree about its exact age, but all agree

that it is at least 600 years old. The tower dates from 1075 and is a curious mixture of styles within its four stages. The original dedication stone of the church bears the date of St George's Day, 23 April 681, and can be found above the tower arch.

A few hundred yards uphill across a pleasant green from the priory, Georgian Jarrow Hall, the oldest remaining house in the town, now serves as a museum dealing with relics from the priory and also as an information centre. Bede Gallery in nearby Springwell Park holds regular exhibitions of contemporary art and the history of Jarrow.

Jarrow received unwanted fame in the 1930s when workers from its redundant shipyards staged a hunger march on Parliament, led by the town's redoubtable MP, Helen Wilkinson. The event is remembered by a plaque at the entrance to the Victorian town hall. Tower blocks and a modern shopping precinct, dominated by a statue commemorating the Viking raids of 793 and 796, now rise above the demolished shipyards. New industries strive to succeed where shipbuilding failed. Jarrow Riverside Park, with footpaths and views of modern shipyards on the north bank of the Tyne, occupies reclaimed industrial wasteland above the Tyne Road Tunnel.

Jesmond Dene *see* Newcastle upon Tyne

Kelloe, *Co. Durham* (8/1B) The village lies southeast of DURHAM, in countryside marred by coal mining and quarrying, but it has antecedents as far back as the Bronze Age. During that period there was a large settlement on the site of what is now Garmondsway Farm.

According to tradition King Canute made a barefoot pilgrimage from Kelloe to Durham in 1017 to visit the shrine of St Cuthbert.

The modern village is further north, mostly miners' cottages and council houses, but it has a heavily buttressed Norman church, where the greatest treasure is the Kelloe Cross. This ancient relic depicts St Helena's vision of the Holy Cross, as well as showing other versions of the saint and an unknown companion. She is also seen menacing Judas Iscariot with a sword, ordering him to dig with a spade and discover the cross.

Elizabeth Barrett Browning was born near by at Coxhoe Hall (demolished in the 1950s) in 1806. She was baptized in Kelloe church, an event commemorated by a monument erected by public subscription in 1897. Another monument is to a terrible mining disaster at Trimdon Grange pit in 1822, when 74 miners were killed.

Kielder, *Northumberland* (3/1A) Forestry Commission village mostly dating from the early 1950s, near the head of the North Tyne valley and close to Kielder Reservoir. It was built to provide accommodation for workers in the nearby Kielder Forests. The surrounding area was once open moorland and Kielder Castle was built in 1775 as a shooting lodge for the Duke of Northumberland; today it forms a palatial working men's club, as well as acting as an Information Centre. The Forest Drive, along a toll road, starts at Kielder Castle and threads its way through 12 miles of conifer plantations, with sections of open moorland, to join the A68 near BYRNESS.

Until 1958 one of the most scenic of railway lines followed the North Tyne river past Kielder and into Central Scotland. It crossed the river below Kielder by a 'skew' viaduct. This still stands, the only tangible reminder of the line, near Bakethin at the head of Kielder Reservoir.

A once important drove road preceded the railway, crossing the border at Bloody Bush, near the head of Akenshaw Burn about 4 miles south-west of Kielder. A stone pillar at this point was a waymark for cattle drovers and the name probably commemorates a Border skirmish.

Kielder Reservoir

The pillar gives details of distances and of tolls levied on the drovers and their cattle or sheep. There is no bush, but instead seried ranks of pines now fill the English side of the Border. It is still possible to follow the line of the drove road on foot, by a forest track above Akenshaw Burn continuing beyond the Forest Nature Trail.

The Kielder Forests (3) Four forests are covered by the Kielder name: Kielder, Falstone, Wark and Redesdale. Together they form one of Europe's largest man-made forests. Shortages during the First World War highlighted the need for Britain to be less dependent upon imported timber. From the 1920s onwards tree planting began under the direction of the Forestry Commission. In 1929 the first trees appeared in the upper Tyne valley as part of the general plan to improve our reserves of home-grown timber. This reafforestation continued, the bulk of it planted between 1940 and 1970, until eventually about 280 square miles of reclaimed heath and moorland on both sides of the Border were covered; but most of the great forest lies within

Northumberland. Maturing forests now provide British industry with over 100,000 tonnes of timber annually.

Sharing a common boundary with the Northumberland National Park, and originally known as the Border Forest Park, Kielder is the largest and perhaps least known British forest. Its most northerly point is high in the CHEVIOT HILLS. Its southern boundary is about 40 miles away, near HADRIAN'S WALL, and it stretches west to the river Irthing on the border between Cumbria and Northumberland. In the east it follows the North Tyne valley north-west of BELLINGHAM and takes in Redesdale as its most easterly limit. The four forests that form the continuous block known today as Kielder cover a total area of around 125,000 acres.

Sitka spruce is the most common tree used by the Forestry Commission, planted in wet, peaty and often exposed sites; Norwegian spruce is mainly used in the more sheltered areas. Both types of quick-growing conifers reach maturity in about 40 years. Valley plantings are often mixed with slower-growing and more attractive trees, such as the Douglas fir, red cedars and larch. More recently the Forestry Commission has adopted a new policy, beginning to replace felled pine forest, especially along river banks, with broadleafed species such as oak, willow, rowan and ash, which in turn are attracting more wildlife into the area.

A popular area for recreation, the Forest offers either peace and tranquillity or space for competitive sports, ranging from orienteering to motor rallying. Brown trout inhabit many of the burns in Kielder, Falstone and Redesdale forests. Rod licences are available from the Northumbrian Water Authority, Yarrow Moor, Falstone, Hexham, and day or period permits from the District Forest Offices. Public access on foot is encouraged by waymarked walks and trails, as well as longer walks. Cars, however, are restricted to the 12-mile Forest Drive from Kielder village to Blakehopeburnhaugh on the A68 near Byrness in Redesdale.Camping andcaravanning facilities are provided at STONEHAUGH and Kielder, with other sites at Leaplish and Byrness. Holiday cabins have been established on sites in the forest.

Kielder Castle Visitor Centre is open during the summer and houses an exhibition covering all aspects of the area; visiting groups can book the services of a Ranger for guided walks. The Northumbrian Water Authority also has a Visitor Centre at Tower Knowe. Kielder Forest supports a large and varied wildlife population and

Kielder Castle

observation hides are available for hire to individuals and groups.

Kielder Reservoir (3) It is fitting that Europe's largest man-made lake should be surrounded by so large a man-made forest. The Kielder Reservoir statistics stretch belief: yielding 250 million gallons a day from its storage capacity of 44,000 million gallons, it is designed to supply the water needs of North-East England well into the foreseeable future. Nine miles long, it covers 125.000 acres of the upper North Tyne Valley and required the felling of 1½ million trees in its construction. The massive earth dam is three quarters of a mile long and the maximum depth of the reservoir is 170 ft. Water flowing from the dam under the pressure created by the reservoir's 9 miles head is sufficient to drive two electricity generators. Further supplies of water are pumped from the Tyne at a point near Riding Bridge, about 27 miles away to the south. The valley's contours have created a lake of a pleasing irregularity of shape, with bays and tiny, twisting estuaries. To prevent unsightly mudflats appearing in the shallower upper reaches of the reservoir during droughts, the smaller Bakethin dam was built to retain an auxiliary reservoir about 1 mile below Kielder Castle.

Almost every likely need and waterborne activity is catered for on and around the reservoir. Information and Visitor Centres exist at Kielder Castle, near the head of the reservoir, and Tower Knowe close to the main dam. Picnic sites are strategically sited either on the shore or in the nearby forest. Car parking is easy and toilets for the disabled are available near most of them. Natural and man-made knolls make excellent viewpoints, and waymarked walks and trails connect several of the main features. The reservoir has been stocked with fish, mostly trout, and angling is permitted either from designated shoreline areas or from boats. Sailing and power cruising enthusiasts have their clubhouses and landing stages on both sides of the reservoir; most cater for day visitors as well as club members. Sailing and cruising activities are controlled by the Kielder Water Club at Leaplish. Non-sailors can enjoy the water by using a ferry service which connects various points along the shoreline; this way walkers and picnickers can enjoy the paths and trails inaccessible from normal motor roads.

Extensive field study facilities have been developed, both for school parties and for visiting naturalists. The reservoir has settled into a naturalized state and wildlife, especially migrant waterfowl, has been attracted to Kielder. Special areas have been kept free from outside pressures and the Bakethin portion of the reservoir has been made into a Nature Conservation Area.

Caravaning and camp sites, which include facilities for backpacking together with attractive holiday cabins, are provided at several places around the reservoir. As well as water sports, cycle trails, orienteering courses, pony trekking, forest walks and guided rambles, and cross-country ski trails have been provided to complete the almost infinite number of activities possible at Kielder.

Useful telephone numbers:	
Forestry Commission Kielder District Forest Office (0660) 20242/3	*Northumbrian Water* *Authority* General: (0660) 40398 Fishing: (0660) 50260
Kielder Castle Visitor *Centre* (0660) 50209	*Tourist Information* *Centre and tearoom* The Manor Office Hexham (0434) 605225

Windsurfers, Kielder Reservoir

Killhope Wheel Mining Centre, *Co. Durham* (5/2A) Derelict lead-mining complex in a moorland setting at the head of Weardale. The site is steadily being renovated and now provides an Interpretive Centre in what was a highly industrialized area. The main and most striking feature of the complex is a giant overshot waterwheel, which powered the crushing machinery. Other restored buildings include the working smithy, which is able to provide shoes for the sturdy Dales pony used in demonstrations of the old methods of transporting lead ore. A miners' 'shop', the bunkhouse where lead miners lived during their working week, often sleeping three and four to a bed, is laid out as a small and interesting museum with working displays and memorabilia of the region. There is also a picnic area near by. Access to the mining centre is from the A689 at the head of Weardale.

Killingworth, *Tyne and Wear* (7/2C) An industrial new town of some architectural merit, 5 miles north of NEWCASTLE UPON TYNE. It is built with direct access on to the A108, the Tyne Tunnel feeder road, and so into the national road network. Killingworth, in common with many new towns, has an old nucleus: the former colliery village where George Stephenson stayed when he was employed as engineman at Killingworth Colliery from 1805 to 1823. A sundial set into the wall of Dial Cottage, now a private residence, where Stephenson lived, is reputed to have been designed by him and carved by his son Robert. Stephenson's first locomotive, *Blucher*, ran from the mine to the Tyne. (A little-known fact is that he also invented a mine safety lamp a month before Sir Humphrey Davy.)

The artificial lake above West Moor is used for sailing and canoeing. The town centre has a modern shopping complex and sports centre.

Kirkleatham, *Cleveland* (8/3B) Historic village on the south-western outskirts of REDCAR and formerly surrounded by a deerpark, but now by the A174 and A1042. The village has managed to retain much of its quiet tranquillity despite the nearby Wilton Chemical Works. Known as *Westlidum* in the Domesday Book the village, or estate as it was then, was owned by William de Percy in the 11th century, then by the Lumley family, and in 1623 it was bought by John Turner of GUISBOROUGH, who had made his fortune from the mining of alum. Of the once grand house, only the stable block and the Old Hall museum remain, next door to the local school. The

Pavilion annexe and rooms in the Old Hall are given over to exhibits of a scientific nature, especially ones related to discoveries and innovations particular to the region. An aviary, a children's play area and an attractively laid-out garden complete this imaginative establishment.

Sir William Turner founded the almshouses now known as the Turner Hospital, Kirkleatham's finest buildings, in 1676. Letters Patent, dated 2 March 1678, speak of the provision of accommodation for 'ten poor men, ten poor women, ten poor boys and ten poor girls'. Although the definition of 'poor' has changed radically since then, the almshouses are still used for their original purpose. The present buildings date from 1742, following their remodelling by Turner's great-nephew Chomley Turner, who also paid for the chapel, thought to be designed by James Gibb.

St Cuthbert's Church has stood on the same site for over 900 years, although the present building dates from 1763. The church has several interesting brasses and a Turner mausoleum as its main features.

Kirk Merrington, *Co. Durham* (6/3B) Colliery village, on high ground north-east of BISHOP AUCKLAND, with its church tower a landmark for miles around. The church is a 19th-century attempt to rebuild the original structure. About 1½ miles south by a minor road is 19th-century Windlestone Hall. Built to a design by Ignatius Bonomi, it was for many years home of the Eden family and birthplace of Sir Anthony Eden, later Lord Avon. It is now used as a school by Durham County Council.

Kirknewton, *Northumberland* (1/3B) Compact Border village at the foot of Yeavering Bell (1181 ft) a northern outlier of the Cheviot Hills. To its north is the floodplain of College Burn and Bowmont Water, salmon streams that join here to form the river Glen, itself an eventual tributary of the Tweed. Safe from the dangers of flooding, local farms enjoy the rich grazing along the valley bottoms. Thick stone cottage walls indicate their former need to withstand attack; in fact the village seems to crouch in on itself, as though still prepared to stave off Scottish raiders.

Inside the village church, a stone carving, thought to be Saxon, shows the Three Magi in the Adoration of the Virgin to be wearing kilts. Josephine Butler, the Northumbrian social reformer, is buried in the churchyard. The church is in the Early English style. Only the tower and nave were altered in an attempt to improve the building in the mid-1800s, leaving a unique tunnel-vaulted chancel and south transept built on walls barely 3 ft high.

South-facing cultivation terraces, on hillsides draining into tributaries of College Burn, are the tangible remains of a civilization which once enjoyed a warmer climate than we do today. **Old Yeavering** is about 1 mile to the east of Kirknewton along the B6351 WOOLER road. Here is the site of the 6th-century timber palace of the ancient kings of Northumbria; a roadside tablet tells a little about its history.

Coupland Castle is across the river Glen. A private residence, it dates from the Union of Crowns; the grounds are open to the public on advertised days.

Kirkwhelpington, *Northumberland* (4/1B) The A696 bypasses the village to the west, leaving behind a tiny cluster of stone houses above the infant river Wansbeck. John Hodgson, the Northumbrian historian, lived here between 1823 and 1832. St Bartholomew's Church was founded in Norman times, but the building is mostly 13th century with later additions, especially in the Victorian era; the tower is built in the Perpendicular style. Sir Charles Parsons, inventor of the steam turbine, lived near by and was buried in the churchyard in 1931.

Ordnance Survey maps refer to the moorland heights above the village as Kirkwhelpington Common, but the locals more attractively call them the Wilds of Wannie, after the name of the local river, the Wansbeck.

Kirkharle Estate is a mile or so to the south-east, on both sides of the A696. The hall is Victorian and the tiny estate chapel dedicated to

Cauldron Snout (see p. 136)

St Wilfrid is a 14th-century building on Norman foundations. 'Capability' Brown, the landscape artist and garden planner, was born near by in 1715 and as a boy developed the foundations of his craft by working in the estate gardens.

Kyloe Hills *see* Belford

Lambley, *Northumberland* (3/2C) Former colliery village in the valley of the South Tyne south-east of HALTWHISTLE. A Benedictine convent stood here until the Scots burned it down in 1296. The valley was once served by a railway line that linked Alston in Cumbria to Haltwhistle and the outside world, but this is now lost. Part of the line has been taken over by a railway preservation society, and so the village is now the northern terminus of the South Tyne Narrow Gauge Railway. Nearby Lambley Viaduct, a 110 ft high monument to railway engineering, is regrettably closed through structural problems.

Lambton Castle *see* Penshaw

Lanchester, *Co. Durham* (6/2A) The Romans built an important fort here on Dere Street, their road linking HADRIAN'S WALL and York. They called it Longovicium, the long fort. Road and fort are ignored by their modern counterparts, the A691 and Lanchester, both having moved half a mile eastwards. Situated about halfway between DURHAM and CONSETT, Lanchester is on both sides of a steep valley and spreads around a wide green. It is dominated by the tall, embattled tower of its Norman and Early English church, a building of considerable architectural and archaeological interest. Of particular note are the number of Roman altarstones and pillars from the nearby fort that are incorporated into the building. Buried among other local notables is the Reverend Dr William Greenwell, DCL, FRS, historian and archaeologist, Canon of Durham Cathedral – but probably best remembered among anglers as the designer of the fishing fly Greenwell's Glory.

Little of Longovicium is visible, for most of its above-ground stones were plundered in the 18th century as ready-made building material. However, several of its altars were saved and are preserved, not only in the village church, but in Durham Cathedral.

A mile and a half along the Durham road and to its south along a wooded side lane, is the Grecian-styled 19th-century Burnhopeside Hall, now a comfortable hotel.

Langdon Beck, *Co. Durham* (5/3B) Lonely farming community in upper Teesdale, regularly isolated by winter snows. There are two pubs in the upper valley, the High Force Hotel and the Langdon Beck Hotel, 3 miles apart, which roughly mark the bounds of this scattered moorland hamlet. Whitewashed farmhouses dotting the fellsides usually belong to the Raby Estate. The story behind them is that the late Lord Barnard was lost in fog while shooting on the moors and came to a farmhouse where he asked for help, only to be turned away because it was not his property. Determined that this should never happen again, he ordered all his properties to be whitewashed.

Cow Green Reservoir (5/2B), 3 miles across Widdybank Fell to the west of the Langdon Beck Hotel, holds back the headwaters of the infant Tees. The reservoir and fell are accessible by a moorland road from Langdon Beck. From the car park you will have dramatic views to the west of Cross Fell (2930 ft), the highest point in the Pennines, and its attendant heights. Many rare subalpine plants, such as the spring gentian, grow in the nearby Upper Teesdale Nature Reserve, where there is also a waymarked Nature Trail, starting from the car park. Downstream from the massive concrete dam wall, the released river surges over the splendid cataract of **Cauldron Snout**. After 6 miles of turbulent meandering beyond the dam, the river reaches **High Force**, the second and equally dramatic stage of its journey to industrial Teesside and the North Sea. Both falls are accessible by footpath, High Force by a short path through the grounds of High Force Hotel, where a small toll must be paid. High Force (5/3B) claims to be the highest (70 ft) above-ground waterfall in England. Low Force is less dramatic, but equally attractive and about 2 miles downstream near Bowlees. 'Force' derives from the Old Norse word for waterfall.

Langley Castle, *Northumberland* (3/3C) A massive Victorian reconstruction of a 14th-century castle on the A686, about 1½ miles south-west of HAYDON BRIDGE. The oblong castle and its four guardian corner towers lay neglected from 1541. At one time or another it was owned by most of the great Northumbrian families, but is now a restaurant used for medieval banquets. A memorial to the ill-fated 3rd Earl of Derwentwater, executed for his part in the 1715 Rebellion, stands close by at the side of the Haydon Bridge road. Not only did the unfortunate earl lose his life, but the castle and all his other estates were sequestered by the Crown.

Lartington, *Co. Durham* (6/1C) Cosy little village about 3 miles from BARNARD CASTLE, sheltering behind a wood to its north and serving the needs of its hall and park. The B6277 skirts the southern boundary of Lartington Park and the Hall, which was built during the reign of Charles I. The present house, privately owned, stands on the site of an earlier building mentioned in the Domesday Book. Lartington Park is the venue for the annual Teesdale Country Fair.

Lesbury, *Northumberland* (2/3C) A straggling village east of Alnwick and built above the river Aln, which is still crossed by a picturesque medieval stone bridge. The village was decimated by the Great Plague in the 17th century, when inhabitants who had the disease were taken out to the nearby moor and left to die beneath crude wicker shelters.

Lindisfarne *see* Holy Island

Liverton, *Cleveland* (8/2A) Farms and cottages line the single street – the B1366 from LOFTUS to the A171 – and its elevated position affords good views seaward across the intervening countryside. The church, dedicated to St Michael, was founded in the 12th century, but altered early in this century. Its finest relic from the past is the Norman chancel arch. Liverton was on the fringe of the Cleveland ironstone deposits and many of the 19th-century cottages date from the time of the mining boom.

The Waterwheel Inn here has a huge wheel over its entrance. Liverton Mill, a link with the agricultural past of the village, stands in the densely wooded valley bottom to the west. Scaling Dam, 4 miles away on the edge of the moors, at the side of the A171, is stocked with fish: angling is available by day permit.

Loftus, *Cleveland* (8/2A) Viking settlers named their *Lopthús* from a house with a loft or upper room. The name has changed at least 13 times since then; the image of Loftus has depended on the fortunes of past owners and industries. Once an important centre for the manufacture of alum, used as a mordant to fix Turkey red dyes, a popular colour in the Middle Ages, its fortunes reached their zenith with the growth of the Teesside iron and steel industry when important deposits of ironstone were found beneath the nearby moors.

This former ironstone-mining boom town is the focal point of the eastern part of the new borough of Langbaurgh. Agriculture has regained its ascendance over industry, especially now that the steelworks across the valley at Carlin How (*see* Skinningrove) has drastically reduced its workforce. But mining is not dead, only changed. Many of the workers from the nearby BOULBY potash mine live in Loftus, spending their working days deep down beneath the bed of the North Sea.

The 20-minute Loftus Dam walk follows the old street pattern to visit the dam and Loftus Mill, now a private house, but once an important amenity for the town.

Handale (8/2A), a remote and tiny hamlet at the head of a deep, wooded valley south of Loftus, is the site of a former Cistercian abbey.

Longframlington, *Northumberland* (4/3A & 7/1A) Village on the A697 about 9 miles to the north-west of MORPETH. The church dates from 1190. Built in Transitional style, its most interesting features are the Norman chancel arch with three detached pillars on either side of the nave and an ancient stone bench. The vestry has a delightfully carved Jacobean chest.

The route of the Devil's Causeway, a Roman road between HADRIAN'S WALL and the Scottish border, can easily be traced west of the village, along what is now a farm lane past Framlington Villa. There is a museum of Northumbrian music in the village, especially devoted to the Northumbrian smallpipe. As the museum is run by volunteers, it is advisable for visitors to telephone in advance: Longframlington (066 570) 635.

Embleton Hall, north-west of the village along the main road, is 18th century.

Longhorsley, *Northumberland* (4/3A & 7/1A) The village clusters around a crossroads of the A697 MORPETH to Coldstream road and a quiet moorland road that links the village to the A1. A well-preserved peel tower dates from the 16th century and stands at the west end of the village. The church is said to the Norman in origin, although the present building is mainly a reconstruction in the early 18th century. About 1 mile north of the village is an early 19th-century manor house called Linden. It was designed by John Dobson of Newcastle, but probably replaced a much older building.

Longnewton, *Cleveland* (8/1C) There is one long main street here and a few shorter ones to either side, just off the busy A66 about halfway between STOCKTON-ON-TEES and DARLINGTON. Modern housing blends well with older and more established properties. The village is linked with the Durham coal-owning family, the Vanes, who acquired extra surnames as their prosperity grew, becoming Vane-Tempests and then later Vane-Tempest-Stewarts, the developers of SEAHAM Harbour and its mine. A grandiose vaulted mausoleum guards the mortal remains of many of them in a church, built in 1856, of otherwise uninteresting appearance. Their home, Long Newton Hall, was to the west of the village street, but only the enclosure wall remains. Behind the church is Longnewton's finest building, the 17th- and 18th-century rectory.

Low Dinsdale, *Co. Durham* (8/1C) Tiny hamlet on a minor road from Neasham that meanders to the south-east of DARLINGTON in the lush lower reaches of the Tees. The river twists and turns on either side, sometimes almost cutting back on itself; here it still flows through attractive countryside before its industrialized entry into the North Sea. The village was once a popular spa and was visited by William Wordsworth and his sister Dorothy in 1799. You can still follow the delightful woodland walk along the banks of the Tees as they did, towards Middleton One Row. The unpleasant smell of sulphur from the spa wells above the riverbank still lingers. This fashion for drinking supposedly beneficial, but foul-tasting waters was very much a late 18th- and early 19th-century affair.

The 16th-century manor house, home of the Surtees family, is built on a mound above a series of dry moats, a reminder that there was once an ancient building on the site. The sandstone church was originally 12th century, but was restored in 1875. Surtees family memorials, dating from the 14th century onwards, are worth investigating. The name means 'dweller by the Tees'; early forms included Super Teise and sur Teyse.

Lynemouth, *Northumberland* (7/2A) Compact industrial town of carefully laid out streets on the south bank of the river Lyne, north of ASHINGTON and about 1 mile inland from the coast. The community developed during the 1920s and '30s and is linked to nearby Lynemouth Colliery, and also the massive aluminium smelting plant. The Miners' Institute is the central point of the village. The river Lyne loops tightly round the village west to north, flowing through an attractively wooded dene. On the sandy coastline fossilized tree stumps sometimes appear after winter gales.

Maltby *see* Middlesbrough

Marsden Bay *see* South Shields

Marske-by-the-Sea, *Cleveland* (8/3B) Ancient fishing village beyond the A174, whose modern streets turn away from the sea. As with many other towns and villages on this exposed coast, there is no harbour and boats are launched from a slipway. The modern shopping centre and housing developments have overshadowed many of the sturdy old stone fishermen's cottages and later ironstone miners' houses near the High Street. One of them is a charming 16th-century cruck cottage standing in the High Street and known as Winkey's Castle. It now houses a small but varied collection of exhibits of local interest related to fishing and mining. The parish church building

The Transporter Bridge, Middlesbrough (see p. 140)

dates from 1866, but a Norman font and a 13th-century wayside cross indicate its earlier origins. Near is Marske Hall, built in 1625 and now a Cheshire Home.

Captain Cook's father is buried in St Germain's, on the clifftop east of the town centre. The church is abandoned and was demolished in 1960, with only the tower left.

New Marske (8/3C) lies a short distance inland and is an overspill town for MIDDLESBROUGH, with a population of 14,000. Errington Park Woods to the south are laid out with woodland walks and picnic areas; there are magnificent seaward views of the Tees estuary.

Marton *see* Middlesbrough

Meldon, *Northumberland* (4/2B & 7/1B) Tiny rural hamlet in lush farmland on a side road off the B6343, about 5 miles south-west of MORPETH. The village and its manor house, Meldon Park, are about 1 mile apart on either side of the river Wansbeck. John Dobson the architect built Meldon Park for himself in 1831. The grounds of the house are usually open to the public on advertised days during the summer, as part of the Northumbria Garden Scheme. July is the best month, when the rose garden and herbaceous borders are at their most colourful stage.

Meldon's tiny village church originates from the 13th century; the present building, however, is 19th century.

Mickleton *see* Middleton in Teesdale

Totem pole outside the Captain Cook Museum, Marton

Middlesbrough, *Cleveland* (8/2C) Before the Industrial Revolution, Middlesbrough was a small farming community on the rich alluvial soil of the lower Tees. Ironstone from the Cleveland Hills, and coal from Durham, were brought together to create an iron and steel industry that changed the local population in a few decades from an agricultural to an industrial-based society. Although both raw materials had been discovered centuries earlier, it was the new technology of such processes as the Bessemer system of converting iron to steel that were developed to meet the insatiable demands of an expanding industrial nation – and Middlesbrough grew with these demands. In the 1800s Middlesbrough took on the look of a boom town. In fact it could be said to be the oldest 'new town' in the North East. In 1862 the Prime Minister, W. E. Gladstone, visited Middlesbrough in 1862 and commented: 'This remarkable place, the youngest child of England's enterprise, is an infant – but an infant Hercules.'

The street pattern of the town centre, based on Albert and Zetland Roads, is reminiscent of the United States, with all its streets at right angles to each other. Fine buildings, most of them still suitable to the needs of 20th-century commerce, wide streets and parks, are a permanent record of far-sighted Victorian planners, such as Joseph Pease, who changed the face of Middlesbrough.

The river has always been the hub of all activity in the area; shipbuilding developed here with the increased demands of coal and iron exports. Today's industries are mostly oil and chemicals north of the river and steelmaking and heavy engineering to the south, on sites that have moved downstream, away from the town, on to what were once salt marshes. To meet the changing requirements of the late 20th century, industrial estates such as Riverside Park have been developed on sites reclaimed from earlier and now redundant industries. The chemical industry, firmly established in the early part of this century, expanded more rapidly after the Second World War and is now producing diverse materials, ranging from animal feedstuffs from methanol fermentation to fertilizers, petrochemicals and various plastics.

In a little over a century Middlesbrough grew from its humble beginnings to become the commercial and administrative centre for Cleveland.

Two bridges, the Transporter Bridge opened in 1911 and the Newport Bridge, which first carried traffic in 1934, cross the river between its flat banks. In order to provide the necessary clearance for shipping, both are unconventional. The Transporter Bridge dominates the skyline downstream and carries a section of road back and forth; upstream, the Newport Bridge lifts horizontally to allow ships to pass. Conventional concrete bridges, built more recently further upstream, now ease the traffic bottlenecks inevitably created by the mobile bridges.

James Cook (1728–79), navigator and explorer, was born at **Marton** (8/2C), now a suburb of Middlesbrough. His birthplace is marked by a granite plinth in Stewart Park, at the start of the Captain Cook Heritage Trail. The trail, with its eye-catching symbols and plaques, visits places associated with Cook's early life in Cleveland. The Birthplace Museum in Stewart Park explains with dioramas and sound the story of James Cook, his exploits and discoveries around the world. Plants from many of the various tropical countries visited by the great man are housed in an adjacent conservatory.

Other museums and places of interest in the area are: the Dorman Museum, which has a collection of pottery made in the district and exhibits that follow the industrial development of the town; the Municipal Art Gallery, which usually has exhibitions of paintings by modern and past British artists; Teesaurus Playground is an imaginative recreation feature with a lifesized *Triceratops* dinosaur, built on reclaimed land close to the Riverside Industrial Estate; Newham Grange Leisure Farm is to the south of the town just off the B1365, where visitors are encouraged to walk round and study the animals and farming methods in a working environment.

The residential suburb of **Nunthorpe** (8/2C), on the south-east side of Middlesbrough, is notable for the 17th-century Nunthorpe Hall, built within the grounds of a 12th-century Cistercian nunnery – but apparently the nuns did not stay long. The house is now an old people's home.

Maltby (8/2C) is a tiny village on the south-west of Middlesbrough, kept independent by conservation and careful planning. It is mainly a double line of well-kept cottages on either side of the country lane linking STAINTON (Cleveland) to the A1044.

Middleton Hall *see* Wooler

Middleton in Teesdale, *Co. Durham* (5/3B) Large village in the pastoral lower reaches of upper Teesdale, north-west of BARNARD CASTLE. Middleton grew in the 19th century and was once the headquarters of the London Lead Company. This had its offices at Masterman Place, and Middleton House to the north-west, and controlled the mining interests in the area. The company had a Quaker background and was a benevolent employer, the first British company to introduce the five-day week. This far-sighted policy encouraged the local lead miners to live on smallholdings in the valleys and – with the odd cow or two and a few pigs and chickens – ensured that they and their families had a secure base and ate a balanced diet. The miners themselves lived in crowded and often insanitary 'shops' between Monday and Friday, so as to be close to their work beneath the high moors.

The most striking feature of Middleton is its wide, grassy main street with the Bainbridge Memorial Fountain at one end, a cast-iron drinking fountain erected in 1877. Cattle auctions, quaint shops and coaching inns complete the rural scene.

The present church is Victorian, replacing an earlier, possibly Norman foundation. Town End chapel to the east is a magnificent piece of Victorian architecture. Stotley Hall is about 1½ miles away, along the Barnard Castle road, a fine and attractive example of a prosperous 17th-century farmhouse.

Mickleton (6/1B) is a linear village of stone cottages 2 miles to the south-east of Middleton, built above the south bank of the Tees. Neolithic burials have been found near by.

Middleton St George, *Co. Durham* (8/1C) Pleasant straggling village above the river Tees about 4 miles east of DARLINGTON and away from the A67. The church stands aloof among fields and is Victorian, but must have been built on the site of an older, Saxon church if the sundial and other relics are anything to go by. Rather incongruous Victorian pews in the nave are more like old-fashioned railway waiting room seats.

The parish covers a wide area, its bounds indicated by the name Middleton attached to Low, West and One Row. Low Middleton Hall is in farmland about 2 miles to the south-east along a winding minor road. An early 18th-century brick house, its best face is to the south where ten sash windows overlook the formal gardens; the front of the house overlooking the YARM road is Victorian Gothic.

Middleton One Row, above the steep north bank of the Tees, is mostly an attractive line of terraced houses above the river where a sulphur spring, discovered by miners in the 18th century, gave rise to a popular spa.

The dramatic situation of its houses gives them unrivalled views south across the Tees and into the Plain of York.

Tees-side Airport (where, for some reason, a hyphen is deemed necessary) is to the north-west with its attendant bonded warehouses; and an industrial estate is within easy access of the A67.

Mitford, *Northumberland* (4/3B & 7/1B) An unspoiled village west of the A1 and MORPETH, above two wooded valleys at the confluence of the river Wansbeck with the Font.

Two stately bridges lead in and out of the village, that to the south leading to Mitford Castle whose ruined five-sided keep, destroyed by the Scots around 1318, dominates the skyline above a steep riverbank.

The Norman church stands separate from the main village; Mitford was moved to its present position after the original village was sacked by King John in 1216. Most of the church of St Mary Magdalene was reconstructed in 1875, but several 11th-century features are still recognizable, including a fine example of a priest's doorway and its typically Norman chevron moulding. A most attractive triple window lights the east end of the church.

A loop of the Wansbeck almost surrounds Mitford Hall. This was built in 1828 to the design of John Dobson, replacing an earlier and less convenient building closer to the village. Little remains of the latter apart from a battlemented tower dated 1673 and other ruins.

Monkton *see* Hebburn

Monkwearmouth *see* Sunderland

Morpeth, *Northumberland* (4/3B & 7/1B) The A1, thankfully, bypasses the town, but inns in the centre still have their coach yards, links with a time when Morpeth was an important stopping place on the Great North Road. Telford built the town bridge in 1831, part of a big improvement scheme for the main road between London and Edinburgh. Modern shop fronts hide the splendid architecture of Georgian buildings in the main street, but Morpeth's spacious tree-lined boulevards still manage to convey the more leisurely aspect of travel in a bygone age. Modern Morpeth has become the main town of Castle Morpeth Borough and also the county town for Northumberland, as well as being a busy market centre for the surrounding countryside.

The town, which straddles the river Wansbeck, once lived under the protection of a castle, but it was sacked by King John in 1216 during the squabble with his barons. Suffering further at the hands of Scottish raiders, its only remains are the 15th-century gatehouse and a motte and bailey on the steep slope above the river in Carlisle Park. Castle Square is situated at the southern end of Telford Bridge and to its east is the massive Court House, a late Georgian building designed by John Dobson, the Newcastle architect.

St Mary's Parish Church is mostly 14th century, but is built on Norman foundations. Following a delightful local custom, the church gates are tied at weddings until the bridegroom pays a toll. A watchtower next to the churchyard was built in 1837 to guard against bodysnatchers, and a nearby clock tower still tolls a curfew bell.

About three quarters of a mile to the west of the town centre, and reached by an attractive riverside footpath, are the ruins of Newminster Abbey, a Cistercian foundation dating from 1137. Ravaged by the Scots soon after its initial completion, the rebuilt abbey became extremely powerful until the Dissolution edict of Henry VIII.

Admiral Lord Collingwood, who commanded the fleet at Trafalgar after Nelson's death, lived in Morpeth, at Collingwood House in Oldgate.

Morpeth has two museums, the Cameo Gallery in King Edward VI School, which holds temporary exhibitions in conjunction with lectures on a wide range of subjects; and on the north side of Telford Bridge the Chantry, which dates from 1296, an eloquent reminder of Morpeth's past. The latter building is also used as a Tourist Information Centre.

One darker note: the name of the town apparently derives from Old English words meaning 'murder path'.

Muggleswick, *Co. Durham* (6/1A) Rural hamlet in a moorland setting above a deep, wooded part of the Derwent valley near EDMUNDBYERS. Its present size belies its earlier importance. The manor house, although now ruined, was once a grange farm belonging to the priors of DURHAM. Its size is indicated by a large stone gable, traceried windows and a massive stone fireplace. The tiny village church is Victorian, but is probably built on the site of a much older building.

Netherwitton, *Northumberland* (4/2A) Hamlet on a minor road north-west of MORPETH, built around a bridge below the widened stretch of the river Font. The present manor house, Netherwitton Hall, is early 18th century, but there has been a dwelling here since the 14th century. Its first tenant was Roger Thornton, a prosperous Newcastle merchant, whose descendant was paid compensation for allowing Oliver Cromwell and a troop of his horsemen to camp overnight in the grounds in 1651.

The remains of a Georgian mill are on the riverbank close to the road bridge, where there is also a good view of the hall. Two miles further to the north west, at the end of a wooded side lane, is where the Newcastle architect John Dobson built Nunnykirk Hall, one of his finest works.

Newbiggin, *Co. Durham* (6/2A) A scattering of farms and roadside cottages on a gentle stretch of the upper Tees. The village was once an important lead-mining centre with its own smelter. Nearby Bowlees Visitor Centre is about half a mile further up the valley from Newbiggin and explains the natural history of upper Teesdale in an easy-to-follow, yet well-documented manner. Gibson's Cave Nature Trail starts from the centre and leads through about half a mile of woodland, to a small cave hollowed out of the surrounding shaly rock by an attractive waterfall.

From Newbiggin a field path leads down to

Scoberry Bridge; across the Tees a riverside path follows the bank upstream to the turbulent waters of Low Force (*see also* Langdon Beck). Wynch Bridge close by can be used on the return. This is built on the site of the first suspension bridge in Europe: the original was put up in 1744 to give access to nearby lead mines.

The name Newbiggin, common in northern England, means 'new building, or house' and is of Old Norse origin.

Newbiggin-by-the-Sea, *Northumberland* (7/2A & 2B) The town seems to turn its back on the sea and concentrates on providing homes for miners who work in collieries further inland, for there is no longer a mine at Newbiggin. The seaward side of the town is a pleasant sandy bay with holiday and camping amenities. St Bartholomew's Church is basically of the 13th and 14th centuries and its tower still acts as a landmark for shipping, but the interior is modern. Erosion is a constant problem along this part of the North-East coast and the church is in danger of eventually falling into the sea.

About a mile outside Newbiggin, along the A197 MORPETH road, Woodhorn church stands beside a little wood. It is Saxon with Norman and Early English additions, but has been redundant since its parishioners moved away following the closure of local pits. The building is now used by Wansbeck District Council as a museum and cultural centre.

Newbrough, *Northumberland* (3/3C) This was a colliery community until the mines were worked out. It lies north-west of HEXHAM, on Stanegate, the east–west Roman supply road that served HADRIAN'S WALL. Newbrough, notwithstanding its name, was obviously well established by the time of Henry III, who granted it its market charter. The parish church of St Peter stands on the site of a Roman fort, built to guard Stanegate.

Neighbouring **Fourstones** (3/3C), too, stands on the line of Stanegate. It is a pleasant village also overlooking the South Tyne and may derive its name from four Roman altars that stood there.

Newburn, *Tyne and Wear* (4/3C & 7/1C) Industrial suburb of NEWCASTLE UPON TYNE, built well above the north bank of the river. George

The Swing Bridge, Newcastle upon Tyne (see p. 144)

Stephenson, of the railway era, was twice married in the parish church of St Michael, about 3 miles from where he was born, upstream at WYLAM. It has an early Norman tower and arcades, together with a 13th-century chancel.

Lemington power station marks the point where the first steam locomotive, *Puffing Billy*, was built by William Hedley in 1813. It ran a full year before Stephenson's *Blucher*. *Puffing Billy* hauled coal from Wylam Colliery, close to Stephenson's birthplace.

The Tyne Riverside Country Park stretches from Newburn to Wylam.

Newcastle upon Tyne, *Tyne and Wear* (7/1C & 2C) The graceful arc of Tyne Bridge dominates the river skyline, making a lasting impression on travellers arriving either by road or rail. The narrow, steep-sided valley of the Tyne was first bridged by the Romans' Pons Aelius, and the legions guarded its northern abutment with a fort. In Norman times it was refortified by a wooden stockade, which became known as the 'New Castle'. The city's prosperity developed steadily despite attacks by marauding Scots; a three months' siege by Cromwell's troops in the Civil War was only a temporary setback.

Newcastle developed first of all, like many medieval cities, on its wool trade. Later salt, lime and coal were shipped down the Tyne. Special collier ships developed to fit the needs of their destinations and were loaded from keel boats, which could operate from the shore at all but the lowest tides. The traditional song 'The Keel Row' is about these busy craft.

Newcastle upon Tyne produced engineering geniuses who met the needs of their time. There was Stephenson with his steam locomotives and his son Robert, who built bridges to carry those locomotives. Lord Armstrong, the armaments king, built a factory on the riverbank at Elswick that has only recently been replaced by the modern Vickers plant a little further upstream. Charles Parson developed the stream turbine and his graceful prototype vessel, the *Turbina*, is now on display in the Science Museum, Exhibition Park, on the Great North Road. Joseph Swan, the inventor of the incandescent light bulb, did his research and development in Newcastle. These men, and many others, forged Newcastle's prosperity, but credit for the actual building of the commercial city must go to three far-sighted Victorian planners and developers: John Dobson the architect; Richard Grainger, a builder; and John Clayton, Newcastle's Town Clerk.

Until the 19th century, Newcastle was a medieval city, altered by one of the finest examples of town planning of its day into an elegant place of solid northern buildings, and spacious streets and squares. Regrettably these developers could not foresee the traffic demands of the 20th century. Until the Scotswood Bridge upstream, the Tyne Tunnel downstream, and an inner city motorway eased the flow, a journey through Newcastle could be a nightmare. The latest traffic management scheme is the Metro, a system of partly underground electic passenger trains linking the suburbs and the redeveloped city centre.

The best way to appreciate Newcastle is on foot. There is no better place to start than the Old Quayside, the oldest part of the commercial city. Walk towards the Swing Bridge and opposite is the Guildhall, an 18th-century adaptation of Robert Trollope's design. A local architect, he built the first hall on the site of an older building in 1658, but the original is masked beneath the alterations and additions made in 1796 and 1823. Inside the Guildhall is the fine hammerbeam-roofed Great Hall as well as the Merchant Adventurer's Court, where the local merchants and dignitaries still congregate on special occasions. Across the street is a grand group of houses known as Sandhill. At the end of the street we come to Castle Stairs, which lead through the South Postern, the last vestige of the Norman castle wall.

On the right is the Moot Hall, venue of the Crown Court, and close by is the County Hall.

The Castle Keep on the left of County Hall is separated from the main gate by the London to Edinburgh railway line. The difficulties the railway developers must have had in siting Newcastle's Central Station are made painfully obvious by the squeals of steel against steel when trains round the sharp curves between the station and the King Edward VII Bridge. The Castle's structure dates from 1172, but some of the present battlements were added by John Dobson during the restoration work that followed the building of Central Station.

To the north of the castle is the cathedral of St Nicholas, dating mainly from the 14th and 15th centuries and notable for its 'Scottish crown' lantern tower, one of two survivors of this style (the other is St Giles Cathedral, Edinburgh). Entering from the north-west porch the visitor first passes a memorial to locally born Admiral Lord Collingwood, friend and successor to Lord Nelson. Moving further towards the nave, you are aware of the Perpendicular architecture and carved heads of people in medieval costume. The magnificent brass eagle lectern is early 16th century, the oldest of its kind in the North of England. Below the transept is a barrel-vaulted crypt, used in the Middle Ages as a charnel house. Returning to the main body of the cathedral, a huge painting of the 'Washing of the Disciple's Feet' dominates the rear wall of the reredos. Windows in side chapels and the east window contain fragments of medieval glass.

The short tour of the city leaves the cathedral and heads towards Central Station. Near by is Westgate road and the Stephenson Monument, a memorial to the father of the railways (1781–1848). The road continues along the line of HADRIAN'S WALL, past Neville Hall and St John's Church, and the graceful Assembly Rooms near Finkle Street. The Assembly Rooms were designed by William Newton in the style of Nash in 1774; the present use as an entertainment centre is something of a let-down for such a splendid building. West Walls, a restored section of the ancient city wall, leads to Stowell Street. Near by is the Blackfriars Centre, on the site of an ancient monastery that dated from 1239.

Further evidence of the city wall appears again and again, near Stowell Street linking Newgate Street, where Grey's Monument acts as a guide back to the city centre.

North along Northumberland street, easy on foot, but a circuitous journey by car around the one-way system, is the modern administrative and shopping centre of Newcastle. Here we have the Civic Centre and its dramatic statue of the Tyne God, together with the realistically sculptured Swans in Flight, both by the prize-winning artist David Wynal. Across Percy Street is the Newcastle University complex and some of the museums and art galleries of which Newcastle is rightly proud. Within the university buildings are the Mining Museum, the Museum of Antiquities, Hatton Gallery of Fine Art and the Greek Museum. The Hancock Museum is on the Great North Road at Narras Bridge and the Science Museum is close by at Exhibition Park on the corner of Town Moor near to Newcastle University. The castle has the Keep Museum and a Bagpipe Museum can be found in Black Gate on Castle Garth. Laing Art Gallery and the John George Joicey Museum in the city centre complete the list of major galleries and museums.

Town Moor is only a short distance north from the city centre. Each June the 'Hoppings' takes place, said to be the largest fair in the country. Freemen of the city still have the right to graze cattle on Town Moor. South across the ring road, Leazes Park and its delightful terrace of houses, built by Grainger, leads back to the city centre.

Gallowgate was where the last public hanging took place in 1844; Newcastle United's football ground gives less barbaric mass entertainment today.

Newcastle is lucky to have the geological feature of **Jesmond Dene** within easy reach of its commercial heart. The dene is a deep ravine cut through the soft sandstones of the underlying rock. It was once owned by Lord Armstrong, who gave it to the city about 100 years ago. Footpaths and a Nature Trail lead through the woodlands and along the river bank.

Industrial suburbs line the bank of the Tyne on either side of Newcastle. Upstream is Elswick, where Armstrong built his factory to produce massive guns for Britain's once mighty fleet. Its modern successor is the Vickers factory at Scotswood. Downstream are densely populated Byker and Walker, and also the start of the Tyneside shipbuilding industry. In summer it is possible to take a ferry tour of about 2½ hours' duration along the river and see shipbuilding at close hand – although today's seagoing vessels are likely to be the service equipment for North Sea oil exploration and development.

Rowlands Gill (4/3C & 7/1C) is a residential suburb of Newcastle in a wooded setting, built high above the scenic valley of the Derwent, the boundary with County Durham.

Newcastle Airport (7/1B) is 6 miles north-west of Newcastle on the A696 near PONTELAND.

Newton, *Northumberland* (4/2C) On a minor road to the east of CORBRIDGE, the place was new in 1346. The pleasant stone houses of this rural village are backed by the sheltering woodlands of Victorian Mowden and Newton Halls. Hunday National Tractor Museum is near by at Stocksfield, with a mixture of old tractors and farm machinery. Many exhibits are in working order, together with scenes of farm life and shops from bygone times. A narrow-gauge working railway completes the attractions.

Newton Aycliffe, *Co. Durham* (6/3B) This was the first of the New Towns developed in County Durham; a place of pleasant groups of houses set among wide greens and open spaces that give the town the atmosphere of a large rural village. Wide roads link the town centre to its suburbs and a spacious industrial estate close to the A167(T). The original Aycliffe and its 12th-century

Norham Castle

church, which has Saxon foundations, is on the south side, off the A167, the Great North Road; the A1 motorway lies to the east.

Newton-on-the-Moor, *Northumberland* (2/2C) Safely bypassed by the busy A1, the Great North Road, the village lies on an elevation between the rivers Aln and Coquet. It is mostly made up of single-storey cottages, one time homes of coal-miners and quarrymen. The village inn has a strange title, the Cook & Barker, apparently the names of the original proprietors. Newton Low Hall, a half mile to the north, was built in 1772 and later altered by John Dobson of Newcastle. The house is private, but the gardens are usually open twice a year under the Northumbrian Garden Scheme.

Newton under Roseberry, *Cleveland* (8/3C) The village is a cluster of houses beneath Cleveland's 'Matterhorn', Roseberry Topping. At 1051 ft the hill is the most prominent feature in the nearby landscape and was used to signal important events, ranging from the coming of the Armada to the Coronation of Queen Elizabeth II. Mesolithic and Neolithic herdsmen sheltered in safety on its summit and left behind traces of their simple technology. Throughout the centuries the hill's name has changed from Othenesberg ('Odin's hill') in 1119 to Onesburg in 1231, becoming

Osburye Toppyne in 1591, the forerunner of the modern title. Footpaths reach this airy vantage point from several directions.

Norham, *Northumberland* (1/3A) Pleasant Border village, built high above the steep southern bank of the Tweed. Grey stone cottages fit snugly on either side of a wide village green where the cross stands on a medieval base. The main street leads on towards a church which was founded in 830 by Eafrith, Bishop of Lindisfarne. He built a wooden church to hold the remains of St Ceolwulf, the converted king to whom the Venerable Bede dedicated his ecclesiastical history of England. The Norman Bishop Ranulph Flambard built the first stone church on this site. Norham was constantly under the threat of attack by Scottish raiders from across the Tweed and at one time even the church was fortified. The present building is mainly 19th century, but a number of Norman parts have survived, notably the chancel, its arch and the south arcade.

Until 1836 Norham was the capital of Norham-shire, part of the County Palatine of Durham. The bridge was built across the Tweed here in 1887, linking England and Scotland.

There is river angling for salmon and trout: enquire locally for permits and available water.

The ruins of **Norham Castle** (1/3A), set high above the river, are now maintained by English Heritage. This 12th-century castle was built by Bishop Flambard as part of the northern defences of the Palatinate of Durham. The castle faces Scotland and had to withstand many Scottish onslaughts in the 13th and 14th centuries. At one time it was considered to be impregnable, but was eventually stormed by the troops of James IV in 1513. Later returned to the English and partially repaired, the final attack came in 1530, after which it was abandoned and had fallen into decay by the time of Elizabeth I, losing its importance with the coming of more peaceful times.

The sturdy bulk of the central keep and the ruins of the castle's perimeter wall still look out over the Tweed. Open daily except Christmas and New Year.

Sir Walter Scott used the Borders for many of his romantic novels and poems. In *Marmion*, first published in 1808, he describes Norham Castle with the opening lines:

> Day set on Norham's castled steep,
> And Tweed's fair river broad and deep,
>   And Cheviot's mountains lone;
> The massive towers, the donjon keep,
> The flanking walls that round it sweep,
>   In yellow lustre shone –

North Shields

North of England Open Air Museum *see* Beamish Open Air Museum

North Shields, *Tyne and Wear* (7/2C) Fishing and industrial centre near the mouth of the river Tyne; the birthplace of the steam trawler which revolutionized the deep-sea fishing industry. The town has a modern shopping centre and a cross-river passenger ferry link with SOUTH SHIELDS. The lively early morning fish market at Fish Quay was first established by the monks of Tynemouth Priory. North Shields is also the terminus for North Sea ferries to Norway and Denmark.

North Sunderland *see* Seahouses

Northumberland National Park England's most northerly National Park, it stretches from the CHEVIOT HILLS and the Scottish border in the north to HADRIAN'S WALL in the south, and covers about 398 square miles altogether. The countryside within the park varies greatly. There is wild heather moorland interspersed by deep secluded valleys in the north that drain towards the wide Northumbrian valleys of the Rede and North Tyne in the centre. Huge man-made pine forests fill the western section. The impressive basalt formation of the Whin Sill, lined by HADRIAN'S

WALL, sits snugly within the southern boundary.

The Northumberland National Park, like all the other nine National Parks of England and Wales, was set up following a 1949 Act of Parliament. Northumberland National Park was designated in 1956. Like all the others, it does not own the land it covers, but its main duties are to safeguard the landscape; set building standards compatible with existing architecture; and encourage the public to appreciate and enjoy this unique area of natural beauty. Not only does the park authority have the duty to protect the environment, but it must be constantly aware that people live and work within its boundaries and must therefore protect these interests, mindful of the attraction created by such a beautiful area. A full-time and part-time Warden Service has been formed to help visitors to enjoy the countryside and also prevent any conflict of interests.

Three great man-made features dominate the Northumberland National Park. The largest feature by far are the extensive plantations of the Forestry Commission's Kielder Forests, which spread west from within the park. Another is Kielder Water, Europe's largest reservoir. Visitor amenities have been created in both features by the cooperation of the Forestry Commission, Northumbrian Water Board and the National Park (see Kielder). The final and most ancient feature is Hadrian's Wall, which crosses the narrowest part of England, from Newcastle upon Tyne in the east to the Solway Firth beyond Carlisle in the west. The best preserved and scenically most attractive portions of the Wall lie within the park. Once Brewed Information Centre is on the B6318, 3½ miles north-west of HALTWHISTLE; provided by the Northumberland National Park it acts as an interpretive centre for Hadrian's Wall, as well as giving local and other information about activities within the park. Housesteads Roman Fort Information Centre, further along the B6318, is jointly run by the National Park and the National Trust.

Roadside parking and picnic sites have been created on many of the scenically interesting roads in the area. The Forestry Commission's 12 miles of Forest Drive (a toll road) is between Kielder and the A68, with picnic sites and waymarked forest walks.

Miles of right-of-way footpaths crisscross the Northumberland National Park and surrounding countryside; the Cheviot Hills in the north offer challenging high-level walks for the more experienced. Organized walks, often with interpretive themes, are led by competent guides throughout the summer months, and to a lesser extent in winter. Details of the walks and other events are given on the *Discovery Walks and Trails* leaflet, available from information centres and local libraries or direct from the National Park Office. Many facilities and amenities in and around the park are accessible to the disabled: see the Northumberland National Park leaflet *A Disabled Visitor's Guide*.

Local rock-climbing areas can be found on the Whin Sill escarpment around Crag Lough and also the SIMONSIDE HILLS near ROTHBURY. Access is not always available and permission should be sought from local landowners.

Horse riding and pony trekking from local stables are both popular in the park; the wide and open nature of the countryside makes it ideal for these activities. Lists of stables and pony trekking establishments are available from the Tynedale District Council (see Useful Addresses p. 180).

Most of the rivers and reservoirs within the National Park are privately owned, but many clubs sell day tickets and Kielder Reservoir has been stocked with trout and other fish. Rod licenses are available from the Northumberland Water Authority (see Useful Addresses p. 180).

A bus service from HEXHAM to Haltwhistle by way of Hadrian's Wall operates Monday to Saturday from the end of July to the end of August.

Nunthorpe *see* Middlesbrough

Old Yeavering *see* Kirknewton

Ormesby, *Cleveland* (8/2C) A suburb of Middlesbrough to the south-east of the town centre and close to the A174, with the oldest parts on higher ground south of that road. The church is late 19th century, but medieval memorials indicate its earlier foundations. Eighteenth-century Ormesby Hall and its park, which is now administered jointly by the local authority and the National Trust, was the home of the Pennyman family from 1600. There is some excellent Adam plasterwork and an attractive stable block designed by John Carr of York.

Open to the public from April to November on advertised days.

Otterburn, *Northumberland* (4/1A) Large village situated in the broad valley of the Rede on one of the main routes into Scotland, the A68(T) DARLINGTON–Edinburgh road. It is an excellent centre for walking and fishing holidays in the area. Two 17th-century gentlemen's houses,

Otterburn Hall and Otterburn Towers, offer accommodation together with the coaching inns that earlier served traffic on the turnpike roads.

The battle of Otterburn (3/3A) was fought near by in 1388. One of the interminable Border frays, it climaxed a bitter quarrel between the Percy family of England and Douglases of Scotland. In the battle, which is commemorated by the English ballad 'Chevy Chase' and by the Scots 'Battle of Otterburn', the young Earl of Douglas was killed. Harry Percy, the Hotspur of Shakespeare's *Henry IV*, and his brother Sir Ralph were both taken prisoner, causing the rout of the English forces. The traditional site of the battle is a field to the south of Otterburn Hall, a site marked by Percy's Cross above the main road. Although parts of the cross appear to be old, it was not erected on the site until 1777. Ancient markers known as Golden Pots indicate ancient routes across the Border; they are probably Roman in origin, but local tradition insists that they were erected at places where the Earl of Douglas's body rested during its journey back to Melrose Abbey.

There has been a mill by the side of the river Rede to the south of Otterburn for at least 700 years. The present mill, renowned for its fine quality tweeds and rugs, is about 150 years old.

Ovingham, *Northumberland* (4/2C) This quiet village has stood on the north bank of the Tyne, 11 miles west of NEWCASTLE UPON TYNE, since Anglo-Saxon times.

A packhorse way once came through the village, crossing Whittle Burn, a tributary of the Tyne, by a small bridge that still stands near the Bywell road.

St Mary's Church was founded by the Augustinian canons; the tower is part Saxon, but although the interior is mostly 13th century, the rest of the building is the result of 17th- and 19th-century restoration. George Stephenson's mother is buried in the churchyard. The vicarage to the south of the churchyard is early 17th-century. Thomas Bewick (1753–1828), the famous ornithologist and engraver, was born at Cherryburn House in Ovingham; several of his exquisitely detailed drawings of birds are on display in the Hancock Museum of Natural History in Newcastle.

Ovingham holds an annual Goose Fair on the third Saturday in June, together with other traditional Northumbrian folk events. There is a caravan site on the edge of Horsley Wood about ¾ mile north-east of the village.

Padon Monument, *Northumberland* (3/3A) Access is by footpath to the north of the unclassified moorland road, 4 miles west of OTTERBURN. The monument is a beehive-shaped stone tower on Padon Moor built, according to local legend, by the followers of the Scottish Covenanter Alexander Padon who held religious meetings on the spot, in an attempt to escape persecution. Each member of the congregation, so the legend continues, carried a stone to every service until the tower was finished.

The Pennine Way, the long-distance footpath from Edale in Derbyshire to Kirk Yetholm over the Border in Scotland, passes a little to the west of Padon Monument. A good viewpoint covering the Border forests and the long line of the CHEVIOT HILLS.

Pelaw *see* Felling

Pelton, *Co. Durham* (6/3A) Mining community of rows of terraced cottages in rolling industrial countryside to the north-west of CHESTER-LE-STREET. There is a jaunty little Victorian Gothic church with tall, narrow pinnacles on its four corners, and a tiny octagonal west tower with a multi-gabled spire. The churchyard is rather large for such a small community and probably serves the needs of other villages in the district.

Perkinsville, an independent suburb of Pelton, is across the A693. It was built in the 19th century by a mine owner whose name was Perkins.

Penshaw, *Tyne and Wear* (8/1A) A straggling place of miner's cottages and red-brick estates, overlooking the woodlands of Lambton Park and an inland stretch of the Wear before it flows through its final and highly industrialized estuary at SUNDERLAND. The one-time colliery village is cut off from its twin, Shiney Row, by the A182.

The church is mock-Norman, built in 1830 and containing, of all things, a stone from the Great Pyramid of Egypt. Dominating the skyline to the north-east of the village is Penshaw Monument, a fanciful Grecian temple, built not as the Parthenon on solid rock, but on a scrub-covered hillock: as a result it looks better from afar. The monument was built to the memory of John George Lambton, the 1st Earl of Durham, in 1844. Public subscription paid for it and John and Benjamin Green of Newcastle were responsible for the design. A waymarked circular walk of about 3½ miles links Penshaw Monument to both natural and industrial archaeological features above the nearby river Wear.

Prudhoe Castle (see p. 152)

Lambton Castle is across the Wear to the west of Penshaw and Shiney Row, a green oasis hemmed in by hurrying traffic on the A1 motorway and the A182. The castle was the home of the Lambton family whose ancestor, as the folk song tells us, went fishing in the Wear instead of attending Sunday church. The song goes on to say that he caught a monstrous worm (or dragon). For reasons known only to young Lambton, he put it in a well where it grew to enormous size and terrorized the neighbourhood. Luckily for him, he was away on a Crusade while the reign of terror took place. Returning, he met a witch who told him how to kill the worm. This meant wading into the river wearing specially protected armour. Another condition was, he must kill the next living thing he saw, or 'the lords of Lambton would not die in their beds for nine generations'. His father released an old dog, hoping – vainly in the event – that this would be the first living creature young Lambton met. Although the ballad is set in the time of the Crusades, it seems to echo old dragon-slaying epics – Beowulf for example. Lambton Castle is basically a 19th-century creation, used at one time as a teacher training college. The present holder of the title lives at Biddick Hall.

Peterlee, *Co. Durham* (8/2A) Arguably the most attractive New Town in the North East. It dates from 1948 and is named after Peter Lee, who was the Chairman of the first Labour-controlled Durham County Council. The town is built in gently rolling country, east of DURHAM and a couple of miles inland from the sea. The hilly nature of the site has been used to full advantage by the planners and designers of the Development Corporation. Spacious lawns and attractively grouped housing developments, well segregated from its industry, make Peterlee a pleasant town which has quickly established its own character.

Castle Eden Dene Nature Reserve fills a narrow wooded valley about 1 mile south of the town. The area was romantically landscaped by Rowland Burdon at the end of the 18th century. Footpaths lead into the valley from Oakerside Dene Lodge Interpretive Centre.

Piercebridge, *Co. Durham* (6/3C) Small village on the site of a Roman fort guarding an important crossing of the river Tees by Dere Street, the arrow-straight road from York to HADRIAN'S WALL. Excavation of the fort has produced many relics that are on display in various museums throughout the North East, and also in the British Museum. Recent archaeological evidence has suggested that the Tees near Piercebridge was partly canalized in Roman times, giving rise to the theory that heavy goods were carried inland by barge rather than hauled by mules or oxen along steeply graded roads.

The bridge carrying the B6275 – the modern Dere Street – is built over three stately arches and dates from 1789. During the Civil War a contingent of Parliamentary troops under Lord Fairfax was routed near here by the Earl of Newcastle's Royalist forces when attempting to cross an earlier version of the bridge.

An interesting feature of the George Hotel in the main street is a grandfather clock that is said by some to be the one alluded to in Henry C. Work's song, 'My Grandfather's Clock'. It actually stopped at the very moment of its owner's death.

Pittington, *Co. Durham* (8/1A) Village north-east of DURHAM that is worth visiting for its church. The church of St Laurence stands at the end of a tree-lined cul-de-sac in the hamlet of Hallgarth. It is originally Saxon with Norman elements that include characteristically bold zigzag decoration, and some later monuments of interest.

Pity Me *see* Barrasford

Ponteland, *Northumberland* (4/3B & 7/1B) Despite its size, the town manages to convey the atmosphere of a rural village. It is now a dormitory suburb of NEWCASTLE UPON TYNE, considerably expanded by the addition of the new districts of Eland Green and Darras Hall. The main A696 follows the river Pont through the town and divides the old from the new. St Mary's Parish Church marks the true town centre, but although it dates from the 12th century, it has been altered many times. Allowing for the later alterations it is an attractive and tranquil place, especially when viewed across the riverside gardens. Opposite the church is the Blackbird Inn, a delightful blend of 14th-century defensive tower and 17th-century Jacobean manor house. Vicar's Pele is in the Main Street, a fortified rectory standing within the grounds of the Council Offices, one of a number of interesting and old buildings still preserved around the town centre.

Darras Hall suburb, across the A696 and river Pont, is a vast residential estate founded in 1910 by a group of local businessmen. Medburn village to its west is untouched by large-scale development and lies within lush agricultural land.

The Northumberland College of Agriculture is

The Octagon Room, Raby Castle (see p. 152)

The Great Kitchen, Raby Castle

about 3 miles to the north of Ponteland, based on Kirkley Hall. The hall was built in 1928 after a fire destroyed an earlier Jacobean building; an obelisk in the grounds commemorates the landing of William and Mary in 1688.

Pow Hill Country Park *see* Derwent Reservoir

Prudhoe, *Northumberland* (4/2C) Former colliery town on the A695 south of the Tyne, but now a NEWCASTLE UPON TYNE dormitory with a large modern industrial estate. The town is old despite its appearance, and had a castle to guard an important crossing over the Tyne. Built in 1173 during the reign of Henry II, the best features are the Gatehouse and a 14th-century Barbican. Castle and town frequently had to withstand attack by Scottish raiders. By the time of the Civil War, however, the castle was falling into disuse; Cromwell's troops are supposed to have damaged the tower. The 2nd Duke of Northumberland made a couple of attempts at its renovation in the early 19th century, but it was never completely lived in ever again. Currently undergoing extensive renovation, the castle is now in the care of English Heritage and open daily except Christmas and New Year.

Raby Castle, *Co. Durham* (6/2B) The A688 BISHOP AUCKLAND road skirts the eastern park boundary to the north of STAINDROP. A medieval battlemented castle, it is set in 200 acres of deer park. Seat of the Vanes and Barnards since 1626, Raby is mostly 14th century and originally owned by the Lords Neville, who forfeited it to the Crown after their disastrous support of the Rising of the North in 1569. The castle retains all of its romantic atmosphere despite the adaptations that later owners have made in the cause of creature comforts. Many of its features are original, such as the 600-year-old Great Kitchen with its collection of Victorian copper utensils. Long vaulted passageways evoke times when the castle was bustling with activity.

The castle is approached across beautiful parkland and entered through its awesome 14th-century gatehouse with its attendant guardian statues. Beyond the gate, Clifford's Tower dominates the view, enough to strike terror into any attackers. Fortunately all is now peaceful and we can walk round the perimeter walls in safety. The Octagon Tower dates from around 1840, part of the 19th-century south front, with the Baron's Hall and Drawing Room on the west front. The Neville Gateway leads towards the main house, built around 1760; the entrance is large enough to allow carriages to be driven through the hall and out beneath Chapel Tower.

Of particular note inside the castle are its medieval features, together with a fine collection of valuable paintings. Carriages and other horse-drawn vehicles in the Coach House were used by the Barnard family. Large walled gardens and ancient yew hedges are an additional link with the past. Check opening times.

Redcar, *Cleveland* (8/3B) Once a tiny fishing village, it grew rapidly when the railway reached it in 1846, bringing early Middlesbrough commuters and also holidaymakers to enjoy its golden sands. The town is unique in having a racecourse almost in its centre and thoroughbreds can usually be seen exercising close to fishing boats drawn up on the harbourless beach. Flat race meetings are held between early May and the end of October.

Amenities for the town are centred on the 9 miles of amost uninterrupted sandy beaches from the mouth of the Tees to the foot of Hunt Cliff, beyond SALTBURN-BY-THE-SEA. Inland, the town has a large modern leisure centre, a boating lake and swimming pool. The Lifeboat Museum on the sea front has as its main exhibit the *Zetland*, the oldest surviving lifeboat in the world. Built in 1800, it saved hundreds of lives on this treacherous North East coast.

Redcar's industry is well away from the town, mainly linked to harbour facilities at the mouth of the Tees. Massive iron and steel complexes, dominated by huge blast furnaces, one of them reputed to be the biggest in Europe, feature along the river. Inland, across the A1085 near Dormanstown, is ICI's Wilton chemical works.

Redmarshall, *Cleveland* (8/1C) A small exclusive village only a mile to the north-west of STOCK-TON-ON-TEES, much favoured by commuting Teesside executives.

The parish church of St Cuthbert is tucked away behind the BISHOPTON road. It is part Norman with later additions dating from the 13th and the 15th century, when the nave was restored. The attractive wooden chancel pews and altar rail are from about 1700. The effigies of Thomas de Lampton who died in 1440, and also his wife, lie in the south chapel; their home was at WYNYARD PARK to the north-east. A Victorian rectory, dominated by its tall gables, is to the east of the church. The popular Ship Inn is also near by; it dates from the early 18th century and the steeply sloping pantile roof is its most eye-catching exterior feature.

Riding Mill, *Northumberland* (4/2C) A small residential town on the south bank of the Tyne with fast road and rail links to NEWCASTLE UPON TYNE for commuters. The Wellington Inn and the Manor House are both 17th century.

Water from the Tyne is lifted, under pressure, from a nearby pumping station. It is needed to augment the stocks of KIELDER Reservoir, about 27 miles to the north-west and 700 ft above the level of the Tyne.

River angling permits are obtainable locally for day fishing or longer periods.

Ridley Hall *see* Beltingham

Rochester, *Northumberland* (3/3A) Small village much troubled by traffic speeding through along the A68 DARLINGTON to Edinburgh road, and the focal point for sheep farmers living on the surrounding moors. The village is dominated by Redesdale Camp and its varying population of army personnel. Artillery ranges and military practice areas beyond Redesdale Camp cover about 70 square miles of wild moorland and the Border heights, stretching to the north-east as far

as Windy Gyle on the Border and to OTTERBURN in the south.

Bremenium Roman fort is near by, the site marked by High Rochester farm. The fort stands on the line of Dere Street, but only parts of the west gateway and outer wall can be traced with any ease.

Rock, *Northumberland* (2/2C) Small agricultural village set back from a pleasant green on a minor road between the B6347 and B1340, about 5 miles north of ALNWICK. The compact church dates from the Norman period, but was considerably altered in the 19th century; the apse is designed by Anthony Salvin. Rock Hall, now a Youth Hostel, is built around the remains of a 14th-century peel tower. Very much altered by subsequent owners, it was originally the home of the Proctors, who were agricultural pioneers and developed a system of using turnips in winter for cattle fodder. The last owners before the YHA were the Bosanquets.

Probably the greatest excitement the village has seen was when the army of Charles I camped at Rock on its march north towards Scotland in the First Bishops' War.

Rokeby Park, *Co. Durham* (6/2C) A magnificent Palladian house built in 1735 by the dilettante and amateur architect, Sir Thomas Robinson, MP, known locally as 'Long Sir Tom'. The park was enclosed and laid out a few years later. Rokeby's pride and joy is Velazquez's *Rokeby Venus*, now in the National Gallery in London, but many other paintings and a unique collection of needlework by Anne Marritt (1726–97) are on display in the compact main buildings. To the east of the house, 14th-century Mortham Tower is glimpsed through the trees. It was the original home of the Rokeby family, but most of the tower and its Tudor additions are in ruins.

Rokeby has been owned by the Marritt family since 1769 and is open Monday and Tuesday from May to September. The house and park can be reached from the A66, 3 miles to the south-east of BARNARD CASTLE.

Romaldkirk, *Co. Durham* (6/1B) Village about 5 miles north-west of BARNARD CASTLE along the B6277. One of the prettiest villages in Teesdale, it takes its name from St Rumwald who built a church there in Anglo-Saxon times. Set in a green and pleasant landscape above the river Tees and backed by rolling moorland, the village is a delightfully haphazard grouping of stone-built cottages around a series of greens and narrow alleyways. The rectory is Georgian and the church a mixture of styles dating back at least to the 12th century.

Roads to the west lead to Baldersdale and Lunedale, with a series of reservoirs, backed by miles of wild moorland.

Rookhope, *Co. Durham* (5/3A) Remote village in Rookhope Dale, a side valley of Weardale. The valley road leaves the A689 at EASTGATE. It is difficult to imagine that Rookhope was once an industrial village, the central point for a large lead- and ironstone-mining area. The straggling village has lost the smelter that once stood at Lintzgarth, to the west of the village (the 'foreign'-looking Lintz- is just an odd form of 'links'). The chimney flue was almost 2 miles long, climbing to poison the surrounding vegetation on Redburn Common.

A railway carried the ironstone and climbed high across Stanhope moors, but it is now a mere cinder track, barely recognizable in places. The line was hauled out of Rookhope Dale by a system of cables, over Horseshoe Hill northwards to

The font, Rothbury Church (Photo by N. Eddershaw)

CONSETT. In its day it was the highest standard-gauge line in the country.

West of the B6278 STANHOPE to EDMUNDBYERS road, the railway is used as the Waskerley Way cycle, footpath and bridle track (*see also* Derwent Walk Country Park). Where mining and smelting once existed, nature is covering the shattered remains with coarse grasses and heather.

Rothbury, *Northumberland* (4/2A) A small residential town on the north bank of the river Coquet, one of the most picturesque settings in Northumberland. The town is favoured by its sheltered position and is built on a series of natural terraces above the river. Easy access to the CHEVIOT HILLS and the NORTHUMBERLAND NATIONAL PARK has naturally lead to the town's development as a holiday resort. Wooded hills to its north shelter Rothbury from all but the harshest winter storms.

To the east, the Coquet flows through a narrow gap called the Thrum, which is dominated by Lord Armstrong's CRAGSIDE.

The town developed in the late 13th century, but it has roots reaching further into the past. Ancient cairns and settlements dot the surrounding heights and Christianity came early to the area. In the church a 17th-century font stands on a beautifully carved red sandstone cross shaft dating from around the beginning of the 9th century (the head is in the Museum of Antiquities, NEWCASTLE UPON TYNE). The cross, possibly made from a pre-Christian standing stone, was found when the church was rebuilt in 1850. The two broad faces of the shaft are carved, one with an Ascension scene, the other with a design of Saxon meshed knot weave. On the narrow faces the Fall of Man is depicted on one side; the reverse shows writhing serpents devouring animals and trapping a naked figure, and speaks of the Anglo-Saxon view of Hell. The town supported the Jacobite cause and the proclamation of James III was read in the market square in 1715. Below the church a medieval bridge, much altered by subsequent widening, still carries the B6342 over the Coquet on its triple arches.

New Town Park, below the SIMONSIDE HILLS south of the town, was enclosed by Robert Rogerson in 1275 as a deerpark. Although occasional wild roedeer can still be seen, little now remains of the wall surrounding this once extensive preserve, except for sections that appear between Lordenshaw and Tosson. Across the Coquet an old peel tower stands in Tosson village to the west, and another is at Whitton, directly above the racecourse. The tower, now Rothbury rectory, was once used as a safe haven in time of attack by Scottish raiders.

Steeplechase meetings are held on the riverside racecourse in the valley bottom, where there is also a golf course and a picnic site.

The area offers many short – or long – walks. Some, using the natural terraces on the northern hillside, wander between Rothbury and the neighbouring village of THROPTON. Across the valley Simonside Hill (1408 ft) is an easy climb by way of a track that starts at Great Tosson and ascends through forest to Raven's Heugh (1385 ft) to reach the summit of Simonside.

There is a National Park Information Centre in the main street of Rothbury. Caravan sites at Whitton, to the south at the top of a steep hill, have reasonable access.

Rowlands Gill *see* Newcastle upon Tyne

Ryhope, *Tyne and Wear* (8/1A) A colliery village 3 miles south of SUNDERLAND on the A1018. It grew inland as any seaward spread was prevented by the coast-hugging Sunderland to HARTLEPOOL railway line. The village has one of the finest monuments to Victorian engineering ability in the North East. Ryhope Pumping Station, designed to lift water from below the ground, is about a half mile inland along the Warden Law road. Superseded now by reservoir supplies further inland, it no longer provides drinking water for the area. Situated inside a huge Gothic hall, its two massive beam engines, dating from 1868, have been carefully restored and operate most weekends throughout the summer. A small museum on the site shows the development of pumped water supplies throughout the ages.

Ryton, *Tyne and Wear* (4/3C & 7/1C) A pretty place despite being near to Tyneside's heavy industry. Standing high above the south bank of the Tyne about 6 miles west of GATESHEAD, the small town has grown southwards from its church, which itself appears to have been built on a site of antiquity even older than Christianity. Broach-spired Holy Cross Church dates from the 13th century and is built in the Early English style. Its pride is the Jacobean woodwork of the chancel screen and oak stalls.

Ryton Willows lies below the town and to its north, part of the **Tyne Riverside Country Park** where a bankside path may be followed for about 2 miles up and downstream. It takes in NEWBURN, THROCKLEY and WYLAM. Massive Stella

Power Station is to the east; its twin is on the opposite bank of the Tyne.

Sacriston, *Co. Durham* (6/3A) Mining community of Victorian terraces and modern housing estates in industrialized country to the west of the A167, between CHESTER-LE-STREET and DURHAM. The unusual name links it to its medieval ownership by the sacrist (the official who kept the sacred vessels) of Durham Cathedral; an old farmhouse at Sacriston Heugh marks the site of the medieval manor house.

Sadberge, *Co. Durham* (8/16) The village is on rising ground a little to the north of the busy A66 DARLINGTON–STOCKTON-ON-TEES road. Wide-ranging views cover the rolling agricultural land between the two big industrial towns. Sadberge was once the centre of a wapentake that stretched from MIDDLETON IN TEESDALE to SEATON CAREW on the coast. (Wapentakes were originally local assemblies that ruled areas of Viking-settled territory; later the areas themselves – corresponding to the 'hundreds' further south.) Its one-time importance is commemorated by a stone on the tree-surrounded village green in honour of Queen Victoria's Jubilee, describing her as 'Queen of the United Kingdom, Empress of India and Countess of Sadberge'. The title is not imagined and dates from the Middle Ages. The church, as befitted a medieval capital, developed early, but only a few fragments remain, incorporated within the fabric of the present building, which dates from 1831. The stones that now feature as part of the south porch were found in a section of the walls of a Darlington public house, but how they got there can only be left to the imagination.

St John's Chapel, *Co. Durham* (5/3A) This is the 'capital' of upper Weardale on the A689 and was once important as a lead-mining centre. Its full and ancient title is St John Weardale. The squat church tower of St John the Baptist looks out over a tiny village green where the diminutive classical town hall is backed by streets of irregularly grouped stone houses and inns. The church was founded in 1465, but the current building dates from 1881. The quiet atmosphere of the place is misleading, for there are important and regular cattle and sheep markets. An agricultural show and music festival, both held once a year, are the major events on the local calendar. The anachronistic organization known as 'The Association for the Prosecution of Felons and other Offenders', a kind of vigilante group, was founded in the

The lighthouse, St Mary's or Bait Island

district to combat sheep stealers and cattle rustlers, in the days before organized police forces. Happy to leave law and order to the proper authorities, the association is now an excuse for an annual get-together of local worthies.

The tiny hamlet of Daddry Shields, half a mile downstream, was once an infamous place where cockfighting took place, but it is now a tranquil, totally law-abiding group of pretty whitewashed stone cottages.

St Mary's or **Bait Island**, *Tyne and Wear* (7/2B) Offshore island connected to the rocky mainland by a short tidal causeway between WHITLEY BAY and SEATON SLUICE. The 126 ft high lighthouse, erected in 1897–8, stands on the site of a monastic cell where traditionally the sanctuary light once acted as a guide for inshore vessels. The island is the haunt of sea birds and is visited by grey seals; its rocks make an excellent vantage point for sea angling.

An interesting 1½-mile-long coastal path from Curry's Point, opposite St Mary's Island, follows the sandstone cliffs as far as Seaton Sluice. Curry was a murderer who was hanged on a gibbet at this point in 1739.

Saltburn-by-the-Sea, *Cleveland* (8/2A) The town sits on a high sandy cliff overlooking miles of golden sand and the North Sea. Saltburn grew during the era of Victorian prosperity and developed rapidly following the arrival of the railway in 1861. Trains deposited holidaymakers literally in the entrance of the Zetland Hotel.

Very much a 'superior' resort in its time, it was planned as one of the leading watering places in Britain, with the deep-cut ravine of Riftswood marking a sort of frontier beyond which ironstone miners from nearby villages were forbidden to pass. The wooded valley has an Italianate Garden and secluded footpaths leading towards the seashore, where a miniature railway and playing fields are a more up-to-date innovation. In more prosperous times a narrow elevated footbridge, known as the Halfpenny Bridge from the cost of its toll, crossed the valley; sadly it became a liability a few years ago and was demolished. At the opposite end of the promenade, another wooded ravine, Hazel Grove, more natural than Riftswood, is again followed by an easy footpath.

Saltburn has the only pier on the North-East coast; once 1400 ft long, it has been reduced to its present 600 ft by storm and accidental ramming in 1924 by a ship, the *Ovenberg*. Saltburn's other unique feature is the Inclined Tramway opposite the pier entrance. It is the successor to a rickety, hoistlike structure, built in 1870 to lift passengers 150 ft from the promenade to the town. The original and potentially lethal structure of wood and guy ropes was demolished in 1883 and replaced by the present water-operated tramway.

The oldest and still recognizable part of the town is centred on the group of cottages that are now incorporated as part of the Ship Inn beneath Cat Nab. Once it was the haunt of smugglers whose activities, despite the watchful eye of the Excisemen, brought illicit supplies of wines and spirits into Cleveland. There was a Roman signal station on Hunt Cliff above Cat Nab; later, its last occupants were murdered by Vikings. Coastal erosion has claimed its site, but a plaque on the present clifftop describes the building.

The Cleveland Way is a 93-mile long-distance footpath which follows the western and northern edge of the North York Moors from Helmsley. Travelling along the Cleveland escarpment above GUISBOROUGH, it joins the coast at Saltburn and follows it as far as Filey Brig.

Brotton, a rather sprawling, overgrown village, lies south-east of Saltburn at the junction of the A173 and A174 coast road, and has a mix of old ironstone miners' cottages and modern housing.

Satley, *Co. Durham* (6/2A) Rural village with one street, on the B6296 LANCHESTER–WOLSINGHAM road. The church is Victorian, but medieval stones in its west wall indicate its much earlier foundations. Hall Hill Farm, along the B6296 to the north-east of the village centre, is open to the public and stages demonstrations of farm skills and crafts according to the season. Steeley Burn flows through a deep, wooded ravine to join the river Browney below the village.

Scremerston, Northumberland (2/1A) Quiet, semi-rural village, thankfully bypassed by the A1(T) and now a suburb of BERWICK-UPON-TWEED, a little over a mile to its north. There was once a coal mine to provide work for the male inhabitants of Scremerston, but it closed some time ago.

During the Great Plague, villagers afflicted with the disease were taken out on to nearby moors and left to their fate.

The coastal nature reserve at Far Skerr can be reached by way of a minor road through the hamlet of Borewell Farm. Saltpan Rocks, between the reserve and Borewell Farm, are probably where salt was made by evaporating sea water.

The pier, Saltburn-by-the-Sea

Seaham, *Co. Durham* (8/2A) Seaham, or Seaham Harbour as it is more usually known, developed in the 19th century to fulfil the need for a convenient harbour to ship Durham coal to markets in London and on the Continent. The foundation stone of the harbour was laid in 1828 and the collier the *Lord Seaham* carried the first cargo of coal 3 years later. At first coal was carried on horse-drawn railways, but later on steam took over. Coal has been a major part of the life of the inhabitants of Seaham and the Vane-Tempest mine is one of the oldest in the district. Terraces of miners' cottages and more modern council estates march inland away from the sea. The peeling stucco of run-down shops in the town centre tells of the declining fortunes of the place.

Most of the inland collieries are closed, worked out or uneconomical; the few remaining mostly exploit reserves beneath the North Sea. The price coal exacts in terms of lives was never more apparent than after the dreadful disaster of 1880, when 164 miners and 181 pit ponies lost their lives. A more recent tragedy to hit the town occurred when the lifeboat capsized and lost its entire crew in 1962.

The church of St Mary the Virgin is over 900 years old and is linked to the original and oldest part of the town. Seaham Hall, on the northern outskirts, used to be owned by the Milbanke family and later by Lord Londonderry, the coal magnate, but it is now a hospital. Seaham Hall also has links with the poet Byron – for it was here he met and married Isabella Milbanke in 1815.

The town is not all grime and industry; it has a number of pleasantly laid-out public parks and open spaces, as well as the long stretches of firm sandy beaches that line the coast. Sea angling is a popular sport in the area, both beach casting and from inshore boats. There is an annual angling 'All Comers' competition held each autumn.

Seahouses, *Northumberland* (2/2B) Holiday and fishing village built on a headland south-east of BAMBURGH. The village did not exist until the harbour was built in 1889 in order to improve the local fishing industry. There is still an appreciable fishing fleet working out of the harbour, and most visitors utilize it to reach the nearby FARNE ISLANDS. Amenities include a yachting and skin diving centre, good beaches on either side of the headland and a well-varied shopping centre. Close by the harbour is the Information Centre, where details and landing tickets for trips to the Farne Islands can be obtained.

Now linked with Seahouses, the older village of **North Sunderland** became something of a backwater when the harbour was built, but it contains many attractive stone cottages.

Seaton Carew, *Cleveland* (8/2B) A former fishing village to the south of HARTLEPOOL that once had hopes of becoming a highly select holiday resort, the northern equivalent of Littlehampton or Bognor Regis. Rows of colourful fishermen's cottages, and attractive Regency and later 19th-century houses, line the sea front and the modest village green. Despite the nearness of industry, the village retains its air of a failed, but still genteel watering place. Miles of wide sandy beaches make it a popular place for a day out from MIDDLESBROUGH.

Seaton Sluice, *Northumberland* (7/2B) Despite the occasional sprawl of bungalows and modern estates inland, this little seaside town remains a pretty place; its red-roofed cottages have appeared on many an artist's canvas. The finest building in the town centre is the Octagon, attributed to Vanbrugh.

The tiny harbour to the north explains why 'Sluice' appears in the name of the town. Coal was mined as far back as the Middle Ages and in due course it was found necessary to construct a harbour on this unprotected coastline. First built in 1628 it frequently silted up, until a cut was made through the solid rock of the sea cliff in the 1750s, to enable Seaton Burn to keep the harbour clear by a sluicing action. Built originally as a port for exporting coal – once it even had a glass

Left: Boat, Seaton Sluice   *Opposite: Seaton Sluice*

industry as well – Seaton Sluice is now a fishing and holiday resort.

A mile inland on the A190 is **Seaton Delaval Hall**, a masterwork of Sir John Vanbrugh, architect of many fine houses throughout the North. It was built in Palladian style for Admiral George Delaval, whose family claimed direct descent from William the Conqueror. Little thought was given to the cost of building this showpiece. Huge Tuscan columns support the portico of the central block and ornate wings project on either side, one being the stables. Twice damaged by fire in 1725 and in 1882, the house fell into disuse. However, its present owner Lord Hastings, a descendant of the Delavals by marriage, has spent a considerable amount of time and effort on its restoration. A Norman church, developed as the family chapel but now used as the parish church, stands in the grounds. House and gardens are open Wednesdays, Sundays and Bank Holidays throughout the summer from May to September.

Seaton Delaval (7/2B) is a colliery town 2 miles inland from the coast at the crossroads of the A192 and A190. Like many of the towns of the Northumbrian coalfield it is striving to attract other industries as an alternative to coal.

Sedgefield, *Co. Durham* (8/1B) This small market town of pantiled cottages and pleasant modern houses fits in the angle of the A177 DURHAM road and the A689 BILLINGHAM to BISHOP AUCKLAND, with lush open country on all sides. Its rural aspect is confirmed by a racecourse on the other side of the A689 from the town. Industrial Teesside, although only a matter of a few miles away, has little or no effect on this quiet place. Even the busy A689 has the grace to bypass it to the south.

St Edmund's Church is 13th century, an impressive example of the Early English style, and overlooks the town centre. The tower was built in the 15th century as a gift by Robert Rhodes, a local philanthropist. The font and memorial brasses commemorating local families are particularly interesting. Sedgefield is one of the few towns in the country to hold a traditional Shrove Tuesday football match, a contest far removed from the modern game. A town walk explores the byways and old buildings and is described in *Walkabout Booklet No 7: Sedgefield*, which is produced by Durham County Council.

The grounds of Hardwick Hall – a 16th-century house with a fine 18th-century front – were landscaped by John Burdon in 1748, on the site of the medieval manor of *Herdewyk*. The park with lake covering 36 acres, a temple of Minerva, as well as follies and a grotto, are all that is left of a grandiose scheme that ran out of money before it was finished. Hardwick was saved from oblivion by Durham County Council and is now a Country Park with a Bog Nature Trail.

Segedunum *see* Hadrian's Wall

Shaftoe Crags *see* Bolam Lake Country Park

Sherburn, *Co. Durham* (8/1A) Village on the B1283, 2½ miles east of DURHAM. It grew rapidly in the 19th century to serve the local colliery. In medieval times it was the site of a leper hospital, founded by Bishop Pudsey in 1181. Later, in 1434, the hospital became an almshouse, altered in the 18th century to become the pleasant group of almoners' houses and master's house, to one side of a grassy quadrangle off the main street.

Shildon, *Co. Durham* (6/3B) Small industrial town on the A6072, a little over a mile to the south-east of BISHOP AUCKLAND. The town grew with the fortunes of the Durham coalfield; and it was the need to move that coal that gave Shildon its place in the story of the birth of the railway system. As the Industrial Revolution reached its peak, coal was in such heavy demand that traditional horse-drawn transportation soon became inadequate. The railway pioneer George Stephenson was invited to build track from Witton Park, via Shildon and DARLINGTON, to the harbour facilities at STOCKTON-ON-TEES. Originally intended to move only coal, the line was so successful that following the demands of the local population, fare-paying passengers began to be carried. The first passenger train, hauled by Stephenson's *Locomotion Number One*, ran on 27 September 1825, beginning its journey from a point close to the home of Timothy Hackworth in Shildon. The first intrepid passengers had to travel in open coal trucks without any protection from the elements, or flying sparks and grit from the engine.

Hackworth was one of the lesser-known founding fathers of the railway system and built the *Sans Pareil*, one of the first engines to be made, which predated Stephenson's more famous *Locomotion Number One*. His home is now a museum and linked by the Surtees Trail to many of the still recognizable features of the original railway. The trail runs from Hackworth's Soho Engine Works to Daniel Adamson's Coach House, the Shildon terminus of a second branch of the Stockton & Darlington Railway. A working replica of *Sans Pareil* stands outside the Soho Paint Shop.

Further relics of the birth of the railway age can be found along an unclassified road to the west linking Shildon with the A68. These are the stone sleepers on the Brusselton Incline, an important section of the original route of the Stockton & Darlington Railway.

A mile to the south-east of Shildon, and in a remote situation, stands Middridge Grange, a 17th-century farmhouse, once the home of the Cavalier, Colonel Anthony Byerley.

Simonburn, *Northumberland* (3/3B) North Tyne village north-west of HEXHAM, on a side road off the A6320. White-painted homes of workers are on the nearby Nunwick House Estate, and older buildings cluster around a large green in this delightful place.

Nunwick House, a private dwelling, is of red sandstone and dates from 1740, reputedly to the design of William Adam, but with later alterations by Bonomi. The garden is famous for its alpines and herbaceous gardens, as well as semi-formal woodlands, and is open to the public on advertised dates.

Simonburn Castle is about three quarters of a mile to the west of the village in the middle of a wood. The ruins of the 14th-century tower house can be reached by a public right of way which starts opposite Burn House.

St Mungo's, the village church, is 13th century, but was rebuilt in the 18th and 19th centuries; its floor slopes towards the altar and gives an indication of its great age. The rectory dates from 1866. A side road opposite the entrance to Nunwick House, about a quarter of a mile beyond Simonsburn, leads towards Wark Forest (*see* Wark). The road passes Ravensheugh Crags along the way and also the enigmatic Goatstones, a stone circle. One of the four stones bears cup markings dating about 1600 to 1000 BC.

Simonside Hills, *Northumberland* (4/2A) A group of round-topped heather-clad hills to the south of ROTHBURY. Access is from a side road off the B6342. Red sandstone crags mark the upper contours of the higher summits (the highest is 1408 ft). Gentler slopes of the moors south of the highest point are covered by conifer plantations known as Harwood Forest.

Access to rights of way and footpaths are from Great Tosson, near Rothbury, or from west of Lordenshaw Farm.

Skelton, *Cleveland* (8/3C) The central village of an elevated complex along the A173 based on ironstone mines. Its population increased dramatically during the boom of the 1800s, and miners' cottages mix haphazardly with older buildings from Skelton's agricultural past. The last operating Cleveland ironstone mine was at North Skelton and only closed a few decades ago. Most of the village is built about 300 ft above sea level and as the land falls steeply away to the east, there are fine views of the North Sea about 2 miles away. William the Conqueror granted Robert de Brus I land in Cleveland and Skelton Castle was the family stronghold. It was rebuilt as a castellated mansion in 1794. The Brus, or Bruce, family were important in English and Scottish affairs in the Middle Ages – Robert the Bruce, King of Scotland, being the most notable. The castle is now the home of the Ringrose-Wharton family; the grounds are open once a year on Daffodil Sunday (variable, but advertised).

An old well and village cross remain, from days when Skelton held a village fair every Sunday in the local churchyard. The church is late 19th century, but replaced one much older.

Skinningrove and **Carlin How**, *Cleveland* (8/2A) Twin industrial villages on the coast north of LOFTUS and the A174, and lining the deep ravine of Kilton Beck before it enters the sea at Cattersty Sands. Their history is linked to the ironstone mines now featured in the Tom Leonard Mining Museum. Named in memory of a local journalist and run by a private trust, the museum is attached to a former drift mine and explains in detail the 'boom-and-bust' life of the Cleveland ironstone industry. Access is from the minor road leading towards the sea from the A174 at the bottom of Loftus Bank.

The scene is dominated here by the hilltop steelworks at Carlin How, where the workforce has been drastically cut and production is confined to special profile steel. It is the only working link with more prosperous times, when ore and finished steel were shipped from the jetty at Cattersty Sands, 240 ft directly below the works.

Cobles on the beach show that the tradition of industrial workers in the North East being spare-time inshore fishermen is still alive here.

Many names in Cleveland derive from the numerous Viking settlements: Cattersty means '(Wild) cats' path'; Carlin How 'Old women's, or witches' hill'.

Snitter *see* Thropton

South Shields, *Tyne and Wear* (7/3C) The town grew around the Roman fort of Arbeia, built at the mouth of the Tyne as part of the seaward defences, and as a supply base for HADRIAN'S WALL, in the 2nd century AD. Modern South Shields developed partly as a colliery town, but also as a Victorian holiday resort, taking advantage of the sandy beaches of Littlehaven and Sandhaven on either side of the southerly twin piers protecting the entrance to the Tyne.

Victorian terraced houses built over the Roman fort have mostly been demolished. Meticulous excavation of the fort has discovered within its walls the foundations of buildings, now carefully preserved and identified as to their original purpose. Roman stones reclaimed from redundant churches and farms in the area have been used to reconstruct the imposing main gate. A simple, but well-laid-out museum on the site has a number of important exhibits – tombstones taken from the site of the nearby Roman cemetery, and many well-preserved household and military objects.

The town has another museum in Acland Road, devoted to South Shields' more recent past. Other interesting buildings and memorials in the town range from the Old Town Hall and Market Square, near Church Way, to the ornate 'new' Town Hall built in 1903. A preserved lifeboat is in Ocean Road, close to Marine Park, a memorial to Henry Greathead and William Wouldhave. They were the co-inventors of the first purpose-built lifeboat, the *Original*, in 1790. A model of the *Original* is in the South Shields Museum. Mill Dam, on a riverside site below the town, was originally a 'job creation' scheme for soldiers returning from the Napoleonic Wars. It developed into a riverside crossroads for traffic and a 'job centre' for seamen seeking work. There was a Customs House and launching ramp here, together with an impressive Port Health Authority Office and ship's chandlers, pubs and waterfront buildings. Between 1960 and 1978 the site fell into disuse, with many buildings, including the Customs House, either being demolished or ready to fall down. Joint schemes, led by the South Shields Borough Council and the Arts and Live Music Association, have restored the site. Today its remaining buildings retain much of the character of bygone times when the river was busy with sail-powered traffic.

Westoe Colliery is close to the centre of South

Marsden Rock, South Shields

Shields, a high-production pit that extends far out under the North Sea. Westoe Village has a number of interesting Georgian and Victorian houses, including the birthplace of Sir William Fox, Prime Minister of New Zealand between 1869 and 1873. The coast south of the mouth of the Tyne is sandy at first, but this soon gives way to high limestone cliffs, the haunt of sea birds. The rocks were laid down about 240–250 million years ago and form a distinctive sequence of strata, ranging from soft buff-coloured limestone, through magnesium-rich layers containing fossils of snails and other molluscs, to a band of hard, grey crystalline limestone. Several 'stacks', or isolated rocks, with Marsden Rock the most prominent, are nesting places for a wide range of sea birds and the whole area is classified as a site of special scientific interest. Constant erosion by the sea makes the cliffs dangerous and they should not be climbed. *Take heed of warning notices.*

Marsden Bay (7/3C) is a popular beach, reached by way of steps from the car park at Velvet Beds. The Grotto, an unusual and unexpected public house and restaurant, is built into the cliffs of Marsden Bay. It was hollowed out in 1782 by a local character, Jack the Blaster, who made a home for himself and his family. Subsequent owners extended the cave dwelling into a 15-roomed house. The red and white-striped lighthouse on Lizard Point marks the southern limits of Marsden Bay.

Spennymoor, *Co. Durham* (6/3B) A sprawl of Victorian houses and modern tower blocks off the A688 to the north-east of BISHOP AUCKLAND. The town developed in open country during the early 1800s to service local coal mines. St Paul's Church (1878) was destroyed by fire in 1953, but has been very pleasantly restored and now stands in a landscaped churchyard.

Hett (6/3B) is a mix of old and new houses around a village green, on a side road off the old Great North Road, north-east of Spennymoor. There are views of Croxdale Hall and its delightful orangery across the London–Edinburgh main railway line.

Staindrop, *Co. Durham* (6/2C) An attractive place of mellow stone houses on either side of a long green, the home village to RABY CASTLE.

The tall-towered village church includes Norman and later elements; narrow, now blocked-off windows speak of its Saxon antecedents. The screen is pre-Reformation, the only one in County Durham. The Lords of Raby are buried

Tomb of the 1st Duke of Cleveland, Staindrop Church

here in splendid tombs: Nevilles in the south-west corner of the church and Vanes in the north-west. The Nevilles lost Raby Castle following their support for the Rising of the North in 1569 and it was bought by the Vanes in 1626. Sir Henry Vane, son of the original purchaser, held Raby for Parliament during the Civil War but later went on to oppose the execution of Charles I. Regrettably, this did not save him from revenge after the Restoration, for he was tried as a traitor and executed in the Tower of London. Staindrop House, a mellow sandstone building on the narrow street leading towards the church, is mostly Jacobean.

Stainton, *Cleveland* (8/2C) A peaceful dormitory village in a lightly wooded setting to the south-west of MIDDLESBROUGH. Older cottages and attractive gardens enliven the modern developments. The parish church of St Peter and St Paul is 19th century and built in the Early English style, but with a 15th-century tower and possibly older sections. The Pennyman family made Stainton their home before moving to Ormesby Hall (*see also* Ormesby).

Stamfordham, *Northumberland* (4/2B) The elongated village of Georgian terraced houses is built around an exceptionally long green above the river Pont. There is a preaching cross dated 1736, and a gaolhouse. The 13th-century church stands at the western side of the village with its part Tudor, part 18th-century vicarage on the opposite side of the river.

Stamfordham, on the B6309 north of HADRIAN'S WALL, is a conservation area and rightly proud of the number of times it has won the county's annual Best Kept Village competition. A Whit Monday fair is held on the village green.

Stang Forest *see* Barningham

Stanhope, *Co. Durham* (6/1A) Small town on the A689 marking the boundary between pastoral Weardale and the wild heather moors to the west. Founded on lead mining, Stanhope is not only an important market town for the surrounding dales and farms, but also the administrative centre for life in upper Weardale. The oldest part of the town sits back from an irregular-shaped square with its ancient market cross. The western end of the square ends abruptly with the rather incongrous battlements of Stanhope Castle. A country gentleman's house rather than a fortified residence, it was built for Cuthbert Rippon, MP for Gateshead, in 1798 on the site of a much earlier castle. Despite its unattractive appearance from the town, it looks very striking from the river. The house has had a chequered career; once a school, it has now been converted into flats. Across the square, the parish church of St Thomas is a much more interesting building. Dating mainly from the 13th century it contains a Roman altar dedicated to the woodland god Silvanus, which was found on Bollihope Common in 1747. The church also has several pieces of medieval stained glass. A fossilized tree stump holds pride of place on the church wall. Found beneath the moors near EDMUNDBYERS, the tree would have looked like a giant mare's-tail plant, growing in the swamplike conditions that covered the area 250 million years ago.

Seventeenth-century Stanhope Old Hall is to the west of the town. Its solid bulk has the appearance of an old mill, probably due to some of the older windows being filled in in the days when a window tax was levied on property. Down a side road, past the swimming pool and across a pretty ford to the south of town, is the strangely named Unthank Hall. An Elizabethan manor house, its name (from an Old English word meaning 'without leave') indicates that it was held by squatters at one time – but when is not known, as the house has been in the ownership of the Maddisons, an ancient Weardale family, for many generations.

Heathery Burn Cave, above the town, was the location of important Bronze Age finds.

The 'battle' of Stanhope took place in 1818 when a group of lead miners, held in the town gaol after being caught poaching by the Bishop of Durham's keepers, were rescued by a group of their friends.

Going westwards and following the wooded banks of the Wear upstream, you come to a 15th-century bridge that carries the road to Teesdale across a narrow gorge. After heavy rain the water level can rise with alarming rapidity. Industry around Stanhope now is mostly quarrying and fluorspar mining.

There is an annual show held the second weekend in September.

Stanley, *Co. Durham* (6/3A) An industrial town of modern housing estates on a bleak hilltop between CHESTER-LE-STREET and CONSETT. The town surrounds a pedestrian shopping precinct and huge windowless supermarket, and an indoor sports complex. Just inside the gateway to the East Stanley cemetery, there stands a sombre granite memorial to 168 men and boys killed in the West Stanley Colliery explosion on 16 February 1909. This was one of the worst disasters in the history of British coal mining.

The surrounding countryside is being grassed over and landscaped as the spoilheaps from opencast mining are removed. Opencast mining is also carried on at neighbouring Annfield Plain.

Harperley Country Park and a caravan site are above the wooded valley of Kyo Burn, on the western outskirts of Stanley.

Stannington, *Northumberland* (7/1B) Pleasant village built both sides of the A1 on gentle slopes to the north of the river Blyth. The church tower rises above a wooded valley and makes a landmark for travellers along the Great North Road. An attractive riverside and woodland walk through Stannington Vale leads along the north bank of the Blyth from Stannington Bridge, eastwards into Plessey Woods Country Park.

Blagdon Hall is 1½ miles south of Stannington. The house was built in 1735, but has been altered over the years, most recently by Sir Edwin Lutyens, who also designed the present gardens. Gardens and park open on advertised days.

Stockton-on-Tees, *Cleveland* (8/2C) There has been a market at Stockton since medieval times and the town developed as a port in the 18th century. You can still find traces of the old warehouses and narrow riverside alleys off the spacious High Street, close by the Green Dragon Yard. Exhibitions of the history of the district are frequently staged at the Green Dragon Gallery and the Georgian Theatre.

It was the railway era that brought almost overnight prosperity to the town, an event usually linked with the opening of the Stockton & Darlington Railway in 1825, the world's first fare-paying passenger steam railway. The old ticket ofice in Bridge Street has been preserved as a museum commemorating the historic railway. Modern Stockton is a mixture, not always comfortable, of old and new. The Town Hall and Market Cross both date from the mid-1700s, but even though they and the parish church are of similar age and make an attractive group, the town tends to be dominated by its tower blocks, its mad whirl of ring roads and complex river crossings.

Stockton has changed radically over the years. At one time it had a castle, the property of the Bishops of Durham during the Middle Ages. Also disappeared are the colourful and often notorious dockside taverns from the town's heyday as an important port. Even though the High Street is an impressive feature, where Georgian façades can still be traced above modern shop fronts, the town centre has been redeveloped on modern lines. There is an excellent sports complex near by, with Ropner and Preston Parks providing open spaces within the boundaries of the town. Shops and houses of bygone Stockton have been collected and rebuilt in the open air museum at Preston Hall. Indoor pavilions are set out with displays ranging from toys to sewing machines and horse-drawn transport.

Stockton has produced its notables – people like John Walker who invented the humble but essential friction match, and died without having taken out a patent. Thomas Sheraton, designer and maker of fine furniture, was born in Stockton in 1751, but he moved to London while still a young man to make his fame and fortune.

Elton (8/1C) is a largely suburban village on the outskirts, south of the A66. Elton Hall, former home of the Ropners, looks Queen Anne, but is in fact of this century and used as offices. The church is a Victorian reconstruction of a Norman building. Its interior is noteworthy, especially the colourful rood screen.

Hartburn (4/2B) is now a residential suburb of Stockton, but the village is avoided by the busy A66 and so retains much of its 17th- and 18th-century charm. Stockton Castle stood near by, but was demolished in the late 17th century, its stones 'recycled' in some of the old houses. Pleasant farmland and streams to the west mark the boundary of town and country.

Stonehaugh, *Northumberland* (3/3B) Purpose-built Forestry Commission village based in Wark Forest. Access is by a remote side road across Broadpool Common, north-west of CHOLLERFORD. Public amenities include a caravan and camp site together with forest walks that include the Warksburn Forest Trail.

The Pennine Way crosses the village access road near Ladyhill, where totem poles, the whimsical creations of local forestry workers, make an amusing diversion. South of the forest the Way passes Comyn's Cross, erected by a Scottish family who owned lands near by in the 13th and 14th centuries. One of their members, John Comyn the Red of Badenoch, was murdered by followers of Robert the Bruce in 1306 when they met at Dumfries in order to settle who was to be the Scottish king.

Streatlam Park, *Co. Durham* (6/2C) Ancient castle and park about 2½ miles north-east of BARNARD CASTLE on the A688 STAINDROP road. The name is pronounced 'Streetlam'. A castle and grand three-storeyed mansion once stood in the park, built around a 15th-century peel tower. Originally this was the seat of the Bowes family, but it fell into disuse after 1922 and was sadly demolished in 1927.

The remaining features of Streatlam, as seen from the road, are the elegant 18th-century gates and twin lodges made in the Classical style, the original entrance to the park.

Sunderland, *Tyne and Wear* (7/2C) Once the largest shipbuilding town in the world, a town that grew around three villages on the banks of the river Wear: **Monkwearmouth**, **Bishopwearmouth** – and Sunderland, from which the town took its name. The first two developed on monastic lands between the 10th and 13th centuries, but Sunderland did not even have the status of a parish until 1719. It grew on land originally 'sundered', or taken, from the monastic estates of Monkwearmouth.

With the coming of the Industrial Revolution, and the need to move coal by sea, the town expanded and soon began to specialize in ship-building. However, following the decline of shipbuilding, Sunderland has come to rely more on the special technology required for oil exploration in the North Sea, as well as marine and heavy engineering. Covered slipways have replaced open-air methods of shipbuilding.

Downstream, twin curved stone piers protect the harbour mouth, a popular spot for sea angling, and the inshore rescue lifeboat is based on the north side below the Roker pier. Sandy beaches stretch either side of the estuary; those to the north are the best and most accessible. Two bridges cross the Wear to take traffic between Southwick, Monkwearmouth and the town centre in Sunderland. Queen Alexandra Bridge is upstream, built in 1909 originally as a double-decker, carrying both road and rail. It makes a good viewpoint for the modern shipyards around Pallion and Southwick. Wearmouth Bridge was opened in 1929 and spans the river with massive steel arches carrying the road south into the now modernized town centre. The centre is built around the sturdy late Victorian and Edwardian commercial heart of the town, where even older Georgian town houses can still be recognized.

St Peter's Church, founded in AD 674 and linked with the Venerable Bede's monastic life, is Sunderland's oldest building. Today it stands in a green oasis on the north side of the river at Monkwearmouth. Originally part of a monastery, the oldest part of the church is in the west end and is probably Saxon. The chancel is 14th century and the rest of the church 19th century.

As would be expected in a town whose growth and development was due to the Industrial Revolution, there are several imaginative museums relating to Sunderland's past. Grindon Close is furnished with Edwardian rooms and ship interiors. Monkwearmouth station has been reopened as the Museum of Land Transport. This was where the 'Railway King' George Hudson, at one time Member of Parliament for Sunderland, brought a branch of the Newcastle railway into the town. The station has been faithfully restored as it was in its Edwardian heyday. Sunderland Museum and Art Gallery in Borough Road has collections of local interest, including models of ships built in the yards here. The North East Aircraft Museum is at Sunderland Airport and has a collection of post-1945 British and foreign planes. Pride of place is given to a Vulcan bomber on external display, together with an internal exhibition of engines and special aircraft parts dating from 1908 onwards.

The Edwardian opulence of the Empire Theatre has been preserved and is now run as a Civic Theatre by a locally sponsored trust. A preserved windmill at Fulwell, by the side of the road to NEWCASTLE UPON TYNE, is the only complete survivor of many that dotted the North East. The remains of 15th-century Hylton Castle are on the western outskirts of the town and consist mainly of the impressive gatehouse tower. The castle was probably a simple rectangular structure. Built by William de Hylton, it is haunted, or so they say, by the 'Cauld Lad of Hylton'.

The Civic Centre stands opposite Mowbray Park. Designed by the Sir Basil Spence, Bonnington & Collins Partnership, it is built of hexagonal blocks and surrounds open courts. Sports facilities in the area range from sailing and waterskiing to indoor amenities at the Crowtree Leisure Centre, and a dry ski slope on reclaimed colliery land at Silksworth.

Tanfield, *Co. Durham* (4/3C & 7/1C) A pleasant haven of rural tranquillity in an otherwise industrial landscape, Tanfield is west of the A6076 where it runs north from STANLEY. The hillside village church is originally 10th century with later alterations; memorials within are to several of the owners of nearby Beamish Hall. Eighteenth-century Tanfield Hall stands immediately to the east of the church and is guarded by elaborate wrought-iron gates.

A preservation society operates the Tanfield Railway in the valley below, and near by is the Causey Arch, the oldest surviving rail bridge. Approach the latter from the A6076, or by a linking footpath from the BEAMISH OPEN AIR MUSEUM.

Thornaby-on-Tees, *Cleveland* (8/2C) The town is now an industrial suburb of MIDDLESBROUGH and STOCKTON-ON-TEES, but officially part of the former. What is left of the original village surrounds a wide green, watched over by its 11th-century church of St Peter ad Vincula, and is now a conservation area. The Green farmhouse is of the 18th century at the rear, but its front dates from the 19th. Sundial House has the date 1621 displayed on its front wall.

Thornaby was originally known as South Stockton, and the town's expansion came when it was linked to Stockton-on-Tees by a bridge in 1771 – at that time the most seaward bridge over the Tees. The 1840s was the time of its greatest expansion, when a glass bottle factory, ironworks and shipyards all opened in rapid succession. In the late 20th century the town continues to spread amid a chaotic jumble of dual carriageways and flyovers. Redevelopment is going on in the area around the railway station and an old Royal Air Force site, to provide space for the new industries taking over from out-of-date shipyards and steelworks. A modern town centre has replaced old industry with new department stores, hotels, and a large sports and social centre called the Pavilion.

Stockton racecourse is on flat land in a triangle formed by the A66, A19 and A1130.

Thorpe Thewles, *Cleveland* (8/1B) The village lies north-west of STOCKTON-ON-TEES and is bypassed by traffic on the busy A177 DURHAM road, so it is an ideal commuter dormitory for Teesside. Two excellent public houses in the village take their names from local colliery and landowning families: the 17th-century Vane Arms and 18th-century Hamilton-Russell Arms. Part of the track of the old Stockton to SUNDERLAND railway line north of Thorpe Thewles has been converted into a long-distance footpath and cycle way, known as the Castle Eden Walkway. The walkway has a number of cuttings that hold snow in winter and has become a popular cross-country ski track when conditions permit.

Throckley, *Tyne and Wear* (7/1C) A dormitory suburb of NEWCASTLE UPON TYNE about 6 miles west from the city centre and set high above the north bank of the Tyne. The small town has good views of the industrial lower reaches of the river. Throckley's main street runs along the line of HADRIAN'S WALL, and houses and shops south of it are actually built over the Vallum. Small sections of both wall and Vallum can still be seen east and west of the town.

The Tyne Riverside Country Park stretches along the banks of the river between WYLAM and NEWBURN, providing waterborne activities and several miles of riverside paths. One such footpath is the Wylam and Walbottle Wagonway, which follows an old railway line associated with George Stephenson and William Hedley.

Thropton, *Northumberland* (4/2A) Pleasant little village above the river Coquet, 2 miles west of ROTHBURY. The village is divided almost equally by the Wreigh Burn, a tributary of the Coquet, crossed by an ancient narrow humpback bridge. Short riverside footpaths and a footbridge over the Coquet can be used to make a delightful exploration of both sides of the village.

Tynemouth Priory (see p. 169)

Thropton Tower, a 15th-century fortified house, stands in the village not far from the attractive 18th-century coaching inn. The church is fairly modern, but worth visiting if only to see the three-arched screen that separates the chancel from the nave.

Oddly named **Snitter** is a hamlet on a steep grassy spur between Wreigh Burn and Back Burn, 1 mile north of Thropton. Snitter Mill used the water of Back Burn to power its wheel.

Tillmouth Park, *Northumberland* (1/3A) A country mansion built in 1822 on the banks of the Till, a large tributary of the Tweed. It is now used as one of the Tweed's leading angling hotels.

The Till is crossed by the single sweeping arch of Twizel Bridge in the north-east corner of the park. Built in 1450, the bridge became a turning point in the battle of FLODDEN FIELD in 1530. The Earl of Surrey's English artillery was allowed to cross the bridge in full sight of the Scottish forces, and as a result dominated the northern flank of James IV's army. The battlefield is about 3 miles to the south, above Branxton village.

On top of a high bank some 200 yd downstream

The Collingwood Memorial, Tynemouth, from North Shields

of the bridge, Twizel Castle's Norman-style ruins date only from the late 18th century, but are built on the site of an older fortification, destroyed in 1496 by James IV, during his attack on Northumberland in support of Perkin Warbeck. A small abandoned chapel near by is said to be one where the remains of St Cuthbert rested on his long journey around the North of England.

Tockett's Mill *see* Guisborough

Tow Law, *Co. Durham* (6/2A) An industrial and former mining town at the junction of five roads on a bleak hilltop in a rural setting south-west of DURHAM. Terraced houses line its long straggling streets, and also those of the curiously named suburbs of Inkerman and Dan's Castle. The local coal mines are worked out, as is the iron ore that once fed the blast furnaces of nearby CONSETT – a town that, like Tow Law, is also struggling to recover from the loss of its life blood.

The church is worth visiting if only to see the delightfully artistic screen made of fir cones, acorns, walnuts and chestnuts, designed and put together by the Reverend Thomas Espin (1888–1934), who also built himself an observatory in the vicarage garden. He was something of an authority on astronomy.

Trimdon, *Cleveland* (8/1B) Three separate mining villages within a mile or so of each other have Trimdon as part of their name. The main village contents itself with plain Trimdon. Off the B1278, about 4 miles north of SEDGEFIELD, it has a wide main street rising to a medieval church, but the rest of the village is mostly modern estates. Trimdon Colliery to the north-east is red brick, but Trimdon Grange, west of it, is more rural.

Tynemouth, *Tyne and Wear* (7/3C) Resort and residential town, where the elegant Georgian and Victorian houses line the central streets and squares above the north bank of the Tyne. On the headland by the river mouth, Tynemouth Priory, once a kind of penitentiary for recalcitrant monks, occupies the eastern cliffs. Linked to it on the shoreward side is a castle, built in the late 13th and 14th centuries to defend priory and rivermouth; the gaunt ruins are now in the care of English Heritage. There is a museum in the recently reopened powder magazines near the ancient fortifications, which were manned by gunners of the oldest volunteer artillery unit in the British army.

Admiral Lord Collingwood's massive statue looks out on shipping leaving the shelter of the Tyne. It is surrounded by guns from the *Royal Sovereign*, flagship at the battle of Trafalgar.

The Volunteer Life Brigade's Headquarters in the nearby Watch House contains relics of ships wrecked along the coast, some as close as on the Black Middens, a vicious skerry below the priory. A short riverside path leads from Collingwood's statue to Fish Quay, originally built by monks from the priory, who founded the local fishing industry. Wooden Dolly, a statue commemorating the local Cullercoats fishwives, originally stood in a passageway leading to the quay, but is now the central point of Northumberland Square in the town centre. Smith's Dock, further upstream, is the largest ship repair dock on the Tyne.

Tyne Riverside Country Park *see* Ryton

Upleatham, *Cleveland* (8/3C) The village is part of the ironstone region which follows the north-facing escarpment of the Cleveland Hills. It never developed as much as its neighbours during the 19th-century mining boom, and as a result has returned more easily to its rural origins. Stone cottages, which give the village its character, look out across the wooded valley of Skelton Beck towards 18th-century Skelton Castle and its parkland (*see* Skelton).

The village church of St Andrew's is said to be the smallest in England. Only 17 ft 8 in by 13 ft, it is part of a larger 12th-century building which had a battlemented tower added in 1644. The main feature inside the church is its attractive 12th-century font.

Ushaw Moor, *Co. Durham* (6/3A) Not a moor, but an industrial village above the Deerness Valley, in a low moorland setting to the west of DURHAM. The abandoned railway along the wooded Deerness Valley has been converted into a footpath. It starts near Billy Row at CROOK and joins the Bishop Brandon Walk, another converted railway track, at the Broompark picnic site near Neville's Cross, between Ushaw Moor and the southern outskirts of Durham.

Vercovicium; Vindolanda *see* Hadrian's Wall

Wall, *Northumberland* (4/1C) The oldest part of Wall is hidden from the main A6079 HEXHAM to Jedburgh road by later development. The original village is a glorious cluster of tiny greens and charming dwellings, an ideal centre to use when exploring HADRIAN'S WALL. The orginator of this timeless tourist attraction has been commemorated in the name of the local inn.

Wall village

Wallington Hall, *Northumberland* (4/2B) Stately home and parkland, bisected by the B6342, to the west of MORPETH. It is owned and maintained by the National Trust together with an estate covering 12,970 acres. The house was built in 1688, but greatly altered in the 1740s. Its interior has fine rococo plasterwork by Italian craftsmen and there is porcelain, needlework, furniture and a collection of doll's houses displayed in rooms ranging from the early Georgian saloon to a late Victorian nursery and kitchen. The central hall, dating from the mid-19th century, was designed by John Dobson of NEWCASTLE UPON TYNE and is decorated with Pre-Raphaelite wall paintings. Outside is a walled garden, with a conservatory specializing in fuchsias, and a coach museum, Chinese pond, lakes and woodlands. 'Capability' Brown began his professional career here. Grounds open all the year; the house on certain days between April and October.

The central hall, Wallington Hall

Wallsend, *Tyne and Wear* (7/2C) An industrial town on the north bank of the Tyne concentrating on heavy engineering and shipbuilding; most of the industry is centred upon the Swan Hunter yards. It was from here that the *Mauretania* first entered the water, an opulent passenger liner which held the Atlantic Blue Riband for 23 years in the heyday of transatlantic crossings.

The name Wallsend refers, quite literally, to its position at the eastern end of HADRIAN'S WALL. Originally the wall only went as far as Pons Aelius, modern NEWCASTLE UPON TYNE, but it was found to be strategically necessary to extend the wall to combat seaborne attack. Little remains of the Roman fort of Segedunum, but it is possible to trace the line of the wall in Richard Dees Park, and also the outline of a tower in a reclamation site not far from Willington Quay.

Wallsend had its own collieries. 'A' Pit, now capped off, was notoriously dangerous and 666 ft beneath the town centre.

Most of the terraced streets of tightly packed

The exterior of Wallington Hall

houses, each with its outside lavatory, or 'netty', have gone, to be replaced by modern estates and tower blocks. The revamped High Street is still the shopping heart of Wallsend, and busy pubs cater for the thirsts of shipyard workers.

The AI takes a wide sweep to the east of Wallsend, missing out Newcastle and GATES-HEAD. A tunnel beneath the river carries its traffic between Howdon Pans and JARROW. To the north the road joins the route of the original AI at WIDE OPEN, and to the south at Birtley.

Walworth, *Co. Durham* (6/3C) Scattered village in gently rising countryside to the north-west of DARLINGTON. King James VI of Scotland stayed at Walworth Castle, on his journey south to London and his eventual coronation as James I of England in 1603. The round towers and once-mullioned windows are of a castle built more for comfort than defence. Dating from around 1600, it was built for Thomas Jennison, Auditor-General for Ireland. South-facing round towers at the corner of the three-storeyed central block give the castle a feeling of strength, and the lower

wings surround a courtyard where Doric and Ionic columns support the spectacular north wall of the main building. The courtward was completely enclosed in the 19th century. Owned throughout its life by many of the leading families of the area, whose monuments feature in the church at HEIGHINGTON, the castle is now part of a special school run by Durham County Council.

Warden, *Northumberland* (4/1C) The secluded hamlet north-west of HEXHAM fits into the confluence of the North and South Tyne, on a side road off the A69. The wooded slopes of High Warden Hill rise above the village and its sandstone summit, 587 ft above sea level, is crowned by an extensive Iron Age fort. The village church is Saxon and Norman, dating from 1050, but incorporates many Roman stones taken from nearby HADRIAN'S WALL.

Boat Side Inn marks the bridge over the South Tyne. To the west is one of the oldest papermills in the country – it dates from 1763.

Wardley *see* Felling

Wark, *Northumberland* (3/3B) The tree-lined B6320, a delightful valley road, follows the North Tyne upstream through lush pastureland. The feature you see on entering this pleasant village of attractive cottage gardens is a steep grassy bank, all that remains of a Norman motte and bailey. The fortification was part of the general defences of northern England, built to prevent southern movement by the unsubdued Scots.

Wark on Tyne – to give the village the full name sometimes used to differentiate it from its namesake on the Tweed – was once the capital of Tynedale, a part of Scotland in the 12th and 13th centuries. The rest of the village spreads from a crossroads surrounded by a pleasant green. A 16th-century farmhouse by the village green is now the curiously named Battlesteads Inn.

Quiet roads to the west lead into Wark Forest, where there are footpaths and picnic sites close to STONEHAUGH, a Forestry Commission village.

Wark-on-Tweed, *Northumberland* (1/2A) Tranquil village on the south bank of the Tweed where the scant remains of a 12th-century motte-and-bailey castle once controlled an important Border river crossing. Guarding a frontier that was rarely peaceful, it has to withstand frequent attacks and sieges by the Scots, and in 1541 it was being described as 'a jewel of noysance' (nuisance).

According to popular legend, in 1346 it was defended by the beautiful Countess of Salisbury and Edward III hurried north to her aid. After successfully driving off the Scots, the king was entertained to a victory ball by the countess. It was during this ball that she lost her garter and the king nobly retrieving it, fastened it to his own leg and uttered the now famous words, 'Honi soit qui mal y pense' (Evil be to him who evil thinks), words that were subsequently to become the motto of the Order of the Garter.

In 1018, the Scots under Malcolm II defeated an English army in open and bloody combat at Carham in a riverside field about a quarter of a mile east of Wark.

Warkworth, *Northumberland* (2/3C) An ancient fortified town within a tight loop of the river Coquet and near its mouth. A modern bridge carries traffic into Warkworth across the river, but does not detract in any way from the beauty of its ancient predecessor a few yards upstream. The twin-arched medieval bridge with its stone guardhouse is only open to pedestrians and makes the best entry into the town. Warkworth is built on a rocky spur and mellow stone buildings line Castle Street, which leads by way of the market square to the still dominant castle.

Warkworth Castle dates from the 12th century, but its stone-framed windows speak of habitation in more settled times. The Percys, who used it as their home until the late 17th century, were responsible for the improvements to the castle. A tall slender central watchtower looks out over the surrounding plain and the sea, still guarding against long-vanished enemies. Warkworth Castle, a singularly splendid ruin, is maintained by English Heritage. Open daily except Christmas and New Year.

The parish church of St Laurence, a fine example of Norman architecture, reputedly built on 8th-century foundations, has a 14th-century stone spire, a rarity in Northumberland. A mile-long pathway follows the steep-sided valley beneath the castle and leads to a hermit's cell carved from the sandstone cliff. In use until the 16th century, the Hermitage has a vaulted ceiling and scenes from the Passion carved into the rock. There is a golf course near by, and a sandy beach, picnic site and a caravan park to the north-east complete the attractions.

Washington, *Tyne and Wear* (7/2C) A New Town created in 1967 and still developing, intended to attract industry into a declining colliery area. In this respect the town has been a success, bringing to it names such as Dunlop, Nissan and the DHSS. The town plan deliberately segregates motor vehicles from pedestrians and, as a result, Washington can be a little confusing to a first-time visitor. Signposts direct motorists to areas described as District No. 3 or District No. 4, none of which can be seen from roads that are mostly confined to cuttings. However, once away from the road the pattern becomes clear and instead of an impersonal town of up to 80,000 inhabitants, each district has developed its own self-contained village atmosphere. Most of the well-designed houses are set in green fields on high ground above the river Wear. Streams and trees have been preserved in an attempt to create natural settings whenever possible, all adding to the maturity of the town.

Washington is built around the unspoiled nucleus of the old village, where 17th-century Washington Old Hall, a National Trust property, has become a place of pilgrimage to visiting Americans. 'Old Glory', the Stars and Stripes of the United States of America, is flown from the

Warkworth Castle

flagpole in front of the hall, proclaiming a doubtful link between Britain and America. The Hall was certainly owned by the Washington family until the 13th century, but there is no proof that George Washington ever visited the town. He lived at Sulgrave in Northamptonshire before emigrating to America. Despite these rather tenuous historical links, Washington Hall is worth visiting in its own right. Mainly a Jacobean manor house, it has some excellent panelling and an oak staircase. Parts, especially near the kitchen, date from the original 13th-century house. Souvenirs of George Washington are on display in rooms set aside for the purpose.

Mining has completely vanished from the area; the only relic is 'F' Pit Mining Museum, to the north of the town and signposted from the A1231. The original shaft was sunk in 1777, making this one of the oldest working pits in the country before it closed in 1968. The winding house and steam engine have been preserved.

Washington Wildfowl Park, an important sanctuary on reclaimed industrial land, is off the A1231, east of the town. It has an interesting collection of wildfowl in a natural setting of 100 acres of ponds, lakes and woods on land sloping to the river Wear. As well as the resident flock, migrants are now making regular visits. Comfortable hides, some suitable for wheelchairs, make it possible to view the birds at close quarters.

Waskerley Way *see* Derwent Walk Country Park

Westgate *see* Eastgate

West Hartlepool *see* Hartlepool

West Rainton, *Co. Durham* (8/1A) There are in fact two Raintons, East and West, divided by the boundary between Tyne and Wear and County Durham. Apart from an open field or two, it is impossible to separate these colliery villages, whose livelihood depended on the east Durham coalfield for many years.

Sir George Elliot, a local lad who made good, was made Member of Parliament for North Durham in 1868. On his return from working as financial adviser to the Khedive of Egypt, Sir George presented the church here with a lump of granite from the Great Pyramid.

West Woodburn, *Northumberland* (3/3A) Straggling village to the side of the A68 and linked with its neighbour, East Woodburn, by a quiet lane following the south bank of the river Rede. Habitancum Roman fort is near by, to the east of a bend in Dere Street. Most of the line of the Roman road is followed by the modern A68, but inexplicably it bypasses Habitancum in a wide dogleg to its east. The fort was one of the first outposts north-west along Dere Street from HADRIAN'S WALL, a day's march from Corstopitum, modern CORBRIDGE. Regrettably, little of the fort can be seen apart from the mound now standing on private land. A Roman milestone has been re-erected to the north of the village and marks the boundary of the NORTHUMBERLAND NATIONAL PARK. It stands close to the junction of the A68 and the minor road that crosses Corsenside Common on its way to Hareshaw Head.

Whalton, *Northumberland* (4/3B & 7/1B) An agricultural village of light-brown houses beside wide grassy verges, where a number of houses, including the rectory, are built around peel towers. The manor house was originally four houses until they were converted into a single dwelling by Sir Edwin Lutyens in 1908. Its gardens were designed by Gertrude Jekyll. The village is designated as a conservation area.

The village church of St Mary is unusually wide for its length. It is Norman in origin, but most of the building dates from the 13th century and was restored in 1908.

Whalton is one of the few places in Northumbria to light a bale fire on Midsummer's Eve. The massive bonfire is probably a link with the pagan past of the Anglo-Saxons and Vikings.

The rural hamlet of Ogle lies 2 miles to the south of Whalton; Ogle Castle is a Victorian restoration of a 15th- to 16th-century manor house, built on to a 14th-century tower house.

Whickham, *Tyne and Wear* (4/3C & 7/1C) Residential and industrial satellite of NEWCASTLE UPON TYNE, built on a steep hillside above the Derwent valley, close to the river's confluence with the Tyne. Across the frantic roar of traffic rushing along the A69, allotment gardens on vacant land near the power station at Derwent Haugh are an island of Tyneside tranquillity. Giant leeks and gooseberries the size of plums, grown by secret methods, are the speciality of Geordie gardeners who, when the time comes round for the annual shows, guard their prize specimens night and day.

The Metro Centre, Tyneside's largest shopping complex and hypermarket, is on the GATESHEAD side of the A69.

Whitburn, *Tyne and Wear* (7/3C) Neat and tidy coastal village, between SOUTH SHIELDS and SUNDERLAND, with a sloping green surrounded by houses of character and a spacious main street. Whitburn is mostly residential since its colliery closed. The church with its narrow buttressed tower is Early English, dating from the 13th century, but with later addition and restoration.

Whitburn Hall stands enclosed in its own gardens south-west of the town centre. It contains a mixture of styles from the 17th century onward.

Lizard Point, 1 mile to the north of Whitburn, is marked by a red and white candy-striped lighthouse. The foreshore is rocky to past Souter Point, but gives way to the sandy beach of Whitburn Bay, south of the village.

Whitfield, *Northumberland* (3/3C) Secluded village in a woodland setting on a side road off the A686, about 6 miles south-west of HAYDON BRIDGE. Whitfield Hall is mid-18th century, but is probably built on the site of an older structure. The village church dates from 1860 and stands close to the northern boundary of the hall. There is access to both from the A686.

Interesting moorland roads offering wide-ranging views in all directions lead out of Whitfield. There is a caravan site at Low Haber to the south across the West Allen river.

Whitley Bay, *Tyne and Wear* (7/3B) The holiday resort and residential town has completely swamped the old fishing village of **Cullercoats**, but fishing boats are still drawn up along the sandy shore. The sands attract holidaymakers or day trippers from nearby industrial areas who come to enjoy the bracing sea air, or spend their money in the Spanish City amusement park. Promenade gardens and sea angling complete the relaxing amenities. The town supports its own ice hockey team, the Whitley Warriors. The view northwards from the promenade below the town centre is of the graceful crescent of Whitley Sands, as far as the prominent white lighthouse on ST MARY'S ISLAND.

The town is old despite its holiday atmosphere. It was founded in the 6th century AD and was certainly established by 1100, when Henry I gave its lands to Tynemouth Priory. Coal led to further development inland, and was shipped from the 'staithes' or jetties at Cullercoats.

Washington Old Hall (see p. 172)

Inland the urban sprawl covers Monkseaton and Shiremoor, and continues almost without a break through Longbenton to NEWCASTLE UPON TYNE itself.

Whittingham, *Northumberland* (2/1C) Small village to the west of the A697 and divided in two by the river Aln. The northern half follows the river on either side of the church. This dates from the Saxon period, and although some work still remains from that time, the church was rather spoiled by over-zealous Victorian 'improvements' made in 1840. A peel tower, Whittingham Tower, across the road from the church, has been converted into almshouses. 'South' Whittingham is across the Aln, a pretty group of houses arranged around its village green. The village holds an annual Games and Fair each August, a popular event for the surrounding area.

The Whittingham Sword, one of a number of Bronze Age weapons discovered at Thrunton Farm to the south-east, is now in the Bagpipe Museum in NEWCASTLE UPON TYNE.

Whorlton, *Co. Durham* (6/2C) Terraced cottages and attractive gardens feature in this riverside village on the north bank of the Tees. The hall and church are Victorian. From the village a hairpin bend descends to a suspension bridge (built in 1829) across the river Tees, making the road through the village a link between the A67 and A66, east of BARNARD CASTLE. A riverside lido and picnic site are situated in wooded grounds on the south bank opposite.

The village is first mentioned as *Queorningtun* in documents dating from 1050. Its church of St Mary has Saxon foundations, but the present structure was built in 1853.

Widdrington, *Northumberland* (7/2A) Quiet village on the A1068, just inland from Druridge Bay. It had its own castle until 1775, when it was dismantled and the stone used locally as building material. To the east lie the ruins of the extensive preceptory of St John of Jerusalem.

Widdrington village was once a much larger place, as witness the isolated church; the old village is now rather superseded by its modern industrial counterpart, a mile or so to the south-west beyond the fireclay works.

In the late 17th century a French privateer anchored in Druridge Bay and a landing party, led by a Jacobite called Thetford, pillaged Widdrington, but thankfully did not venture inland.

The Nature Reserve, Witton-le-Wear

Wide Open, *Tyne and Wear* (7/2B) A suburb of NEWCASTLE UPON TYNE, to the north of the city, the central of three adjoining overspill areas. Its neighbour, Brunswick Village, is across the A1 and Seaton Burn, the oldest of the group, is to the north. The A108 Tyne Tunnel feeder road intersects the A1 about a half mile to the north. Woodland and water link the town to agricultural land beyond the A1. Big Waters Nature Reserve has a 4½-mile nature trail and the circuit of the lake is approached across the A6125, by a signposted road from Seaton Burn.

Wilton, *Cleveland* (8/3C) A small 'estate' village of pleasant cottages off the A174 east of MIDDLESBROUGH. It is centred around Wilton Castle, once the home of the Bulmers, defenders of the North against the Scots.

The present castle was built in 1807 by Sir John Lowther. It is now the property of Imperial Chemical Industries and used as the company's Teesside administrative headquarters.

The church is dedicated to St Cuthbert and was originally built in the 12th century, but 'improved' in the 19th. Effigies of two long-dead Bulmers decorate the porch. Several interesting old buildings are near by, despite intrusions by

the Middlesbrough commuter belt: 17th-century Lackenby Hall has some fine mullioned windows; Lazenby farmhouse was built in the early part of the 19th century and is now a private residence.

Winlaton *see* Blaydon

Winston, *Co. Durham* (6/2C) Charming village above the tree-lined rocky banks of the river Tees. The parish church of St Andrew, though partly rebuilt in the 19th century, is mostly 13th century. Inside is an unusually designed medieval font with carvings of dragons fighting each other. Memorial brasses feature in the nave. Aaron Arrowsmith (1750–1823), the international cartographer, came from Winston.

The Tees below the village is spanned by a single stone-arched road bridge. When it was built in 1764 it was the longest of its kind (111 ft) in Europe. A mile west along the A67 DARLINGTON–BARNARD CASTLE road Stubb House, a handsome building dating from 1750, is hidden among trees at the end of a long drive and is now a school run by Durham County Council.

Witton Gilbert, *Co. Durham* (6/3A) The 'G' in Gilbert is pronounced soft, as in 'ginger'. The village, north-west of DURHAM, developed in the

19th century as a mining community above the river Browney and was built on medieval foundations. The church has a double belltower and was rebuilt in 1863. Even so, it retains much that links it with its Norman origins, especially on the south side of the nave and in the chancel. The Hall was once a leper hospital, traces of which still remain, including a 13th-century window.

A mile or so beyond the village, and in dense woodland to the north of the Burnhope road, lie the sad ruins of Langley Hall. This was a 16th-century courtyard house built by Lord Scrope of Bolton, but abandoned by his descendants in the 18th century.

Witton-le-Wear, *Co. Durham* (6/2B) A village of great character and antiquity built around a narrow green on a south-facing slope above the river Wear. A peel tower, part of a medieval manor, is at the upper end of the village and dates from less peaceful times. The church is 13th century, but it was rebuilt in the early 1900s.

Floodplains and woodland around the river Wear to the east have been designated as a Nature Reserve, haunt of both woodland birds and waterfowl.

Witton Castle across the Wear from the village is a mix of additions, but the 14th-century keep, built by Sir Ralph de Eure, is the original portion. There is an attractive camping site and a caravan park within the grounds.

Witton Park, to the south-east, is a run-down industrial hamlet that grew in the 19th century around a coal mine.

Wolsingham, *Co. Durham* (6/2A) Small industrial town in central Weardale, a mixture of old stone cottages and modern developments in a rural setting. One or two buildings are of special note: namely the 18th-century Whitfield House, a three-storeyed town house with an almost French provincial air; and next to it, and in complete contrast, is Whitfield Place, a 17th-century building with attractive mullioned windows. The tower of the parish church is 12th century, otherwise the main body is mid-Victorian in Early English style.

Wolsingham holds an annual show in the first weekend in September, which is quite an ambitious affair for such a small town. There is fishing in the Wear (brown as well as migratory trout and salmon). Tunstall Reservoir, 2 miles to the north of Wolsingham, is stocked with brown and rainbow trout. Rod licences and day permits are available locally.

Wolviston *see* Billingham

Wooler, *Northumberland* (2/1B) Market town serving the rich pasturelands and moorland farms north of the CHEVIOT HILLS. The quiet atmosphere of Wooler belies its turbulent history. Built between its river, Wooler Water, a tributary of the Till, and the massive flanks of the Cheviots, it sits astride one of the ancient routes into England. Warring Scots and Border reivers (cattle thieves) came this way on their forays into England, and the English in their turn marched northwards in revenge. In more settled times an important drove road passed through, along which cattle, sheep, and even geese, were walked south to feed the burgeoning populations of the industrial centres of the North and Midlands, or even London. Today, Wooler is a market town where cattle and sheep from the nearby moors and dales are brought for sale and moved on to their ultimate destinations by lorry. Some of the lorry drivers will be related to the cattle drovers of old.

Wooler is a good base for walking in the Cheviot Hills. Walter Scott stayed near by in a small cottage at Langleeford in 1791, building up his knowledge of the Borders. There is salmon and trout fishing in the Till and tributary burns: enquire locally for permits and for information about available waters.

People have lived around Wooler for thousands of years: prehistoric fortresses on top of Harehope Hill and on Earle Whin, and other hillforts in the area, are mute testimony to long-dead lifestyles.

Despite its ageless appearance, Wooler has no buildings of great age, as the town was twice destroyed by fire, once in 1722 and later in 1862; few if any buildings are older than 19th century. Friendly market town pubs line the streets in the central area and the shops cater mostly for local needs. There is a permanent display of the history and geography of the area at the Cheviot Field Centre and Museum in Padgepool Place, Wooler, and an Information Caravan is permanently sited in the bus station.

Middleton Hall (1/3B) is not a stately home but a tiny hamlet just south of Wooler. To reach it, follow Cheviot Street from Wooler town centre.

There is a sheltered picnic site beside a small pond, where there are usually families of waterfowl.

Wylam, *Northumberland* (4/2C) Small town on the north bank of the Tyne 10½ miles upstream of NEWCASTLE UPON TYNE. The railway age can claim Wylam as its true birthplace, for it was here in 1813 that William Hedley built his *Puffing Billy* to haul coal from Wylam Colliery to a pierhead at Lemington Staithes, 4 miles down the Tyne.

Stephenson is, of course, the better known of the two pioneers. He was born at Wylam, in a cottage a mile to the east of the town. The cottage still exists and is a National Trust property, although it is not open to the public. Stephenson went on to build his *Rocket* and later *Locomotion Number One*, which hauled the first passenger-carrying trains. His only son Robert was the designer of the Royal Border Bridge at BERWICK-UPON-TWEED. He and Stephenson's nephew, George Robert, became great civil and locomotive engineers, designing bridges and tracks to carry the new form of transport all over the North. The railway no longer runs through Wylam; the town that saw the birth of steam locomotion has to make do with the more modern line following the south bank of the Tyne.

The Wylam and Wallbottle Wagonway follows the track of the old railway through the Tyne Riverside Country Park.

Wynyard Park, *Cleveland* (8/2B) This 19th-century mansion is in rolling countryside barely 2 miles north of the conurbation of STOCKTON-ON-TEES and BILLINGHAM. Wynyard was the home of the Marquises of Londonderry, descendants of the Vane-Tempest-Stewarts, one of the big colliery-owning families in the North East. The house, park and farmland are sheltered from public gaze by cleverly planted mature woodlands along the minor road linking the A177 to the A689.

The present house was erected in 1841, under the supervision of Ignatius Bonomi and John Dobson, Wyatt's 1822 design having burned down; but there has been a manor house on the site since the Middle Ages. It is built on the grand scale: a six-columned Corinthian portico dominates an entrance that leads to great and sumptuous galleries and the state room. The latter overlooks Wynyard's formal gardens, from whose terrace a lake winds towards woodland.

Royalty and men and women of power and high society have visited Wynyard Park. At the highest point in the park an obelisk commemorates the visit of the Duke of Wellington in 1827. Edward VII was a frequent visitor and all the royal family, including the present Queen, have followed his example.

Yarm, *Cleveland* (8/1C) Cleveland's history is condensed into the little town of Yarm, which is tucked into a sharp bend of the Tees 3 miles

south-west of STOCKTON-ON-TEES. At one time Yarm was a sizeable port, dealing with farm produce, coal and lead, with shipping coming up the river to avoid the inhospitable saltflats and marshes where modern MIDDLESBROUGH and BILLINGHAM now stand.

Before the rise of Stockton and Middlesbrough, Yarm was the most important town on the river Tees. It was granted a charter by King John in 1207 to hold a weekly market and two annual fairs. During the 18th and 19th centuries, it had an amazing variety of industries ranging from brewing, clockmaking, tanning, papermaking, ropemaking and shipbuilding to the manufacture of barrels and nails. Elegant Georgian merchant's houses built on the prosperity of this industry still dominate the southern end of the High Street, but the industry disappeared with the growth of the new towns closer to the sea.

There was a Civil War battle fought around

Yarm's bridge in 1634 and casualties were buried in local churchyards. The ancient bridge dates from 1400, when Bishop Skirlaw of Durham ordered its construction. Its northern arch was replaced by a drawbridge during the Civil War to hold back Scottish troops – the local rector was responsible for pulling it up each night. The parish church of St Mary Magdalene is mostly as it was rebuilt in 1730. There are, however, much older parts around the west end; of special note is the curious 'fish-eye' window. A Dominican friary first stood on the site of the Friarage, built in 1770, the only relic of the older building being a Tudor dovecot. The octagonal Methodist chapel in Capel Wynd was built in 1763, a building much admired by John Wesley when he visited Yarm on his great treks around the country.

Twentieth-century Yarm is a small town with a delightful mixture of buildings lining its wide, cobble-edged main street. The town is made all

Wooler (see p. 177)

the more interesting by a trail following its old streets and 'Wynds', which takes in all the best features. Being on what was an important coach road to the north, the High Street has its fair share of interesting old inns. The 18th-century George and Dragon was used as the meeting place for promoters of the Stockton and Darlington Railway, but it is perhaps the Town Hall that is the most interesting building in the town from an architectural point of view. Built in 1710 in the Dutch style, it was originally a court house and is now, since Yarm was merged with Stockton, the meeting place for the Parish Council.

The Teesside branch of the north-eastern arm of British Rail crosses the Tees at Yarm by a 43-arched viaduct. An attractive riverside walk that passes the church is known locally as the 'True Lovers' Walk'.

Bibliography

Birley, A. R. *Hadrian's Wall*. HMSO, London 1970

Birley, E. B. *Research on Hadrian's Wall*. Wilson, Kendal 1961

Blair, P. H. *Northumbria in the Days of Bede*. Victor Gollancz, London 1976

Bleay, J. *Walks in the Hadrian's Wall Area*. Northumberland County Council, National Park & Countryside Department. 1982

Breeze, D. J., and Dobson B. *Hadrian's Wall*. Allen Lane, London 1976

Daniels, C. M. (ed.) *Collingwood Bruce's Handbook to the Roman Wall*, 13th edn. Harold Hill, Newcastle upon Tyne 1978

Davies, H. *A Walk Along the Wall*. Weidenfeld & Nicolson, London 1984

Dobson, B., and Breeze D. J. *The Building of Hadrian's Wall*, 2nd edn. University of Durham 1970

Ekwall, E. *The Concise Oxford Dictionary of English Place-names*, 4th edn. Clarendon Press, Oxford 1960

Fraser, C. *Northumbria*. Batsford, London 1978

Frere, S. S. *Britannia: A History of Roman Britain*. Routledge Kegan Paul, London 1967

Godfrey, L. *Complete Northumbria*. Ward Lock, London 1979

Graham, F. *The Farne Islands: A Short History and Guide*. F. Graham, Newcastle upon Tyne 1972

—*The Roman Wall: A Comprehensive History and Guide*. F. Graham, Newcastle upon Tyne 1979

Grierson, E. *The Companion Guide to Northumbria*. William Collins, London 1976

Harlech, Lord *Northern England* (Vol. I of *Illustrated Regional Guides to Ancient Monuments* series). HMSO, London 1951

Harrison, D. *Along Hadrian's Wall*. Cassell & Co, London 1956

Hopkins, T. *Northumbria National Park* (Countryside Commission Guide). M. Joseph, London 1987

James, B. *A Kingdom by the Sea*. Hodder & Stoughton, London 1967

Lillie, W. *The History of Middlesbrough*. Central Library, Middlesbrough 1968

Magnusson, M. *Lindisfarne: The Cradle Island*. Oriel Press, Stocksfield, Northumberland 1984

Mee, A. (ed.) *The King's England: Durham*, new edn. Hodder & Stoughton, London 1969

—*The King's England: Northumberland*, new edn. Hodder & Stoughton, London 1964

Ord, J. W. *The History and Antiquities of Cleveland*. Patrick & Shotton, Stockton-on-Tees 1972

Pevsner, N. *The Buildings of England: Durham*. Penguin, Harmondsworth 1953

Pevsner, N., and I. A. Richmond *The Buildings of England: Northumberland*. Penguin, Harmondsworth 1957

Ridley, N. *Portrait of Northumberland*. Robert Hale, London 1965

Ross, A. *Pagan Celtic Britain: Studies in Iconography and Tradition*. Routledge Kegan Paul, London; Columbia University Press 1967

Salway, P. *The Frontier People of Roman Britain*. Cambridge University Press, 1965

Sharp, T. *Northumberland*, 3rd edn. Faber & Faber, London 1969

Stevens, C. E. *The Building of Hadrian's Wall*. Wilson, Kendal 1966

Tegner, H. *The Magic of Holy Island*. F. Graham, Newcastle upon Tyne 1969

Thorold, H. *County Durham*. Faber & Faber, London 1980

Tranter, N. *Portrait of the Border Country*. Robert Hale, London 1972

Victoria County Histories: *Durham County* and *Northumberland*

Wade, H. O. *Discovering Northumbria*. Shire Publications, Aylesbury 1975

Watson, G. *Northumberland Villages*. Robert Hale, London 1976

Woodhouse, R. *Castles of Cleveland*. A. A. Sotheran, Redcar 1975

Wright, G. N. *View of Northumbria*. Robert Hale, London 1981

Useful addresses and telephone numbers:

Northumberland National Park
Eastburn
South Park
Hexham NE46 1BS tel: (0434) 605555
Forestry Commission
Walby House
Rothbury NE65 7NT tel: (0669) 20569
and
West View
Bellingham NE48 2AH tel: (0660) 20242
Northumbrian Water Authority
Northumbria House
Regent Centre
Gosforth
Newcastle upon Tyne NE23 3PX
tel: (091) 284 3151
Tyneside District Council
Tourist Information Centre
The Manor Office
Hallgate
Hexham NE46 1XP tel: (0434) 605225

Information Centres:
Ingram tel: (066 578) 248
Rothbury tel: (0669) 20887
Once Brewed tel: (049 84) 396
Kielder Castle tel: (0660) 50209

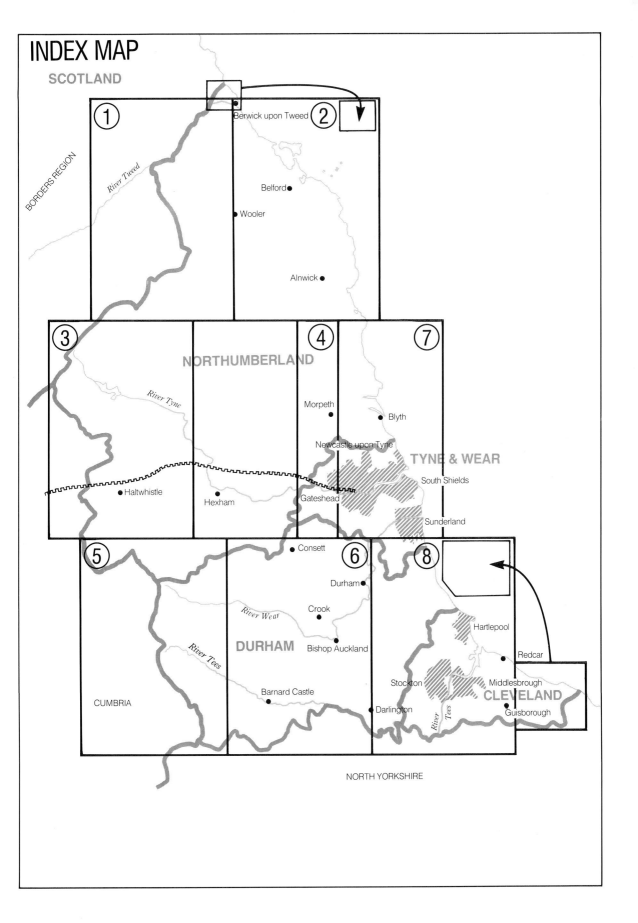

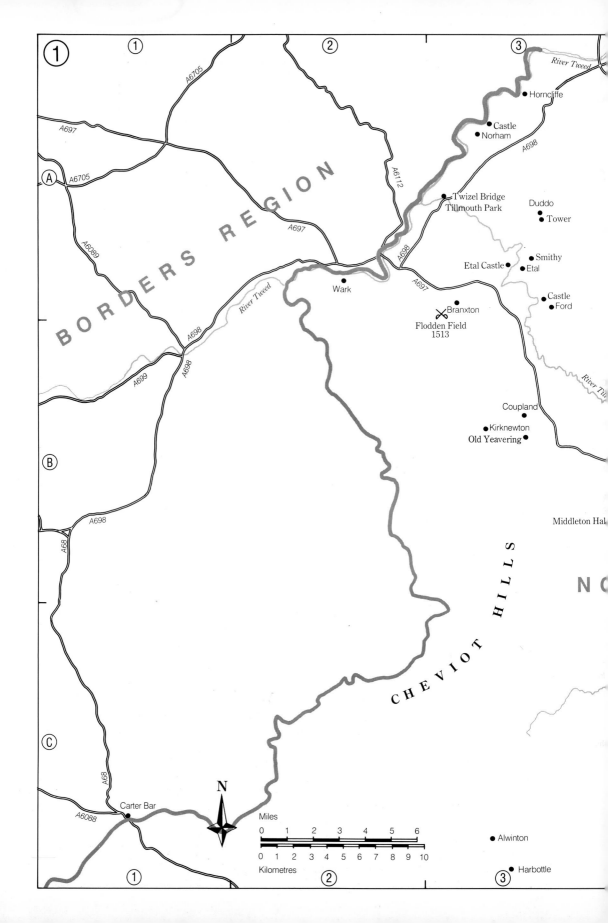

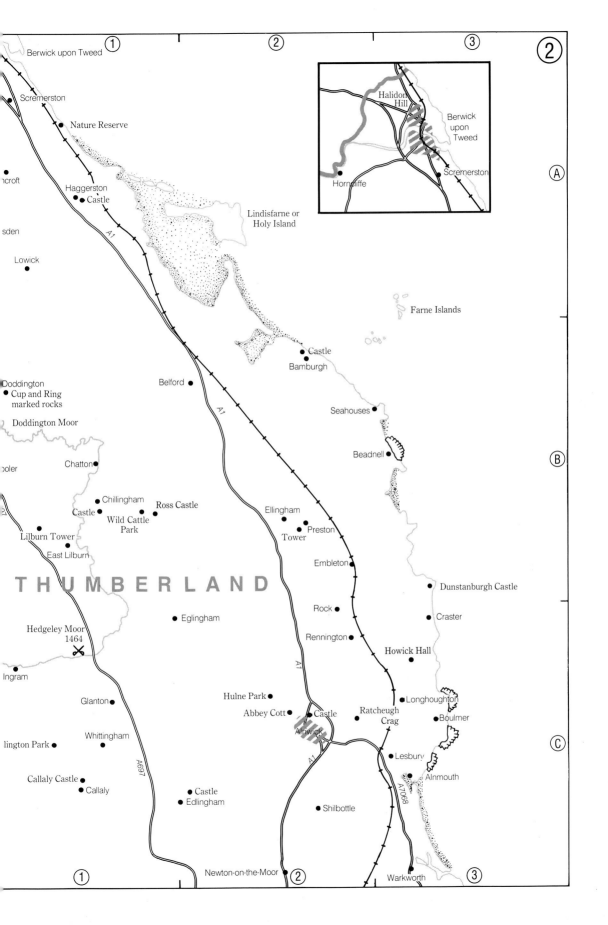

Berwick upon Tweed

Scremerston

Nature Reserve

ncroft

Haggerston
Castle

sden

Lowick

Lindisfarne or
Holy Island

Halidon
Hill

Berwick
upon
Tweed

Horncliffe

Scremerston

Ⓐ

Farne Islands

Doddington
Cup and Ring
marked rocks

Belford

Doddington Moor

Castle
Bamburgh

Seahouses

Beadnell

Ⓑ

oler

Chatton

Chillingham
Castle
Wild Cattle
Park

Ross Castle

Ellingham

Preston
Tower

Lilburn Tower

East Lilburn

Embleton

THUMBERLAND

Dunstanburgh Castle

Hedgeley Moor
1464

Eglingham

Rock

Craster

Rennington

Ingram

Howick Hall

Glanton

Hulne Park

Longhoughton

Abbey Cott

Castle

Ratcheugh
Crag

Boulmer

lington Park

Whittingham

Alnwick

Ⓒ

Lesbury

Callaly Castle

Callaly

Castle
Edlingham

Alnmouth

Shilbottle

A697

A1

A1

A1068

Warkworth

Ⓐ

Miles
0   1   2   3   4   5   6
0 1 2 3 4 5 6 7 8 9 10
Kilometres

Byrness

A68

Rochester

Elishaw
Blakehope
Battle
Otterbu
1388
Percy's Cr
M

Monument
Padon Hill

Kielder • • Kielder Castle

N O R T H

Kielder Forest

Kielder Reservoir

West Woodbu

• Falstone

Hareshaw Linn •
• Bellingham

Kielder Forest

Ⓑ

River

Wark •   *North*

N

Stonehaugh •

Chipchase Castle

Tower •

Simonburn •

Mile Castle 3

Mile Castle   Brocolitia
33

Housesteads •

VERCOVICIVM
Roman Fort

Fourst

Newbrough •

Cawfield Crags   • Twice Brewed

Gilsland •

Bardon Mill •

Ⓒ

Blenkinsopp Hall
Haltwhistle   A69

Beltingham •

Haydon Bridge

Lambley •

Langley Castle •

Featherstone Castle •

A689

River East Allen

A686

Whitfield Hall •

Allendale Town •

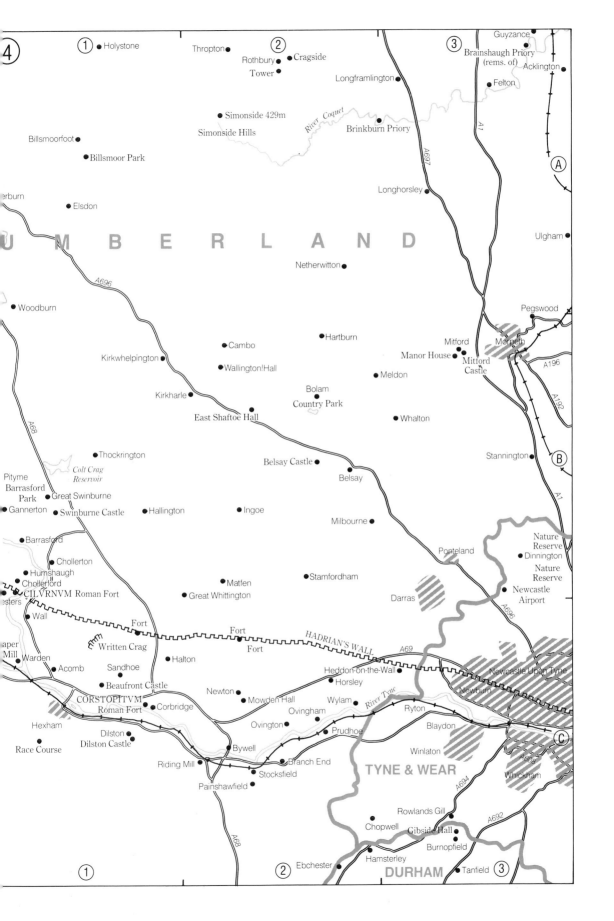

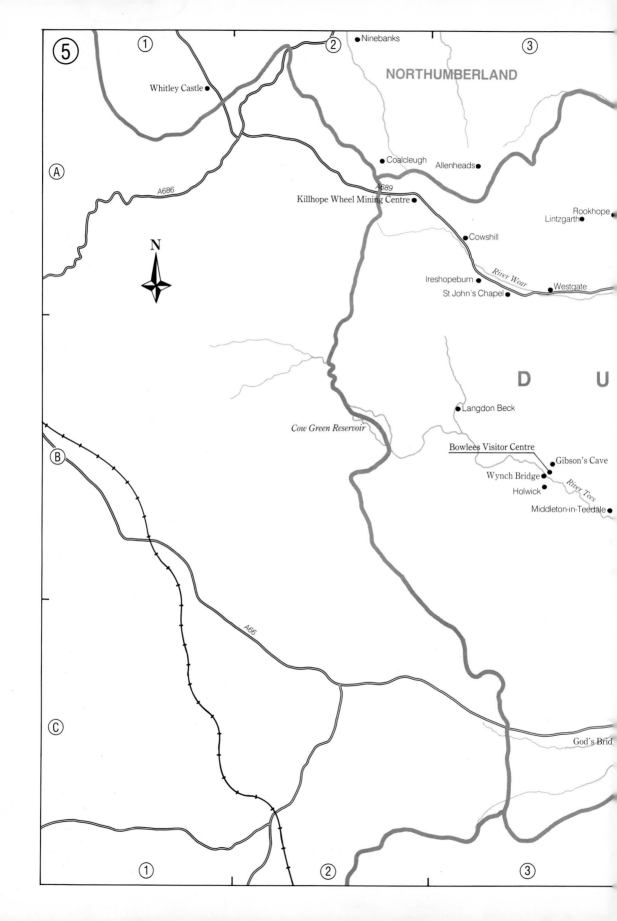

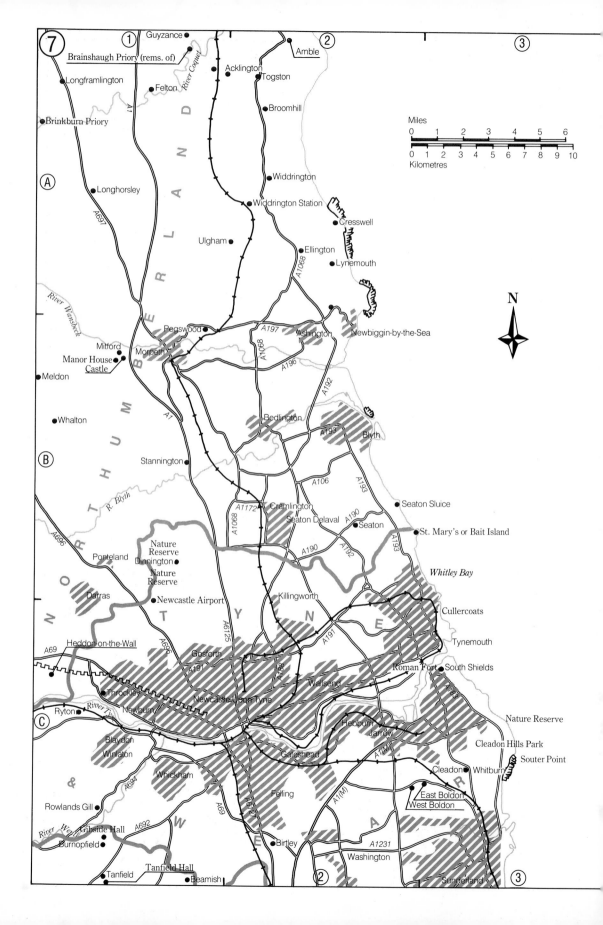

① Guyzance
Brainshaugh Priory (rems. of)

② Amble

③

●Longframlington
●Felton
Acklington
Togston

●Broomhill

●Brinkburn Priory

(A)

●Longhorsley

●Widdrington

Widdrington Station

Cresswell

●Ulgham
Ellington
Lynemouth

River Coquet
A1
A1068

N O R T H U M B E R L A N D

River Wansbeck

Pegswood
A197
Ashington
Newbiggin-by-the-Sea

Mitford
Morpeth
Manor House
Castle

A1068
A196

●Meldon

●Whalton

A1

Bedlington

A192

(B)

●Stannington

A193
Blyth

R. Blyth

A106
A193

A1172
Cramlington
Seaton Delaval
A190
●Seaton Sluice
St. Mary's or Bait Island

A1068
A190
A192

Nature
Reserve
Dinnington
Nature
Reserve

A696

Ponteland

Datras

●Newcastle Airport
Killingworth

Whitley Bay

Cullercoats

A6125
A191
A66

Tynemouth

Heddon-on-the-Wall
A69
A696
Gosforth

Roman Fort ●South Shields

T Y N E

Throckley
Newburn
Newcastle-upon-Tyne
Wallsend

Nature Reserve

Ryton
River Tyne

(C)

Hebburn
Jarrow

Cleadon Hills Park
Souter Point

Blaydon
Winlaton

Gateshead

A1(M)
Cleadon Whitburn

Whickham

Felling
A1(M)
East Boldon
West Boldon

A694

W E A R

Rowlands Gill

A69

Gibside Hall
A692
Burnopfield

River Wear

Birtley
A1231
Washington

Tanfield Hall
●Tanfield
●Beamish

②
Sunderland
③

Miles
0 1 2 3 4 5 6
0 1 2 3 4 5 6 7 8 9 10
Kilometres

N

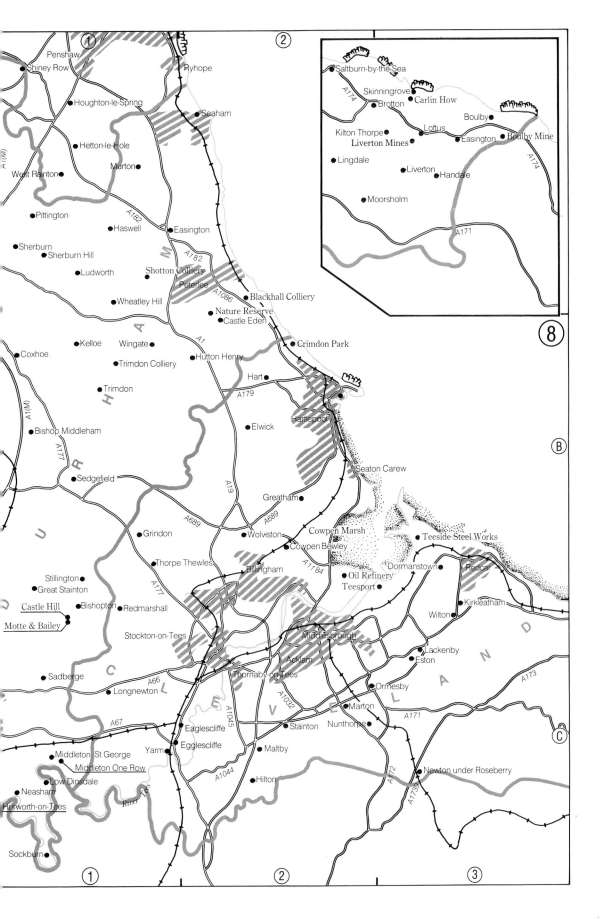

Index

Numbers in *italics* refer to illustrations